W9-AAG-942

ARCADIA FALLS

Arcadia Falls

A Novel

CAROL GOODMAN

RANDOM HOUSE
LARGE PRINT

Copyright © 2010 by Carol Goodman

All rights reserved.
Published in the United States of America by
Random House Large Print in association with
The Random House Publishing Group, New York.
Distributed by Random House, Inc., New York.

Cover images © Wally Stemberger/Shutterstock (forest),
Michel Legrou/MPG (woman)

The Library of Congress has established a Cataloging-in-Publication record for this title.

ISBN: 978-0-7393-7759-8

www.randomhouse.com/largeprint

FIRST LARGE PRINT EDITION

Printed in the United States of America

10 9 8 7 6 5 4 3 2 1

This Large Print edition published in accord with the standards of the N.A.V.H.

For Andrew and Katy

Acknowledgments

Thanks to my first readers: Gary Feinberg, Scott Silverman, and Nora Slonimsky. Lisa Huber was especially generous in sharing her knowledge as a folklorist.

Thanks to my agent, Loretta Barrett, and her associate Nick Mullendore for making it possible for me to write; to my inestimable editor, Linda Marrow, for her insight and friendship; and to all the people at Ballantine whose care and efforts made this book possible: Gina Centrello, Elizabeth McGuire, Kim Hovey, Dana Isaacson, Brian McLendon, Lisa Barnes, and Junessa Viloria.

Finally, I couldn't have written this book without the love and support of my family—my mother, Marge Goodman, my husband, Lee, my brothers, Bob and Larry, my niece and nephew, Andrew and Katy, and my step-daughter and daughter, Nora and Maggie.

ARCADIA FALLS

CHAPTER 1

"We're lost," my daughter tells me for the third time in an hour. "I told you we should have gotten GPS. Lexy's mother has it and they **never** get lost."

"We're not lost," I reply, biting back the urge to tell Sally that one, we can no longer afford the things Lexy's mother can, and two, the only places Lexy's mother drives to are the Americana shopping center and the hair salon, two destinations within a five-mile radius of their Kings Point home, and so she is not likely to get lost. Instead I say: "We're taking the scenic route."

Sally rolls her eyes, throwing her head, neck, and shoulders into a gesture so practiced it has attained the grace of a yoga asana. I told her this a few weeks ago, making a joke of it. It was the kind of thing she and I used to joke about: eye-rolling teenagers. Instead of laughing, she asked me with exaggerated patience not to **try** to be funny anymore. And would I please stop comparing everything to yoga, she added as she plugged her iPod buds into her ears.

"Scenic would imply that we were able to **see** something. How **remote** is this place?"

"It's only two and a half hours to the city."

"There's a train?" Sally asks, stretching her neck and sniffing as if scenting the air for freedom. When she sits up straight you can see how lovely she is—like an exotic wading bird craning its long neck.

"Well, no, I don't think so. There might be a bus."

"Oh," Sally says, slouching back into her more characteristic slump. She pulls her long legs—in the prefaded jeans that cost more than the rent on my first apartment—up to her chin and plugs in her iPod. "Great. A bus." I may as well have suggested she take a coach and four. Good thing. The last thing I want is Sally running off to the city.

She has a point about the limited visibility of this **scenic** drive, though. As soon as we got off the highway a low-lying fog had settled on either side of the narrow two-lane country road snaking up into the mountains. I could point out that she used to like fog, that I used to wake her up early on foggy mornings so I could walk her to school. We'd pretend that we were lost in the woods. I'd be Hansel to her Gretel, the Woodsman to her Little Red Riding Hood. She **liked** the idea of being lost. Her favorite stories were about children lost in the woods and the tricks they used to find their way home—bread crumb trails and yarn unraveled from sweater cuffs. It was a game you could enjoy when you knew what the ending would be: a lighted cottage window shining through the dark, all disfiguring spells broken, and the world restored to what it should be. I couldn't blame her for losing faith in that kind of storybook ending.

It isn't much fun being really lost, which we are now. Although I printed out the directions from the school's website, they'd seemed a little unclear to me. When I called for clarification, Ivy St. Clare, the dean, had laughed. "Oh, we consider it part of the application procedure. Only those who can **find** Arcadia belong here." Then she had gone on to give a series of impressionistic route suggestions. "By all means take the scenic route that follows Wittekill Creek. Turn right when you see an old decrepit barn—you're a mile from the school when you see that—and then up a steep hill and past the apple orchard where we used to have concerts on summer evenings." Then she had gone into a ten-minute reverie on the days when the Arcadia School was still an arts colony with famous musicians, poets, and painters who all **collaborated** (a word she used frequently and invested with some magical import). Even Virgil Nash, the famous painter and one of the first teachers at the colony, had played the mandolin. Over the phone, I'd had to listen to a long anecdote about Virgil Nash and some women potters before getting a momentary chance to ask her what I did after we passed the apple orchard (**Turn left at the sign of the White Witch**). I have the directions on a Post-it note affixed to the dashboard (**Poor man's GPS**, I quipped to Sally earlier, forgetting her banning of jokes), but they won't do me much good if I can't see the orchard or the sign.

"Do those look like apple trees?" I ask, not really expecting a response from my plugged-in daughter. She gives herself away, though, by glancing out the window at the hobble-branched shapes looming out of the fog on the left side of the road.

"Hey," she says, peeling the buds out of her ears, "those remind me of that story you used to read to me when I was little. **Trees like gnomes on crutches marching through the mire.**"

"They are those trees," I say, trying to keep my voice flat. Enthusiasm, another emotion under interdiction, is a surefire way to scare off any nascent curiosity in Sally. I'm thrilled, though, that she remembers the story. "Remember, I told you that the two women who wrote and illustrated the story, Vera Beecher and Lily Eberhardt, lived here."

"Oh yeah, the lesbians you're writing about."

"We don't know that they were lesbians, honey," I point out, wondering what her current stance on lesbianism is. Last year there was a flurry of nervous e-mails among the mothers of Sally's friends about a new trend in bisexual experimentation, which basically boiled down to Jessica Feingold having made up a story about two girls making out at her Sweet Sixteen. When I asked Sally about it, she dismissed the whole incident as fallout from a recent TV episode, which featured two girls kissing. Then she told me I was no longer allowed to use the words **sexuality, gender,** or **making out.**

"Unmarried women often lived together back then. That's how the art colony was started. Some women artists from the city banded together to live up here so that they could work as artists instead of having to get married and spend their time raising families." I pause, wondering if I've just made it sound like having children and pursuing an artistic career are mutually exclusive and how I could explain that back then—in the twenties and thirties—they often were. "These women met at an art school in New York and decided they could pursue careers as artists better if they didn't marry. One of them, Vera Beecher, offered her family estate. Then a bunch of other artists joined them—"

"Like a hippie commune?" Sally asks.

"Sort of, only this was in the late twenties and early thirties, way before hippies. They called themselves bohemians or socialists. It was even before beatniks—"

"I know, Mom, like Audrey Hepburn in those Gap ads."

"Yes, well, anyway they called it Arcadia—after the town, of course, but also because Arcadia was a place in Greece where life was supposed to be perfect."

"And was it?" she asks.

"Was it what?"

"Was life here"—she rolls her eyes—"perfect?"

"Well, nothing's perfect," I begin, but then I realize how often I have given her this speech over the last ten months. She doesn't have to roll her eyes; I'm as bored with the concept as she is. "For a time, yes. They were able to live off money they made doing illustrations for fashion magazines and children's books, which gave them the freedom to do paintings. Vera Beecher was commissioned to do the murals for a college in Pennsylvania and together she and Lily Eberhardt wrote and illustrated fairy tales. That one I used to read you—"

"**The Changeling Girl**—was that what it was called?"

"Yes," I say, hardly daring to say more, so glad am I that she remembers our old favorite bedtime story. "That was their first fairy tale. They went on to write others and they became so popular that they had enough money to start the school. The proceeds from the fairy tales still fund scholarships for high school students who are talented in writing, visual arts, or music." Like you, I'm tempted to add, but I don't because the last time I told her she was talented she told me that it felt like I was pressuring her. "Do you remember how **The Changeling Girl** went?"

"Oh, oh, oh . . . **There once was a girl who liked to pretend she was lost until . . . until . . .**"

"**Until the day she really lost her way. She liked to play—**"

"**In the old orchard and pretend the trees were gnomes on crutches marching through the mire,**" Sally finishes, her voice ranging through all the forbidden emotions of glee and delight. "**Until one day she met an old witch dressed all in white**—ohmygod, stop, stop!" Sally shouts, pounding on the dashboard so hard I almost swerve off the road. "There she is! The white witch!"

Out of the fog a pale shape careens drunkenly—a cut-out tin woman with a witch's hat and broom. Rust has covered the painted metal sign, but clearly this is the White Witch, the only remnant of a Prohibition-era speakeasy that was here when the artists first moved up from the city.

"This is the way," I say, turning the car up a narrow private drive. Instantly we are plunged into a twilight so deep I have to stop the car . . . and it stalls, reminding me that Jude's temperamental eleven-

year-old Jaguar is past due for its service appointment. But instead of adding and subtracting figures
in my head—what I'd get for the car, how much it
would cost to replace, how much is left in savings,
how much we needed to live on in Great Neck, how
little we could live on somewhere else, what could I
get for the house, how much would Sally hate me
for making her move before her junior year of high
school—a process that's become second nature over
the last few months, I look up at the arched canopy
of trees overhead, their branches intertwining like
clasped hands, and listen to the sound of water dripping from their dappled limbs. Then I let out a
breath that I feel like I've been holding for the ten
months since Jude's secretary called to tell me he'd
collapsed during his weekly squash game and been
taken to St. Francis Hospital because they had the
best cardiac care.

   "It's the crystal path that the lost girl takes after
she meets the white witch," Sally says, her voice clear
as crystal itself. They're the first words untinged by
bitterness or regret I've heard her say in months.
"See, the trees look like **girls in torn dresses** because
of the way the bark's peeling and **they're holding up
their freckled arms to make a canopy to protect
the lost girl on her journey.** And when the sun
comes through the trees it catches on the fog
droplets and turns them to crystal—oh!" Sally grabs
my hand. My heart thuds so hard in my chest that
I'm afraid she'll lose a second parent—a thought

that, along with the column of figures, keeps me up nights counting my own heartbeats along with the grocery bills and mortgage payments. The life insurance policy is just one of the policies Jude borrowed against in the year before he died. But then I see what she sees. The eastern sky is still a stormy blue, but a sliver of sunlight has appeared at the horizon low in the west. A stream of sunlight brightens the tops of the trees, catching the drops of water among the leaves and making them sparkle like candles in a darkened church.

I look at Sally and see light there, too, a light of wonder that illuminates her face. For the moment, it erases the dark circles under her eyes, the rashy skin around her mouth, the hacked-off ends of her dark auburn hair, and the torn cuticles on her hands. She could be the lovely child I remember from a year ago.

Cautiously, I start the car, praying the engine will turn over smoothly for a change—and it does! Maybe this place **is** perfect, I think. "Do you remember the rest of the story?"

"Yeah, but you tell it. You always told it so well."

"Okay," I say, scarcely believing my luck. I can't remember the last time I did anything right in Sally's eyes. "After the lost girl meets the white witch she takes the crystal path into the woods and there at the end of it she finds the witch's cottage. The witch takes her in and tells her that if she works for her for a year her family will have everything they need—a warm home, enough to eat, rich suitors for her sisters, beautiful clothes for her mother.

" 'But won't they miss me?' the girl asks.

"But the witch explains that she will send in her stead a fairy changed to look just like her."

"The changeling girl," Sally says.

"Yes. All the girl has to do is go to the old copper beech tree at the edge of the meadow and dig up a root—"

"Is that a copper beech?" Sally asks, pointing up the hill through a gap in the sycamores where a single tree with wine-colored leaves stands on a green lawn before a stone Tudor mansion. I shiver at a detail I always left out when I read the story to Sally—that the beech's leaves were red with the blood of the changelings that lived in its roots. This whole part of the story always struck me as creepy, but I go on, not willing to waste a minute of Sally's attention.

"Yes, it is," I tell her. "The girl digs until she finds a bit of gnarled root shaped like a tiny baby. She takes it out of the ground and wraps it in a piece of calico cloth, which she tears from her own dress—"

"That's why the sycamore trees are like girls with torn dresses," Sally crows. I steal a glance at her. She's sitting up in her seat, the white buds of the iPod tangled in her lap—like naked roots, I think with a little shudder—her eyes shining.

"You know, I never thought of that," I say, "but I think you may be right. Anyway, the witch had told her that she must wash the root in well water, not the water from the stream, but the well is a long way off and the girl knows that the bucket will be hard to haul up. As she's walking toward the well she crosses over the stream—"

As if on cue, the Jag's tires bump over a wooden bridge and Sally thumps the window with her hands in her excitement, the rings on her fingers chattering against the glass like loose teeth. "This is it! This is it!" she cries. "And of course the girl—like all stupid girls in fairy tales—disobeys the witch and washes the root in the stream. And then she goes back to the witch's house and she has to sleep with the root tucked up in bed next to her. Ugh! Remember how that used to scare me? I'd wake up sure that the root was in my bed and that it had come alive in the night, but it would just be one of my stuffed animals, and Dad would have to come in and search through my whole bed."

"He'd take off the sheets and shake out the blankets," I say, stealing another look at Sally to see how she's taking the introduction of her father into the story. The therapist I've taken her to says I ought not to be afraid of sharing anecdotes about Jude, but once again the effect has been to clam her up. She hunches her shoulders, making the bones around her neck stick out. How much weight has she lost since Jude died? When did I last see her eat a real meal? She ordered blueberry pancakes at the diner we stopped at in Rockland County this morning, but she only ate half of one. What kid ever left a pancake unfinished? I wonder if I should say something else about her father here—how he loved her so much that he'd have searched through all the beds in all the world to make sure they were safe for her, that the fact that he up and died on us with debts and second mortgages and borrowed-against life insurance doesn't mean he didn't love us.

But I soldier on with the fairy tale, as the road climbs steadily through a dense pine forest that is as dark and mysterious as the forest where the witch lives.

"In the morning, the root has grown into a perfect likeness of the girl—right down to the freckles on her arms and the tear in her calico dress. The witch sends the changeling down the crystal path, out of the forest and to the cottage at the end of the woods where the lost girl's family lives, so she can take the lost girl's place. The girl stays at the witch's house, working as hard as she can to please the old witch. Not only does she do the ordinary housework like cooking and cleaning and washing the clothes, she also does extra things to make the witch's house beautiful. She spins the wool from the wild goats in the mountains into yarn and weaves the yarn into beautiful rugs for the floors and tapestries to cover the walls. She chips the broken glass out of the windowpanes and fits in pieces of colored glass in beautiful patterns so that the light in the cottage glows like scattered jewels. She gathers wood in the forest and carves it into comfortable chairs and sturdy tables. She digs clay by the stream and fashions it into vases to hold the wildflowers she picks in the fields.

"But no matter how beautiful the girl makes the house, she still dreams of her own home every night and counts the days until her year of service to the witch is over. When that day comes the witch gives her back the dress she came in, only the torn piece has been patched with cloth of gold. They wait on the porch for the changeling girl to come back. They wait all day. At last when evening comes the witch turns to the girl and asks, 'You didn't, by any chance, wash that root in running water? Because you know, that gives the changeling running legs and she'll never come back again.' "

It's not the end of the story, but we've come to the end of our trip. At the top of the steep road I see a sign marked FLEUR-DE-LIS. This is the cottage Ivy St. Clare told me Sally and I could stay in—the free housing that made the job impossible to turn down. (Not that I, with an incomplete English doctorate and a mountain of unpaid debts, could afford to turn down any job at all.)

We pull up in front of the cottage in silence. It's so well camouflaged in the trees that it takes a moment to really take it in, but slowly I begin to notice that the slate tiles are furred with moss and that many are missing. The rough pine walls are stained and moldy-looking, many of the windows cracked and covered with spiderwebs. A detached garage with a crooked roof slumps against the right side of the house. This could be the witch's cottage before the lost girl comes and fixes it up—the hut still under the spell of disfigurement. Nothing has been restored. Sally's father is still dead of a heart attack at forty-two, and I'm still the bad witch who's sold her childhood home—her castle and her rights to the kingdom—and banished us to this peasant's hovel. I turn to Sally, looking for any glimmer of the light I saw shining in her eyes just minutes ago, but she's slouched back down in her seat, stopped her ears up with the iPod buds, opened her cell phone, and put her sunglasses back on. I've lost her again right before my eyes.

CHAPTER 2

"It's quaint, don't you think, like something in a fairy tale?"

But Sally is done with fairy tales for the day. "I'm not getting service," she says. "This place does get cell phone service, doesn't it?"

"I'm not sure," I lie. The dean had, in fact, told me that the campus lay in a cellular dead zone, but I hadn't had the heart to tell Sally that yet. I was hoping that if she spent a little less time texting her friends she might occasionally talk to me.

"What about wi-fi?" she asks. "I mean, you can't drag me away from all my friends and then not give me IM."

From the look of it, the house is more likely to have black mold and a mouse infestation than electricity and a working phone. It certainly doesn't match the image I've held in my head these last few months, through each painful stage of divesting ourselves of our old lives, of a tidy white clapboard house with a front porch and a small garden. **Nothing too big,** I said to myself as I put our Great Neck McMansion on the market. **Nothing too new,** I thought as I tag-saled the Danish modern furniture Jude and I had bought at Roche-Bobois. Nothing more than I can take care of by myself, I lectured myself as I let go the housekeeper and the gardeners.

I got the **nothing** right. The house is built of the same rough pine as the surrounding forest and the same granite as the hillside it backs up against. The only color is the faded green and russet of the trim on the pointed eaves. The whole house is tinted the colors of a pheasant seeking to camouflage itself in the undergrowth of the forest. I have the feeling that if I blink it will disappear.

"The library will have wi-fi," I finally think to tell Sally. "All private schools do these days."

"Not private schools for losers." Sally slumps farther down in her seat. She makes no move to get out of the car, and neither do I. We seem trapped in the driveway of our new home, as if thorny hedges blocked our way. Perhaps Sally thinks if she doesn't get out I'll put the car in reverse, drive back through the pine woods, down the sycamore-lined road, out to the county route, and to the highway. We'll retrace our steps until we get back to Great Neck and like clever children who've unraveled their sweaters to mark the way home, we'll unspool time until we're back in our lives of a year ago. I'll be the wife of a prosperous hedge fund manager. Not the kind of suburban housewife I despise—the ones like Lexy's mom who spend their days gliding in their BMWs between the hair salon and Burberry's—but one with literary interests and just enough time to nurture our talented daughter. Last September I was taking the last course requirement for my Ph.D. in English literature at City University Graduate Center. Sally was starting tenth grade. She belonged to the art club and the literary magazine and had been inducted into the National Honor Society. The hedge fund was in its third year. Jude had quit his trading job at Morgan Stanley three years before. I knew that we had borrowed heavily to start the fund—and to support the lifestyle that, Jude assured me, was necessary to look successful—but I thought it was worth it to have Jude home more and looking less stressed. He hadn't looked so young and carefree since his sophomore year at Pratt, where we had met. He didn't look like a man who had less than three months to live.

If I could unravel time and change that, I'd drive

in reverse all the way down the New York State Thruway to Long Island.

"Why do you think it's a school for losers?" I ask. "It has a very good reputation—especially in the arts. Its graduates go on to Ivy League colleges and the best art schools. Remember Grandma always said she wished she could have gone here?" I don't mention that my mother was always bitter that her own mother hadn't let her attend the Arcadia School, even after she got a full scholarship. When I heard about the job—as a last-minute replacement for a new teacher who'd gotten another job somewhere else—I felt that coming here might somehow heal that old wound. Right now we can use all the healing we can get.

Sally lets out an exasperated sigh and holds up a finger—a habit of Jude's, this counting on fingers. "One, it starts in August."

"That's so the students have time to get to know one another."

"Please, there are only six hundred students here. I'm sure they get to know each other all too well. Two, it's full of rich, spoiled kids."

I have to suppress a laugh that after living in materialistic, prosperous Great Neck she would worry about such a thing, but I reply soberly, "They have a scholarship program for gifted art students and only let in qualified students, whether they can pay or not. Remember, we had to send your portfolio for you to get in?" I hadn't let Sally know how relieved

I'd been when she was accepted because it meant I wouldn't have to pay for private school or send her to the public school in the town of Arcadia Falls. "I think you'll really like the art classes here."

"I liked the art classes at my old school. And three, it was founded by hippie lesbian witches."

"Witches?" I repeat only the last part because I've heard the accusation of **hippie** and **lesbian** already.

"I looked it up online. Do you know that there's a legend that the town of Arcadia Falls was founded by a group of witches who were thrown out of the Dutch settlement in Kingston?"

I should be glad, I suppose, that Sally's taking an interest in American history and that she's bothered to try to find out anything about our new home, but I would prefer she'd chosen some other feature of the local landscape, like the history of bluestone quarrying or the short stories of Washington Irving. "That sounds like a pretty outlandish story, but even if there was some truth to it, that's the town, not the school. The school was founded by artists—"

"Who were drawn here by the whole witchcraft thing. I've been looking at the Facebook profiles of the students here. They're all into Wicca and voodoo. They even teach it here."

"That's the folklore class, Sally, which is why this is such a great place for me to teach. Not many high schools have classes in my field."

"Maybe that's because it's a field for **losers,** no offense. And four, it's almost all girls here."

"The school went co-ed in the seventies," I say, ignoring the hurt of my own daughter labeling the discipline I've devoted myself to for the last eight years as a field for losers. When did she start dividing the world up into winners and losers, anyway? And when did I land on the losing side of her score book? I can't help but remember, though, that when I chose my specialization—fairy tales in nineteenth- and twentieth-century women's fiction—eight-year-old Sally thought it was **cool** that I was going to get to use the stories I read to her at bedtime for **schoolwork**. So did I. "It's sixty-forty now. Not that I think you should be worrying about boys anyway."

"Why don't you just lock me up in a convent?" Sally screams, her voice reaching into registers that are as painful to my ears as they must be to her vocal cords. The enclosed space of the car (**A two-seater, Jude, what were you thinking?**) can't hold her anymore. She opens the passenger side door (which has made a wrenching noise since a Hummer grazed it in the Food Emporium parking lot three months ago) and steps out while issuing her last invective.

"Just because you can't have sex anymore doesn't mean no one else should be allowed to."

Leaving the door open, she stomps up the weed-choked path and sits down on the cracked front step. I get out of the car to let her in. Sally's fury has released us from the spell of inertia and that, I suppose as I approach the threshold of our new home, is probably the only kind of magic we're going to get for a while.

Inside I find Sally poking around in the packing crates I had shipped up ahead of us.

"Pew! It smells like shop class in here!" Sally complains.

"Pine wood," I say, opening all the windows to let out the stale, musty air. They're the old-fashioned double-sash kind, like the ones in the first apartment Jude and I shared on Avenue B in the East Village. Jude had called them guillotine windows. These make a sound like a Frenchwoman having her head chopped off when I pry them open.

"Do we have to live with this gloomy furniture? I told you we should have kept our old stuff."

I could point out that our massive leather sofa wouldn't have fit into this tiny living room, but that would be calling attention to how very small the house is. The parlor is about the size of the laundry room in our old house.

"This is Arts and Crafts style," I say instead, patting a Morris chair upholstered in a design that appears to be lettuce leaves wilting on a ground of fresh-turned soil—a dreary pattern that is unfortunately repeated in the wallpaper and curtains. A puff of dust rises from the chair like the ghost of the last person who sat in it, which must have been a few decades ago, judging from the dust that lies over everything. What had Ivy St. Clare said on the phone? **I haven't had the heart to go into Fleur-de-Lis since Vera passed**. That was ten years ago. I hadn't realized she meant **no one** had gone into the cottage. "The Arts and Crafts style was popular in arts colonies in the early part of the century—the twentieth century," I correct myself before Sally can remind me that we're not living in the twentieth century anymore. "Colonies like Roycroft, Byrdcliffe, and Arcadia made their own furniture. Some of this stuff might have been made here at Arcadia—"

"They couldn't afford to buy furniture?"

"It was part of the ideal of the Arts and Crafts movement that the artists be able to work in practical mediums and produce their own goods. They raised sheep for wool to make their own rugs and clothes and made furniture from the native hardwoods. They even used indigenous trees and flowers in their designs. See—" I wipe a layer of grime from the armrest of the chair. "There's a beech tree carved into this side and a lily on the other. I think the same pattern is on the fireplace," I say, pointing to a wood carving of a beech tree on the mantel. "And on the hearth tiles." I wipe the soot off the ceramic tiles that frame the fireplace until a crackled blue-green glaze appears. The pattern of beech tree and lily repeats across the length of the hearth, but the tiles are badly cracked. Especially the ones decorated with lilies.

"It looks like someone took a fire poker to them,"

Sally says. "Probably after being driven mad by the wallpaper . . . Hey, isn't there a short story about some woman who goes crazy because of her wallpaper?"

" 'The Yellow Wallpaper' by Charlotte Perkins Gilman," I say, delighted that Sally has remembered a bit of the nineteenth-century fiction I'm always telling her about. "I know she stayed at the Byrdcliffe Colony in Woodstock. Maybe she visited here, too."

"Yeah, and maybe she got the idea for the book from this gross wallpaper."

"It will look better once we clean it up and wash the curtains . . . maybe get some new slipcovers." I look around at the dreary room trying to imagine it looking like anything other than an undertaker's parlor.

"Good luck with that," she says, grabbing a box labeled SALLY. "I'm going to go look at the bedrooms. They can't be worse than this."

I smile encouragingly, glad that Sally's showing any interest in the house, but I'm afraid of what her reaction might be if she's wrong. What if the bedrooms **are** worse? Suddenly I'm not up to hearing another tirade. Cowardly as it is to run from a sixteen-year-old's displeasure, I find myself plotting my exit strategy.

"I should tell my new boss I'm here . . . and see if I can figure out where to get some food and cleaning supplies. Do you mind if I leave you here alone?"

"Whatever." Sally's voice is studiously nonchalant. We both know she's had nightmares since Jude died. "It's not like the place is haunted, right?"

"Of course not, sweetie," I say quickly. It's a measure of how frayed our relationship has become that I'm actually thrilled she's asked me a question I know how to answer. But as I leave, I think of those battered lilies over the fireplace and wonder if the house is completely free of bad spirits.

Ivy St. Clare told me that her office in Beech Hall was an eleven-and-a- half-minute walk from Fleur-de-Lis Cottage.

"I know because I made the trip so often when Vera was still alive." She had expelled a sigh that, even over the phone, managed to convey both grief and the fortitude she had employed over the years to bear up under it. "Vera used to say I was uncommonly light on my feet. 'My little sparrow,' she called me."

She must have been. It takes me a good five minutes just to find the path. (**It starts between two old oak trees that are catty-corner to your front door. You take the one that branches to the left to reach Beech Hall.**) I'm on the narrow, pine-bordered path for a good fifteen minutes before I come out onto the lawn in front of Beech Hall. I pause there to take in the scene. In front of the stone and half-timbered Tudor hall, the lawn slopes down toward the copper beech Sally and I saw from the car. The late-afternoon sun turns the tree's leaves a glossy purple—not at all the color of blood. The grass beneath it is strewn with students who, taking advantage of the late afternoon respite from the rain, are sprawled out on blankets and towels, some reading and some sitting in small circles talking. The girls—and it's mostly girls, making me wonder if that "sixty-forty" figure has been exaggerated—are stripped down to sports bras and shorts or tank tops and rolled-up jeans. Quite a few have tattoos.

At the city colleges I've adjuncted at over the last few years I've noticed a steady increase in the amount of tattooed flesh amongst my students, but I'm surprised to see tattoos on high school kids. Would Sally deem the tattooed student body at Arcadia **gross**, or would she end up wanting one herself? Or, knowing Sally, both? I'll have to decide between putting my foot down by saying no—in which case Sally will probably sneak off to Kingston and get needled in some unhygienic biker parlor—or agreeing in order to get some say over where it's done and how much exposed skin gets inked. For about the millionth time this year I wonder what Jude would do. The interior silence that greets the question is almost more painful than his physical absence. I used to be able to predict what Jude would do in most situations. His death didn't take that away, but what I learned in the aftermath of his death did.

When I enter Beech Hall it takes a moment for

my eyes to adjust to the darkness after all that sunlight and brightly colored skin. The only light comes from two narrow stained-glass windows on the second floor landing, which is directly above me. When my eyes adjust I make out a small bronze statuette of a naked woman standing in a recessed niche to my right. She's looking over her shoulder, her long hair streaming down her back into a pool of water lilies at her feet. She seems as if she's giving the last person who opened the door a reproachful look for letting in a draft. I don't blame her. Even on this summer day I can feel the chill of the stone floor through my thin-soled sneakers and a draft tickles the sweat at the nape of my neck.

It occurs to me that I should have dressed better before reporting to Ivy St. Clare. The hall, as it emerges from the shadows, is imposingly formal. It's not what I expected from a private school founded as an art colony, but then I remember that Beech Hall was originally Vera Beecher's family home. I hadn't appreciated the scale of her gift until now, standing in this large drafty hall, staring up at the Beecher family arms—a beech tree, of course, that's carved in the dark wood paneling of the second-floor landing. What a refuge this must have been for impoverished artists during the Depression! Arcadia must have seemed like a paradise.

As if filling in for the parts of "impoverished artists in paradise" a cluster of girls bang through the door and swarm past me. "Excuse me," I say as they pass by me. One of the girls flings back her waist-length black hair to reveal a heart-shaped face that looks at me with all the impassivity of a fox, but she continues past without speaking. Another, a tall blond girl, stops.

"Can I help you?" she asks in tones so polite I'm momentarily startled into muteness. When was the last time one of Sally's friends spoke to me so politely? Then she does another amazing thing. She looks right at me. Direct eye contact.

"Yes, thank you, I'm looking for the dean's office."

"You must be the new English teacher," she says, extending her hand. "I'm Isabel Cheney. I'm going to be in your folklore class. I've done all the reading already and I'm looking forward to it."

"Isabel!" A voice calls from the upper landing. It's the girl with the foxlike face. "Stop sucking up and come on. Ms. Drake is waiting to make the adjustments to our costumes. Unless you want to be tripping over yours, you'd better hurry up."

"My costume already fits fine, Chloe, because I'm not a midget."

The girl on the landing—Chloe—scowls. "But we still have to hand in our paper, too."

"I've got **our** paper right here." Isabel holds up a bright orange folder. "I'm just going to show Ms. Rosenthal to the dean's office and then I'll meet you in the Reading Room."

Chloe casts a lingering look at the orange folder, as if she'd like to swoop down and pluck it out of

Isabel's hands, but then she throws up her hands, utters the teenager's favorite rejoinder—"Whatever!"—and turns away from us.

"Sorry," Isabel says, turning back to me.

"Really, you don't have to take me. I don't want to make you late for—" I'm about to say class, but then I realize that classes haven't started yet.

"It's just the fitting for First Night and, as I said, **my** dress already fits. Chloe's just pissed because I won't show her the paper we were supposed to do together, but that I did all the work on. She's afraid she might have to answer questions about it, but she should have thought about that when she let me do all the work."

We pass through a long echoing hall set up with easels, go up a short flight of stairs, along a corridor lined with glass-fronted cabinets that I imagine were once meant to hold the family china but are now full of art supplies, down another short flight of stairs, and across a small parlor where a fair-haired girl is curled up on a rose velvet settee sound asleep. Charcoal sketches of nude figures are scattered on the floor beneath her, their shadowy limbs intertwined in a dreamlike orgy. "Wow," I say, "I **am** glad you're showing me the way. The house seems to be set out like a maze."

"That's because the Beechers were a secretive family," she tells me. "They suffered persecution in England for their religious beliefs and when they immigrated to Massachusetts, Hiram Beecher was accused of witchcraft. That's why they settled here on the edge of the wilderness and that's why they built their houses with twisting hallways and secret hiding places in case they needed to hide from persecution."

"You're quite the historian," I say.

Isabel beams with pleasure. "I love history! I plan to double major in history and poli-sci at Brown or Cornell. I'm working on a senior thesis on the history of Arcadia."

We've come to a pair of wide oak doors, which I assume must, finally, lead to Ivy St. Clare's office. "I've been researching the history of Arcadia, too," I say. "Perhaps we can compare notes."

"Yes, I read the article you published on the historical sources of Lily Eberhardt's fairy tales. I liked it . . . but . . . well, I think you'll change your mind about the real meaning of the fairy tales when you've learned more about her life."

"Well," I say, a little taken aback by her presumption, "that's why I'm here." I give her a tight smile that I hope disguises the chagrin I feel at being corrected by a teenager. It's the arrogance of youth, I remind myself, she'll find out soon enough that life isn't just about doing well in school and being right . . . and that not everybody will respond as kindly to her smugness. "Thank you for showing me the way here," I add with more genuine warmth.

"My pleasure," she says. "Good luck with the dean. She can be a little intimidating." With that last warning, Isabel Cheney turns around and goes back the way we came. I watch her go, envying the certainty of her youthful confidence—the confidence of thinking that everything will go according to one's plans. I could use a little of that confidence now as I knock on my new boss's door.

CHAPTER 3

A soft but penetrating voice from inside calls, "Enter."

As I cross the threshold into Ivy St. Clare's office I have two conflicting impressions at once. One is that I've walked into a crowded party; the other is that the room is empty. I quickly see that my first impression comes from the murals. Monumental figures of women dressed in medieval robes line the walls. Some play musical instruments, while others carry sketch pads or artists' palettes. One sits at a loom, while another kneels beside a chunk of marble, a mallet raised to strike the stone. At the center of the painting, directly above the desk chair, a golden-haired woman holds a pen in one hand and a sketchbook in the other. She looks straight out at the room as if she were about to draw the viewer's portrait. The Muse of Drawing, I remember, recognizing the work as **The Arts,** a famous mural painted by Vera Beecher in the 1940s. It's a smaller version of the one she was commissioned to paint for a college in Pennsylvania. I've seen photographs of both versions, but none had captured how the figures fill the room, making it seem inhabited even though the chair behind the massive oak desk and the two seats in front of it are empty.

I glance over at the windows, imagining that my new employer must have slipped out to play a trick on me. Perhaps it's another initiation rite, like not giving coherent road directions. But then I detect a slight bulge in the heavy drapes.

"Dean St. Clare?" I say to the drapery, which happens to be of the same wilted lettuce print as the curtains in my cottage. "I'm Meg Rosenthal."

"Yes, yes, just give me a moment. I've almost got her."

I step forward and a little to the right to find a diminutive woman curled up on the ledge of a bay window, legs tucked beneath her, with a fat sketchpad balanced on her knees. Her head is bent to the pad, a wing of perfectly white hair concealing her face. I look out the window to see what she's drawing and find that after all the twists and turns Isabel led me through we're somehow facing the front lawn again. Most of the students have vanished from it, except for one girl who has fallen asleep lying on her side, facing the copper beech. Her long strawberry blond hair spills over the grass like a cascade of autumn leaves.

I look down at the sketchpad and see that Ivy St. Clare has perfectly caught the line of the girl's hip, the splay of her long legs, and the fall of her hair—all framed against the massive tree towering above her. In the drawing, though, there are other shapes sharing the lawn with her—hips and elbows and shoulder blades roiling just below the surface of the grass. The image is so powerful that when I look back out the window I half expect the scene to be suddenly populated by the artist's imaginary cohorts. The lawn, of course, is empty, but now I see the origin of those underground figures. The roots of the beech tree snake across the lawn, here and there breaking the surface of the grass and then diving back underneath. Once you look at the scene as the artist has drawn it, it's hard not to see them as bodies beneath the ground.

"There! I think I've captured it as best I can for now. The sun's gone behind a cloud." She shivers and cranks closed one of the two narrow casement windows that flank the wide central window. Then she flings the pad down on the ledge and looks up. The white hair falls back to reveal a wizened face, the color and texture of a walnut shell, that seems too small for the large brown eyes that stare up at me. When she uncoils herself from the window seat I see that all of Ivy St. Clare has been pared down to the essentials. She can't be more than 4'11" and she's as slim as a pixie—an impression enhanced by fawn-colored capris and a dark green tunic with a wide portrait collar that shows off her sharp collarbones and sunken chest. A round silver brooch, engraved with a design of two women encircled by a ring of ivy, is pinned to her collar. Her hair is cut in the same helmet bob I remember from photographs of her in the forties, but it's turned from chestnut brown to ash white.

"I see you found us all right," she says, cocking her head to one side. "Are you all sorted out in Fleur-de-Lis?"

"My daughter's unpacking. I thought I'd come over and let you know we'd gotten here."

"I'm glad you did. I was just about to ring for tea. Please, have a seat."

She perches on the edge of the desk, pushes an intercom button on a sleek office phone, and asks someone named Dymphna to bring the tea.

"I hope the cottage isn't too run-down. I sent some students over to clean it out. . . ." She pauses, no doubt seeing the look of surprise on my face. "Oh no, don't tell me, it hasn't been cleaned?"

"It really doesn't matter—"

"Of course it matters! We pride ourselves on our self-sufficiency here at the Arcadia School. The students all have jobs and the two I sent to Fleur-de-Lis were let off kitchen duty last week because they were supposed to have the cottage ready for you. I'll have to speak to them when we're done. . . . Ah, there's Dymphna now." Ivy St. Clare slips down from her desk, responding to some signal from outside the door that I have failed to hear. She's right, though. A stout woman holding a heavily laden tray is standing in the doorway. The dean tries to take the tray from her, but the woman ignores her efforts, slowly trundles across the carpet, and sets it down on the desk.

"Dymphna, who did I send to clean Fleur-de-Lis?"

"Chloe Dawson and Isabel Cheney," she answers as she pours out the tea. "But I'm not surprised if they didn't do a thorough job of it. They're both caught up in getting ready for the First Night festival."

Ivy St. Clare lets out a long, drawn-out sigh. "I thought they'd compete to see who could do the most cleaning, but I guess the festival was more important to them." She turns to me. "We always start the year off with a fall festival which we call First Night. Chloe and Isabel, as the two seniors with the highest class rankings, have the lead roles in it. Since they were here early I thought they could also do your cottage. I'll have to have a word with them."

"It's really all right," I say for the second time,

wishing I'd managed to lie about the state of the cottage. I hate to think that the two girls will think I complained about them—especially Isabel Cheney, who was so helpful to me. "I just met Isabel Cheney," I add. "She was nice enough to show me the way here. She struck me as a very responsible and intelligent girl."

"An aggressive and ambitious girl," Dean St. Clare says with a little shudder. "She's probably already planning to ask you for a college recommendation. I imagine she thinks she's **above** having to do her cleaning chores, but it's part of our philosophy here that each student takes part in the day-to-day running of the school. Dymphna, do you know where the girls are now?"

"They're upstairs in the Reading Room. Miss Drake is making the last adjustments to their costumes. Do you want me to send them down here?"

The dean tilts her head for a moment, considering. She looks, I think, like a robin cocking its head to the ground to listen for worms beneath the earth. "No," she says. "I'll go up so I can have a look at the girls' costumes. Thank you, Dymphna. That will be all.

"Well, then," Ivy St. Clare says after Dymphna has left, "I imagine you'd like to know more about the classes you'll be teaching."

"Yes." I take a sip of what turns out to be a bracing black tea—Darjeeling, maybe?—with some kind of spice. "I'm so happy to have the opportunity to teach a folklore class."

"And we are glad to have you to teach it," she says, handing me a plate of buttered brown bread and apple cake. "The minute I saw that you were writing your thesis on Vera Beecher's fairy tales I was interested in your application. I was also interested to see that you were a fine arts major in college. Do you still draw?"

"Not really," I say. I pause to take a bite of the apple cake—which has delicious chunks of tart apples in a buttery yellow cake flecked with cinnamon and pecans—and to wonder if I should tell her the truth and say I gave it up when I had Sally. But I'm never sure how other women—especially women without children—will react to that, so I skip over it. "But when I went back to school I was interested in combining the study of visual arts and language."

"That's exactly what we look for here at Arcadia. I enjoyed your paper on Dante Gabriel Rossetti's illustrations for his sister Christina's poem 'Goblin Market,' by the way. It's one of my favorite poems. Vera used to recite it in the evening." St. Clare puts down her teacup, closes her eyes, and recites in a low contralto so unlike her own high-pitched voice that I have the uneasy feeling that Vera Beecher is speaking through her: "**We must not look at goblin men, / We must not buy their fruits: / Who knows upon what soil they fed / Their hungry thirsty roots**." She pronounces the last line with such relish that I feel a chill I haven't felt since the first time I read Rosetti's poem of demonic seduction.

"I'll certainly cover Rossetti in the nineteenth-century fiction class, as well as the Brontës, Thomas Hardy—"

"Good, good . . . and for the folklore class, I would expect that in addition to the usual texts you will also use Vera Beecher's **Tales of Arcadia,** especially since it's the subject of your thesis—which I trust is near completion?"

"Oh yes," I say with what I hope sounds like conviction. The truth is that with Jude's death, dealing with the estate, looking for a job, and relocating I've done barely any work on my dissertation all year.

"Good. Most of our teachers have their Ph.D.s, but the board and I felt that in view of your interest in Vera Beecher's fairy tales—"

"The fairy tales by Vera Beecher **and** Lily Eberhardt, you mean? They were written and illustrated by both women. One of the goals of my thesis has been to figure out who drew and wrote what."

Ivy purses her mouth, making her face look even more pinched than before. It occurs to me that interrupting my new boss while she was pointing out my professional shortcomings hadn't been the best idea. "I think you'll find most of the artwork was done by Vera, who was by far the superior artist of the two. As for who wrote them, Vera liked to give Lily the credit, especially after Lily died. Lily had a trove of childish tales she had heard from her mother that she liked to tell around the hearth side in the evening. It was her contribution to the community. Vera would write them down in her notebook and then later transform them into works of art. Believe me, I heard the original tales and then read the finished product. There's no doubt who really **wrote** them."

"But you didn't come here until 1945," I say. "And you were only . . . what . . . sixteen?" I know from my research that Ivy St. Clare was one of the first scholarship students at the Arcadia School. "And Lily was here from the late twenties. How do you know the collaboration worked the same all those years?"

"Because Vera asked me to transcribe all the early versions of the fairy tales. It's all in the notebooks."

"Vera's notebooks? I can't wait to see them. Are they in the archives in the school library?"

"No, they're far too precious . . . and fragile. I keep them locked in the Reading Room upstairs, here in Beech Hall."

"Those notebooks would be invaluable to my work."

Ivy St. Clare fixes me with her bright brown eyes and I have to try hard not to squirm. It's like being stared at by a hawk. I feel sure she's not only going to turn down my request, but that she's going to fire me on the spot. And then what will I do? After selling our Great Neck house and almost everything in it to pay back the debts that Jude had accrued, I have nothing but an eleven-year-old car and an unfinished doctorate. I'm thirty-eight years old and haven't held a job since waitressing during college.

This job is the only chance I've got for supporting Sally and myself. I take a deep breath, preparing to plead if I have to.

But Ivy St. Clare doesn't fire me. She smiles and says, "Of course you'll have access to Vera's notebooks. It's half the reason I hired you. It's about time she received her proper academic recognition. In fact, we can go upstairs to the Reading Room right now. I have to have a word with Chloe and Isabel anyway."

"Thank you." I wonder why I don't feel more relieved. For a moment I had pictured Sally and myself driving away from here and for the second time today it had seemed like a good idea. But that's probably just anxiety over a new job—my first **real** job.

Ivy St. Clare gets to her feet and I'm startled again by how tiny she is. "While we're getting the notebooks, I'll tell Dymphna to wrap up some cake and sandwiches for you to take back to your daughter. If she's like most teenagers, I know she's probably ravenous."

She says **ravenous** with a glint in her eyes, as if the appetite of the young fed something in herself.

"Thank you, that's very kind." When she's on the intercom with Dymphna, I wander back to the window and look out at the lawn. The day has turned overcast again and the sleeping girl is gone. Before I turn away, my eye falls on Ivy St. Clare's sketchpad still lying on the window seat. Her last touches to

the drawing had subtly changed the figures beneath the ground. It's clear now that they are heading toward the sleeping girl. The one closest to the
girl has reached a hand up out of the grass and is
about to pull her down to join the rest of them.

CHAPTER 4

I follow Ivy St. Clare back through the rose parlor, from which the sleeping artist and her charcoal sketches have vanished, and then up a narrow flight of stairs to the second floor.

"This was the Beecher family's winter parlor," she announces as she opens the double oak doors. "Vera loved to read here on snowy days." The scene inside the parlor might be a pageant entitled "Snowy Day." Girls in white dresses lounge on settees and chintz upholstered chairs. Swaths of transparent tulle lie on the floor or are draped over tables and bookshelves. In the center of all this white froth Isabel Cheney stands still as a statue in a long white Empire-waist dress while a woman with silvery hair—Ms. Drake, I assume—kneels at her feet. Isabel looks every bit a goddess, but the woman at her feet is not worshipping her—she's letting down the hem.

"I don't understand," Isabel is saying as we enter. "The length was perfectly fine yesterday."

"Maybe you grew another inch." The comment comes from the dark-haired fox-faced girl I saw earlier—Chloe. She's draped across a love seat, her white dress spread out around her so no one else can sit next to her. She's surrounded by a circle of girls sitting on the floor and balancing on the arms of the love seat who giggle at her next remark. "Around the waist, that is."

"Is that why you two failed to clean Fleur-de-Lis in time for Ms. Rosenthal's arrival?" The dean's crisp voice cuts across the laughter. "Because you were wasting time arguing?"

Isabel Cheney looks from the dean to me, her face pinking with embarrassment. Although I've only just met her I feel I've betrayed her trust.

"I don't know what you're talking about," Chloe says. "**I** cleaned upstairs. Isabel was supposed to be cleaning the downstairs, but when I came down I found her with her nose in a book **as usual.**"

"You said you'd clean the downstairs if I did the

whole research paper for our group!" Isabel counters.

"You would have done it all yourself anyway since you think you're smarter than anyone else."

"Girls!" Dean St. Clare's voice silences the girls. "You were **both** responsible for the cleaning of the whole cottage and you were supposed to work on that research paper **together.** Here at Arcadia we are not allowed to barter chores."

"But Dean St. Clare, I've done some really interesting original research—" Isabel begins, but Ms. Drake stands up and interrupts her.

"Dean St. Clare," she says, removing a pin from her mouth. "I'm afraid this is all my fault. I've pushed the girls to work so hard on First Night. And Isabel has done such a good job researching the old festivals here. Perhaps if you take a look at her paper—" The woman leans down to retrieve an orange folder—the same one I saw Isabel Cheney carrying earlier—from a chair, but Dean St. Clare holds up one hand.

"I'm sure Miss Cheney has done an admirable research job—she always does—but that is not the point. This school was founded on the spirit of collaboration and cooperation. Women helping women to achieve their artistic goals. And you two"—she levels an icy stare on Isabel and then Chloe—"have utterly failed. I have half a mind to replace you in tonight's festivities—"

"That's not fair!" Chloe stands up, her too-long

white dress poofing out around her. She looks really upset. "Isabel got to be the goddess since last May. She's stepping down tonight and I'm just starting. So it's not an equal punishment."

Goddess? I think, beginning to wonder what sort of festival is planned for tonight. I remember that the founders of Arcadia put on elaborate festivals—May Day dances and winter solstice pageants—but I didn't know they were still celebrated. Maybe Sally was right about this school being a little **off.**

"Perhaps if the girls agreed to come by tomorrow to clean," I say, "and I can get those journals later."

Dean St. Clare looks at me as if she has not only forgotten my presence but who I am. Then she shakes herself. "Those are both good ideas, Ms. Rosenthal. I'll collect the material you need and have it ready for you tomorrow. And you two—Chloe and Isabel—come downstairs to my office. I'm not done with you yet."

"Chloe still needs her dress altered," Ms. Drake says. "Why don't you take Isabel first and I'll send Chloe down as soon as I'm done with her?"

"Very well," the dean says. She suddenly looks tired. "Come with me, Isabel. And Ms. Rosenthal, don't forget to stop by the kitchen for the food Dymphna is packing for you."

She turns to lead the way back to her office with Isabel in tow. I follow because otherwise I'll have no idea how to find the kitchen again. I stay back a few yards, though. When the dean turns a corner Isabel turns to me. "I'm really sorry about the cottage not being cleaned," she says.

"**I'm** really sorry I said anything, Isabel."

She grins at me. "It's okay. I'm used to being in trouble. The kitchen's just down this hall, by the way." She turns to go and I watch her straighten her shoulders as she follows the dean. I hope I haven't gotten her in too much trouble. She is, after all, the first friend I've made here.

In the kitchen I find Dymphna standing at a massive cast-iron stove, ladling stew into a plastic container. "Please, that's way too much," I tell her.

"Don't argue, she'll only give you more."

The voice comes from a man sitting at a butcher block table against the far wall of the kitchen. He's wearing a navy blue windbreaker emblazoned with a shield that reads ARCADIA FALLS SHERIFF'S DEPARTMENT. He looks up from a bowl of stew and smiles crookedly at me. His face is lined enough to mark him as a man in his forties, but the glint in his pale green eyes is boyish.

"Dymphna's like the witch in Hansel and Gretel. Always trying to fatten you up."

"Aye, leave off, Callum Reade, why do you come out here if you're not after my cooking. I know it's not my beauty," Dymphna says in an aggrieved voice, hiding the smile on her broad face by leaning down to smell the stew.

"Ah, you underestimate your charms, Dymphna, you witch." He lifts the bowl to his lips and tips the last bit down his throat, stands up, and brings the bowl over to the sink. I notice the glint of a sheriff's badge under the jacket and, when he leans into the sink, the dull metal gleam of a pistol handle at his waist. "But I'm afraid I'm here tonight to see your boss. She free now?" He looks toward me and I realize he's asking me, not the cook.

"Um, she just called a student into her office," I say, wondering why the town sheriff is on the campus. Has there been a crime?

"Which student?" the sheriff asks.

"Isabel Cheney."

"Really?" The sheriff exchanges a look with the cook. "What did she do? Tongue-lash the opposing team in debate club? Hack into the school's computer and sabotage Chloe Dawson's GPA?"

"She and Chloe Dawson were supposed to clean my cottage and they didn't. What is it between those two girls? They were at each other's throats."

"Beats me," the sheriff says, running his hands through his hair until it stands up straight from his scalp like fresh-mown wheat. "I'm just a small town sheriff, not an adolescent psychologist. But I'll tell you this—I wouldn't get between those two when they go at it." He winks at me and shoulders his way out the swinging door.

"Are the local police always so involved with the school?" I ask looking down at the large plastic vat of stew to hide the blush I can feel heating my face. I can't remember the last time a man winked at me.

"Well, there was some trouble at the First Night festival last year. Now the dean likes to enlist the cooperation of the sheriff beforehand. Besides, Callum Reade likes to keep an eye on things. Here." She hands me the large container of stew.

"That's really too much," I try to tell her again but she shakes her head.

"You can freeze what you don't eat tonight. You've got a growing girl and"—she gives me a quick up and down look and shakes her head again—"you look like you haven't had a decent meal in a while yourself."

"I haven't had much of an appetite since my husband died last fall," I say, surprising myself with my own honesty. The only one in Great Neck who'd noticed the ten pounds I'd lost was a mother at a field hockey game who asked what my secret was. Grief, I'd wanted to tell her, and the stacks of bills I can't pay, and finding out that my daughter's college fund was spent a year ago without my consent. Instead I had told her I'd cut down on carbs. But to plump, motherly Dymphna I say now, "Everything just tastes like dust."

She clucks her tongue while pulling a loaf of bread out of a tin bread box. "That's how Miss Vera took on when Miss Eberhardt died back when my mother was head housekeeper here. Wouldn't touch nary a crust for a fortnight," she said. She begins cutting thick slices of the brown, grain-flecked bread with a serrated knife in her right hand while using her left to slather each slice with butter from an earthenware crock: a balletic display of coordination I'm tempted to applaud. "My mother said that she nearly starved herself to death, and that she wasn't really herself for a whole year—not until she got the news that Virgil Nash had killed himself. Then she started eating again."

"Really? Are you sure that was the reason?"

Dymphna pauses in her cutting and buttering of bread, both knives arrested in midair. "My mother told me she called her to her office that day and told her to take down a painting of Nash's that hung in the dining room. 'I'll not have the work of a suicide hanging over our girls,' she said to her. And that night she came down to dinner for the first time since Miss Eberhardt's death and ate everything put in front of her. My mother never had no trouble with her appetite again."

Dymphna rests both knives on the counter and brushes crumbs from her apron. She wraps the buttered bread in wax paper and puts it and the plastic vat of stew into a canvas sack that she hands to me. "There's nothing like revenge to sharpen the appetite."

I leave Dymphna's kitchen laden with foodstuffs. Before I could get out she'd added an apple cake, a dozen apples, a tin of oatmeal, coffee beans, and a quart of milk to my sack. I feel a little like the girl in Rossetti's poem who returns from the Goblin Market with forbidden fruits to tempt her sister's appetite. As I'm walking through the front door of Beech Hall, Chloe Dawson brushes by me in a cloud of white fabric. In addition to her own dress she has another white dress draped over her arm.

"Chloe," I say as she rushes by, "stop a minute, please."

She turns around and I see that her heart-shaped face is swollen and tearstained.

"I just wanted to say that I'm sorry about what happened. I never meant to get you and Isabel in trouble."

"It's not your fault," she says, "it's Isabel's. She **wanted** to do the research paper by herself. Now we're both going to get Fs on the paper. Do you know what that will do to my GPA? I'll never get into an Ivy now. Have you seen her, by the way?"

"No," I say, scanning the lawn. "But there seem to be some students gathering over there under that tree."

"Yeah, that's First Night. Maybe she's there."

"Honey," I say, putting my hand on her shoulder. "Why don't you forget about the fight with Isabel and your GPA for tonight and have a good time?"

"That's exactly what I plan to do, Ms. Rosenthal," she says with a brilliant smile. "I plan to have a good time getting back at Isabel."

I walk back to the cottage chilled by Chloe Dawson's gleeful anticipation of revenge. I've certainly witnessed competitiveness and nastiness among the girls at Sally's high school. Last year a few girls posted insults and embarrassing pictures on the Internet. The Burn Thread, as it became known, was the subject of half a dozen assemblies and letters home from the principal. I'd hoped, though, that the Arcadia School, which promoted "the collaborative spirit" on its website, would be free of such mean-spiritedness.

But then there's a long history of betrayal and rivalry at Arcadia, from its beginnings when Vera Beecher met Virgil Nash in New York in the 1920s when he was a poor but promising artist teaching at the Art Students League. When he lost his job there—over an incident in which he allowed one of his students to pose nude—Vera Beecher invited him to come to her childhood home at Arcadia to start an artists' colony with her and a handful of other students, including Lily Eberhardt, in whom Vera was rumored to have taken a particular interest. It was also rumored that Virgil Nash and Lily Eberhardt had had an affair. Nash left the colony abruptly after its first summer. His career after that had gone in an unexpected direction. He'd become a society portraitist, patronized by a rich clientele. He became wealthy but dissolute, a man who had traded his talent for commercial rewards. In the late forties, though, he had returned to Arcadia and painted a series of portraits of Lily Eberhardt, which were altogether different from his society portraits. He was just beginning to receive acclaim for his new work when Lily died—killed when she fell into a ravine during a snowstorm. According to the local gossip picked up by the press she'd been on her way to meet Nash and run away with him. Two weeks later her body was found buried in the snow. A year later Nash killed himself, many believed over grief at the death of his muse.

When I see the lights of the cottage at the end of the path I imagine Lily Eberhardt setting off from there in the middle of the blizzard. I've always wondered why she would have risked the storm. Had she been that desperate to get away? Had she been afraid Nash would leave without her?

I'm thinking so hard about Lily Eberhardt that when a white-clad figure flits between the trees ahead of me I stop dead in my tracks, sure I've conjured her ghost. The apparition—if that's what it is—stops, too, then glides off the path into the woods and disappears. I hurry to the end of the path and scan the trees but all I see is a slim white birch tree tilting among the surrounding pines. Is that what I saw? It must be, I think as I leave the woods. If it was a person why would they hide from me? I can't quite banish the feeling, though, that I've summoned Lily's ghost.

When I walk into the cottage I go straight to the fireplace and look at the cracked tiles. Vera had the cottage built for Lily. Fleur-de-Lis is a reference to the flower Lily was named for. The two women made each other tokens of the other's name—tiles decorated with lilies and beech trees, cabinets engraved with those symbols, tapestries and rugs woven with interlocking tree and flower patterns. Examining the tiles above the fireplace again it's clear that only the ones decorated with lilies have been cracked. Did Vera do this when she learned that her protégée—and, some believed, lover—had announced that she was leaving? If so, it might have been that final act of violence that drove Lily out into the storm.

I shiver thinking of poor Lily wandering lost in the middle of a snowstorm and dying by herself in the cold. When I can't stop shivering I realize why I'm so cold. I left all the windows open and the afternoon, waning toward evening, has become chilly. I'd forgotten that even summer evenings this far north can be cold. Dymphna's stew will be a welcome comfort.

I call Sally's name while unpacking the food in the kitchen. She doesn't respond, but then that could be because she's plugged into her iPod, asleep, or just ignoring me. Pausing to listen, I hear the faint sound of music coming from upstairs—something by the Decemberists, I think. So she's not plugged in, but listening to music on her laptop. Hopefully while unpacking. I head toward the stairs but stop myself. The therapist we saw in Great

Neck said that repeatedly calling for Sally when she didn't answer me just enabled her helplessness. "Just put dinner on the table and let it get cold if she doesn't come down for it," she had told me. I've watched a lot of food congeal—and Sally grow thinner—over the last year. Still, I might as well unpack the boxes marked "kitchen" and get dinner ready before calling again.

Although I sold off all the good china on eBay and left the high-end appliances with the house, I've kept most of the everyday china and cookware. It didn't have good resale value, I figured. Who would want someone else's used pots and pans with the ghosts of past meals clinging to them? What stranger would want to braise pork chops on the tarnished copper-bottomed saucepan with the burn on its rim from when Jude stole up behind me while I was sautéing shallots and kissed me so long I let them burn? I can still smell the charred onion when I lift the pan from its nest of packing paper—a smell as intimate as the memory of sex. It would be like selling our marriage sheets. And how could I sell the blue-glazed Le Creuset casserole, a housewarming present from my mother, chipped on the lid from when I dropped it during a fight? It was in the apartment on Avenue B, two weeks after I had told Jude I was pregnant. He came home and announced that he'd dropped out of the MFA program at Pratt and taken a trading job with Morgan Stanley.

"Good thing I'm good at math as well as art," he

said just as I lifted the lid off the casserole. I looked down at the coq au vin I'd spent half the day making from a recipe in Julia Child and felt suddenly queasy. **Morning sickness,** I thought, even though it was night. When I picked up the pot to bring it to the table my arms went limp. It fell to the stained linoleum, splattering wine sauce and chicken bones everywhere.

"Shit, Meg," Jude said, surveying the carnage, "if this is how you react to my first real job I'd better not bring home a Christmas bonus."

As I pour Dymphna's stew into the pot I touch the place where the iron shows through the blue glaze. Whenever I look at it I wonder what I might have said to change things. Should I have offered to get an abortion? Should I have told him we'd scrimp by on an art teacher's salary? Or that surely with his talent he'd be a famous artist someday? Should I have suggested we borrow from his parents? Or move to the country and raise goats for a living? Should I have recognized the look in his eyes as defeat and not pretended that giving up his dreams to support me and our unborn child was a good idea?

I turn on the gas under the chipped pot, but it hisses without catching. It takes me a long moment of smelling gas to realize that the stove is so old it needs a match to start. There's a box of Diamond Tips in a rusted tin box screwed into the cabinet right above the range. I light one and step back as the flame lashes out like a cornered cat.

My hands are still shaking as I start unpacking the everyday china: the blue-and-white Marimekko Jude bought at the Scandinavian Design store our first married Christmas together. What a kind man, I had thought. The average guy his age would have spent his Christmas bonus on stereo equipment or a bigger TV set, not plates and bowls and saucers for his hugely pregnant wife who had burst into tears the week before because the paper plates she ate on made her think she wasn't grown up enough to be a mother. I still remember how bright and cheerful it all looked laid out for Christmas breakfast. And even though the white glaze is scratched and the blue rims have faded it's all still here—service for eight. "For our growing family," Jude had said. Now it seems like a lot of crockery for just me and Sally.

I lay plates and bowls on the table and fish out spoons and knives from the jumble of flatware (the good silver went in February to pay the heating bill), and then sink down onto a spindly kitchen chair that creaks under my weight. A wave of exhaustion settles over me like the lead apron the dentists make you wear when you get your teeth X-rayed. How am I going to unpack all these boxes when every single cup and saucer carries the weight of all the mistakes I've made? Checking first to see that Sally hasn't come downstairs, I lay my head down on the table.

It's surprisingly cool. I'd thought the top—white with a trim of green leaves and brown pinecones—was painted wood, but with my cheek on its smooth surface I realize it's actually enameled steel. My grandmother had a table like it in her Brooklyn kitchen. It had two folding leaves like this one that could be let down and then, when you sat underneath it, you felt like you were in a little house. The scalloped edges of the leaves looked like the trim on the cottages of fairy tales. A word was stamped on the underside of the table: Porceliron. I had thought it sounded like a fantasy kingdom, but my grandmother told me it was the brand name of the table because the top was iron coated with an enameled layer of porcelain. That was why I loved those Le Creuset pots when I grew up; they had that same odd marriage of delicate porcelain over hard steel. Right now the cool surface of the table feels like my grandmother's hand on my forehead when I had a fever. The aroma of some herb in Dymphna's stew steals out of the pot on the stove and I feel the fatigue lift off me just a little. Enough to get me to my feet. I'll go get Sally and serve us dinner on our old scratched dishes. Hot stew and homebaked bread with coffee and apple cake for dessert. We'll be okay, I say to myself for what might well be the millionth time since Jude died. We'll get through this.

The narrow stairs are pitched so steeply I can feel the muscles in the backs of my legs pinching by the time I reach the second floor. What a strange little house. Nothing about it—windows, door frames— seems to be built according to any standard. It feels like a child's playhouse put together from odd bits and pieces. The steps creak and bow in the middle. The newel post at the top of the stairs is carved in the shape of an owl. The second-floor hall slopes down to a narrow window seat squeezed under the sharply pitched eaves. Peering through one open door I see an empty bedroom that's all angles and corners. Good thing I ditched our old bedroom set—nothing would have fit. Besides, it looks like there are cabinets and shelves built into all those nooks and crannies.

It's charming in a way, and I find myself hoping as I knock on the second bedroom door that Sally has found it so. Probably it's a good sign that she's shut herself into her new room. This could mean she's settling in. I knock again, louder, in case she's plugged in to her iPod or fallen asleep, but the only sound coming from behind the door is the Clash singing "London Calling." She must be asleep. I turn the knob—tarnished brass with some design of vines and leaves—and open the door.

Whatever image I'd had in my head of Sally settling in is instantly vanquished by the bare mattress and unopened boxes on the floor. The only light in the room comes from Sally's open laptop where her screensaver cycles through images of outer space. Nebulae bloom and gas giants explode in the time it takes me to realize that the room is empty. Sally's gone.

CHAPTER 5

It takes only a few minutes to go through the whole cottage: two upstairs bedrooms crammed under the sharply sloping eaves, a bathroom fitted with a stained clawfoot tub (no shower—what must Sally have made of that?), then kitchen, parlor, and pantry downstairs. I even check the closets. I don't check the basement because there's no way Sally would ever go into one of her own free will. Ditto the garage, which I haven't even had the nerve to go into yet. The thought that her absence might **not** be of her own free will licks at the corners of my mind with the same darting stealth as the flame on the gas range, but I draw back from it just as quickly.

No, this is just Sally punishing me for bringing her here. I can already imagine her defense: **I thought you wanted me to get acquainted with our new home.** I'll yell at her for not leaving a note, and she'll shrug and say she forgot. It's such a familiar scenario that I'm almost comforted until I step out into the darkness that's fallen over the campus.

Beyond the wedge of light spilling out from the cottage door, the night is as dark as the outer reaches of space moving across Sally's laptop screen in the empty room above me. Darker. There are no exploding gas giants here to light my way. When I close the door behind me and step off the front stoop I can't even see as far as the car.

The car. Was it still in the driveway when I came back from the dean's? I can't remember. Does Sally have a spare key? I remember now that Jude had had a spare stashed somewhere in the house, but I hadn't been able to find it before moving. Had Sally? Has she been secretly holding on to it all this time and planning her getaway?

It's an elaborate plot I never would have suspected her capable of a year ago, but she's done a lot I wouldn't have thought her capable of over the last year. She's memorized my credit card number and ordered concert tickets over the phone and then taken the train into the city to see the concert while claiming to be at the local movie theater. She's hidden report cards, intercepted phone calls from teachers, forged my signature, hacked into my AOL account to buy several hundred dollars' worth of CDs and XBox games from Amazon.com, and impersonated me on the phone to get her out of taking the bio Regents. She's become such an expert at subterfuge and clandestine activity that I might have suspected car theft would be her next move.

I stumble down the front path in the direction where I left the Jag, tripping twice over the uneven flagstones, and run straight into the jagged edge of the broken passenger door. The pain is almost welcome. At least wherever Sally is she's on foot, not trapped in a twisted metal wreck.

On the other hand, if she'd taken the car I could at least have called the police and given them a license plate to track down.

The thought of the police reminds me that there is a town sheriff somewhere on the campus: the blond, green-eyed man I saw in Dymphna's kitchen. I even recall his name—Callum Reade. I get out my cell phone from the car before remembering that there's no service, which means that I won't be able to reach Sally on **her** cell phone. I could go inside and call the police, but what will I say? My sixteen-year-old has been missing for—how long? I have no idea when she left the house. I imagine the amused and condescending look that will appear in the sheriff's eyes. I'll look like an idiot, when probably all Sally's done is go looking for me at Beech Hall . . . or gone to the library in search of a wi-fi connection. The thought cheers me up for the three or four seconds it takes to remember that she would have brought her laptop along if that's where she was going.

Still, I decide it's worth looking in the library before I call Sheriff Reade and brand myself a nervous, neurotic mother in front of the whole town and my new colleagues.

I remember that Jude always kept a flashlight in the glove compartment. I take it out and switch it on, amazed that it works. Jude must have changed the batteries not long before he died; it was the kind of detail he attended to. I also get out an old Pratt sweatshirt from the trunk, less to keep me warm than for its smell of motor oil that reminds me of Jude.

The library, I recall, is the imposing Gothic edifice I saw looming behind the copper beech tree. I consider driving there, but if Sally's already coming back on the path I'll miss her. And since I've already walked the path once it shouldn't be too hard to find my way on it. At least I'm beginning to get adjusted to the dark—aided by a full moon just risen over the tree line.

It turns out, though, that even finding the entrance to the path in the dark is a chore. **Between two oak trees catty-corner to Fleur-de-Lis's front door** is hardly a map. Would it kill them to nail a sign to one of these precious trees with a destination and an arrow—MAIN CAMPUS THIS WAY? Under the beam of my flashlight the line of trees appears unbroken and monolithic, a legion of forest guards standing at attention. Their rough bark faces stare back at me impassively, defying me to find a hole in their ranks to slip through. For a moment I have the ridiculous notion that the path I took earlier today somehow closes at nightfall, sealing the cottage off from the rest of the world. Then I realize that the idea comes from a line in **The Changeling Girl. As she approached the witch's house she thought she heard the trees moving behind her and when she came out of the woods and turned around she saw that the path had vanished and she had lost her way home.** I picture Sally on that path now, being swallowed up by the woods.

But then my flashlight finds a space between two broad trunks that are smoother than the pines'—oaks, surely—and I dive into the gap as if it were going to vanish if I don't move fast enough.

It's like stepping into an unlit closet. The dense canopy of pine trees blocks the moonlight. There's not a single light marking the way. Really, I think as I aim my flashlight onto the pine needle–covered path and start walking, what boarding school doesn't light their paths? No doubt Ivy St. Clare would cite some harebrained rationale along the lines of electric light diminishing the sylvan idyll, but hasn't she heard of campus crime and date rape? Sally was right; this **is** a school for losers.

And what a crock that eleven and a half minutes was! There was no way that anyone could make this walk in under fifteen minutes no matter how light on their feet they were—no matter whose **little sparrow** they were!

My anger at Ivy St. Clare and the Arcadia School in general speeds my steps and keeps my fear at bay for a little while, but then I start to picture some of the ways Sally could come to harm: she could have been attacked by a local psychopath or she could have fallen and be lying at the bottom of a steep ravine. Wasn't that how Lily Eberhardt had died? And somewhere near here. As my heart starts to race at these images I recall something my mother used to say to me when I woke up at night screaming because I was convinced there were monsters under my bed and lurking in the closet. "You have a powerful imagination. You can use it to tell good stories or you can use it to tell bad ones." I'm pretty sure my mother would say that imagining Sally dead is telling bad ones.

It is not my imagination, though, that the path has lengthened since I took it during the day. **A journey in the night always seems longer than one in the day.** The line appears in my head and it takes me a minute to remember that it's also from

The Changeling Girl. It's from the part I didn't get to today in the car. The rest of the story comes back to me now as I travel the dark path.

After the witch told the captive girl that she had given the changeling "running legs" by washing the root in running water instead of well water, the girl waited every day at the edge of the woods for the changeling to come back. She watched the leaves on the trees turn red and gold and then fall to the ground, she watched snow fill up the woods and hang heavy in the pine boughs, and then she listened to the slow drip of the melting snow, always listening for the sound of footsteps coming through the woods, waiting for the changeling girl to return. Could her family really have accepted her as a substitute? Wouldn't they have noticed she was a thing made out of wood and magic and not flesh and bone? One day the girl saw a flash of color in the woods and thought that it was the changeling girl's calico dress, but it was only a patch of wildflowers spreading over the forest floor. The cool blue and white and purple flowers of early spring turned into the blazing red and yellow and orange of high summer and still there was no sign of the changeling girl's return. On the day the first leaf changed color, the witch came to her and told her that her family had accepted the changeling girl now as their own. There was no sense waiting for her any longer.

But the girl could not believe this. That night she stole a lantern from the witch's larder and filled it with hazelnut oil. She had overheard the old witch muttering to herself that the only way to find one's way back through the forest was to light the path with a mixture of hazelnut oil and a drop of one's own blood. So the girl pricked her finger and let a drop of her blood fall into the oil. The light that fell from the lamp became a ghastly red that frightened the girl, but when she held the lantern up to the trees they parted before her, showing her the path back to her home at last. As soon as she stepped onto the path she could hear a heavy shuffle behind her. The trees were closing the way back. But she didn't care. She never wanted to go back to the witch's house. She held the lantern before her and followed the blood-lit path deep into the woods. The way seemed much longer than it had when she had first made the journey, but a journey in the night always seems longer than one in the day, she told herself. She went forward bravely until the light from her lantern began to wane and, looking inside, she saw that almost all of the oil was gone. Only then did she realize that if she burned through all of the oil before she made it home she would be trapped inside the forest forever.

I'm beginning to feel that I'm going to suffer the same fate. Much more than fifteen minutes have gone by and the path hasn't come out onto the lawn in front of Beech Hall. Could it be the wrong path?

I recall now that the path branched in two directions. Had I taken the wrong branch? Or could it be, as in the fairy tale, that the trees have rearranged themselves at the witch's orders to confuse me? The latter idea, although patently ridiculous, lights a spark of fear in my brain. I even imagine that I can hear the trees behind me closing rank, sealing me into the woods forever, and that the light from my flashlight glows a garish red on the pine needle–littered path. I should, I know, turn back if this is the wrong path, but instead I go faster, breaking into a run. When the path slopes suddenly down—proving it's the **wrong** path since the one I took today was level—I lose my footing and land on my hands and knees in the dirt. The flashlight flies out of my hand, rolls into the woods, and goes out, leaving me in the pitch-black dark.

But not alone. Now that the noise of my steps is silenced I realize that I hadn't been imagining the sound of footsteps after all. I hear them crunching through the underbrush somewhere behind me. Sally, I think hopefully. But as I listen to the heavy footfalls I recall that Sally hasn't worn anything but flip-flops in months, and these steps sound as if they were made by heavy workboots. Or, my frantic imagination suddenly insists, like trees uprooted and dragging their heavy limbs together to trap me in the forest. Another sound is beneath the sound of the footsteps, a low roar like some kind of wild beast growling.

Still crouched on my hands and knees I turn

around to stare into the woods behind me, but of course I can't see anything in the impenetrable dark. I can hear the steps approaching me, though, and feel their vibration through my hands pressed against the ground. Suddenly I remember the picture that Ivy St. Clare was drawing today—of the beech roots turned into creatures that swarmed beneath the sleeping girl.

Something skitters across my hand and I scream. The footsteps crash through the trees and then I'm blinded by a flash of light. Behind it the woods flare into looming shadows that bear down on me. Tree-shaped and man-shaped shadows. I get to my feet and step backward. The man-shaped thing stops and lowers the blinding light. A face that looks like it was carved out of pine wood, with hair like gold pine needles standing straight up, emerges out of the gloom, its eyes gold in the flashlight's beam.

"Stop right there," the man tells me. "Don't move another inch."

"What do you mean?" I ask, my fear turning into outrage at the man's brusque tone. "I haven't done anything wrong." I notice that the lettering on the man's jacket reads ARCADIA FALLS SHERIFF, and the fringe of blond hair and pale green eyes are familiar. "Reade, isn't it?" I say. "You're the town sheriff. I'm the new English teacher."

"Yes, I know who you are, but I don't think you know **where** you are. If you'll stand still for a second . . ." He holds up his hands as if he were approaching a skittish horse and takes a tentative step in my direction. When I don't move he approaches me cautiously. I feel ridiculous, but something in his intent pale eyes keeps me rooted to the spot. When he's reached my side he holds his high-powered lantern over my head, illuminating the woods behind me.

But there **are** no woods behind me, only empty space. Three feet from where we stand the ground falls away into a deep chasm hewn out of black rock. The roar I'd heard before was the stream of water that leaps from rock to rock like a silver snake and crashes somewhere far, far below us.

"Witte Clove," the guard tells me. "Two more steps and you would have broken your neck down there. What in hell are you doing wandering up on the ridge at night?"

"I'm looking for my daughter, Sally," I say, trying to hold on to the anger I felt a minute ago to steady my voice. "She wasn't at the cottage when I got back there. I thought she went to the campus, but I must have taken the wrong path. . . . Oh my God, if Sally took this path . . ."

"How long has she been gone?" Reade asks me. He lowers the lantern and rests his other hand on his holster. The gesture, perhaps meant to reassure me that he's able to protect us from predators, makes me wary instead. What is there in these woods that we would need protecting from? I wonder suddenly what kind of **trouble** Dymphna was referring to earlier today.

"Since before dinner . . . I think. I mean, I thought she was there when I got back, but then she wasn't. . . ."

"So you really don't know how long she's been gone?" He crosses his arms and leans back on his heels. Then he rocks forward and sniffs the air. With a flash of anger I realize he's checking my breath to see if I'm drunk.

"What difference does that make? She's out here somewhere wandering around an **unlit** campus. Haven't you people heard of security lights? This campus is a crime scene waiting to happen!"

A smile tugs at the corner of his mouth, but he purses his lips to hide it and nods his head. "I've voiced the same complaint to Dean St. Clare. You're absolutely right. Why, right now the rival gangs of Arcadia Falls, New York, are getting ready to rumble. I haven't seen anything like it since my days walking the beat in the South Bronx."

"Oh, so you're a retired city cop. I should have known. So what did you do to get yourself exiled up here to the boondocks?"

He flinches as if I'd hit him and hardens his mouth. "I'm sure you wouldn't find it as interesting as the fairy tales you've been hired to teach. And besides, I thought you wanted to find your daughter. I have a pretty good idea where she's gone off to."

"You do?" I'm so grateful for that news that, obnoxious as he's been, I'm tempted to throw my arms around his neck. But he's already turned on his heel and taken off down the path away from me. The path descends steeply now and I have to hurry to keep up with his long strides. The last thing I want is to be left alone in the dark again. It's only when I catch up to him that I think of a question.

"Hey, why were you following me anyway?"

He turns and stares at me, his eyes flashing like cat's eyes. "My God, you intellectuals are all alike. You think the sun rises and sets on you. I wasn't following you. I was taking a short cut through the woods to keep an eye on that." He jabs his finger in the air toward an opening in the trees. When I look in the direction he's pointing, I see why his eyes are flashing. We've come out in the apple orchard. The stunted, misshapen trees look even more like gnomes in the strangely glowing fog that surrounds them. Above the field the copper beech looms like a giant marshaling his troops together. I can see it clearly silhouetted against the night sky because it's surrounded by flames.

CHAPTER 6

"What in the world—?"

"It's the First Night bonfire. Year after year I tell the dean it's dangerous, but she says it's **tradition.**" He snorts the word and shakes his head. Etched against the fire, his high forehead, crooked nose, and strong jaw look like the features of a Roman general struck on a bronze coin. His eyes, turned gold in the firelight, are set in a determined expression as we approach the circle on the hill, where dark shapes sway before the lurid orange and red flames in the same rhythm as the pulse of the fire.

As we get nearer, I strafe the crowd for Sally but don't see her. I can hear the roar and crackle of the burning wood and something else—a whispering that seems to be coming out of the fire itself, the way water caught in wood steams and hisses as it escapes. But it's not the fire, it's the circle of fire worshippers chanting something as they dance around it—the girls in the white dresses I saw them trying on earlier, the boys in loose white shirts over their jeans. Although I know they're the same teenagers I saw lounging around the lawn earlier today, there's something disturbingly pagan about the scene.

"What in the world are they supposed to be celebrating?"

"Beats me. One of the students tried to explain it to me last year. It has something to do with the changing season and ancient fertility rites."

"Fertility rites?" I squawk, imagining Sally rolling around in the hay with some gangly teenaged boy. I still can't make out her face in the ring of figures surrounding the fire. They all look alike in the glow of the flames, eyes wide and mouths open in some song, the words of which I can't make out.

"Well, it's not as bad as the one they have in May," Reade says. "Beltane, they call that one. Then there's a kind of marriage ceremony between the fertility goddess and what they call the corn god. Here they just celebrate the departure of the summer goddess and the beginning of the autumn goddess's reign . . . or some such nonsense."

It's hard to tell in the fitful light from the fire, but the sheriff appears to be blushing. I wonder what he's embarrassed about: the nature of this high school spectacle or how much he actually knows about it. I look away from him to the circle around the fire.

We're close enough now that the anonymous figures have begun to acquire distinguishing features. I see that there are some teachers here as well, including the teacher who I saw in the reading room, Ms. Drake. The figures that stand out are the two girls sitting on thrones made out of hay on opposite sides of the fire. One is blond Isabel in a long flowing white dress and with a crown of flowers on her head. The other is petite, dark-haired Chloe, in a dress identical to Isabel's but wearing a crown of russet leaves and acorns.

"It looks like they're both being honored," I say, remembering the rivalry between the girls. Then, recalling Chloe's vow of vengeance against Isabel, I ask, "They don't have to duke it out to see who gets to be goddess, do they?"

"Duke it out?" Sheriff Reade asks, cocking one eyebrow up. "No, it's a purely symbolic sacrifice, though it does tend to get a little frisky. Last year Autumn pulled out a handful of Summer's hair. I had no idea girls could be so mean."

"Tell me about it. Last year after my husband died a girl in Sally's class posted a rumor on Facebook that he had killed himself."

"That's horrible. . . . I'm sorry to hear about your husband. Did he . . . ?"

"It was a heart attack," I say briskly, both because I don't feel up to hearing the sheriff's awkward attempts at sympathy and because I've finally spotted Sally. "Excuse me a second."

Sally is sitting behind a gangly boy with lank dark hair falling over his eyes. She's huddled behind his long, gawkily folded legs as if she were trying to melt into the shadows outside the circle.

As Reade speaks to the group—an address that manages to combine tips on fire safety, underage drinking penalties, and the New York State laws on controlled substances—I make my way around the perimeter of the circle until I've reached Sally. I crouch down next to her.

"Having fun?" I ask.

She rolls her eyes at me, but I notice there's a pink flush in her cheeks I haven't seen in a while. "I thought you wanted me to make new friends here, so when Clyde came and asked me to come out to the bonfire I knew you wouldn't mind."

"Clyde Bollinger," the boy says extending a hand to shake mine. I don't know whether to be impressed by his manners or suspicious of his desire to ingratiate himself with me, but I take his hand. "I'm in your folklore class, Ms. Rosenthal. I hope it's okay

that Sally's here. I didn't want her to miss the first
festival of the school year, so I came by Fleur-de-Lis
to invite you both. Did you find the note we left on
Sally's laptop?"

So the note was hidden in plain sight behind
the Orion Nebula. Leave it to a teenager to find
some perfectly obvious-to-them place to leave a
note where no parent would ever think of looking.

"No, but I ran into Sheriff Reade in the woods
and he said you'd probably be here."

Sally and her new friend Clyde exchange a look,
the meaning of which is unclear to me. She's
known this boy for a couple of hours at best and already they're trading tacit signals like an old married couple.

"I hope you'll let Sally stay, Ms. Rosenthal. First
Night is the traditional beginning of the school year
and sort of the unofficial initiation into Arcadia.
She'll really feel more a part of the community if she
stays. You're welcome, too, of course." He finishes
with such a charming smile that I almost miss the
half-heartedness of the invitation. But it would
be hard to miss the look of alarm in Sally's eyes. She
certainly doesn't want her mother hanging out with
her new friends.

"Well, it's just that Sally doesn't know her way
around the campus yet—"

"I'll walk her back," Clyde offers. The ghost of a
smile flits across Sally's face, but then she purses her
lips and glares at me, daring me to turn down Clyde's

perfectly polite and reasonable offer. We haven't been here for a full day yet and already Sally's figured out that it's going to be tough for me to curtail her freedom on this campus.

"That's very nice of you, Clyde," I say. And then, turning to Sally. "Better make it by eleven. Classes start early tomorrow and you wouldn't want to keep Clyde up late."

Sally opens her mouth to object, but Clyde answers for her. "Sure thing. This breaks up pretty soon anyway. I'll make sure that Sally's home by eleven."

"Great," I say, getting to my feet. I've made my point, but clearly I've also been dismissed. I move from the circle, instantly feeling the chill of the night away from the warmth of the fire. I turn to go—and find the police officer standing right behind me.

"I see you found your daughter," he says, nodding toward Sally, who's laughing at something that Clyde is saying to her. "Everything okay?"

"Everything's fine." I start to walk away from the bonfire. The last thing I want is for Sally to think I'm talking to a police officer about her. The worst scene we had last year occurred after I called the police when she didn't come home one night. "It was a misunderstanding. I just didn't see the note she left. I'm going to go back now. She'll be all right here . . . won't she?"

He shrugs—not exactly the gesture of reassurance I was looking for. "Probably. The whole thing's pretty harmless . . . usually. I'm going to stay to make sure the bonfire's put out after they're done. If you'd like to keep me company . . ."

I look from him to the bonfire to see if Sally is watching me, but she's completely absorbed in Chloe, who's holding up some kind of doll crudely made of corn sheaves and shaking it over her head.

"She won't even know you're here," Sheriff Reade says, guessing my concern. "I've got the perfect spot." He points to a bench in front of Beech Hall, partly hidden in the shadow of the beech tree.

"Sure," I say, thinking that a cold bench seems more desirable than the empty cottage waiting for me.

When we're seated he digs in the pocket of his jacket and produces a thermos. "Dymphna's tea," he says, pouring some steaming liquid into the plastic thermos cup. I accept it gratefully. It's hard to believe Sally and I were in the middle of a sweltering Long Island summer just this morning; it must be fifty degrees here, which doesn't bode well for the coming winter. I shiver at the thought and take a long swallow of the tea. It has the same hint of spices—clove? cinnamon?—I'd noticed in the tea I had in the dean's office.

"I'm curious to see the festival. I met the two girls who are playing Summer and Autumn earlier. They didn't seem exactly friendly."

Sheriff Reade laughs. "That's the understatement of the year. Dymphna tells me they've been at each other's throats since they got back to campus last week. The girls chosen to play the two goddesses are always the ones with the highest averages. So I guess it's no wonder they're competitive."

"I thought the whole idea of Arcadia was that everybody was supposed to collaborate and support one another, especially the women."

He gives me a long measuring look. "Weren't you the one just telling me how mean girls can be?"

"Yes." I sigh, keeping my eyes on the bonfire so the sheriff won't see the pain in my eyes. "Only I'd hoped things would be different here." As soon as I've said it I realize how much I'd been hoping that **everything** would be different here. That coming here would be a truly new start for Sally and me. Only now do I realize how foolish a hope that was. I look back at Sheriff Reade and catch him staring at me. He looks away, no doubt embarrassed by the emotion in my voice, and points to the bonfire.

"Look, Isabel's going to make a speech."

Getting to my feet for a better view, I see that the students have also all risen to their feet. Isabel Cheney stands up on her throne of hay. She holds in her hand another one of the dolls made out of corn sheaves, which she shakes like a rattle. In response the others in the circle hold up their own corn dolls and shake them at the fire.

"My subjects," Isabel says, her clear voice ringing through the rowdy crowd. "I have been honored to be your leader since May Day. Before I came to Arcadia all I ever thought about was how I could do better than everybody else." Mock expressions of surprise come from the crowd. Isabel smiles. "But since I've been here I've learned that there's more to life than being on top—and before you say anything, Justin Clay"—she points to a handsome red-haired boy who has his mouth open to speak—"that's not the kind of top I mean."

The crowd laughs, but I notice that Ms. Drake, who's standing on the edge of the crowd, has pursed her mouth in disapproval. "As part of my responsibilities as summer goddess I researched the history of the Arcadia School. I learned that the women who founded the school wanted to create a place where women would be free of domestic responsibilities so they could have the time and energy to pursue their creative goals. But I also found out that they weren't any more free of everday rivalries and jealousies than we are."

I notice that Isabel is no longer looking into the faces of the students around her. She's looking over their heads toward Beech Hall. I follow her gaze to Dean St. Clare's window. It takes me a moment to make out a figure standing in the darkened office beside an open window.

"It looks like the dean is watching the festivities, too," I remark to Sheriff Reade.

"She's always watching," he replies.

I shiver and turn back to Isabel, who I now realize is addressing the dean as well as the students.

"I discovered a lot of things about the women

who founded this school that weren't entirely admirable, but in spite of the mistakes they made the school survived, giving future women—and men, now that the school is co-ed—Thank God!" Isabel pauses a beat for the laughter that follows and I feel sure she's timed the crowd's responses into her speech. "Giving us all a chance to discover our strengths and talents as well as our limitations and weaknesses. And that's really the important thing. Coming to Arcadia has been the best thing that ever happened to me. The friends I've made here are like my family. This is my last year here and I felt sad about that because there are times I think that these years will turn out to have been the best of my life. I'm afraid sometimes that nothing will ever be as good."

She stops for a moment, her voice cracking with emotion, and a silence falls on the revelers. A melancholy seems to have pierced their wildness, as if they have all glimpsed the sad truth of youth: that this night and nights like it might indeed be the happiest moments of their lives.

Callum Reade hands me a handkerchief and I realize to my great embarrassment that my face is wet with tears. Isabel, though, has managed to shake off her melancholy.

"So I say, if these are the best times of our lives, then let's be the best that we can and leave regrets behind us. And speaking of leaving things behind us, if you think you're going to sacrifice me . . . well, you'd better move fast!"

Isabel leaps off the hay throne and bounds past

the revelers, who shriek with surprise. She pauses at the crest of the hill and turns back to the crowd. She holds her arms wide, the sleeves of her white dress billowing in the wind. The image reminds me of the glimpse of white I saw in the woods on the path to my cottage. A girl in a white dress—tall like Isabel. Had it been Isabel? But what would she have been doing near my cottage? The question is driven from my mind when Isabel leans backward and disappears over the edge of the hill.

I jump to my feet, sure the poor girl has fallen to her death, as a dozen or so of the students surge over the hill. When I reach the top of the hill I see Isabel sprinting across the apple orchard. She disappears behind one of the bent and crooked trees. The students stream down the hill and fan out into the orchard, their shapes soon melting into the twisted shadows of the trees.

"What are they doing?" I ask Callum Reade when he reaches my side.

"A bunch of them are supposed to escort Isabel to the edge of campus to ensure that the spirit of the summer goddess isn't angry she's been sacrificed. There's Chloe, leading the others, but it looks like Isabel's gotten a good head start on the rest of them, so hopefully there won't be any hair-pulling incidents." He turns toward the bonfire, where many of the students are still gathered. They're throwing the little figures made of corn onto the fire.

"That's another part of the tradition," Sheriff

Reade says. "You're supposed to throw out all your bad habits and regrets from the last year and wish for what you want this year."

I'm glad to see that Sally is part of this crowd and not the group chasing Isabel in the orchard. I watch her as she tilts her head up and squeezes her eyes tight just like she used to when she blew out her birthday candles or threw a penny into a fountain. Then she cocks her arm—exactly as Jude taught her to for softball—and throws the corn doll into the very heart of the fire. I think I know what she's wishing for, but it's the one wish no one can ever grant her: for time to go backward and restore her old life.

CHAPTER 7

As soon as the sacrifice of the corn dollies is over I leave the bonfire, eager to make it back to the cottage before Sally and Clyde. Sheriff Reade offers to walk me back, insisting he's going that way anyway to patrol the woods for bonfire stragglers. "Although they usually stay out of the woods."

"Really? I'd have thought it would be a popular spot for clandestine activities."

He smiles—a sly smile that makes him look devilish. "This generation tends to prefer their **clandestine activities** indoors. Certainly not in a haunted wood."

"Haunted?"

"According to local legend," he says. "This is one of the oldest tracks of virgin forest in the state. The Dutch wouldn't cut down the trees because they thought it was inhabited by wood elves and moss maidens. When I was growing up, boys would dare one another to spend the night in these woods. They said the **wittewieven** would eat you alive."

"The **wittewieven?**"

"The white woman. It's an old Dutch myth, from the first settlers who explored the clove. They thought they saw a ghostly white woman in the mist from the falls. It's mixed up with a story about a woman from Kingston who died in the clove. Just something kids used to scare each other witless. . . . anyway . . . here we are. Will you be all right on your own or do you want me to walk you to your door?" I don't relish the idea of going on by myself even though I can see the lights of my cottage, but when I see the sheriff's teasing smile I don't want to give him the satisfaction of thinking he's scared me with the local folklore.

"I'll be fine. I don't think the white woman will get me between here and my front door." I mean it to be a joke, but then I recall that I glimpsed a woman in white earlier tonight. Or I thought I did.

I almost ask him to escort me to the door, but he's already saluting me with his flashlight and turning up the path that leads to the ridge. As soon as he's gone, I realize I never did retrieve my flashlight when it fell earlier tonight, and now I'm alone in the dark. I fix my eyes on the lighted windows of the cottage and walk toward them, ignoring the sounds of the trees creaking behind me and trying not to think of white women and changelings and other things that inhabit the trees of folklore. Only when I get to my door do I risk turning around . . . and catch my breath at the sight of slim white shapes swaying in the woods. But then I see it's only a stand of white birches among the pines.

To keep myself from watching the clock until Sally comes back, I go upstairs to do some more un-packing. I unpack the boxes marked SHEETS AND BLANKETS and make up my bed and Sally's. Then I open a suitcase and put nightgowns and underwear in the cupboard drawers and hang up shirts and dresses in the closet. When I'm done I lift up the suitcase to put it on the top shelf of the closet, but I notice that it's still heavy. Putting it back down I see that one of the outer zippered compartments is bulging. I unzip it. Inside I find Jude's old Rolex watch, a fifth of Jack Daniel's, and a handful of round, speckled stones.

I put the stones and the bottle on the night table and sit down on the bed, the heavy gold watch cra-dled in my hands. I looked for it off and on for the last ten months until I concluded Jude must have had it on when he was taken to the hospital and that someone stole it from him. It had seemed a final indignity—the thought of someone removing the expensive watch from his still-warm wrist—and I feel absurdly grateful knowing that's not what happened. He'd used this suitcase for a trip he'd taken just a few weeks before he died and left the watch in the zippered compartment. It was a strange oversight, though, since he usually wore the watch. A sign, perhaps, that he was under stress.

I slip the gold band over my wrist where it dangles loose and surprisingly warm against my skin, as if it still held the warmth of his flesh. It's still ticking. It's kept time all these months, outlasting its owner's heart.

The idea is so painful that I instinctively reach for the bourbon and take a long burning swallow. I pick up one of the stones and close my eyes, trying to imagine where Jude found it, what exotic beach or mountain stream, but all I feel is the cold, smooth empty weight of it in my hand. When I open my eyes I'm looking at the watch face. It reads 11:20.

Okay, I think, she's a little late. No big deal. She was with polite, well-mannered Clyde Bollinger. I get up and look for a place to hide the bourbon. I stopped keeping alcoholic beverages in the house after some friends of Sally's broke into the liquor cabinet last year and Lexy Rothstein threw up all over her mother's BMW. Sally might invite some of her new friends over and I don't want a repeat of last year's debacle, especially with kids who will also be my students. It's going to be a little tricky having Sally socializing with my students. How will I deal with Clyde, for instance, when he finally gets here with Sally? Should I mention that they were late even if it's only twenty—I look down at the watch—well, forty-three minutes late?

I go to the window, the bottle still in my hand, to look for them coming up the path, but I can't see a thing. I turn off the bedroom light so I can see better—and so Sally won't find me framed in the lit window when she comes home—but all I can see are those white birches swaying in the wind. I open the window to listen for Clyde and Sally's voices and hear the wind instead.

I can't remember the last time I heard wind like this—not in our Avenue B apartment where the city sounds of traffic and sirens drowned out every natural noise, and not in our hermetically sealed, climate-controlled Great Neck house. My new home, though, seems to be engaged in a duet with the wind. Gusts whoosh out of the pine forest and fling themselves onto the house, which sighs and moans as if it were being caressed and then, as the wind sweeps back into the forest, keens like an abandoned lover. The white birches thrash like women tossing their long hair over their shoulders.

I take another gulp of bourbon and imagine Sally out on this wild night, buffeted by the elements.

Just when I think I can't bear to sit another moment I catch a flash of light between the pines, hear a scrap of laughter, and then Sally and Clyde emerge from the woods. I look down at my watch. It's midnight. A full hour late. I can't let that go. Swallowing the last half-inch of bourbon, I head down the stairs. They're coming in the front door just as I reach the bottom step and I see in the two sets of eyes that stare up at me how I must look: a deranged woman shaking her hand at them. Clyde flinches as if he thought I was going to slap him.

"I believe we agreed on eleven," I say, trying to keep my voice calm.

Sally looks from me to Clyde and then, heaving a disgusted sigh, lifts her hand so I can see her wristwatch. "It **is** eleven, Mom."

I start to object, but then, looking down at Jude's watch, I understand. The last time he wore the watch was in Japan where, no doubt, it is now twelve o'clock in the afternoon. I consider making a joke about how late she would be if we were in Japan, but she's already stomping up the stairs, leaving me with an embarrassed Clyde.

"I'm sorry," I say. "It's my late husband's watch so it's set to a different time." Only when Clyde's gone do I realize that what I've said sounds like the dead are on a different time zone.

Sally is still angry in the morning. I bring her orange juice—the only thing she'll ingest before noon—as a peace offering, but she tells me she promised to meet Clyde and Chloe for breakfast in the cafeteria at—she holds up her watch—"eight o'clock standard sane person's time."

"I said I was sorry, Sally. You don't have to be mean—"

"You were mean to embarrass me in front of Clyde," she snaps. "If you don't want me to make any new friends here we might as well have stayed in Great Neck."

"Of course I want you to make new friends—"

"Good. Then I'd better go unless you don't think I'm capable of walking to campus by myself."

I concede that she can find her own way to campus.

And truly, in the light of day finding the spot where the trail splits—left to the campus and right to the ridge and Witte Clove—couldn't be clearer or more straightforward. Once on the trail to campus, I deliberately slow my steps so that I have time to calm down from the scene with Sally and to think over how I want to open the class.

I had planned to simply go over the course outline, which will take us from primitive animal bride tales to Greek myth to the seventeenth century French salons to Marvel and DC superheroes. But now? I don't want to start with chronologies and bibliographies; I want to start with the raw panic I felt in the woods last night. I want my students to hear the trees moving behind them, to see the fleeing peasant girl in the shadows of the pines—to hear her heart beating as she races from the witch's house to reclaim her stolen life. I want them to experience the fairy tale as a living, breathing organism, not some quaint story in an illustrated children's book.

As I enter Beech Hall and walk to my classroom, it strikes me that this was Vera Beecher and Lily Eberhardt's achievement. They created a life here at Arcadia Falls crafted out of their dreams and visions—a fairytale kingdom where artists could come and paint and draw and write and compose amidst the beauty of nature, free from society's demands and the stress of commerce and industry. They were changelings, I think as I enter the classroom, who refashioned themselves into the heroines of their own stories. They had come here to reinvent themselves. Perhaps that was part of the reason I'd applied for the job here. I remembered my mother once saying that if she'd come here to school her life would have been different. She would have been a different person. I think that I'd hoped that Sally and I might be able to become different people here.

I stand in front of the class, looking out at the young faces that last night had glowed in the light of the bonfire. I recognize Chloe and Clyde but am disappointed not to see Isabel. I recall what she said last night: **let's be the best that we can and leave regrets behind us.**

"What if," I say now, "you could start completely fresh as someone new?"

"As anyone?" The question comes from a slight girl in the back row. I noticed her when I first came in because she's striking in an unusual way. She has the oval face, high forehead, and almond-shaped eyes of a Botticelli madonna. She's wearing an embroidered peasant dress and purple tights. "Absolutely anyone," I answer.

"Any personality would be an improvement for you, Hannah," a girl in the front row says.

I quickly look down at my roster and find the name Hannah Weiss. Then I look up at the girl who's just spoken. She's wearing faded jeans that hug the curves of her hips and accentuate the length of her legs. From the stitching on the pocket I recognize the brand as one coveted by Great Neck teenagers. A backless sheepskin slipper dangles from her right foot; she taps it against her heel. "And who would you trade places with?" I ask her.

"Oh, I'm perfectly happy with who I am," she says, flipping her waist- length, perfectly straight brown hair over her shoulder, "unless . . . well, I wouldn't mind trading places with Angelina Jolie if it meant I could be Mrs. Brad Pitt."

A few of the girls giggle, but Clyde Bollinger straightens up in his chair and pushes the hair out of his eyes. "Why would you pick a mindless celebrity, Tori, when you could change places with someone truly extraordinary. Like Stan Lee, or the Coen brothers, or Stephen Hawking."

"Well, at least if you were Stephen Hawking you'd

finally score a set of wheels, Clyde." This remark comes from a red-haired boy sitting next to Tori—Victoria Pratt, I guess from the roster—who wears identical jeans and a polo shirt with its collar popped up. He's the boy that Isabel joked with last night, Justin Clay. He and Tori exchange a high five as Clyde turns pink and slouches back down in his seat.

"Hey," Hannah chirps, "if Clyde did trade places with Stephen Hawking, would that mean that Stephen Hawking would have to take Clyde's place? I mean, that would probably be cool for him because he could walk around and be in a regular body—" Hannah begins to blush as she realizes she's trapped herself into discussing her classmate's body. I notice that Clyde seems to be breaking out in hives. I decide to jump in before he goes into anaphylactic shock.

"Exactly. In fact, it would be interesting to see if Stephen Hawking would want to ever go back. He might find life at the Arcadia School too appealing."

This sets off a round of speculation on how the British physicist would take to life at Arcadia: how he'd like the food, whom he might date, what sports he'd go out for, and whether anyone would notice that he was inhabiting the body of Clyde Bollinger. Just when they've exhausted all the scenarios they can envision, Hannah Weiss pipes up with another identity.

"J. K. Rowling," she says. "I'd like to be J. K. Rowling for a month."

"So you can live in a British castle?" Clyde asks.

"No! Well, not **just** for that. I'd like to see what it feels like to have that kind of imagination. And to look at all her notes to see what she plans to write next."

A number of students second Hannah's choice and I'm grateful to see that the teasing has abated. Instead of Hollywood celebrities the names of famous writers are bandied about. In addition to J. K. Rowling, Stephen King and Dan Brown lead the list, but also included are the graphic novelist Alan Moore and "that guy who wrote **Fight Club.**" Internet tycoons follow—Steve Jobs, of course, but also Mark Zuckerberg who, I learn when I admit my ignorance, made so much money from inventing Facebook that he dropped out of Harvard. The final celebrity candidate is Bono, the lead singer of U2, both for his musical talent and humanitarian work. I'm about to move on when Chloe, whose full name on the roster appears as Chloe Lotus Dawson, raises her hand. She's been unusually quiet all period. I assume she's tired from last night's revelries. She looks pale and her light blue eyes are rimmed with red. "Yes, Chloe?"

"Does it have to be a celebrity?"

"Not at all," I answer, grateful for the question.

"Could it be . . ." Chloe's voice trails off and she looks out the window toward the giant copper beech tree. Just visible beside it are the smoldering remains of last night's bonfire. "Could it be yourself, only yourself yesterday? Like a past version of yourself?"

Chloe's question strikes me dumb, and the entire class as well. I've been studying the changeling story in fairy tale and folklore for a couple of years now and I've never come across a version in which the changeling trades places with another version of itself. But as I think about it I realize that there is an element in some of the stories that the changeling itself was a child deprived of a normal childhood and that by stealing another child's place it gets to re-experience its own childhood minus its flaws and heartbreaks.

"You mean so that you could relive your past . . . more perfectly?"

"Like a do-over," Clyde says, looking toward Chloe. Chloe glances at Clyde and blanches. Then she looks away from him and meets my look.

"Yeah, like a do-over."

"I don't see why not. After all, this is your fairy tale and fairy tales are nothing if not flexible. Look at what Vera Beecher and Lily Eberhardt, the founders of this school, did with them. They took the old changeling story and rewrote it to tell the story of the young women who came here to Arcadia in the thirties and forties and were able to reinvent themselves. How many of you have read it?"

I'm expecting at least a few raised hands—after all, the story was written by the school's founders—

but no one responds. Then I realize that it's not in the collection that Vera published after Lily died— **Tales of Arcadia.** It was only printed in a limited edition.

"Huh," I say, trying to think how I can continue with the assignment I planned to give the class—the assignment that all of this talk is supposed to have led up to. To buy myself a few minutes I rummage through my book bag and retrieve my old, worn copy of **The Changeling Girl.** It's the copy I first found at my grandmother's house in Brooklyn and which I'd read over and over again sitting on the linoleum floor beneath her kitchen table. As soon as I take it out, I feel the eyes of my students lock onto the cover. The illustration chosen for the cover is one of the most striking in the whole book. It shows the peasant girl kneeling beneath the bloodred copper beech at sunset, cradling the root she's just dug up in her arms as if it were a baby.

"It looks just like our copper beech," Hannah says.

"I'm sure Vera and Lily used the tree as a model. Would you like to hear the story?"

I'm not expecting an enthusiastic response. The teenagers who a few minutes ago debated the relative merits of Angelina Jolie and Natalie Portman surely don't want to hear a bedtime story. But I'm wrong. The tapping of laptop keys and shuffling of bodies stills. Even Tori Pratt stops slapping her bedroom slipper against her bare heel and sits up a little straighter.

Leaning against the edge of a desk, I cradle the book in my left arm so that the class can see the pictures. Luckily, I remember the story so well I hardly need to see the words. "**There once was a girl who liked to pretend she was lost,**" I begin. When I get to the part in the story where the peasant girl is running through the forest at night, the trees closing in around her and her lamp running out of oil, I feel the hairs at the back of my neck stand on end and, looking out at the class I meet Chloe Dawson's wide, bloodshot eyes. She looks as if I've just described her worst nightmare. I consider stopping—it's well past the hour we've been allotted—but when I start to close the book for just a second Hannah Weiss squeaks.

"You can't stop now. Does she make it out of the forest alive?"

"Yes, but just barely. This last part, though, is a little . . . squicky," I say, using one of Sally's favorite words. Nobody objects to **squicky.** They only lean in closer.

"**When she saw that the light in her lamp was failing, the peasant girl took her knife out of her belt and, cutting a deep gash in her arm, added more of her own blood to the remaining oil. The light flared up again, only now it was as red as the cooper beech leaves at sunset, as red as the heart of a hearthfire, as red as heart's blood. The pine trees stomped and thrashed behind her, their resiny breath hot on the back of her neck, their boughs lashing her face. Her legs felt heavy and** wooden and when she held up her arms she saw that her skin had roughened to bark. A lock of hair brushed against her face with the feathery touch of pine needles. And when a single tear rolled down her face it was sticky as tree sap. She was becoming a tree. The wind that moved through the forest chanted an invocation: 'Stay with us. Live through the centuries with us.' When she picked up her feet, roots clung to them. She felt so tired. Would it be so bad to become a tree?

"But then she caught a glimpse of light at the end of the path. The sun was rising in the fields beyond the forest. She could hear birds singing on the fence posts and smell the smoke of the farmhouse's cookstove. She smelled bread and coffee and the heather that grew in the fields around her old home . . . and then she heard her mother's voice calling her name. She ran, tearing the roots that clung to her feet and leaving bloody footsteps behind her. She ran for the gap between the trees that had shrunk to a mere slit, and leapt through it, the bark flaying her skin into peeling strips. But she didn't care. She could see her childhood home, her mother standing on the stoop, her arms held open . . . and then she saw her. The changeling girl. Like herself, only grown taller and more beautiful. The changeling stepped into her mother's embrace—her mother's!—and bent her golden head down to kiss the old woman's weathered cheek, and her mother lifted her face to the changeling as if she were lifting her face toward the sun.

"The girl saw then that in the year that had lapsed her mother had gone blind. She saw, too, that the humble farmhouse she left behind had become a stately manse. Her sisters, who came out from the barn carrying pails of milk and baskets of eggs, were dressed in fine clothing. Everything the witch promised had come true. In exchange for her year in the witch's cottage, her family had been granted wealth and prosperity. Nowhere did she see any sign that she had been missed. Her sisters greeted the changeling with kisses and embraces far more fervent than any sign of affection she ever received from them. They preferred the changeling to her, she realized as she got to her feet. She looked down at her own torn clothing, her scratched arms and bleeding feet. But it was her hands that looked different. Her hands that had learned to paint and carve, mold clay and weave yarn. They weren't the hands of a milkmaid anymore. Did she really want to spend her days milking the cows and gathering eggs?

"But what choice did she have? The path back to the witch's house had closed behind her. She turned around to face the wall of trees, but instead she found herself face-to-face with the witch. The witch held a lantern up in her hands;

the light pouring out of it was the red and gold of sunrise. The girl turned one more time to look at the farmhouse, but her mother and sisters had all gone inside. Only the changeling girl stood on the threshold, her eyes wide and frightened.

" 'If you choose, you can turn her back,' the witch said. 'All you need do is sprinkle her with the soil from the roots of the beech tree and she will become a root again. I have the soil here.'

"The peasant girl turned back to the witch and saw that she was holding a handful of black dirt. It was the dirt that the changeling was staring at. She knew it held the power to change her back. The witch was offering the peasant girl the freedom to choose between her old and new life."

Before turning to the last page of the book, I look closely at the picture. The peasant girl stands on the edge of the forest framed by two women—the witch and the changeling. In all the other pictures of the witch, her face is hidden in shadows, but in this one the light of the lantern falls on her and illuminates her face, revealing features very much like the photos I've seen of Vera Beecher.

I sense the class waiting for me to finish the story, but instead I close the book.

After a moment's silence, Hannah Weiss explodes. "Is that how it ends? What does the peasant girl do? Does she go back with the witch or to her family?"

"What do you think?" I ask, slipping the book back into my bag.

"You're not going to tell us?" Clyde asks.

"I thought I'd let you figure it out," I say. "Of course you can probably find the story on the Internet, but in the meantime, I'd like you to think about what you would do. Would you stay with the witch or go back to your old life? It might help you to finish the two assignments for this term, which are . . ." I pause to give them time to pick up pens or resuscitate their laptops. "One, research the lives of Lily Eberhardt and Vera Beecher and tell me why they wrote this version of the changeling story; and two—" Before I can give the second half of the assignment, though, a bell rings. Although they don't get up, most of the students are already shoving books and laptops into backpacks. I can see that they're eager to be gone. "It can wait till tomorrow," I say.

When they've gone I look down at my roster. As each student had referred to another by name I had found them on the roster and added a few notes to help remember them later. By the end of the period I'd checked off all but one of the students signed up for the class: Isabel Cheney. It seems odd to me that a girl as ambitious as her would miss the first day of school.

I add the roster to my book bag and straighten up to leave. My eyes are drawn, inevitably, to the red glow of the copper beech tree outside the window. A gray insubstantial figure stands beneath it. I quickly realize it's a reflection in the glass, but that does little to make it less chilling. The figure is Ivy St. Clare standing in the doorway of my classroom, silently watching me. I can't be sure how long she's been there, and I can't help but recall what Sheriff Reade said last night. **She's always watching.**

CHAPTER 8

I wait to see if the dean will come in, but after a moment the ghostly figure vanishes from the glass. I'm left with the unsettling feeling of having been spied on. It's not the way I wanted to start out my first day on the job. I shoulder my bag and decide to track the dean down at her office. If she's been observing my class, I want to know why.

Before I get there, though, I meet Dymphna Byrnes, whose

large figure effectively blocks the hallway. "There you are!" she exclaims as if I've been hiding from her. "Dean St. Clare sent me to give you this." She hands me a cardboard hatbox with the name VIOLET DU LAC, MILLINER printed in faded gilt letters on a deep purple background.

"What's this?" I ask. If Dymphna were to pull out of the box an outlandish hat and declare that Arcadia tradition demands that I wear it while teaching, I'd hardly be surprised. The Arcadia School is shaping up to be that strange. But instead she provides me with a perfectly rational explanation.

"Why, Miss Vera's letters and journals, of course. You asked to see them, didn't you? Well, here they are. Dean St. Clare says to be careful with them. They're irreplaceable. **And** she told me to remind you that you need to give the library your reserve list by four o'clock today and not to forget the faculty tea at four-thirty."

"Of course I won't forget," I say, instantly sorry for how peevish I sound. The truth is I **have** completely forgotten the tea and the deadline at the library. "I'd like to see the dean—"

"That's just not possible. She personally oversees the freshman orientation all day."

I'm about to say that she apparently had time to spy on my class, but I stop myself just in time. No need to sound paranoid as well as testy. "I guess I'll just have to wait for the faculty meeting then."

"The tea," Dymphna corrects me. "The dean is

quite adamant it be treated as a social occasion. She likes everyone to **dress** for it as well," she adds, casting an appraising eye on my outfit. I'd chosen a slim black skirt and a pinstriped button-down shirt for my first day. It looked professional enough when I left the cottage this morning, but looking down I see that the shirt tails have slipped out of the waistband, probably because the skirt is two sizes too big. I haven't worn it since Jude's funeral and I didn't think about all the weight I've lost until I put it on this morning. Then it was too late. All the clothes I have are two sizes too big.

"Of course I'd planned on going back home to change," I lie. "Um . . . what do the teachers generally wear to tea?"

Dymphna's brusqueness melts at my admission of wardrobe confusion. "Haven't you got a tea dress?"

I shake my head. "Tea" hadn't been big on the Great Neck housewife's list of social outings, which might include soccer games, bar mitzvahs, lunch at the Americana mall, or a trip to the pedicurist. It wasn't that women in Great Neck didn't spend a fortune on their clothes, but if you didn't work you could make do with a pair of well-tailored chinos, a pair of Tod's loafers, a Burberry quilted jacket, and whatever expensive bag was in style at the moment. But then I recall that I bought a lovely floral print dress at Anthropologie for Sally to wear to Lexy's Sweet Sixteen last summer. Sally declared it lame after wearing it once, but I hadn't been able to throw it out. She looked so pretty in it. I've lost so much weight that I can probably fit into it now.

"I think I have something," I tell Dymphna.

She looks relieved. "Well, I should hope so. A pretty lass like you. You can change when you bring Miss Vera's papers back to your cottage for safekeeping. Don't forget. Dean St. Clare will have your head if anything happens to them."

But I'm not able to get back to the cottage right away. By the time I've finished discussing my wardrobe shortcomings with Dymphna, I have only ten minutes to get to my Senior Lit Seminar. Unfortunately, it's in another building—Briar Lodge. So I tuck the heavy hatbox under my arm and take it with me.

The walk to Briar Lodge proves longer than the campus map led me to believe. It's on the western side of the apple orchard, on the edge of the woods below the ridge where I'd gotten lost last night. It was Virgil Nash's residence and studio when he came back to Arcadia. This is where he was living when Lily died. When I get to the Lodge I see that there's a path that starts beside the building and goes up into the woods. It must lead to the ridge trail that I inadvertently took last night. I wonder if Lily took that trail to meet Nash on the night she died, and fell into the clove just as I almost had. The memory of how close I came to meeting the same fate she did makes me feel a little light-headed.

When I walk into the first-floor parlor where the

class is to be held, the feeling only intensifies. Designed to take advantage of the southern exposure, the room feels like it's made out of light, from the wide plank oak floors to the vaulted ceiling. Most striking of all are the paintings. When Dymphna Byrnes told me that Vera Beecher had ordered Nash's painting removed from the Dining Hall I had assumed that all of his paintings had been purged from Arcadia. But that was not the case.

Three large oil paintings hang over the couch at the end of the room. They're in Nash's "late style," when he was moving away from the traditional society paintings from which he'd made his living. Instead of posed, formal portraits, these are stark and vivid renderings of a woman. The center painting is a close-up of her face. Framed by lank blond hair, pale blue eyes defiantly stare straight at the viewer. The painting on the left shows the same woman standing nude in a doorway of a barn. Strips of light coming through gaps in the barn wall ripple over her body, but her face is in shadow. The last painting is of a naked woman lying on grass beneath a tree, her body dappled with late-afternoon sunlight filtered through the leaves. From the color of her hair and the angularity of her figure, I guess it's the same woman as in the other two paintings, but since she's turned away from the viewer it's impossible to tell for sure.

"Lily has that effect on everybody," a dark-haired young man seated on the couch says. "That's why

I'm sitting under her, not facing her. I'd never be able to concentrate on what you're saying. . . . no offense."

"No offense taken," I say, taking a chair opposite the couch and putting my book bag and the purple hatbox on a low oak table. "These are amazing paintings. I've always heard that Nash's late portraits of Lily were remarkable, but I've never seen these. I don't think they've ever been reproduced."

"Vera Beecher would never allow it during her lifetime." This comes from a young woman seated in a straight-backed chair to my right. She pushes black-framed glasses up her nose and adds, "And Dean St. Clare has followed her wishes. In order to use them for our senior thesis we have to study them in situ."

"Which is why we're meeting here," the dark-haired young man says. I look from the young woman to him and notice that they're nearly identical—same black hair with pronounced widow's peak, same pale skin and wide-set gray eyes.

"You two must be Rebecca and Peter Merling," I say, taking out my roster. "You're—"

"Twins," they both say at the same time.

"I was going to say that you're writing your senior project on Nash's paintings," I say with a small smile. "I wondered what you hope to get out of this seminar."

Peter glances toward his sister. She raises one perfectly arched eyebrow at him and he nods as if something has been agreed on. "Becky and I are working on our senior project together: 'Fairy-Tale Resonance in Twentieth-Century Painting and Literature.' Miss Pernault, our adviser, suggested we look at the use of the Grimms' fairy tale 'Brother and Sister' in Margaret Drabble's novel **The Witch of Exmoor.**"

"Especially its animal bride motif," Rebecca adds.

"Because of the image of the brother transformed into a deer—"

"Which is echoed in Nash's late paintings of Lily."

"How is the animal bride motif echoed in Nash's painting?" I ask, mostly to interrupt Rebecca and Peter's Tweedledum, Tweedledee performance.

The twins exchange another look and then Rebecca answers. "Look at her. At the way the light falls on her skin. Do you notice anything unusual about her?"

I look back at the paintings. In the one of Lily reclining nude beneath the tree, her skin is dappled by light falling through the leaves. The tint of the leaves has dyed her skin a tawny copper except where the light shines white. I get up and move closer.

"She looks like a deer," I say at last. "Like a young fawn."

"Exactly," Rebecca says. "And in the standing pose—"

I laugh before she can finish. "The stripes of light make her look like a zebra."

"Yes!" Rebecca and Peter say together. They sound

as though they're pleased with me. I realize that although I'm the teacher they've been assessing me since I walked in the door and I've just passed some test they had devised together. Instead of resenting them, though, I feel the warmth of being welcomed into their little circle of two.

"So you see why we're interested in studying the animal bride stories," Peter says. "Even though Virgil Nash abandoned the obvious trappings of fairy tales in his last portraits of Lily Eberhardt, he was still depicting her as an animal bride. . . ."

Peter pauses to let his twin finish the sentence for him. I almost feel as if they've rehearsed this bit. "Which makes the fact that he killed her all the more fascinating."

By the time I leave Briar Lodge I still feel a bit dizzy. Even after I made them explain their shocking allegation against Virgil Nash ("She died running away with him, didn't she?" Rebecca had asked) their habit of finishing each other's sentences was maddening. My neck has a crick in it from looking back and forth between the two of them. It was like watching a tennis match. At the very least, I'll have to make them sit next to each other.

In comparison Junior British Lit goes well. Some of the students—Clyde Bollinger, Hannah Weiss, Fleming Sedgewood—are also in my folklore class, so I feel from the beginning that I've got advocates. I'm grateful to hear that many of the students have already started reading **Jane Eyre.** We spend the class talking about the fantasy fiction that the Brontës concocted during their dreary childhood winters on the Yorkshire moors. When I assign them the next two hundred pages of **Jane Eyre** there's not a murmur of complaint. I end the class ten minutes early so I'll have time to get to the library to turn in my reserve lists.

The library's gray granite tower is clearly visible looming over the copper beech tree, but, like almost everything on this campus, it turns out to be a little farther away than I'd thought. I'm beginning to realize that the paths are not designed to get you to your destination quickly, but rather to take the most scenic route. Besides, the library wasn't originally part of the estate at all. Vera Beecher's parents built it in the 1890s as a gift to the town of Arcadia Falls, but when Vera decided in the 1940s to found a school on the site of her childhood home she used a loophole in the lease to appropriate the building. It couldn't have endeared the school to the town, I think, when I arrive, slightly breathless, at the top of the rise—on top of the same ridge I was on last night, only farther south—and see the town of Arcadia Falls for the first time. It lies in a cleft between two hills, hidden from the highway and most of the campus. Hidden, too, it appears, from the twenty-first century. The white church steeple, the town green, and the white clapboard houses could have come from the eighteenth century. It looks like a village forgotten by time—a place where Rip van Winkle might have laid down to take his hundred years' nap.

I pull away reluctantly, promising myself that I'll explore the town when I have more time, and enter the library . . . and leave Brigadoon behind for thirteenth-century England. Vera Beecher's parents were ardent medievalists and followers of William Morris. They had their library built to resemble a cross between a castle and a Gothic church, complete with turreted bell tower. And as in most Gothic buildings of the Perpendicular style, my eyes are immediately drawn upward as I enter the central entrance hall, past carved stone arches and rich tapestries toward clerestory windows glazed with stained glass.

I stand in a spill of sapphire and ruby light that falls on the calm gray stone, looking up first at the carved wood ceiling, each panel engraved with the Beecher family crest. Then my eye drifts midway down the wall to the tapestries. There are four, each depicting a stately beech tree at a different season: tender green buds for spring, the full green plumage of summer, a fiery red tree at fall, and bare limbs covered with snow in winter. If not for the secular nature of the tapestries I would think I was in a church. I **do** feel like I'm in a place of worship, only here the gods are trees and books.

"I hope you're here to hand in your reserve list." The voice brings me down to the ground level, where a woman with mousy brown hair unbecomingly cut in a pageboy sits behind a long desk beneath the tapestry of the tree in winter. "You're the last one, you know."

"No, she's not," another voice announces as the front doors bang open. "That would be me. I absolutely demand my customary status as last to hand in her reserve list!" Ms. Drake floats in, her muslin smock and frizzy gray hair billowing around her. She's waving a piece of paper in her hand.

"But you have yours all ready," I say, pointing to the paper in her hand. "And I don't. So really, you have to go ahead of me."

"Aha! You must be new here. Tell me, Birdy," the woman says to the librarian. "Is this poor shred of paper acceptable to you?"

"You know it's not, Miss Drake. The reserve list must be entered on the reserve list form—"

"**Of course it must!** In triplicate, the white copy to go to you, the pink to remain with the instructor, and the yellow to go to the dean. Correct?"

"That's right. And I distributed those forms in the interoffice mail last week, Miss Drake. You could have had them all filled out already."

Ms. Drake sighs and shakes her head, but when the librarian turns to retrieve the forms she looks up at me and crosses her eyes. I try to swallow the laugh that bubbles up and end up coughing instead.

"It's all the dust from all the old books," Ms. Drake says, slapping me heartily on the back. "I'm Sheldon Drake, by the way, but everybody calls me

Shelley . . . well, except for Miss Bridewell here.
Birdy, why is it that I call you Birdy, but you never
call me Shelley?"

"I've no idea, Miss Drake. Perhaps for the same
reason that you are always the last one to turn in
your reserve list. It's our natures."

"Hm . . . you mean I have slovenly habits, I suppose. Or derangement due to inhalation of toxic
paint fumes." Shelley holds up her hands and wrig-
gles multicolored fingers. They're spotted with paint
and smell like turpentine. "Or perhaps it's due to
the artistic temperament's tendency toward left-
brainedness . . . or is it right-brainedness? I lean to
whatever side it is that can't remember the difference
between them."

"It's no excuse," Miss Bridewell says, handing
each of us a stack of forms. "Shall I show you how to
fill it in?" she asks me.

"I'll show her," Shelley volunteers. "I think even
I have mastered the intricacies of the reserve list
form by now."

The librarian looks dubious, but Shelley Drake
grasps me by the elbow and steers me into a small alcove off the entranceway. She upends a bag of books
on the table and sits down, gesturing for me to do
the same, which I do while formally introducing
myself.

"The new English teacher! My drawing class was
all in a twitter over you. I saw that you attended the
bonfire with Sheriff Reade last night. . . . Oh, and

you must be Sally's mother! She's in my Intro Drawing class. She's got a great eye. She really should be encouraged."

"I've always encouraged her—" I begin.

"Oh, I didn't mean to suggest you hadn't. It's just that I get the sense from her work that she's holding herself back—as if she's afraid of what might come out if she really let herself go. Just a first impression, of course, but I'd like to challenge her a bit this semester, if you don't mind—oh, here, make sure you alphabetize your list for each class. Birdy's a real bear for alphabetizing. Have you got the call numbers? She'll send it back, in triplicate, if you don't. You can look them up on the computer catalog. I write them down on my own copies of the books so I don't forget."

For someone who claims to be disorganized, Shelley Drake is quite efficient. She fills out her forms in about three minutes and then helps me with mine, all the while keeping up a nonstop patter about the land mines of bureaucracy to avoid at the Arcadia School. She talks so relentlessly that I don't have a chance to ask her how, exactly, she plans to challenge Sally. When she's finished both our forms she stands up and gives my outfit a skeptical stare.

"That won't do for tea, you know." She looks at her watch. "Do you have time to go home and change?

I look at my watch—Jude's watch, which I haven't been able to take off and which is still set on

Japanese time. When I subtract an hour, I see it's 3:45. "I'd better run. I have to bring this box back to my cottage. . . ." I look down at the table. My canvas book bag is there, and the stack of color-coded reserve forms, but no purple hatbox.

"What's wrong?" Shelley asks, her freckled face creased with worry.

"I've lost Vera Beecher's journals."

CHAPTER 9

"Close your eyes," Shelley Drake orders me.

"What?"

"Just do what I say. Close your eyes."

I'm not sure why, but I obey her. For all her daffiness, Shelley exudes a certain authority.

"Good. Now, picture the hatbox. Do you see it?"

In my mind's eye I see the round purple hatbox embossed

with faded gold lettering. I even remember the name of the milliner: **Violet du Lac.** "I do," I tell her.

"Good. Where is it?"

In my mind's eye I look up from the box and into the painted blue eyes of Lily Eberhardt, her face striped with light.

"In the studio at Briar Lodge where I taught my senior seminar with Rebecca and Peter Merling. Damn, I must have left it there." I open my eyes and am startled to find another pair of blue eyes staring at me—not Lily Eberhardt's, but Shelley Drake's. "I don't remember taking it with me, but then I was feeling a little dizzy."

"The Merling twins have that effect on people. The good thing is that hardly anyone ever goes to Briar Lodge. Your box is probably still there. Come on."

"You don't have to come with me—" I begin as Shelley grabs both stacks of forms, hers and mine, and sweeps back into the library's entrance hall.

"I know a shortcut," she says, tapping the edges of the forms on the desk in front of the librarian. She's deftly plucked the pink sheets from each form before the librarian can get ahold of them, but not before she can complain.

"But I need to stamp those—"

"Don't worry," Shelley calls back as she pulls me out of the library. "I've got a copy of your stamp in my studio."

We leave the astonished Miss Bridewell sputtering behind her desk and burst out into the late-afternoon sunshine, Shelley collapsing against my shoulder in a fit of laughter. "Oh, dear," she says, nudging me off the path that goes down to the campus and through a gap in a bordering hedge. "I'll pay for that later, but it was worth it to see the expression on her face."

"Do you really have a copy of her stamp?"

"Absolutely. I carve them out of rubber. You wouldn't believe the time it saves. . . . This way now . . ."

She directs me by leaning against my arm and pushing me through the shrubbery. At first, though, I think she must have gotten the wrong path. We're blundering through a dense thicket of thorny bushes that scrape my arms as I follow her.

"Sorry," Shelley says, holding a thorny branch out of my way, "I haven't used this trail in a while and it's grown up a bit since. We've had a lot of rain. . . . oh, look, blackberries! They're almost ripe. . . . Ah, here we are. The rest of the way's a bit clearer."

We emerge from the blackberry thicket onto a narrow footpath that follows the same ridge I was on last night. The campus lies to the east in a gentle declivity. Far below the steeper western ridge is the village of Arcadia Falls, separated from the school by a deep cleft in the mountain, which the Dutch called a clove. Witte Clove, I remember Callum Reade called it last night. As we approach it, I hear the roar

of the cataract that gives the village its name: Arcadia Falls. We're suddenly at the head of the falls,
looking down into a dark, shadowed gash in the
ridge filled with large boulders and cascading water.
It makes me feel dizzy again just to look at it.

Shelley points toward an old weathered barn
that's listing to one side in an overgrown field beyond the clove.

"That's the barn Nash used for those late paintings of Lily Eberhardt," she says. "She was on the way
there to meet him the night she died. Her body was
found down in the clove. I've always wondered why
she tried to get across it in the middle of a snowstorm." Shelley shakes her head and then turns away
from the view of the barn, taking a path that leads
down to Briar Lodge.

I stay for a moment looking down into the deep
clove that lies between the ridge and the barn. It looks
only slightly less sinister in the daylight than it did in
last night's moonlight. There's a ledge about twenty
feet below the ridge where the water pools, and then
a steeper second cascade that plummets another
hundred feet. There's a path that winds down to the
left of the falls that looks like it would be a challenge
to a mountain goat. If you lost your footing, you
could fall and break your neck on one of those pro-
truding rocks. How much more dangerous would it
be navigating it at night? And in a snowstorm? Shelley's right; it didn't make any sense for Lily to try
crossing the clove that night—unless she'd been so

frightened of Vera's anger when she told her that she was leaving with Nash that she was afraid of spending the night with her in the cottage.

I turn away from the clove and follow Shelley, keeping my eyes on her white smock as she makes her way through a dense stand of pine trees that cover the eastern slope of the ridge. Sunlight pours through the trees, catching a drift of pine needles falling through the air. For a dizzying moment the summer scene evaporates and I see a winter night and a lone figure making her way down the hill through the snow. But then I dismiss the image from my mind. For one thing, according to the story, Lily never made her way back down this hill from the barn.

The hatbox is right where I left it on the table in the parlor. "Oh, thank God," I say, pouncing on the box. "I can't believe I was so stupid. Dean St. Clare would have had my head."

"She **does** take the legacy of Vera Beecher quite seriously." Shelley stands with her back to me, staring up at the paintings of Lily Eberhardt while I open the box to check that the letters and journals are still there. Since I didn't open it earlier I have no way of knowing if anything is gone, but the box is full to the brim with letters and clothbound journals. It certainly doesn't look as if anything's missing. Lying on top of everything is a photograph of three women standing beneath a blossoming apple tree, their arms wrapped around one another's waists. I recognize the slim blonde on the left as Lily, but I don't know the other two. I start to turn it over to see if their names are written on the back but am arrested by Shelley's next statement. "Sometimes I think that's all this school is to her: a reliquary to preserve the rotting corpse of Saint Vera."

I close the box, startled by the harshness of the sentiment. But when Shelley turns around she's smiling. "But you've found the box, so you don't have anything to worry about . . . except, of course, getting to tea on time. We've got twenty minutes, which is what it'll take me to scrub the paint off my hands. I'll see you there."

She disappears before I can thank her for helping me find the hatbox. What a strange person, I think as I hurry back to my cottage. I can't quite decide how much her "disorganized artist" persona is an act and whether I like her. But I'm sure of one thing: I'd never meet anyone like her in Great Neck.

I manage to make it back to the cottage by taking the ridge trail the rest of the way. I stow the hatbox in my bedroom closet, change into Sally's dress—which fits perfectly—and make it to Beech Hall by 4:30 on the dot. So what if I'm panting and sweating underneath the thin cotton lawn dress? Tea is held in the Rose Parlor, which gets its name from the faded pink upholstery, the roses on the wallpaper, and vaguely roselike designs etched into the glass French doors.

The teachers themselves are arrayed in tight bouquets around the room. I approach a group of women who are all wearing nearly identical A-line dresses in tastefully muted colors, upswept hair, and pearls. "I teach twentieth century art," a woman who introduces herself as Miss (not Ms.) Pernault tells me. After polite introductions to a math and biology teacher, I forget their names almost as quickly as I hear them. They return to the conversation they were having when I intruded: a bitter comparison of Arcadia salaries to those at other private schools.

I drift over to a contingent of more brightly dressed people, younger and of mixed gender—I can't help noting that the faculty body is clearly dominated by women—and find that they are the **fine** arts and English teachers. They're complaining about budget cuts. I'm beginning to suspect why it was relatively easy to get this job. The Arcadia School is apparently the cheapskate of the Northeast.

After a few minutes of listening to one woman bemoaning the high price of gouache, I detach myself and approach the only person standing by himself: a tall, gangly thirtyish man standing near the entrance to the room. He looks like he dressed as hurriedly as me. I can see the comb marks in his damp hair and a piece of tissue is clinging to a shaving cut on his neck.

"I'm Meg Rosenthal," I offer, holding out my hand.

"Colton Briggs, math department," he says,

switching his teacup to his left hand to grasp my hand with his long damp fingers.

"I'm teaching English," I say, pretending he actually asked.

"I see," he says, and then stands there looking at a spot two inches above my left shoulder.

"How did you decide to be a math teacher?" I ask, reverting to strategies I learned from teen magazines. **Ask the boy what he's interested in.**

"I'm just teaching here while I finish my Ph.D. in economics," he whispers, leaning closer to me. Then he leans back and glances nervously side to side as if he's just revealed his true superhero identity.

"Oh," I say, smiling encouragingly. "What area of economics do you specialize in?"

"Randomness and improbability," he answers.

"Oh, like the Black Swan theory. My husband, who died last year, was a hedge fund manager. He loved to talk about the Black Swans—"

"Well, no," Colton Briggs says without even the usual sympathetic murmur I get when I parade my recent widowhood. "My work does not primarily concern the Black Swan concept; it focuses more on Burton Malkiel's 'random walk' theory. . . ."

He proceeds to deliver a lecture on the economist's discovery that a stock chart and the steps a drunken Frenchman took in crossing a deserted snowy field at night traced similar patterns without pausing to ascertain my interest level or comprehension. When he's done I half expect him to give me a quiz. Before he can, I excuse myself to get a cup of tea.

"Arcadia blend or herbal?" the girl behind the middle urn asks when it's my turn.

"What's Arcadia blend?"

"Something Vera Beecher made up. I think it's half darjeeling, half assam, and some kind of spice. It's pretty good."

In the spirit of fitting in, I agree to give it a try. I recognize the tea I had yesterday in the dean's office and which Sheriff Reade had in his thermos. I still can't identify the spice, but it's certainly growing on me. I wander over to the French doors and pretend to be fascinated with the view. After being lectured by Colton Briggs I'm not quite ready to reengage with anyone. It occurs to me that this is one of the few social occasions I've been to in sixteen years that doesn't revolve around either Sally's education or Jude's business. Perhaps I've lost the knack of being myself.

I scan the room for Shelley Drake, but she's missing from the scene. I feel a twinge of guilt that I might be the reason she's late.

I turn back to the French doors, wondering if anyone would notice if I slipped out, and immediately catch sight of Shelley on the lawn in front of the copper beech. The bright halo of kinky gray hair would be hard to miss even if she weren't flailing her arms in the air. She's talking to two students whom I also recognize: Chloe Dawson and Clyde Bollinger. Chloe looks like she's crying, while Clyde, his hands in his pockets and head bowed down, seems to be trying to make himself small. What, I wonder, could the two of them have done to make Shelley Drake so angry? She hadn't struck me as a particularly strict teacher.

"Someone must have tampered with Shelley's art supplies."

I turn and find a short man who, despite the heat, is wearing a three-piece velveteen suit. Even if the suit weren't bottle green, his pointy ears and sharp cheekbones would make him look like an elf.

"I met her earlier and she seemed so . . . easygoing."

"Ha!" The barking laugh is much louder than anything I would expect to come out of such a diminutive person. "Shelley's got the whole freespirited artiste thing down to a tee, but unfortunately she's also inherited the curse of the Sheldons—what they called nerves when her great-great-aunt Honoria took the rest cure with S. Weir Mitchell, and manic depression when her mother took poetry classes with Anne Sexton at McLean, and what we call bipolar disorder now." Moving closer, he stands on tiptoe to whisper in my ear. "Dean St. Clare made her agree to having her meds monitored by the infirmary before letting her back this year." Although I'm half-repulsed by this man, I find myself leaning in when he whispers again. "Not that she's the only one."

I should, I realize, feign disinterest and get away from this malicious gossip, but instead I raise an eyebrow and ask, "No?"

The little man grins and sidles next to me so he can indicate whom he's talking about. "You see the rumpled tweedy fellow talking to St. Clare? That's Malcolm Keith."

"**That's** Malcolm Keith? Didn't he publish that famous story in **The New Yorker** back in the early eighties that everyone thought was brilliant?"

"Yep. He got a six-figure contract from Knopf on the strength of one story and then never wrote another word. He's on Antabuse to keep him from drinking. He's also got to report to the infirmary to make sure he's taking his medicine."

"Gosh, I feel a little left out. The party's obviously at the infirmary. I guess I could sign up for B_{12} shots. I have been a little anemic."

"That's the spirit," my new friend says, clapping me on the back. "I go for bee allergy shots once a week, more to see the mental health parade than to protect against anaphylactic shock. I'm Toby Potter, by the way. I teach art history—eighteenth-century painting's my area: Boucher, Fragonard, great fluffy nudes and girls in pink dresses, that sort of thing."

"Meg Rosenthal. I'm interested in fairy tales in nineteenth- and twentieth-century literature. . . ." I stumble a bit, unused to identifying my academic interests as my area of expertise rather than some eccentric pursuit to keep a bored Great Neck housewife entertained, but Toby Potter beams, turning his ugly face almost beautiful.

"Marvelous! You'll find nineteenth-century children's literature good preparation for this place: it's mad hatters and goblins all around. Oh, speak of the devil, there's Shelley now, collaring the dean. I hope she's not going to make a fuss."

But Shelley Drake seems to be doing exactly that. She looks like a wild woman—Cassandra on the walls of Troy warning her countrymen to lock the gates against that monstrous wooden horse. Her crinkly silver hair is floating around her face like an electric cloud; two feverish spots stain her cheeks. She's practically giving off sparks. She goes straight to the dean and interrupts her in the middle of a conversation with Colton Briggs. At first Dean St. Clare looks annoyed, but then Shelley whispers something in her ear and the dean's expression changes abruptly. They both rush from the room, leaving Colton Briggs standing by himself, awkwardly shifting his weight from foot to foot. He lifts his teacup to his lips, but, apparently realizing it's empty, spins on his heel and heads back to the urns.

"Now what do you think all that was about?" I ask Toby Potter.

"I don't know. The last time I saw St. Clare so rattled was when that biographer from England came asking questions about Vera Beecher. Look . . . there they are on the lawn. It must have something to do with those students."

I turn back to the French windows and see Ivy St. Clare crossing the lawn with a gesticulating Shelley Drake in tow. Halfway across, just past the copper beech and near the ashes of last night's bonfire, they meet Chloe Dawson and Clyde Bollinger. Chloe does all the talking, swiping tears away from her eyes. Clyde stands with hunched shoulders, his eyes darting nervously back and forth between the dean and his friend. A small crowd has begun to gather around the quartet. I recognize a few of my students from Folklore and Junior Brit Lit, as well as the Merling twins, who stand off to one side whispering to each other. I also see Hannah Weiss, who is leading a group of new students on a tour of the campus. Then I notice that Sally is one of the students in Hannah's group.

"That's my daughter," I say, turning to Toby Potter, but I find that the little man has disappeared. Well, if he can abandon the party, so can I, I think, slipping through the open glass doors. Sally's a perfect excuse.

Halfway across the grass I start to wonder if approaching Sally is really such a good idea. She's talking to an Asian girl who's wearing an **Invader Zim** T-shirt—one of Sally's all-time favorite cartoons. She'd often complained that no one in Great Neck had ever heard of it. I don't want to barge in if she's just found a soul mate.

But when I get closer I can see that the color has drained from her face and she's biting the ends of her hair—two sure signs that she's upset. I head toward her, unable to stay away.

"Are you okay?" I ask when I reach her. "Has anything happened?"

"Sheesh, Mom! Why would anything be wrong with me?" She shakes her head so hard the damp ends of her hair swing against her face. "Haruko and I are just trying to find out what all the excitement's about."

Figuring that this is as close as I'm going to get to an introduction to her new friend, I turn to the girl in the **Invader Zim** shirt. "Hi, Haruko, I'm Sally's mom, Meg . . ."

"Ms. Rosenthal, yeah, I wanted to take your class when I saw you had Neil Gaiman on the reading list, but it was closed out. Maybe next year."

I smile, immediately liking the girl, and say a little prayer that this year Sally will hang out with smart, polite kids who have something on their minds other than boys and designer clothes. And aren't into pagan sacrifices either, I think, glancing at the crowd that's now gathered around the embers of last night's bonfire. The scene eerily mirrors last night's festivity, with Chloe at the center making supplicatory gestures toward the stern figure of Ivy St. Clare. The only one missing is Isabel.

"Has anyone seen Isabel Cheney today?" I ask Sally.

She shakes her head. "I heard some girls commenting that she wasn't at breakfast."

"She didn't show up for my classes either. I'd better go talk to the dean."

I leave Sally and Haruko and approach the little circle gathered around Chloe. "Is this about Isabel Cheney?" I ask. "She wasn't in class today."

Ivy St. Clare turns her head toward me and snaps, "Perhaps you should have told someone."

I open my mouth to defend myself, but Shelley Drake speaks up instead. "Apparently no one noticed the girl was missing until lunchtime. She's not in her room, she hasn't gone to any of her classes, and no one's seen her since she left the bonfire last night . . . isn't that right, Chloe?"

Chloe Dawson sniffles and shakes her head. "The last time I saw her was in the apple orchard when we were all chasing her. She was headed into the woods . . . and . . . well . . ." Chloe looks up nervously at the dean.

"The woods behind the Lodge are strictly off-limits," the dean says.

"That's right," Chloe says, widening her eyes exactly as Sally does when she's lying. "So of course I didn't follow her. Isabel doesn't think the rules apply to her." She looks as if she's about to start in on a tirade about her rival's failings, but then she thinks better of it. "You think she could have fallen in the woods and hurt herself?"

I immediately think of the treacherous ravine— Witte Clove—behind Briar Lodge. When my eyes meet Shelley Drake's I can tell she's thinking the same thing. "It's possible," she says, turning to the dean. "We should start searching the woods now, before it gets dark."

"Shouldn't we call the police?" I ask.

The dean looks momentarily startled by my suggestion but then nods. "Yes, of course. I'll go to my office and do that immediately. But I see no reason to wait for them to start searching. It's awful to stand by and do nothing. I'm sure the students will want to help look for their friend."

"Really?" I ask, surprised that the Dean would send her teenaged charges into the woods. But then I notice how upset she is and realize she's probably remembering the days after Lily Eberhardt went missing. After all, she was only a teenager herself at the time. "That drop off the ridge is dangerous," I point out very patiently. "Another student could get hurt."

"Meg is right," Shelley says, once again coming to my defense. "If we do allow the students to take part in the search it should be supervised by adults— at least one for every five students, I think. I'll be happy to organize the search at the Lodge while you go call the police." Then, turning to Chloe, she adds, "Why don't you help me, Chloe? You can show me where you last saw Isabel."

I see immediately that Shelley's giving the overwrought girl something to do to help calm her down. And it seems to work. Chloe wipes the tears from her face and takes a long breath. The dean, too, looks calmer and more reassured.

"And you, Meg," Shelley says before she leaves with Chloe. "You ought to change into long pants before you go, don't you think?"

I'm about to object but then, remembering the thorn bushes in the woods, decide she might be right. I tell Sally that I'll be back in twenty minutes and **not** to start until I get there. No matter what precautions they're taking I don't like the idea of her wandering around in those woods without me. Then I take off at a sprint, determined to match— or better—Dean St. Clare's eleven and a half minutes to the cottage.

CHAPTER 10

I manage to get back to the cottage, change into jeans, and get back to Briar Lodge in a little under half an hour. I'm amazed at how much has been accomplished in that time. At the edge of the forest Shelley Drake is pacing in front of a long line of students and teachers like a general surveying her troops. There's a teacher or staff person for every five students and each group leader has been given a whistle and a bright pink bandana.

"The bandanas were left over from a breast cancer benefit walk," Shelley tells me, handing me my bandana and whistle. "Find a couple of students who don't have a leader and make sure you keep a good eye on them. We can't afford to lose another one."

Could we afford to lose the **first** one? I think, but I keep it to myself. Shelley is clearly harried. Her cheeks are as bright pink as the bandanas and her eyes nervously dart everywhere, as if she could rein in the chaos by sheer willpower. In addition to the students, there are two ambulances parked in front of the Lodge, half a dozen EMT workers, and, holding a German shepherd straining at his leash, a man in camouflage hunting clothes who is talking to Sheriff Reade. A little past where Reade stands I see Sally with her new friend Haruko, Clyde Bollinger, Hannah Weiss, and Chloe Dawson. I look around the crowd for another group to lead. As much as I'd like to keep Sally in my sights, I don't want to crowd her. But then she looks up and waves me over.

"Why don't you join our cell?" Clyde asks when I reach the group. "Professor Drake thought it was a good idea for the older students to mix with the new ones because we know the area better."

"Clyde and I were both in the hiking club last year," Hannah adds. "And Chloe wrote a paper on the history of the woods—"

"That doesn't mean I know my way around

them," Chloe snaps. "We're not **supposed** to go in them without a supervised hiking group."

"I didn't say you had—" Hannah begins, her voice rising in annoyance. They're all overtired, I realize, like toddlers who haven't had their naps, and will soon be squabbling if I don't interfere.

"Oh look," I say, "Sheriff Reade is making an announcement."

Sheriff Reade has mounted an old stone wall to speak to the search parties. One of the EMTs offers him a bullhorn, but he turns it down. I see why when he speaks. He has a deep, authoritative voice that instantly silences all chatter in the line. "We've got three hours till nightfall. That means three hours to find this girl. I'm calling all civilian searchers in at dusk. We need to cover as much ground as we can in that time. Proceed directly west toward the ridge with your group leader. At the quarter hour we'll all stop and call Isabel's name for one minute, then observe total silence for four minutes."

"Why?" someone asks. "Shouldn't we just keep calling?"

"How do you expect to hear her answer if the woods are full of people shouting?" Sheriff Reade asks. "For the rest of the time, keep your voices low. If you find **anything**—a piece of clothing, an object that might belong to Isabel—blow your whistle once and wait. I'll find you. If you find Isabel, blow your whistle three times. Remember, stay with your groups and watch your footing. When you reach the ridge, turn back. We're putting together a climbing team to search there. It's too dangerous for civilians."

Reade lifts his left hand up and checks his watch. "I've got six-fifteen. Check your watches and make sure that's what you've got."

I look down at Jude's old Rolex, still set on Japan time—or, as I've been thinking of it, Jude time. Jude would be the first to tell me that it's more important now to be in sync with the rest of the search party, so I twist the stem until the watch reads 6:15 and push it in. When I look up, I notice Sally staring at me. "Let's go," I say. "Let's find her."

Although we have three hours of daylight left, the sun is low enough in the western sky to cast our shadows, and the shadows of the trees, behind us. Climbing the ridge I feel as if we are advancing through the ranks of a retreating army: the ghosts of those who have gone before us. It's an image that can't help but remind me of the last scene in **The Changeling Girl.**

The peasant girl looked from the witch, who stood at the edge of the woods holding the handful of dirt that would give her the freedom to return to her old life, to the changeling who stood in the doorway of her old home. As she watched, another figure appeared in the doorway—a man. She recognized the young shepherd who courted her, only he had grown stouter in the year she'd

been away. He'd become a prosperous gentleman. He put his arm around the changeling girl and squinted out into the dusk, but he didn't see his old sweetheart. His eyes were dazzled by the changeling. She'd made him her own, just as she'd made everything in the peasant girl's old life her own. Only now she had the power to take it all back.

The peasant girl turned to the witch and held both hands out, cupped together. The witch poured the soil into her hands. It was warm and loamy, like soil newly turned for spring planting. It was full of life. Feeling its power in her hands, she knew what she must do.

She lifted her hands up over her head and, twirling in a circle, tossed the soil into the air. Instantly, a wind caught it and carried it into the woods, lifting the cloud into the topmost boughs of the oldest trees and then letting the grains rain down through the branches. The wind sighed and the trees swayed and creaked, sounding like old bones coming to life. The tops of the pines tossed and thrashed like girls drying their hair . . . and then they were girls, stretching their arms, tossing their hair, and shaking out the cramps in their legs. Dozens of girls . . . hundreds . . . come to life. All the changelings that had been forced into alien shapes for time out of mind, now free to move.

The peasant girl looked at the witch and saw that she was smiling. She was no longer a witch, but a beautiful woman in a long white dress: the queen of the changelings. She held open her arms to welcome all her children back and the peasant girl turned away and began climbing the hill toward the high ridge that marked the boundary of the valley. The sun was setting beyond the ridge, staining the sky rose and violet. The girls who were once trees were black against that light, shadows who passed the peasant girl as she climbed the hill. As they passed her, they reached out their hands to touch her, their fingers grazing her lightly like pine needles brushing against her skin, their voices whispering in her ears in the cadences of the wind, thanking her for setting them free. When she reached the top of the ridge, she had been brushed clean and given all she'd ever need to go out into the world and make a new life. At the top of the ridge, she turned back to wave goodbye, but the woods below her were filled with a dark mist that hid everything below the tree line. She turned and faced the setting sun, the next valley, and her future.

The last picture in the book shows the dark figure of the peasant girl silhouetted against a lilac and pink sky, bravely setting off into the unknown. Although she stands alone, her hair and dress are tossed by invisible breezes that I had always imagined were the voices of the changeling girls whispering their parting wishes to her. Their breath like the touch of white pine needles . . .

A hand brushing my hand startles me out of the

fairy tale and into the reality of our mission in the woods tonight. "It's seven-fifteen," Clyde is reminding me. "Time to call."

I signal to Sally and Haruko, who are on my left while Clyde alerts Chloe and Hannah to the right, and we stop. All around us the quiet woods fill with myriad voices calling Isabel's name. Then at 7:16 the woods fall silent again. Even the birds, no doubt frightened by our voices, are quiet in the ensuing hush. For four minutes there's only the sound of the wind sifting through the tops of the white pines. There's no answering cry.

"If she were out here and conscious she would have answered by now," Clyde points out as we resume our upward trudge. I'm sure it's what we're all thinking as we get close to the top of the ridge: if we don't find Isabel on this side, she has probably fallen into the clove—and if that's what happened, how likely is it that she's still alive?

"Maybe she's not even in the woods," Hannah says. "Isabel was a real wuss—she couldn't even watch a scary movie—I just don't see her going into the woods."

"But you saw her go in, didn't you, Chloe?"

Chloe doesn't answer right away. Instead she looks down at Clyde's feet. "Your shoe is untied again," she says with a long drawn-out sigh and a pained look on her face.

Clyde's face turns red as he stoops to retie his black Converse high-top. His shoelaces have come

untied so many times that I've been tempted to tie
them in double knots like I used to do for Sally.
We've stopped in a swatch of golden early evening
sunlight that streams through a break in the canopy
that was made when the tree Clyde has his foot
propped on came down. It must have fallen years
ago, because its upturned root plate is furred by
moss, making it look like a huge hairy spider—an
impression that I imagine would be magnified at
night. I don't envy Isabel if she came this way.

"Come on," I tell Clyde, "we'll waste the ten minutes we get to walk. At this rate we won't make it to
the ridge by dusk."

Clyde drags his foot down from the root and
something white flutters in the air. A moth, I think,
but when it settles on the ground I see it's a piece of
white cloth. Chloe reaches out and fingers the material before I can stop her.

"It's the same cloth Ms. Drake used to make our
dresses," she says in a shaky voice.

"It could have been from someone else's dress," I
say, "but I think I'd better blow the whistle. Sheriff
Reade will want to see this."

I lift the whistle to my mouth. It takes me a moment to find the breath to blow it. We're only a few
hundred feet from the ridge and I'm suddenly afraid
of what we will see when we look over it into the
ravine. When I do find my breath the whistle
sounds like someone shrieking. The woods are unnaturally silent afterward. No one speaks while we

wait for Sheriff Reade. Fortunately, he doesn't take long.

"There he is." Clyde points up the hill. I look up and see Callum Reade silhouetted against the western sky. Of course, I realize, he's been patrolling the ridge. He'd want to find Isabel before anyone else. Well, at least now he'll have a narrower area to search. When Reade reaches us I hold up the piece of torn cloth. As it ripples in the breeze I feel absurdly like a medieval lady saluting her knight. Sheriff Reade takes the cloth from me with all the gravity of a knight accepting his lady's favors.

I describe how we found it and turn to Chloe to confirm that it's the same cloth that the dresses were made from. Reade nods and says: "Right. I need you kids to go back down to the Lodge. Tell any teachers you meet to meet me on the ridge—you can use this fallen tree as a landmark—and send all the students back to the Lodge."

"But why can't we help?" Chloe cries.

"Because I can't go fishing anyone else out of the clove. If Isabel's down there, she could be seriously hurt. We can't afford to waste any time."

Chloe looks as if she is going to argue, but Clyde leans down and says something in a low voice. Her eyes widen and I'm afraid we're in for a scene, but she gets to her feet and meekly follows Hannah and Clyde down the hill. Haruko turns to go, but Sally hesitates—as if she were suddenly unwlling to be parted from me. The thought that she might actually prefer for me to stay with her for once—that she **needs** me—makes me reluctant to go with Sheriff Reade. I'm about to tell him that I'm going back with my daughter when Hannah comes back up the hill and lays a hand on her arm.

"It's okay," she tells Sally in a lilting voice that seems more mature than her years. "We'll all stay together at the Lodge. You'll see—the good thing about this place is that we all stick together."

Sally nods and, without looking back at me, turns to follow Hannah down the hill.

"It looks like your daughter has made some friends," Reade says as we start walking up the hill.

"Yeah, I hope so. It's been a rough year for her, and the friends she chose in Great Neck were no help. She started hanging out with a group who went into the city to clubs and used their parents' money for alcohol and pot. I was hoping the kids here would be different. Less . . . shallow."

"Because it's an art school?" Reade asks, barely disguising the derision in his voice.

"Well, at least they might care about something other than the latest Marc Jacobs bag or who has an iPhone."

"The affectations and poses may be different here, but they're still affectations. I'd keep a close eye on who your daughter hangs out with."

"Really?" I say. "And where do you get your parenting experience? Do you have kids?"

Instead of answering he suddenly grabs my arm.

I let out an offended squawk and he immediately lets go and holds up his hands, palms out. "Sorry! I wasn't trying to interfere in your parenting, just keep you from walking over the edge. You seem to have some peculiar attraction to the spot." I look past him and see that we've reached the ridge and, once again, I've almost walked right over the edge. It's a particularly steep fall from this point and the drop-off is obscured by a blackberry bush. Below us the Wittekill leaps from rock to mossy rock, golden in the last rays of the setting sun. Between the rocks are deep patches of fern and hanging mosses.

"She could be right below us and we wouldn't be able to see her."

As if in answer to his words a breeze ripples the surface of the clove, parting the greenery on the ledge above the second cascade and revealing a patch of white. "There!" I point at the ledge about twenty feet below us. "Did you see that? I saw something white."

Reade leans farther over the edge, staring at the spot I'm pointing to, but shakes his head. "I don't see it, but if you're sure—"

"I'm not sure, but if it is Isabel—" I don't need to finish my sentence. We're both thinking the same thing. If there's any chance that Isabel's still alive, there's no time to lose. The sun has sunk below the ruin of the barn in the valley below; there's only another half-hour of sunlight left. Sheriff Reade takes his walkie-talkie off his belt and asks someone named Kyle how far he is from the ridge. I can't make out the blast of static that comes out of the machine, but he nods and says, "Over."

"They'll be here in ten minutes," he says, stripping off his jacket. "You show them where to go."

"Shouldn't you wait—" I begin, but he's already swung his legs over the edge of the rocky precipice. The man's infuriating, I think as I watch him crawl down the steep, rocky slope, using roots and rock outcroppings as handholds. He must see himself as some kind of hero. Still, I can't take my eyes off him. I lie flat on the ground and lean my head over so I can watch his progress, as if the force of my attention will keep him from slipping. When at last he makes it down to the ledge where I spotted the patch of white I let out a breath I didn't know I was holding.

Reade looks up and waves to me, then he turns and wades into the ferns, which come up to his waist and are now entirely in shadow. I hear footsteps and voices behind me. I get up so that the EMTs will see me, but I don't take my eyes off Callum Reade. He looks like a man wading into deep water, and I have the uneasy feeling that he might suddenly go under and then I'll have to know exactly where he is to save him. It strikes me that even though I've only known this man for less than twenty-four hours—and for most of it, I've found him bossy and prickly—I have no doubt that I'd dive in after him to rescue him.

Which is what I think I'll have to do when Reade trips and falls to his knees. The brambles close around him like hungry wolves. I cry out and fall to my own knees, ready to scramble down, but he holds up one hand and yells, "Wait!"

How, I wonder, did he know I was already on my way down?

"I've found her," he says, turning around. The blood has drained from his face; the only color left is the green reflection of the leaves, giving him the complexion of a drowned man. "You can send the EMTs down. But tell them there's no need to hurry."

CHAPTER 11

The last light has drained from the sky by the time they bring up the broken body of Isabel Cheney from the clove. The EMTs and police have brought floodlights to the edge of the ridge and aimed them down into the ravine to help the rescue crew see what they are doing. A few of the teachers stayed on the ridge, but most went back to the Lodge, where the students had gathered.

"If we let them go back to their dorms, they'll just brood on their own," Ivy St. Clare tells me. She arrived soon after word went out that Isabel's body had been found. Now she stands on the crest of the ridge, a little apart from the teachers, her left arm wrapped around her tiny waist and cradling her right elbow, a cigarette held in the right hand. I stand next to her as we wait for the medical examiner to give the okay to move the body, and we wait while Isabel is strapped onto a stretcher and painstakingly carried up the steep slope. I stand next to St. Clare the whole time even though I'm soon freezing and footsore. If an octogenarian doesn't need to sit down, I figure I don't. I do take a jacket offered by an EMT after the dean turns it down and put it over my shoulders. "I'm glad you're keeping them all together," I tell her. "I don't have to worry where Sally is."

"Of course," she says, squinting at me through her cigarette smoke. "This must make you feel worried for your daughter's safety. I imagine many of the parents will feel that way. I'll have to send a letter out first thing tomorrow, assuring them this was an unusual accident and delineating the steps that will be taken to make this part of campus off-limits. I've always thought that the ridge should be fenced off. I told Vera that after Lily died, but she said these woods were too old and too beautiful to ruin with fences and gates."

Watching the men lifting Isabel's body out of the

ravine, I understand why Ivy looks so haunted. "Was this where Lily fell?"

"Yes, it's exactly the same spot. We found her body just down there—" She points to the ledge where Isabel's body was found. I can't imagine how she can be so sure; there are no landmarks in the clove except for tumbled, moss-covered boulders and deep patches of fern and hanging moss. "It took weeks to find her because of the blizzard. She gave me her farewell note to give to Vera. When I told Vera that Lily was gone with Nash she collapsed. We thought Lily had left with him from the Lodge. We never guessed she was crossing the clove to meet him in the barn. We might not have found her until spring if Nash hadn't had his paintings of her sent back to Fleur-de-Lis. That was when we realized that she wasn't with him."

"You mean he didn't tell anyone when she didn't show up at the barn?"

"No. He figured she had changed her mind about leaving with him. His male ego was so wounded, he sulked off to the city. As soon as his show was over, he sent the paintings of her back here and then he went off to Europe."

"Are those the paintings hanging in the Lodge?"

"Yes. Vera couldn't bear to look at them. I don't think Nash could either, which is why he sent them back. I remember how Vera's face turned white when we got Nash's note. 'These belong with the woman who inspired them,' he'd written. 'She's not with him,' Vera said. 'She must have changed her mind.' Vera was so happy." Ivy sucks deeply on her cigarette and then drops it to the ground and crushes it beneath her foot. They're French cigarettes, I notice. Gauloises. I imagine she only smokes them in private, away from the students. "But then Vera realized what must have happened. She ran up here, through snowdrifts that reached to her waist, and I ran after her. I was afraid she'd throw herself from the ridge. I made her wait for me to call from the Lodge and get men from the town to look for Lily, but she insisted on searching with them. It took all day to find her and half the night to bring her body up. We used the toboggan that Vera had brought back from Switzerland as a present for Lily because it was something she remembered from her childhood in the country. The men wouldn't let her help carry it, so Vera ran back to the Lodge and collected candles. She made a path from the Lodge to the ridge of lit candles to light their way as they carried her body down the hill."

She looks behind us as if she were expecting to see that candlelit path now . . . and we both gasp at the sight of lights moving through the woods.

"Fireflies," I say, recovering first. "They're just fireflies."

Ivy turns to me, her face bleached white by the floodlights, her eyes huge and shiny as an owl's. "Of course, they're just fireflies," she says as though I were a child, "but when Vera came up here in the summer she said they were the ghosts of the lights that lit Lily's way back to the Lodge that night. **That's** the real reason she wouldn't fence off these woods. She believed that Lily's spirit was wandering lost and that she'd someday find her way back. On the anniversary of her death, Vera would lay out the candles just as they were on that night so that Lily could find her way home. I was tempted more than once to tell her that if Lily's spirit was looking for anything, it was the path to the barn and Virgil Nash. That's where she was going when she died— not back home to Fleur-de-Lis."

The bitterness in her voice is unmistakable. If I didn't know better, I'd think the body being carried up toward us was Lily Eberhardt's. But it's not. It's Isabel Cheney's. As the men finally reach the ridge with the stretcher, I pick up one of the flashlights and approach them. Other teachers think to do the same. We form a protective circle around them to light the way through the woods down to the Lodge. It's not a path of candles, but it's enough like one to make me feel as if we are reenacting an old rite—something even older than the procession of Lily Eberhardt's body. The burial procession of the summer goddess, sacrificed so that the autumn goddess might rule over the land.

The same spirit seems to have moved those waiting in the Lodge. Candles have been lit in the windows and a group of students, including Sally, and teachers stand outside holding lit candles. Word must have gotten to them that Isabel is dead because the mood is somber. The assembled crowd is silent as we pass. Glancing at the faces of Isabel's classmates I recall those faces last night in the glow of the bonfire. They look as if they had all aged overnight from innocent children into careworn adults. I remember Isabel's speech. "There are times I think that these years will turn out to have been the best years of my life," she'd said. Had she had some presentiment that they would turn out to be the last years of her life?

The thought of someone dying so young makes me want to be with Sally, but when I ask her if she's ready to go home she tells me no. "The other kids are going to stay here at the Lodge and talk. It's kind of a tribute to Isabel. I know I didn't really know her, but I'd like to stay."

The last thing I want is for Sally to be out of my sight, but then I remember that I promised her she could be just like any other kid at the school. That it wouldn't make a difference that her mother was a teacher here.

"Are you all staying in the Lodge?" I ask, scanning each of their faces in turn, trying to detect any sign that they're planning to do something else.

"Oh yes," Hannah Weiss assures me. "Ms. Drake and the dean will be here, too."

"And Sally can stay in my dorm room afterward," Haruko says. "My roommate never showed up."

Both Hannah and Haruko seem like good prospective friends for Sally. How can I say no? "Okay," I say. "Come back in the morning to get dressed though, okay?"

I leave before I can reconsider. Two more police cars have arrived—one with the Arcadia Falls insignia on it, one that has the markings of the state troopers. An officer is cordoning off the edge of the woods and telling students to stay out of the area. I imagine that in the morning they'll search the woods for any other clues to Isabel's demise. In the meantime, the campus is so well populated by law enforcement that even I can't imagine how Sally could come to any harm here. I can go home and get some sleep.

When I finally make it to my bedroom in the cottage, though, I realize that it's not going to be easy to fall asleep. As soon as I close my eyes I see Isabel's body being lifted out of the ravine. When I open my eyes the bathrobe hanging over the closet door becomes that ghostly white figure flitting through the woods. The white woman.

I flip on the lamp on my nightstand, banishing the shadows back into the corners, but I still feel them lurking there. When I got like this when I was little, my mother would read to me; only a story would calm me down. It didn't matter if the story was frightening. I liked fairy tales in which children lost their way in the woods. As long as they found the way back, I could go to sleep. On my bedside table now is my old copy of **The Changeling Girl**—the one that belonged to my grandmother—but for once I don't think that'll help. It's become too real in this place where it was written.

Instead, I reach for the purple hatbox with Vera Beecher's journals and letters. I open the box and take out the picture of the three women that lies on top. I turn it over now and find, in ink faded to pale lavender, the words **May Day, 1928. Lily Eberhardt, Gertrude Sheldon, and Mimi Green.**

I turn over the picture and look more closely at the three women. I've seen pictures of Lily Eberhardt from the thirties and forties, but never one of her this young. Nineteen twenty-eight was the first year of the colony. Lily would have been only nineteen years old. She looks radiant, in a long white dress and with a wreath of daisies around her loose, waist-length hair, her face bathed in soft early-morning light. She's holding her right arm out as if inviting someone just outside the frame of the picture to join the threesome. She looks as if she wants to embrace the whole world, as if the joy inside of her is about to overflow. It's almost painful to look at someone so young and happy, knowing that she would die alone in a frozen ravine twenty years later. That look reminds me of Isabel's face last night—but at least Lily had another twenty years.

I recognize the woman in the middle, Gertrude Sheldon, from histories of the period. She was a wealthy arts patron who went on to found the Sheldon Museum in New York and to shape the careers of many prominent mid-twentieth-century painters. I hardly recognize the society matron in this wild maenad in medieval-style dress and messy hair, but I do recognize someone else. Shelley Drake. Her granddaughter, perhaps?

The third woman is dwarfed by Gertrude Sheldon's statuesque form. Her face is half-hidden by a square-cut helmet of hair—the style favored by Louise Brooks and any number of 1920s flappers. I vaguely recall reading about an artist named Mimi Green who was at the Art Students League and who later worked on a mural with Lily Eberhardt, but she's absent from the later records of Arcadia. Perhaps there's more about her in Vera's papers.

I prop the photograph against the lamp on my night table and turn back to the box. I pick up the first book, which is bound in brown cloth stamped with a beech tree, and something falls into my lap.

At first I think it's a leaf. It looks as fragile as one and it's pale green. It crackles when I touch it and releases a scent that's instantly familiar. Lily of the valley. It's the scent my grandmother always wore. It was a popular scent in the 1920s.

I unfold the page gingerly; it's like forcing open a flower bud. I'm afraid that the paper will crumble to dust in my hands. But it doesn't. The thin spidery lines of script on it are so faint that they might be the veins of a leaf instead of handwriting. The ink may have been blue once, but it's faded to pale lavender—the same color as the writing on the back of the photograph. I have to hold the page under the bedside lamp to read it.

> My darling,
> As I write this I am afraid it might already be too late and that I have lost your love. My Lily Among the Thorns, you once called me. I am afraid that I have been little more than a thorn to you, but I don't want you only to remember the thorns. The only way I can think to tell you how much you have meant to me is to tell you the whole story. I have written it these last few months because, after all the stories we have told each other all these years, I knew it had come time to finally tell **my** story. My hope is that it will explain to you why I have done what I have, but failing that, at least it should show you how much you have meant to me. You are my heart. I have left my story for you in the heart and hearth of our lives together.
> You have my love always,
> Lily
> December 26, 1947

I stare at the date. It's the night that Lily left Arcadia to run away with Virgil Nash, never to make it to their meeting place; she died in a cold ravine not a quarter mile from the cottage she shared with her **darling** Vera. **You are my heart.** A strange thing to say to someone when you're leaving her. And the next line was stranger still. **I have left my story for you in the heart and hearth of our lives together.** What could that mean?

I pick up one of the brown journals and flip through it. There are lots of lists: lists of artists who came to the colony each summer, lists of art supplies needed and workshops to be taught, even lists of food items to be ordered for the kitchen. A wealth of the minutiae involved in the running of an art colony. I'm sure Vera's journals will be an invaluable resource for my thesis, but they're not what I'm in the mood for right now. What I want to read right now is the story Lily promises in her farewell letter to Vera.

I unload the hatbox onto my bed—making separate piles of Vera's journals, inventory books, letters, and photographs. There's no journal belonging to Lily. Perhaps Vera burned it. I picture her doing just that, smashing the tiles on the mantelpiece and then throwing the journal into the fireplace . . . into the **heart and hearth of our lives together.** Is that what Lily meant in her letter—that the journal was hidden in the hearth? And is that why the mantelpiece tiles were broken, because Vera had been looking for it?

Although I don't have any real expectation of finding anything, I get out of bed and pad downstairs in my bare feet. I examine the tiles over the fireplace, looking behind each of the broken ones.

There's enough room to hold a book, but there's nothing there. Of course not—whatever was there must have been removed by Vera on that night in 1947. And then she must have smashed the tiles in anguish over her betrayal . . . or had it been frustration? What if she had been looking for the journal and hadn't been able to find it?

I run my hand over the wooden panel above the tiles, along the beech tree carved in the center. Its roots snake into the ground beneath the tree and there's something buried deep within the twisted roots. I look closer and then rear back when I see that it's a tiny baby curled up into a ball. The changeling baby of the story. It's a disturbing image, but somehow it also draws me to it. I touch my finger to the perfect curve of the sleeping child . . . and the panel pops open. I'm so surprised I step back and nearly trip over the rug, but I catch my balance and peer into the narrow slot behind the panel . . . and then I pull out a slim green leather book embossed with a gold fleur-de-lis. Lily's journal. Somehow still here after all these years. Any thought of sleep is gone now. I sink down into the musty old chair by the fireplace, open the book, and begin to read.

CHAPTER 12

The first time I saw Vera
Beecher at the Art Students
League I thought, "But I know
her, she's the girl in the stories I've
been telling: the maiden in the
tower, the queen of the forest, the
enchanted damsel."

Not that she'd be everybody's
idea of a fairytale princess. Her
face was square and strong-jawed,
not heart-shaped and dimpled
like the heroines of the fairy tales

in the illustrated Grimm's my oma brought over from the old country. Her hair was brown—nut brown, I called it to myself—not the spun gold flax of Rapunzel. And she was tall, more like a Valkyrie or an Amazon than Cinderella or Rose Red. But as the light from the studio windows fell on her, I recognized her as the heroine of my stories—the ones I had been telling and drawing as long as I could remember. Instead of being surprised, I remember thinking that it made sense I would find her here. After all, it was my storytelling and drawing that had led me to the Art Students League in New York City in the fall of 1927.

I grew up on a dairy farm in Delaware County, New York, in the town of Roxbury, the eldest of five girls. Because my mother was needed to help with the milking, it fell to me to watch the younger ones while doing my chores. I saw that the children minded me best when I told them a story. Each morning, while I stoked the fire and stirred the oatmeal, I would begin one of the fairy tales that I'd read in Grimm's and tell it piece by piece all day through, so that the little ones did everything I said and followed me about to hear the story till its end. Before long I began making up my own stories and fitting them up with pieces of our lives. The cow Posey would become an enchanted fairy godmother and the farmer's son in the next dale would be the prince of a great kingdom. My sisters, Rose, Marguerite, Iris, and Violet (my mother had a weakness for floral names), would each in turn feature as the heroine of the story. In the evenings as we sat around the fire sewing the girls asked me to draw pictures to go with the stories and I happily obliged.

But a funny thing happened when I began to draw the characters of my stories. The heroines looked nothing like my sisters or like me. We were all blond and small and would have done well enough for fairy princesses with a little cleaning up and nicer clothes, but the women I drew were regal and tall, slim but sturdy. They looked, to me, like they wouldn't wait in a tower for a prince to rescue them or sleep in a castle for a hundred years until the huntsman hacked his way through the briars. They—or, rather, she, because I soon saw she was the same woman in each story—looked as though she could wield a sword herself. And so she did. My heroine mounted her own steed and rode off looking for adventures. After my sisters fell asleep, I stayed up late into the night drawing the pictures to go with the stories I had made up during the day. Each story would end the same way: my heroine standing on a ridge overlooking the next valley, a dark silhouette against a rose and lilac sunset.

The day the farmer's son from the next dale

asked me to marry him, I packed up all my
drawings and my best dress and boarded the
train that took our milk to the city. I left a
note promising my parents that when I found
work I would send money back to make up for
my labors on the farm. To my sisters, I
promised I would send them more stories. I
told them all that I was very sorry, but I had to
find the girl in my stories. When I saw Vera
Beecher for the first time, I knew that I had.

She was, I soon learned, already a heroine
to many at the Art Students League. Mimi
Green, who worked at the magazine where I'd
found some work doing fashion illustrations,
told me that Vera Beecher had studied in Paris
and won prizes for her work. Virgil Nash, the
League's most famous teacher—and the hand-
somest, the girls all swooned over him and said
he looked like Rudy Valentino—always singled
Vera out for praise and held her work up as an
example to the rest of us. That made some of
the students speak against her, especially the
men, who, for all the equality the League
boasted of, still considered themselves the only
serious artists. Everyone knew what Eugene
Speicher had said to young Georgia O'Keeffe
when she wasn't eager to pose for him: "It
doesn't matter what you do, I'm going to be a
great painter and you will probably end up
teaching painting in some girls' school."

Even though Eugene Speicher was proven wrong, a lot of the teachers still treated the women students as inferior. They resented the debutantes and socialites who came to the League to fill up their days and hobnob with "the bohemians," women like Gertrude Sheldon who was married to one of the richest men in New York, Bennett Sheldon, but spent her days at the Art League taking classes and flirting with the teachers. And she couldn't even draw well. The other girls made fun of Gertrude. They said the reason she wasted her time with art was because she couldn't get pregnant and her husband had grown tired of her. But no one made fun of Vera Beecher. She came from a wealthy family, too, but she was talented and she never used her wealth or position to gain unfair advantage over the other students. Mimi told me that when Vera won the **William Randolph Hearst Prize** from the Art Institute of Chicago she had insisted that her prize money be given to the artist who had come in second because he was in more financial need than she was. She taught art classes to poor children on the Lower East Side and volunteered at an orphanage in the Bronx.

Saint Vera, Mimi called her one night when we were riding the subway downtown to a party in the Village. I knew Mimi meant it as an insult, but a picture flew into my head of

Vera Beecher as Joan of Arc. That night I
stayed up drawing a sketch of her in that role.
The next day in Life Drawing I positioned my
easel so I might surreptitiously draw Vera
Beecher instead of the model. (In those days, it
was the custom at the League for senior students to take the first row, nearest the model,
while newcomers such as myself hung back in
the last rows.) I drew her as the young martyr
when she first hears the voice of God calling
her. She stood in a ray of sunlight, her fine,
broad forehead bathed in light. When
Mr. Nash came by to look at my work, I saw
his eyes traveling from my drawing to Vera
and back again. I was afraid he'd say something to embarrass me or be angry I wasn't
drawing the model—a voluptuous vaudeville
dancer named Suzie. Instead he commended
my sense of line. It was the first compliment I
ever received from the great Mr. Nash and I
nearly burst out laughing when I caught Mimi
looking cross-eyed at me.

But if I thought I'd been spared embarrassment, I was wrong. I watched in horror as
Nash walked straight over to Miss Beecher and
whispered in her ear something that made her
turn in my direction. **He had told her!** I crim-
soned with mortification. I would have fled
the room right then, only when her gray eyes
met mine I suddenly couldn't move. I felt like
a field mouse trapped in the barn owl's gaze.

But even as I trembled, a part of my brain was thinking how lovely it would be to draw Vera Beecher as gray-eyed Athena! How well the owl's helmet would sit upon that noble brow! Even as she put down her pencil and approached me, I remained transfixed.

She came and stood behind me. The room had become unnaturally quiet. The usual chatter and gossip had ceased; even the whispering of pencils on paper had died down to nothing. All I could hear was my own heart beating and the sound of her breath.

"Is that really how I look?" she asked.

I thought she was criticizing, but when I looked over my shoulder at her I saw that her eyes were shining. "Yes," I said with a confidence born from her eyes—from the way she looked at my work. "That's how you look to me."

She smiled then and introduced herself—as if I didn't know who she was!—and after a few minutes went back to her easel. But at the end of the class she caught up to me and asked where I was walking to. Embarrassed to give my address—I was living in a room at the Martha Washington Hotel on East Twenty-ninth Street—I told her I was walking to Central Park to sketch.

"What a marvelous idea!" she said. "May I join you?"

It wasn't a marvelous idea at all; it was a

very cold day. But of course I said that I'd be honored to have her company. We entered the park at Fifty-ninth Street, through the Merchants' Gate, and followed the path past the dairy—which was so clean and pretty that it resembled no dairy I had ever seen—and through the Promenade. It had rained earlier in the day and then the temperature had dropped, freezing the water droplets that hung from the bare limbs of the great elm trees on either side of the Promenade. The sun came out as we walked beneath them, and Vera gasped and grabbed my hand.

"Look, how beautiful! Like trees carved of crystal. They remind me of the Sycamore Drive at Arcadia."

I asked her what Arcadia she spoke of, and she told me about her childhood home—hers since both her parents had died eight years ago in the 'flu epidemic. She spoke of it as an enchanted land she had been exiled from. I wondered aloud why she didn't live there all the time.

"All it lacks," she told me, "is the right sort of company. I have thought sometimes of inviting a few like-minded artists to come spend the summer there and of engaging an instructor to give classes in drawing and painting **en plein air.**" She looked at me with those placid gray eyes that seemed to see **everything.**

"Perhaps you would want to come, since you are so dedicated to drawing out of doors." She tapped the sketchbook which I held pressed against my chest and I blushed to remember the excuse I had given for our present stroll—and that we had yet to stop and draw anything!

"Yes, I do love drawing from nature. . . ." I stammered and then, casting my eyes around for a suitable subject, found the perfect one. "But today I wanted to draw **her.**" We had come to the end of the Promenade, to the upper terrace overlooking the lake and the Angel of the Waters fountain. I pointed to the angel. "I saw her the first week I was in the city and have come here often since, whenever I feel alone."

"Ah," Vera murmured as we walked down the steps to the lower terrace. "'Now there is at Jerusalem by the sheep market a pool, which is called Bethesda . . . and whoever then first after the troubling of the waters stepped in was made whole of whatsoever disease he had.' You've picked the right place to come to be healed." We sat on the rim of the empty basin and looked up at that grave bronze face. I took out my sketchpad and began to draw. "Do you know her story?" Vera asked.

"You mean the angel's story?" I asked.

"No, the sculptress's story."

When I shook my head she went on. As she
spoke I kept my eyes on the bronze face above
me, but I could feel the gaze of the flesh-and-
blood woman beside me. "The sculptress was
Emma Stebbins, who studied in Rome under
John Gibson. There she met and formed a deep
attachment to the actress Charlotte Saunders
Cushman. They lived together very happily
until Charlotte became ill with a cancer of the
breast. . . ." I could see out of the corner of my
eye that Vera had lain her hand over her own
breast as she talked of Charlotte's illness, and I
felt a corresponding tug in my own breast as if
she had touched me there. "Emma took loving
care of her, taking her to spas for water cures. I
am sure that's what she was thinking of when
she sculpted this statue—that she made it in
thanks for Charlotte's cure."

"Was she cured?"

"Yes, but sadly, Charlotte died of pneumo-
nia three years after Emma made this statue."

I turned to her then, my own hand flying
to my heart. I felt as if I'd been hit there and
that all the air had been driven out of my
lungs. "What became of Emma?" I asked.

"She lived another six years," Vera answered. "But she never made another sculpture."

I turned back to my drawing, unsure of
what to say in the face of such love and grief. I

wondered what it felt like to care that much for someone and what it would feel like to be loved like that. Although the farmer's son had asked me to marry him, he had switched his attentions to my sister Margeurite soon after I left. My mother had written to tell me that they would be married in the spring. It hadn't hurt me. I could barely remember what his face looked like. I looked down at my sketchpad and saw that instead of the features of the statue, I had drawn, once again, Vera's face.

"I see why you are drawn to her," Vera said.

I hugged the sketchpad to my chest, afraid she'd see what I had done, but she was pointing at the angel's left hand. I looked up and noticed for the first time what she held in it. "A lily," Vera said. "Sign of purity." She put her hand over mine and I felt her touch course through me down to the core of my being. "We'd better go," she said. "Your hands are as cold as ice."

From then on we walked in the park after class, no matter how cold. If it rained or snowed we sat beneath the Arcade and sketched the patterns in the ceiling tiles. Vera said she wanted to make tiles like them for a cottage at Arcadia.

She often spoke of Arcadia and drew pictures of it for me, so that I began to feel as if I

knew the place. She told me about the
Sycamore Drive and the old stand of woods on
the western ridge, which had been there since
before the first European settlers had come to
the mountains. The villagers had superstitions
about the woods which Vera laughed at, but I
noticed that she knew each tree that grew at
Arcadia and spoke of them as though they
were old friends. She may have laughed at the
idea of tree spirits, but she seemed to revere
them as much as any druid ever had. The tree
she loved the best, though, was a great
copper beech that stood on the main lawn.
I drew a picture of it with Vera's own features
imprinted in the bark and entitled it **Vera,
Druid Priestess of the Beeches.** She drew me
as a lily, my head nodding over my easel, my
eyes drooping, half-asleep.

We sent these little drawings back and forth
in class and soon others noticed. I heard them
whispering, but I didn't care. I didn't care that
the girls giggled when Vera brought me presents: scent from the apothecary Privet and
Sloe in thick green glass bottles stamped with
fleurs-de-lis, nosegays of violets, a hat trimmed
with lilies of the valley in a purple hatbox.
One of the girls who had gone to a woman's
college said Vera was my **smash.** Even Virgil
Nash noticed and made jokes about how
close we set up our easels together and how

all our portraits turned into pictures of each other.

"Miss Eberhardt," he said one day with an elaborate, drawn-out sigh, "you might as well come up here and pose because you are all Miss Beecher will draw anyway."

Gertrude Sheldon tittered and said something to another girl that made her blush. I saw Vera growing angry and was afraid she'd make a scene. It was her one flaw, my poor darling, her temper. And I knew that Gertrude Sheldon particularly irritated her. I think it was because Vera was, quite unfoundedly, afraid that what people said about Gertrude was true of her: that she was a rich, idle woman who was only playing at art.

"Very well," I said, putting my pencil down. "I will."

The class was perfectly silent as I walked to the front of the room. The model had come in, but she hadn't disrobed yet. I climbed onto the raised dais where a musty old settee draped in moth-eaten shawls served as background and pedestal for our models. Turning to face the room, I was surprised at how different it looked from this perspective, as if I had climbed a high mountaintop and was looking down upon a valley. It reminded me of the finales I had drawn in my fairy tales, the heroine silhouetted against the setting sun. Instead of a sunset, an embroidered Chinese shawl hung behind me, but I imagined I had become the heroine of my old stories. The girl who was not afraid.

I took off my muslin smock and began to unbutton my dress.

"Miss Eberhardt . . ." Virgil Nash began, approaching the dais. "The rules state . . ."

"That Life Drawing class be provided with a model. Does it say who that model should be?" I asked, all the time undoing the buttons down the front of my dress. "Am I any different from Suzie, here? Are any of us?" My hands were shaking, but my voice was steady. I thanked God that I had recently given up wearing a corset . . . and then smiled to think what an odd thing that was to thank God for! It was the smile that saved me. I saw it reflected in Vera's face. Her gaze held mine as I peeled back my shirtwaist and camisole in one movement. I let them fall loosely around my waist as I sat on the settee and faced the class. Vera was the first to pick up her pencil and begin to draw. I kept my eyes on her for the rest of the class and imagined that she and I were alone in the room. That's what kept my spine straight and my chin held up for the next hour. She gave me the strength. No one spoke. Even Virgil Nash had taken up pencil and begun to draw instead of circulating and critiquing. The room was filled with the soft whicker of pencil on paper. It sounded like snow falling through pine trees. I felt as though I had **become** a tree, a great white pine standing in the forest, snow sifting through my needled boughs. . . .

I could have stayed there forever. The hour ended sooner than I thought it would. Only when I tried to stand did I realize I had lost all feeling in my legs. Vera came to my rescue and held my muslin smock up in front of me as I fumbled the buttons of my shirtwaist. She carried my sketchpad for me and whispered in my ear that I must come to her house for tea. She was afraid I'd catch a chill if I didn't. I readily agreed, but as we were leaving Mr. Nash asked me to stay a moment "for a word." I nodded to Vera that it was all right and said that I'd meet her downstairs.

I expected a lecture and was prepared to tell him that I'd never do it again, but instead he turned his easel around so that I could see the drawing he'd begun. What I saw took my breath away. While Vera had drawn me as her drooping lily, Virgil Nash had captured how I felt up there on the dais. He'd drawn me as the girl from my stories, the heroine I'd made up and come to the city looking for.

"I'd like to finish this," he said. "Would you consider posing for me privately?"

It did not occur to me to say no.

As it turned out, it was the least that I could do for Mr. Nash. When it came out (I've always suspected that it was Gertrude Sheldon who complained to the board) that he had allowed a student to disrobe and model in class, he was fired. Vera was so incensed that she withdrew her membership from the League and proposed to Mr. Nash that they form their own art school. Her home at Arcadia Falls would be the perfect setting. He readily agreed.

I've always wondered if his decision was influenced by the fact that I would be there. By then Vera had asked me to come to Arcadia, not just as a fellow student, but as her companion. Should I have suspected that Nash's interest in me went beyond the aesthetic? Should I have told Vera **not** to include him in our "sylvan idyll"? Would things have been different if Vera and I had gone to Arcadia without him? Perhaps. But the seeds were sown that day I peeled away my outer layers in front of the Life Drawing class. What Vera saw was her lily—a symbol of purity held by an angel. I'm not sure that Virgil Nash saw me more clearly, but he saw me as I liked to think of myself and I wasn't willing to give that up. Not even for Vera. We came to paradise already carrying the seeds of its destruction, but I'm afraid that is the way of all paradises.

—

Beneath this line, Lily had drawn a small fleur-de-lis signaling the end of this first section. It seems like a good place to stop for the night. I go upstairs, hugging the journal to my chest, place it on the nightstand, and turn off the light. I listen to the wind in the pine trees that surround the cottage. It is gentler than last night's keening. Tonight it sounds like pencils on paper, and I fall asleep with the strange notion that all of Arcadia Falls is a pencil drawing and each night it draws itself anew.

CHAPTER 13

When I wake up the next morning, my dream of Arcadia as a drawing seems to have come true. Fog shrouds the woods surrounding my cottage, turning the view from my bedroom window into a lightly smudged charcoal sketch. Lily's journal lies on my nightstand, a lilac ribbon marking where I stopped reading last night. I touch the worn cloth cover, recalling the last lines I read: **We came**

to paradise already carrying the seeds of its destruction. And yet, she and Vera had lived here happily for nineteen years before disaster struck. What kind of love triangle smoldered so long before bursting into flames? I pick up the book. In the still of the fog-locked house, I have the feeling that all I have to do is open it to populate this cottage—and the surrounding woods and the campus—not only with the three main players in that drama, but all the fairytale maidens and monsters that Vera and Lily created together.

And as soon as I turn to the marked place in the book I **do** hear the creak of a door opening downstairs, and a voice shouting . . . but it's not a character out of one of Vera and Lily's stories. It's Sally.

She's already in her room by the time I get out into the hall, pulling jeans and T-shirts out of her suitcases. "You're not dressed yet?" she asks when she sees me standing in her doorway. "You're going to be late for class."

It's exactly what I've said to her every morning for the last year. Have we changed places overnight? "Um, I wasn't sure there would be class," I say.

"They announced at breakfast that classes would be held as usual," Sally says, finally settling on a T-shirt silkscreened with images of little girls in short dresses, Mary Janes, and bobby socks. Across the back is the name of the band the Vivian Girls.

"You've been to breakfast?" I ask, more stunned at that news than at the dean's decision to hold classes on the day after a student's death. Sally has refused breakfast for the last year, claiming that it made her nauseated to even think about food before noon.

"Sure, everybody goes," Sally responds distractedly as she rejects one pair of jeans in favor of a seemingly identical pair. "They've got waffles and blueberry pancakes with real maple syrup. Hannah says that they make their own maple syrup in the spring and everybody helps. Anyways, I'd better go. I promised to meet Haruko before art class to show her my cartoons."

She's gone before I can ask how she's dealing with Isabel Cheney's death, but really, it's not necessary. Clearly, she's fine. I can only hope that the rest of my students are doing so well.

In Folklore class I start out by asking if anyone has anything they want to share about Isabel. After a moment of silence, Hannah Weiss raises a timid hand. "I feel bad that I never got to know her better. She was always working so hard—"

"What you really feel bad about is that you didn't like her better," Tori Pratt says.

"That's not fair," Hannah cries, blushing. "I didn't **dislike** her, it's just that she was a hard person to get to know."

"She was," Clyde says from behind the curtain of his hair. He's hunched so far over that I can't make out his eyes. But then he rakes the hair off his face and I see that those eyes are bloodshot and ringed with dark circles. He seems to have taken Isabel's death especially hard. "You had the feeling when you talked to her that she was planning her future. And you weren't in it. It's funny that she wanted to study history."

A pall of silence falls over the class. Perhaps they're all thinking—as I am—about what a waste it is: a smart, talented girl with her whole future ahead of her, gone because of a careless slip. Or perhaps they've just run out of things to say. I'm about to go on with today's lesson when Chloe, who's been silent so far, raises her hand. She looks even worse than Clyde, her greasy, unbrushed hair hanging lank around her face, her eyes rimmed with red.

"Yes, Chloe?" I ask.

"I wrote a poem," Chloe says in a small voice. "I call it 'The Death of Summer.' "

"Would you like to read it?" I ask.

Chloe nods and opens her laptop. The machine chimes as it powers up—like a bell tolling for Isabel's death.

" 'The Death of Summer,' " she reads.

Indifference kills in this cold world: a flower ignored by rain in early spring will die, and even in midsummer heat, a sigh of love's ephemeral, dies with the hour.

And when love's just a glance, brief touch, mere smiles, and cruel fate kills, love's never harvested,

**but love yet lives in memory; we're wed
now, all of us, by youth's tremors and trials
and will remain so in our lifelong thoughts,
the same way sunshine often floats
on rivers, streams, amidst the breezestrewn air,
in sudden aftermath of violent storms.**

**There is a dark side to us, cruelty warns,
but also art and love. If we could dare.**

The class is silent when she's done. "That's lovely, Chloe," I say at last, although in truth there's something about the poem I find unsettling. Perhaps it's the idea of the bond between the two girls lasting for eternity. After all, they hadn't even seemed to like each other.

"We should have some kind of memorial," a girl whose name I've forgotten says. "With poems and songs and art about Isabel. After all, this is supposed to be a school for the arts."

Others chime in, volunteering suggestions for projects honoring Isabel's memory: a slide collage of pictures of her, a compilation of her favorite songs, poems written in her honor.

"We should have it on the autumn equinox," Chloe says.

I'd have thought they'd all have had enough of pagan ceremonies, but a murmur of consent moves through the room. Chloe jots down notes and takes names of volunteers. Clearly she's become the leader of this new group, just as she was the leader of the First Night festival. If I don't say anything, the rest of the class will become a meeting of the Equinox Club.

"I'm glad you've all found a way of expressing your loss over Isabel," I say loudly enough to capture their attention. "Using words and images to reframe real life seems to be a tradition at Arcadia." I'm thinking of what I read in Lily's journal last night, how she had seemed to first invent Vera and then herself out of the stories she told and drew for her sisters, and then how she had spent her last months at Arcadia trying to make sense of her life by writing it all down in her journal. In between she had coauthored fairy tales like **The Changeling Girl.** Had that, too, been a way of telling her story? Had the fairy tale told how Lily had left her old life behind on the dairy farm for the life of an artist in the city? And if that were true, had Vera Beecher been the witch?

"Yesterday I told you that your first assignment for the term was to find out what in Vera Beecher's and Lily Eberhardt's lives led them to tell the changeling story as they did. Your second assignment is to write your own changeling story. If you could exchange your life with someone else's, would you? Whose life would you choose? Would you ever want to go back to your old life? You might want to think about how the changeling story describes the death of an old life in exchange for the birth of something new."

"The way the summer goddess dies and is reborn as the autumn goddess?" Chloe asks.

"Something like that," I say. Although I'm reluctant to subscribe to the pagan theology that seems to be so popular here at Arcadia, I can see how it might help them to deal with Isabel's death to think about it in these terms. Would it have helped Sally accept her father's death? I wonder. Maybe not, but it might help her accept that the old life we had with Jude is gone. "Certainly it's an idea you can explore," I conclude.

I spend the rest of the class discussing the changeling story in European folklore. I start by reading them a story from the Grimms in which a child is removed from its crib. In its place is left a changeling with a thick head and staring eyes who would do nothing but eat and drink. When the mother seeks advice from a neighbor she's told to boil water in two eggshells in front of the baby. If the baby laughs, she'll know it's a changeling. As soon as the mother sets the eggshells filled with water over the fire, the changeling says:

Now I am as old
As the Wester Wood,
But have never seen anyone cooking in shells!

Then the baby laughed so hard that he rolled out of his high chair. Finally, a band of elves appeared with the mother's rightful child. They gave it to the mother and took away the changeling.

The class laughed at the story, as I had hoped they would. I told other stories just like this one, some of which employed different tests to expose the changeling. Many of the tests were designed to surprise the creature into speech, but some were harsher and involved putting the changeling into a fire.

"But what if it was a real baby?" Hannah asks, her eyes wide.

"Then it would call out to its mother to be saved. But in all of these stories the creature turns into smoke and goes out a hole in the ceiling, or changes into its real shape and runs out the door. Still, it's a good question. **What if it was a real baby**? And why do you think people told these stories?"

"To explain why a baby might change all of a sudden?" Hannah, again, provides the answer even if it is in the form of a question. "I mean, babies sometimes change, right? My youngest halfbrother seemed fine until his second birthday and then we found out he was autistic."

"Absolutely," I say, wondering if this is why Hannah seems so personally connected to this subject. "Autism is one of a number of developmental disorders that might explain what happens in these tales. Asperger's, cerebral palsy, brain damage from a fall or fever. A seemingly healthy baby becomes listless. Perhaps it's not getting enough to eat. In a number of the tales, the changeling is insatiable. It eats and eats but fails to grow. Imagine a poor family, a mother who's not getting enough food to produce adequate milk, a baby who cries and cries and can't be comforted. What's to be done?"

"You mean they might abandon the baby?" Hannah asks, appalled.

"Many cultures practiced infanticide. Of course it's a horrifying thought, so how better to mask it than by creating a myth about changeling babies? It's not a real baby, the story reassures the mother, it's an impostor, a **demon**. And in order to get her own baby back, she must sacrifice the changeling."

"But in real life, that's not what would happen. There was no **real** baby to get back," Chloe Dawson points out.

"Of course not," I say. "But the sacrifice of a baby who wasn't thriving might mean the survival of older children, or the possibility of the mother having another—healthier—child. The story masks a harsh reality, as many of these stories do. For the next class, I want you to read 'Cinderella' and think about what social circumstances that story masks." They scribble the assignment in their notebooks as the eleven o'clock bell chimes. As they file out, I hear several of them talking about the lesson and about other fairy tales. I was afraid that the changeling stories might be too morbid a topic for today, but I see that I've succeeded in getting them to think about the stories in a different way, **and** I've managed to get them thinking about something other than Isabel Cheney's death. The only one not talking is Chloe Dawson.

"Chloe," I say as she attempts to slink by me, "could I have a word with you?"

She flinches as if I'd slapped her. Clyde Bollinger stops halfway through the door and turns back. "You're not going to ask her more questions about Isabel, are you? She already told the sheriff that she didn't see Isabel after she went into the woods. Can't you all just leave her alone?" He finishes by giving Chloe an adoring look. When, I wonder, did Clyde Bollinger become Chloe Dawson's champion? It seems an unlikely pairing. "I have no intention of interrogating Chloe. I just want a word with her. **Alone.**"

Clyde bristles at my emphasis on the last word. "I'll save a place for you at lunch," he says, and then lopes away, but not before giving Chloe a glance filled with a naked longing that instantly transports me back to the first time I saw Jude in Drawing class at Pratt. I remember feeling as if I'd seen him before even though I knew I hadn't. It was as if I'd **invented** him out of all the inchoate longings of my teen years. How had Lily put it? That Vera Beecher was the girl in the stories she'd been telling all her life.

"You wanted to talk to me?" Chloe asks. To my embarrassment, Chloe has come out of her reverie more quickly than I.

"I just wanted to ask how you were doing. You look like you've been crying. I know it must be especially hard for you since you and Isabel worked on that project together—"

"But we didn't really," she says, cutting me off. "Isabel liked to do things on her own. It's not like we were tight or anything. So really, you don't have to worry about me. In fact, I wish everyone would just stop worrying about me." She concludes so emphatically I can't think of anything else to say, except for the last resort of clueless adults everywhere: "Well, if you decide you want to talk about anything—"

She's out the door before I can finish, leaving me feeling like the girl in Rumpelstiltskin after she guessed the wrong name.

I hurry toward Briar Lodge for my next class, but when I get there I find a note from the Merling twins telling me that they had to leave campus for a "family emergency." I'm annoyed that they didn't e-mail me to save me the trip, but then I remember that Sheldon Drake said that her studio is in the Lodge. Since seeing the May Day picture with Gertrude Sheldon last night I've been wondering how Shelley Drake is related to her—and if she knows anything about the early days of the colony that would be useful.

I find the studio at the back of the Lodge in a sunlit, high-ceilinged room. Although I expected to find the studio full of students, the room is unoccupied. The entire west wall is a glass window that frames a view of the woods. Right now the woods look placid and innocent, but later in the day they'll fill with the long shadows I saw yesterday. That must be when Shelley paints, I think, because the large painting on the easel is of the woods in the late afternoon. Standing in front of the canvas, I'm transported back to yesterday when we first began the search for Isabel. Carpeted with dried pine needles, the forest floor glows an eerie gold, broken into tawny stripes by the long shadows of the trees that reach toward the viewer. Perhaps that's what makes this painting so unnerving. The shadows seem to be reaching out from the canvas, like long fingers that will wrap around your neck and pull you into the grasp of something lurking behind the trees.

"It's not done." The nearness of the voice makes me jump. Spinning around, I see Shelley Drake, wearing a muslin smock and holding a paintbrush, standing only a foot behind me.

"I didn't hear you come in," I say to explain my nerves. Somehow I don't want her to know that it's her painting that has set me on edge.

"I never wear shoes when I paint," she replies, pointing down to her bare feet. "It makes me feel grounded."

"Oh," I say, unsure of how to respond to such a peculiar confession. I turn back to the painting, thinking that having invaded her studio, I should say something about her work. The art has only become more disturbing, though, as if its shadows had used the minute my back was turned to creep a little closer. "It's scary," I say, opting for the truth. "Did you do this after we found Isabel?"

"No . . . actually I was working on it yesterday morning. When they found her body out there . . ." She lifts her chin to indicate the woods, but because the easel stands between her and the window she could be referring to the woods in the painting just as easily as the real ones behind the window. "Well, I had the feeling that I'd painted this because her body was out there."

"You had a suspicion?"

"A premonition. I have them sometimes and they emerge in my paintings. Things I paint sometimes come true." She must see the skepticism on my face because she shrugs and laughs. "I'm sure it's just a subconscious thing. Or what Jung would call the collective unconscious. If I really had that power I'd try my luck in the stock market."

This at least reminds me of what I wanted to ask her. "I wondered if you were related to the art patron Gertrude Sheldon. I came across a photograph of her last night and I thought I detected a resemblance."

"She was my grandmother—but I hardly think I look like her!"

I'm taken aback by the vehemence of her reaction. Clearly, she doesn't consider a family resemblance flattering. "Perhaps it was the similarity of names that made me think you were related. And you're both artists—"

"You don't think I **paint** like her?"

I recall that according to Lily, Gertrude Sheldon

was the butt of everyone's jokes at the League. "I've never even seen her work," I answer.

"Well, that's a relief. I'd hate to think my work looked anything like hers." She walks to a shelf, takes down a large clothbound book with faded lettering on its spine, and hands it to me open to a color plate. "This is Gertie's **Ancient Priestess Worshipping at the Feet of Artemis.**" The painting shows a scantily clad girl laying flowers at the feet of a corpulent woman dressed in flowing robes. The goddess is gazing skyward with an abstracted look on her face, meant, I imagine, to invoke otherworldliness but suggesting peevishness instead. The colors are muddy, the anatomy awkward, and the composition clumsy. I try to think of something nice to say about it. "The flowers are well done," I say.

Shelley laughs. "Yes, Gertie could do flowers! She should have stuck to floral still lifes. In fact, she did after a League artist lampooned her painting in the 1921 Fakirs show."

I recall that the Fakirs was what the League artists called the show they put on each year to raise money. They would lampoon the work of more established artists, or even each other's, to provoke interest and, perhaps, to make their own artistic preferences known.

She flips the page to show an almost identical painting of a young girl kneeling at the feet of a matron, only here the girl is dressed in a maid's uniform and she's holding a nail file and scissors. A thought bubble, rising from the matron's distracted face holds the words, "I think I'll have Cook make a jelly for dessert." I have to suppress the urge to laugh. The lampoonist has captured the worst features of the original and magnified them to comic effect.

"I've read it was considered an honor to be lampooned by the Fakirs," I say.

"Gertie was not honored. She tried to make her husband, Bennett Sheldon, buy the painting—no doubt so she could destroy it—but instead Vera Beecher bought it. My grandmother was so upset about the incident she had a breakdown and had to check into a sanatorium for a few months—the first of many such 'retreats.' She loathed Vera and Lily after that, and Virgil Nash, too, because he took their side. She thought Vera founded Arcadia to compete with her plans to found a museum in the city."

"According to something I was reading last night, Arcadia was founded because Virgil Nash was fired from the League over an incident when Lily modeled for a Life Drawing class."

"Yes, well, that's the story Lily liked to tell because it put her beloved Vera in a better light. That the high-principled Miss Beecher founded this place on principles of artistic freedom. Now, if you don't mind, I left my class sketching **en plein air** in the apple orchard so that I could steal a little time to finish this."

"Of course," I say, thinking that it seems a bit unfair to her students, but then maybe that's how a real artist manages to get her work done. "They must be a very self-directed class," I say.

"I find if you give them the right direction they do quite well on their own. I told them about the final project today—a special assignment I give each year. Sally seemed quite taken by it. I think you'll find that she grows in some unexpected ways this term."

"I'm glad she'll have you to guide her," I say, smiling and trying to ignore the little pang of jealousy I have at the thought of someone else having that role in Sally's life. I turn to go, but then something else occurs to me. "Does it bother anyone in your family that you're teaching here? I mean, considering the hostility between your family and the Beechers."

Shelley laughs. "They **hate** it. Which is one of the main reasons I do it."

I leave her standing in front of her painting, arms hanging limply at her sides, head tilted in contemplation. It's as if she were waiting for the shadows to tell her what to do next.

I head back up to Beech Hall, noticing on my way Shelley's drawing students scattered through the apple orchard, each holding a sketchpad on his or her lap. The ground is still wet so they're sitting on rain ponchos. The sky is still overcast. The outlines

of the apple trees are blurry and indistinct—hardly
the best models for drawing. The air certainly isn't
very clear. I wonder if Shelley would have told the
class to draw outside if she hadn't wanted to work
herself.

I see Haruko and stop to look at her drawing.
She's drawn an anthropomorphic tree picking the
fruit off its own boughs and stuffing them into its
mouth. "I love that," I tell her truthfully. "What was
your assignment?"

Haruko grins. "Draw whatever we see in the
mist. This is what I see. But then," she confides, "it
might just be because I'm hungry."

I laugh and continue up the hill. When I pass
Hannah she presses her sketchpad to her chest so I
can't see what she's working on, but says hello
brightly.

"I hope today's subject wasn't upsetting to you,"
I say, encouraged by her greeting to stop. "It must
have been hard for your family finding out your
brother is autistic."

She nods. "Yeah, my mom and stepfather have
three other kids so it's really hard for my mom to
spend time working with him. That's why she and
my stepfather thought it would be better if I came
here."

"Oh." I'm not sure what else to say. It seems
colossally selfish to me to send one child away for
the sake of another, but then, what do I know about
dealing with a handicapped child? Hannah must see

the look of pity on my face because she smiles rue-fully. "It's okay," she tells me, "I really like it better here."

What a brave, generous girl, I think, walking on to the top of the hill where I find Sally sitting with Chloe Dawson. I wonder why she's with the older girl instead of her new friend Haruko, but then I guess it doesn't really matter. Sally's drawing so quickly and furiously on her sketchpad that it's un-likely she knows who she's next to. Her back is to me as I come up behind her. I don't intend to sneak up on her, but she's so absorbed in what she's drawing that she doesn't hear me approaching. I shouldn't peek, but I can't help wondering what subject has so inspired her. I look over her shoulder and down at her pad. What I see there takes my breath away. She's drawn a portrait of her father—Jude as I can barely stand to remember him, his face radiant with love, but slightly blurry and out of focus, as if he were slowly fading into the mist.

CHAPTER 14

In the weeks that follow I notice
that Sally spends more and more
time with Chloe Dawson and the
little circle she draws around her:
Clyde, Hannah, Tori Pratt, and
Justin Clay. It seems like an odd
collection of personalities. Tori
and Justin seem shallow and con-
ventional, while Hannah Weiss is
ethereal and selfless. Clyde is
bright and funny but reduced to
wordless adoration around Chloe.

I can only guess that they're drawn together by the shared trauma of Isabel's death. Unlike the crowd Sally had fallen in with last year, Chloe's circle is studious, polite, and, as far as I can tell, not into drugs or alcohol. In fact, Sally becomes less confrontational over the next few weeks, less likely to snap at me when I remind her to do her homework or pick up her room. Instead she agrees placidly with whatever I say and then goes on doing exactly what she was doing—drawing, mostly.

She draws nearly all the time. It's as if the inchoate grief that had been bottled up inside her for the last year has been jarred loose by Isabel's death and is coming out now in a flow of images from pencil, pen, and paint. The pictures aren't all of Jude. She draws self-portraits and landscapes, still lifes and abstract designs. In the third week of the term she begins an oil painting of the copper beech tree as we saw it the day we arrived at Arcadia: lit by the late afternoon sun against a gray-blue storm-laden sky. The tree seemed to be glowing from the inside out, as if it possessed the secret of life.

"Your daughter's really on fire," Shelley says to me one morning in the Dining Hall. "I looked at her portfolio from last year and there's nothing there remotely like what she's doing now."

"Thank you," I say, as I always do when someone compliments Sally—as if I had anything to do with it. "I'm sure your instruction is responsible."

"It's not instruction," she corrects me. "The stuff

she's doing can't be taught, but I do like to think that I have a knack for tapping into the young artist's deeper potential. Sally is unbottling, as we say. I'm just trying not to get in her way."

I, too, try not to get in Sally's way. In the evenings after dinner she goes to the art studio at the Lodge to work. At first I felt uneasy about her going there at night, but then I learned that she isn't alone. A dozen or so students are usually there working late. Apparently it's an Arcadia tradition. They all walk back to the dorms together and usually Sally calls me to ask if she can stay with Haruko, whose room-mate never did show up. The one time we do fight is when she asks if she can room in the dorms full-time. There's an empty single in Chloe and Tori Pratt's suite.

"But they're seniors," I tell Sally. "I don't think it's appropriate for you to room with older kids."

"They're **one** year older! If you didn't want me to have a dorm experience then why did you bring me to a boarding school?"

"Couldn't you room with Haruko?" I ask instead.

Sally squinches up her face for a moment to consider this apparently brand-new idea and after a few minutes declares, "Okay. I'll room with Haruko."

Only later, when I find out that Haruko's room is between Chloe and Tori's suite and Hannah's single, do I realize that this was her goal all along. But by then it's too late to go back on my word.

And so I spend my evenings alone in the cottage

grading papers, preparing for class . . . and reading Lily Eberhardt's journal. What I discover there is that Sally isn't the first young person to experience a sudden flowering of her imagination at Arcadia.

The apple trees were just beginning to bloom when we arrived at Arcadia in the last week of April and soon the air was full of their petals, like a warm and fragrant fairy dust that enchanted everything. We stayed in the Hall that first summer, along with the other women. Mimi Green had quit her job at the magazine so she could come (she could get by on free-lance work, she said) and she'd brought two women she knew from the Village who wanted to start a pottery studio: Ada Rhodes and Dora Martin. Vera said she hoped the pottery kiln would become a place for the artists to gather in the evenings: "the heart and hearth of the colony" as she called it.

We hadn't planned to have men—except for Virgil Nash, of course—at first. Vera and Mimi agreed that in order for a woman to truly make something of herself as an artist she must remove herself from all domestic obligations. Women were trained to subjugate their needs to men. "It's easy for the men," she once told me. "They can marry and gain a helpmate for their work—a wife to wash their brushes and cook their meals while they paint. But for a woman, marriage is the death of art. A man might say he'll allow his wife to paint—even claim that he'll encourage her—but the first time his dinner's late or the house untidy or his precious progeny slips on the stairs, he'll demand she give up her art for the sake of the household. No, we women must band together to support one another as artists."

But Nash invited a number of his cronies, and so Vera decided to let them all stay in the old hunting lodge. The trophies her grandfather had mounted on the walls of slaughtered prey gave the place a masculine feel, she felt. Virgil Nash set up his studio there and said he liked to sleep close to it in case he woke up in the middle of the night seized by inspiration.

"You don't want to meet me stumbling around the place half-naked," he told Vera right from the start. To which Vera answered, "I sleep with a loaded shotgun beneath my bed, so I don't think you'd like to meet **me** in those circumstances."

Nash invited the painter Mike Walsh to come as well. Walsh was a big, rawboned fellow from Kansas City who sloshed paint onto giant canvases in the manner of the Expressionists. He also favored working in the middle of the night and working half-clothed. Also bunking in the Lodge were two Russian brothers, Sasha and Ivan Zarkov.

There were others there that summer, League students who came and went for a few weeks at a time. Even Gertrude Sheldon put away her jealousy and animosity to come for a fortnight. And of course there was Mrs. Byrnes, the Beecher family housekeeper, who kept house for us with help from a couple of Irish girls from the village. That was another reason, Vera said, to keep the accommodations separate: to stop the villagers from spreading rumors about us.

Whatever the reason, the separation was no hardship that summer. Rather, it lent a certain piquancy to our days. There was plenty of going back and forth. Ada and Dora set up their pottery studio down in the Lodge and that's where drawing classes were held. So every morning, after breakfast, we girls trooped down through the apple orchard to the Lodge, our long dresses trailing in the dew, the apple blossoms falling in our hair. To announce our arrival, one of the Zarkov brothers would play a tune on his balalaika when he saw us coming and the other would sing a Russian song which he said the villagers sang on May Day. Something about maidens washing their faces with dew and meeting their true loves at sunrise.

That might have been when we first got the idea of celebrating May Day, the first of our

rites. It came up one night at dinner and
Mrs. Byrnes, overhearing us as she served the
soup, said we wouldn't be the first in these
parts to celebrate the **old rites,** as she called
them. She told us that the first settlers of the
village had practiced the old religion. Not just
May Day, which they celebrated on May Day
eve and called Beltane, but Lammas—what
they called Lughnasadh in her village back in
Ireland—and Samhain on All Hallow's Eve,
and the Winter Solstice instead of Christmas.
Vera sniffed at the idea of celebrating some
Old World superstition, and said such things
had nothing to do with art, but Mimi and
Dora were excited by the idea.

"It's just that you think you'll look pretty in
a white May dress," Ada Rhodes said with a sly
smile to Dora that made her blush. I'd realized
since the two of them had arrived that their
bond was more than mere affectionate friendship. I heard sounds like doves cooing coming
from their room at night.

"Oh, let's do it!" Mimi said. "Let's have fun
while we're here. In the winter we'll all have to
go back to the city and our dreary jobs and
have to worry about money."

"Ah," Virgil said, "the realm of filthy lucre!
What would we do without it?"

"Of course, we'd all starve!" Mimi said.
"Well, maybe not Vera here and it's her patronage, her generosity in providing a haven

for us this summer that makes it possible for us to pursue our art without worrying about making the rent or scrounging meals. . . ."

"Hear, hear!" Virgil Nash tapped his butter knife against his salad plate and held his wineglass up to toast Vera. "To Vera Beecher. But for May queen I propose the lovely Lily."

"And I suppose you'll want to play the May king, Mr. Nash," Vera said dryly.

"Only if it's a paying job," he answered, winking at me. "God knows I could use the money."

We all laughed at that. It was well known that Nash was in debt up to his ears and that his paintings, although brilliant, never sold. At least not until that next winter, when everything changed for him and his portraits were suddenly in demand. It's hard not to look back on that moment and not see poor Virgil Nash's downfall written in it. It was during that first summer at Arcadia that Gertrude Sheldon nagged Nash into doing her portrait. He did it to make a few dollars, so he said, but it was so successful that all of Gertrude's society friends wanted their portraits done by him thereafter. That was the work that would eventually make him both wealthy and famous, but he was forever haunted by the notion that he had given up his true vocation as an **artist** to become a society painter.

But I get ahead of myself. I had no presen-

timent of doom that night. Instead, I saw the
May Eve celebration as a way of thanking Vera
for bringing me here. I needed some way to
express my gratitude. Since we'd arrived, I'd
felt a certain reserve from her . . . as though
she were half-frightened of me. Indeed, she
seemed shy of receiving any notice of her generosity and didn't like, I think, to be reminded
of her wealth and position. For instance, when
we arrived at the house I was surprised to find
that although her mother had been dead for
many years, she still slept in a little room next
to her mother's old room. She told me that she
had stayed in it during her mother's illness so
that she could attend her at night. I thought
perhaps that she wanted to leave her mother's
room as it had been, but she had it all redone
for me to stay in! Each night she came to the
door that communicated between the two
rooms to wish me goodnight, but she would
not cross the threshold.

When she came to the door that night,
though, she saw I was sitting up in bed sketching. She asked me what I was drawing and I
told her to come see. She came and stood by
the side of my bed, but when I showed her
what I'd drawn she gasped and sank down beside me. I had drawn a May Day scene, with
all of us dancing on the great lawn in front of
Beech Hall, but instead of a maypole we

danced around the copper beech, which had
come to life as an Amazon with flaming
copper-colored hair streaming behind her. I'd
given her Vera's face.

"This is quite remarkable. . . . You've made
so much progress since we came here . . ."

"It's this place," I told her. "It's magic. I
owe you so much for bringing me here."

The moment I mentioned my debt to her, I
felt her bristle. She rose stiffly to her feet. "You
owe me nothing," she said coldly. But then,
softening as she looked back at the picture I
had drawn, she said, "An imagination like
yours deserves a place to flower. I am merely
the gardener . . . the soil. . . ."

She turned a bright shade of pink then and
swiftly turned on her heel and left without
even a goodnight. But when she went back to
her room she didn't shut the door between our
rooms, and when she was in bed she called out
her goodnight to me.

I realized that night that Vera was afraid of
demanding an intimacy of me that I might feel
compelled to give out of obligation to her. I
mention this because I know that many people
will look at the friendship we had and think
that because Vera was the wealthier and older
woman, she made the advances in our friendship. But that isn't how it happened at all. I realized that night that Vera's discriminating

scruples would always keep her aloof from me. It would take some great convulsion to break down her reserve . . . and I began to hope that May Eve would provide that convulsion.

And so I threw myself into the planning of it. We all did. Mimi and Dora sewed the costumes I designed. Nash and Walsh went out into the woods and cut down a birch sapling to use as our maypole. Mrs. Byrnes baked and her helpers wove flower wreaths for us to wear. Word spread to other artists at the League and a few dozen arrived before the last day in April. There was a feeling in the air that we were starting something important here at Arcadia.

Instead of a dress for Vera, I designed a costume based on the picture of Robin Hood in an illustration by N. C. Wyeth. I made a green velvet tunic and matching green cloak with a fringe of purple and copper. I sewed gold and purple fringe on high leather boots and long leather gloves so that when she moved she looked like an aspen quaking in the wind. And I made a jaunty green cap adorned with a long pheasant feather. The green brought out her hazel eyes and the red highlights in her chestnut hair.

We held the festival on the last afternoon of April, the eve of May Day, as Mrs. Byrnes told us the pagan Celts celebrated it. We danced

around the maypole and then sat down to a
banquet which Mrs. Byrnes and the girls from
the village had prepared for us. I sat beside
Vera, but I felt Nash's eyes on me. When it
grew dark, we lit a bonfire on the crest of the
hill above the apple orchard. When the full
moon rose, it turned the orchard into a silver
pool. We drank wine and sang songs around
the bonfire and the Phipps-Landrews, who had
recently come back from Morocco, passed
around a sweet-smelling pipe filled with something that Vera said was **hashish.** I only took
the smallest puff of it, but the smoke was in the
air, mixing with the fire and the scent of apple
blossoms. When I looked outside the circle of
lit faces, forms seemed to be moving in the
shadows. I thought it was my imagination, but
then the shadows came closer and sprouted
horns. One of the horned creatures pounced
on Dora Martin and she screamed.

"It's only those Russian boys," Vera told
me, wrapping her green cloak around me because I was shivering. "They've taken the
antlers down from my grandfather's trophy
room and turned themselves into some kind of
pagan creatures."

There were more than two of them,
though. One by one, the horned figures invaded the circle, pouncing on a girl, who
would then leap up and flee down the hill into

the apple orchard. I wasn't sure if Vera would go along with this part of the game and I knew it was only a matter of time before one of the horned figures came for me. Already a chant had risen for the May queen to take part in the chase.

"How fast can you run, Lily?" Vera asked me, squeezing my hand. When I saw the grin on her face and the spark in her eyes I told her how I used to run races with my sisters on the farm.

"I can certainly run faster than any of these city boys," I said.

"Good. Then meet me in the woods behind the Lodge. We'll double back to the Hall together."

I just had time to nod yes when a shadow of branching antlers fell across my lap. I sprang up and leapt clean across the fire. I heard gasps in my wake, but I didn't pause to bask in my accomplishment. I ran full speed down the hill into the orchard. The ground between the trees was so thick with petals that it looked as though the orchard was covered with snow, but this snow felt silken and exuded sweet perfume against my bare feet. The air was full, too, of the giddy cries and laughter of the hunters and the hunted. To catch my breath, I hid behind a tree and watched. The shadows of the horned pursuers and the trees melted into one another until it seemed as if the trees themselves had come to life and were chasing the girls in their white dresses, who flitted like fireflies from tree to tree. But because I had on Vera's dark green cloak I was better able to blend into the shadows. I stalked from tree to tree until I reached the edge of the woods and then I slipped into those darker shadows.

Even in the denser woods the moonlight found its way and spilled down the slim birch trunks like waterfalls of light. I heard steps behind me and guessed it was Vera come to keep our rendezvous, but something kept me moving. The moonlight was traveling up the hill and I followed it, with the sound of Vera's footsteps behind me. I felt as though the moon was drawing both of us up and that we could climb this silver ladder into the sky. But when I reached the top of the ridge, I saw that the moonlight was a wave that crested the hill and then broke over the ridge. It became the waterfall that spilled over into the clove and filled the ravine and the valley with silver light.

In the valley below there was a barn whose old wood planks glowed silver. That's where I would lead Vera. I knew that this was where I had been heading all along—since my childhood dreams of a fairytale heroine and from the moment I had met Vera Beecher. This was where we were meant to celebrate our marriage to each other. I had been looking for a convulsion to break her reserve and this was it: the crash of moonlight on this silvery shore.

The moonlight laid a path through the clove and to the barn, and I followed it. Later I would realize how dangerous it had been to attempt that steep path in the dark, in bare feet, after all the wine I had drunk and the hashish I had inhaled. But I felt, then, as if I were borne forward by the moonlight, like a current in a stream, and that nothing could happen to me. And besides, I could hear Vera's footsteps behind me. If she thought it was dangerous wouldn't she call me back?

The door of the barn was open. It was empty save for the chaff from last summer's haying and dark except for a circle of moonlight in its center. Looking up, I saw that the moonlight fell through a circular window in the cupola above me and pooled into the circle. I recalled the story Vera had told me about the pool of Bethesda, how the angel came to whoever first stirred the water and healed her of whatever plagued her. I wanted to be healed—to be cleansed of the feelings I had for Virgil Nash so that I could come to Vera pure and whole. I walked toward the circle, wanting to feel that moonlight on my skin. When I reached the edge of the light I heard a footstep on the threshold. I shrugged off my cloak and stepped into the circle as though stepping into an enchanted pool that instantly turned my limbs into the pure white of marble. I turned around, holding my arms out to call her into the circle.

Only it wasn't Vera on the threshold. It was Virgil Nash.

CHAPTER 15

After I read the part where Lily and Nash became lovers, I put Lily's journal aside. I was disappointed in her. Clearly she loved Vera, but she was also drawn to Nash and eventually she would leave Vera for him. Did she see him as a hedge against childless spinsterhood? Was she afraid of committing to an unconventional relationship? Perhaps I would find the answers in the rest of her journal, but for now I was compelled to hear Vera's side of their story. So I turned to her letters and notebooks.

I found none of the personal confession in Vera's papers that I had found in Lily's journal (she spoke of Lily as her **dear friend and companion,** never hinting at a more intimate or physical relationship), but I found instead a strong-willed, idealistic woman dedicated to creating a haven for artists—especially women artists. Vera's diaries for the summer of 1928 were full of plans to make the colony of Arcadia self-sufficient. "Each artist should know that she is capable of sustaining herself, rather than feel that she is the object of charity," she wrote, "as nothing infantilizes a woman more than to feel herself **dependent.**"

No wonder Vera flinched whenever Lily thanked her for her generosity.

To that end, Vera planned to establish craft workshops that could produce fine handmade wares to be sold commercially: furniture, textiles, hand-bound and printed books, and pottery. It was the pottery studio that she was most enthusiastic about and that she hoped to launch first. To that end, she had invited Ada Rhodes who was a master potter; she had studied with Clarice Cliff and exhibited at the National Arts Club in New York. Vera's notebooks were full of praise for Miss Rhodes's expertise and sketches of designs for pots and vases that the Arcadia Pottery would produce. If Vera also hoped that Ada and Dora, who had lived together for ten years by 1928, would serve as a model for the kind of romantic friendship she wished to have with Lily, she didn't record the sentiment.

According to the account books the pottery was the most successful of all the commercial ventures launched by the Arcadia Colony. It provided a small but steady income through the years of the Depression and the war until 1947—the year Lily died. When the summer of 1948 rolled around, the pottery didn't reopen. In her notebook Vera recorded, **The Misses Rhodes and Martin have found accommodations for their studio elsewhere.**

Where? I wondered.

And what had become of the pottery studio that they had put so much work into? I noticed that ceramics was oddly absent from the present-day Arcadia School curriculum, as were the other crafts practiced at the beginning of the colony. One night at dinner, I ask Dean St. Clare about the lack of a ceramics class. She sniffs and says that when the colony turned into a school Vera felt that they should focus on the fine arts rather than **arts and crafts.** It seems a rather odd prejudice given the proletarian beginnings of Arcadia, but St. Clare's attitude makes it clear that she has nothing further to say on the subject. Dymphna Byrnes catches my eye and tells me to come by later to pick up some leftover scones.

It isn't unusual for the housekeeper to slip me leftovers. She seems to always cook more than what is needed for each meal, and she distributes the excess to the teachers and staff she deems both worthy and wanting. As a widow and single mother, I must fall under the **wanting** category. On this particular night, though, I'm pretty sure that Dymphna is offering more than baked goods. There's a hot cup of tea waiting for me along with my packet of still-warm scones.

"I heard you asking about the pottery," she says when I sit down to the tea. "You see, there was a falling-out between Ada Rhodes and Vera Beecher after Lily's death. Ada and Dora Martin stopped teaching at the school, but they had bought a little house in town the year before. When they fell out with Vera they simply moved their studio there. It's called Dorada Pottery and it's still there."

"Still there? But Ada Rhodes and Dora Martin were in their thirties when they came here in 1928. They must be long dead."

"Dead, aye, but not so long. They both lived into their nineties and died within two months of each other—Ada first, then Dora, in 1982 or thereabouts."

"And they lived together that whole time?"

"Oh yes, in a sweet little bungalow just off the town green with their studio in back. They adopted a niece of Ada's who still lives there and still runs the pottery. Beatrice Rhodes. She's seventy-three but she fires up that kiln every day and teaches a ceramics class on Saturdays at the Guild Hall. You should go visit her, it's just past the square—" She stops when she sees my blank expression. "Don't tell me you haven't been to town yet?"

"Well, no, I haven't had a chance, and with your excellent cooking and generous leftovers"—I point to the packet of scones—"I haven't needed to."

Although she glows at the compliment she swats me with the dishtowel. "That's no excuse. You've been here a whole month now!"

I'm startled to realize she's right. It's already the third week of September and I haven't left the campus once. Something about Arcadia makes you forget that the outside world exists. Even the way the school sits in its own little valley against the side of a mountain, surrounded by wooded slopes on three sides and a long vista of mountains, gives one the feeling that the rest of the world has vanished. I realize, though, that for someone like Dymphna, whose family comes from the town, it must seem snobbish to completely ignore it.

"Maybe I'll go in this weekend," I tell her.

She sniffs and takes a sip of her tea. "If you go into the Rip van Winkle Diner, tell my cousin Doris I sent you and ask for the apple pie."

Charged now with a mission, I feel honor-bound to go, but first I ask Sally if she wants to join me. Since she's moved into the dorms, I hardly see her, and when I do she's always bent over a sketchpad, feverishly drawing. When I approach her, she hugs the pad to her chest or closes it so that I can't see what she's drawing. It's frustrating because Shelley keeps telling me how much progress she's making and—I have to admit—I'm jealous that the art teacher gets to share this new stage of Sally's development while I'm shut out. An afternoon together away from campus seems like the perfect way to reconnect.

But when I ask her, even dangling the prospect of a trip to the malls in Kingston and a McDonald's stop, she tells me that Clyde and Chloe have asked her to work on the preparations for the Autumn Equinox Festival. I suppose I should be glad that she's caught up in school activities and has made new friends, but it's a little alarming that she would turn down a shopping expedition to weave corn wreaths and sew costumes out of felt.

I drive in alone after breakfast on Saturday. Descending the mountain, I pass a farm stand selling tomatoes, corn, and squash and make a mental note to stop there on the way back. A little way back from the road stands—or rather **leans**—the barn where Lily and Nash met on May Eve in 1928 and where, years later, he painted her. It's crumbling into itself now, its gray planks leaning against one another like drunken friends standing in a field. The cupola that Lily wrote of tilts to one side and looks as if it might at any moment crash through the roof. I wonder what patterns the moonlight makes in the barn these nights, what enchanted pools and eddies.

In another five minutes, I reach the village. I'm startled by how close it is and also how pretty it looks, nestled into a fold of the mountains, the kind of quaint rural village that travel guides feature on their covers. Beyond the church steeple there's a central green with a gazebo and a bronze statue of a cloaked figure, all surrounded by white clapboard houses that drowse behind rose-covered picket fences and deep front porches. But when I park my car on the corner of Main and Elm and get out, the impression fades. The church steeple and the clapboard houses need paint, the picket fences are being held up by the weed-choked rose bushes, and the front porches list crookedly. The village green is more yellow than green, covered by an encroaching fungus where it's not swamped by weeds. The statue is so tarnished I can't tell if the cloaked figure is a man or a woman and the plaque underneath it has been defaced so badly I can't read it. Clearly the once-pretty town has fallen on hard times. Walking along Main Street I pass two boarded-up shop windows and one so begrimed with dust I can't see through it. When I come to an open shop with clean windows I'm sorry that I can see in. It's a taxidermy shop featuring stuffed local game that also doubles as a tattoo parlor called Fatz Tatz. A reclining dentist's chair, like something out of a Frankenstein movie, sits beneath a stuffed moose head and a suspended stuffed Canada goose. I shudder at the thought of needles piercing flesh in such unhygienic surroundings and move on, passing the town bar (the Hitchin' Post!) and a gift shop called Seasons that sells crystals, incense sticks, and Tibetan prayer flags. Thank goodness I didn't persuade Sally to come with me. The dearth of retail options might make her Great Neck–trained mind reel. There is, though, an art supply store that looks well stocked, and delicious bakery smells come from the Rip van Winkle Diner. Through the diner's well-washed windows, I can see a Dymphna-shaped waitress pouring coffee for a table of old men in plaid jackets.

I check the directions Dymphna gave me to Dorada Pottery and see it's only two blocks off Main, so I decide to go there first before eating lunch at the Rip van Winkle. I turn down Maple Street (clearly the town fathers were so struck by the surrounding forests that they couldn't think past the trees for their street names) to look for Beatrice Rhodes's house and studio.

Away from the sadly diminished Main Street, the town regains some of its initial charm. Many of the houses still could use a fresh coat of paint, but the yards here are tidier, full of flowers, and the bones of the old houses shine through. I recognize several Dutch Colonials that must have been built when the town was first settled in the early eighteenth century, a stately Greek Revival, and then, farther down the street, several lovely Queen Anne Victorians that represent the town's last flowering of prosperity in the early nineteen-hundreds. One of the Queen Annes has been stripped of its old paint and is in the process of receiving a new sky blue coat. A ladder leans against a steeply pitched gable above the front porch. There's an elaborately carved relief within the gable featuring a woman's face surrounded by swirling acanthus leaves, fruits, and flowers. Sadly, half of the woman's face has been destroyed by the elements. Her one remaining eye stares at me balefully beneath a sunflower crown. She's clearly some kind of nature goddess—Persephone or Pomona, perhaps. Coming through the open front door, along with the smells of fresh sawn wood and new paint, are strains of Irish folk music. Someone is renovating the house, maybe a couple from the city.

I remember that Jude and I used to talk about doing that someday. When we still lived in the city we would spend our weekends driving around upstate, looking at old farmhouses and dilapidated Victorians in forgotten Catskill towns, and dream of buying and renovating one. But when I got pregnant with Sally and Jude took a job on Wall Street, it made more sense to buy a new house in Great Neck, where the schools were good and the commute into Manhattan under an hour. "Someday when Sally graduates high school," Jude used to say, "and I can work more from home, we'll buy an old house to fix up in some little town upstate."

I pause in front of the Queen Anne, inhaling the scent of freshly sanded wood and new paint. A few late-summer roses still bloom on the fence and heavy viburnum clusters are turning the color of old paper on a tree in front of the porch. Through an arbor gate I spy a deep, shady backyard that slopes down to a stream. I can imagine sitting in that back- yard in a lawn chair, watching the sky go from blue to lilac to dark purple as the fireflies come out. . . .

I pull myself out of that little domestic reverie when I realize I don't know who would be sitting in the lawn chair next to me. Not Sally, surely. She'd be barricaded upstairs in her room plugged into com- puter and iPod—or at the school working on her art with Shelley Drake. And then in just under two years she'd be off to college. What would I do with a big old house like this one now? I ask myself as I continue down the street. It's not even something I can daydream about anymore.

Two houses away is a small Craftsman bungalow painted butter yellow and covered in late-blooming roses. A sign on the front gate for Dorada Pottery di- rects visitors to a meandering stone path, around the side of the house, and down a flight of stone steps to a little studio that hangs over the edge of the stream. The front door is propped open by a large glazed urn planted with fragrant herbs. Smaller urns and pots surround it, some containing herbs or flowers, others holding smooth stones or shells. A wind chime hanging beside the open door moves lan- guidly in the light breeze, its music braided into the trill of running water.

I step inside the small shop. The walls are lined

with shelves holding ceramic ware in shades of green and blue, some unadorned, others painted with flowing abstract designs. The shapes are elegant and simple, their curves inviting one to touch them. I move toward a vase with a sinuous shape embedded into the clay under a matte green glaze. Its impossible to tell if the swelling curve is a flower or a woman's hip or some other shape. I reach for it, but then hesitate, unsure if I should handle the wares in the unattended store.

"Go ahead," a voice calls from the back of the shop. "They're made to be touched."

I let my hand fall on the cool, creamy glaze and turn the vase around. The swelling shape turns out to be both woman and flower: a nude figure unfolding from thick petals.

"That's Dorada." A woman in a dark blue linen smock, her long silver hair swept up, steps out of the back room. She's wiping her hands on a blue-and-white-striped dishtowel, but there are smudges of clay still on her forearms, smock, and even one long gray-green swipe on her cheekbone that makes her eyes glow a deep cobalt blue.

"Dorada?" I repeat, trailing my finger along the line of the woman's hip as it slips into the folds of the petal. Is it the name of the woman, I'm wondering? But then I recognize the name. "Oh, Dorada Ware. It's the name of the line of pottery, not the name of a woman."

"Well, it's both. Actually it's the name of two

women: my aunt Ada and her partner, Dora. Dor-Ada."

"You must be Beatrice Rhodes, then," I say, holding out my hand. "I'm Meg Rosenthal. I teach at Arcadia and I'm writing a paper on the fairy tales of Lily Eberhardt and Vera Beecher. I came across your aunt's name in a journal and I thought you might be able to answer a few questions."

Beatrice Rhodes shakes my hand with a surprisingly firm grip for a septuagenarian. Her skin, though, is soft as velvet. All that time soaking in clay, I suppose.

"I'm happy to tell you whatever I can, but I came here the year before Ada and Dora stopped teaching at the school, and they didn't have much to do with Vera Beecher after that. Lily died right about the time I arrived."

"Did your aunt and—" I stumble for a moment, unsure of how to identify Dora's relationship to Beatrice. The old woman smiles.

"I called them both **aunt.** They treated me equally as kin. But now that I've gotten old as they were, I think of them as Ada and Dora."

"Did Ada or Dora ever say why they left Arcadia?"

"You mean why they left Vera Beecher's colony, don't you? As you see, they stayed right here in Arcadia Falls." She holds her hands up to indicate the little studio full of their pottery, and I realize that she doesn't just mean that they stayed in Arcadia for the rest of their lives, but that their spirits still reside here. "I still use their molds and their recipes for clay and glaze. Of course, I do my own designs as well, but when I sit down at the wheel I can still feel Aunt Ada's hands over mine as she taught me how to throw my first pot." She laughs and a cloud comes over her blue eyes. "It was a disaster, that first pot! A lumpen mess. But Dora said that it had the shape of my hands in it and insisted on firing it anyway. She kept it on her dresser to hold her hairpins to the day that she died." She ducks her head to pull out a leather-bound album from beneath the counter. "Here, I've got pictures of all the designs we've made over the years."

I politely turn the pages even though my interest is in the women and not the pots they made. They're lovely to look at, though, long-necked vases that bloom into flowers at the rims, perfectly round bowls whose shapes echo bird's nests or rounded river stones. I notice that a number of the designs incorporate lilies.

"Your aunts must have been very fond of Lily Eberhardt," I say. "Do you think they left the colony because they didn't want to be reminded of her?"

Beatrice looks at me, her blue eyes now clear as a flame. "No," she says. "They left because they blamed Vera Beecher for her death."

CHAPTER 16

"I thought Lily was running away with Virgil Nash when she got killed. Shouldn't they have blamed him?" I ask, remembering that this was the Merling twins' point of view.

"They thought that Vera drove Lily away and that if they hadn't argued she wouldn't have tried to cross the clove in the middle of a snowstorm. They would have nothing to do with Vera or the

colony after Lily died. I heard them talking sometimes about how intolerant and exacting Vera could
be—how she ran the colony—and then the school—
like a dictator. In the years after they left the school,
neither if my aunts was ever asked to speak or teach
a class there."

"That's too bad," I say, closing the album. "In
Vera's notebooks she says that she hoped that the
potter's kiln would be a 'communal hearth' for the
colony, and Lily spoke fondly of them in her journal." I blush remembering what she'd actually written: that the sounds coming from their bedroom
sounded like the cooing of doves. It's not my embarrassment that Beatrice notices, though.

"Lily's journal? You've read Lily's journal?" she
asks, her eyes wide with amazement.

"Just the first twenty pages or so. I stopped to
read some of Vera's notebooks—"

"But where did you get it?"

I realize that I shouldn't have mentioned the
journal, but it's too late now. "I found it in the cottage . . . Fleur-de-Lis. That's where I'm living. . . ." I
stop, noticing how agitated the old woman has become. Two bright pink spots have appeared on her
cheeks and her eyes look feverish. She's twisting the
dishtowel in her hands. "Why is that so strange?"

"Because Lily's journal disappeared after her
death. Ivy St. Clare came here to ask Ada and Dora
if they knew anything about what happened to it. I
remember it because Dora, who never raised her

voice to me once in forty years, screamed at Ivy to 'get out and never come back.' The aunts found me later hiding in a closet and Dora told me she was sorry for raising her voice, but that when a person accused someone you loved of stealing, you really had to stick up for her."

"So you think Ivy St. Clare accused Ada of stealing Lily's journal?"

"She must have. And to think it was in the cottage all along. Right under Ivy's nose!" A ripping sound draws both our attention to the dishtowel in Beatrice's hands. She's torn it clean in half.

"But she didn't know about it because it was hidden."

"She should have looked more thoroughly before she accused my aunt of stealing." Beatrice carefully folds the torn dishcloth into a small neat square. Her hands are shaking. "My aunts would have loved to have had a look at that journal. I heard them say once that if they did have Lily's journal they might know why Lily left that night. . . ." Her voice trails off and an abstracted expression comes over the blue eyes that seemed so sharp a moment ago. Then she shakes herself. "Have you found out anything from the journal about why Lily left?"

"Not yet. I haven't gotten to that part. But I promise that I'll tell you when I do." I lay my hand over Beatrice's soft weathered one. It seems little enough to promise an old woman after upsetting her.

I walk back to Main Street, noticing that the carved relief in the gable of the Queen Anne is gone. Without the placid face of the goddess the house looks strangely forlorn, even though it has acquired a few more yards of sky blue paint. There's still no sign of the housepainter, making the progress seem as if it had been done by helpful elves. When I enter the Rip van Winkle Diner, though, I find my housepainter. Not an elf at all, but Sheriff Reade in sky blue paint–splattered T-shirt and faded jeans. I hesitate, wondering if I should join him in his booth. He seems happily engaged in a book and it's not as if we exactly hit it off on the two occasions that we've met.

But when he looks up from his book and sees me, he breaks into a smile so spontaneous that it would seem rude to ignore him.

"Mind if I join you?" I ask.

"Not at all," he says, laying the book facedown.

I glance at it, but the front cover is ripped and the spine too creased to read the title, so that conversational gambit is out. "You've been painting, I see," I say, opting for the obvious. "You're working on that Queen Anne on Maple Street?"

"That's the one. How'd you know it's a Queen Anne?"

"The spindle work, the half-timbering on the front gable, the decorative shingles . . . and it's the most common type of Victorian, so it's a safe guess."

He laughs. "Well, you're right. It was built in 1885 by Eliphalet Nott, who ran the town newspaper back when there was one. Sadly, the Nott family lost all their money in the Great Depression and the house hasn't had a fresh coat of paint, a window caulked, or floor varnished since then. The roof needs reshingling and there's water damage in the basement."

"But it has great bones," I say. "Are you planning on living there?"

"Me? I'd rattle around in there like bones in a casket. It's an investment property. I'm fixing it up to sell to some likely couple from the city. Since Nine-Eleven there's been a steady influx of New Yorkers moving up here."

"I'm surprised that the town sheriff has the time to do all that work. There must not be a lot of crime in the area—"

I'm interrupted by the appearance of the waitress, who refills the sheriff's iced tea without asking and asks me what I'd like. I order a grilled cheese with tomato, iced tea, and a slice of apple pie.

"Are you Doris?" I ask. "Your cousin Dymphna said to try the apple pie."

"She would," the woman says, shaking her head so that her pink cheeks wobble. "She bakes 'em."

"I guess Dymphna's moonlighting," I say to Sheriff Reade when Doris leaves.

"Most of the folks around here do more than the one job," he says. "It's not easy to make ends meet, and I doubt the school pays Dymphna what she's worth. Maybe you teachers do better."

"No . . . I mean, I was glad to get anything, considering I hadn't worked since college and I don't have my certification or Ph.D. yet, but the salary is low compared to other schools. I figured it was because Arcadia is relatively new. It hasn't had the time to acquire a big endowment."

"Vera Beecher left the school very well endowed. It's just that Ivy St. Clare is stingy. Since it's the biggest employer in the area—practically the only employer—she can get away with paying the locals low wages. Sometimes I think that St. Clare's taken the medieval theme of the school to heart and believes we're all her vassals. I've had to remind her a number of times that the Arcadia Falls Police Department is not a department of the Arcadia School and that I'm not in her employ."

"She must not like you questioning the students, then."

"No," Reade says with a grin. He leans forward and lowers his voice. "She's pressured me to have Isabel's death declared an accident, but I'm not convinced that it was. Until I am, I'll question anyone I think has information, including the students."

"Like Chloe, you mean. She was very upset after you questioned her."

He groans and shakes his head. "You make it sound like I waterboarded the poor kid—"

He's interrupted by Doris Byrnes delivering my

order. She gives me a suspicious look, clearly un-
happy that I've annoyed the local sheriff, and puts
my sandwich and pie plates down so hard they clat-
ter on the linoleum surface of the table. When she
leaves Reade leans back over the table.

"I knew Isabel Cheney a little," he says. "She
came into the station last year to interview me for a
story she was writing for the school newspaper." He
breaks out in a grin at the memory, transforming his
face from severe to handsome in an instant. "I felt
like I was being interrogated by the CIA! She was
very thorough—and very level-headed. I just don't
see her running willy-nilly into the woods and
falling over the edge of a cliff."

"You think Chloe Dawson pushed her?" I ask,
appalled that a girl who's spending so much time
with my daughter is under police suspicion. "Isabel
Cheney was nearly twice Chloe's size."

He swears under his breath and runs his hand
through his hair—a habit I notice he has when he's
thinking. It makes his short blond hair stand up like
dried pine needles, bristling with electricity. "That
wouldn't mean much if Chloe surprised her. I do
know that there's something she's not telling me. . . ."
He stops and cocks his head at me. "Just like I know
that there's something you're not telling me right
now."

"Me?" My voice comes out high and squeaky.
The fact is that I have remembered something. "It's
nothing," I prevaricate. "Just something Chloe said

the night of the bonfire. But kids are always saying things like that—"

"Like what?"

I sigh. "She was angry that Isabel had told Dean St. Clare that she'd done all the work on their paper. She said she had a plan to get even with Isabel."

"And you didn't think this was worth telling me when Isabel showed up dead the next day?"

"I'm sorry," I say. "I honestly didn't remember it until now."

He makes a disgusted noise and gets up. "Do me a favor," he says, peeling a few bills out of his wallet and laying them on the table. "The next time you have information about a murder investigation, come and see me right away. Okay?"

I nod numbly as he walks out of the diner. I had no idea that Isabel's death was being treated as a murder. I push away the half-eaten apple pie, my appetite spoiled. How can I keep Sally at a school where a girl was murdered? Should I leave? But go where?

I leave the diner in a haze and start toward my car, but I'm not ready to go back to the campus. Instead I wander into the first store I see—the little New Agey gift shop, Seasons. I'm greeted by the sounds of clattering bamboo, running water, and birdsong, as if I'd stepped into a Buddhist meditation garden. The store is dim after the bright sunny street, the sunlight filtered through colorful madras curtains. When my eyes adjust I realize that the sounds are coming from a recording. There's no bamboo grove, although there is a bamboo curtain screening an alcove full of crystals, candles, and books. At first I don't notice the saleswoman behind the counter. The kurta she wears blends in with the wall hanging behind her as do her short, pixie-cut sandy hair and freckled skin. She sits still as a baby deer gone to ground. When I make eye contact, she presses her hands together in front of her chest and inclines her head in my direction, but she still doesn't speak. I smile and step through the bamboo curtain into a dimly lit alcove lined with books. **Celtic Wisdom**, I read from one spine; **Making Magic with Gaia** is another. While my back is turned, I hear the door open and a burst of laughter and loud teenage voices disrupt the bamboo-grove quiet.

"Chloe said we had to get the candles **here,**" one of the girls says. The voice is familiar, but I can't at first place it.

"If you ask me, Chloe's gotten pretty damn bossy. Ever since she got picked to play the goddess, she thinks she is one. I think we should let someone else play the goddess for the equinox."

The second voice is also familiar. I half turn, shielding my face with a copy of **Seasons of the Witch** to get a look at the two girls. It's Hannah Weiss and Tori Pratt—an unlikely pairing even though I knew they hang out with Chloe. Tori is a type familiar to me from my years in Great Neck: a preening queen bee, groomed within an inch of her life from her artificially straightened hair to her pedicured toes (visible now in flip-flops). She's the one complaining about not getting her turn to be goddess.

"I just don't buy Chloe's argument that it has to be the same goddess for the whole cycle."

"You do have a point," Hannah, who's wearing a plaid flannel jumper, orange tights, and corduroy Mary Janes, says, "It is a **cycle.** That means it doesn't have a beginning or an end."

I have to give Hannah points for Geometry 101, but it still strikes me as passing strange that these girls are arguing not about a part in a play or getting to be prom queen but assuming the role of goddess in a pagan rite.

"Well, tell that to Chloe. She thinks that since Isabel died it means she was a real pagan sacrifice and so the cycle is really **charged** or something."

"That's sick, Tori."

"Maybe, but I'm not going to be the one to tell Chloe that, especially now with her insisting we have the equinox thing on the ridge. She might push **me** off this time."

"Don't say that! Chloe didn't push Isabel off the cliff."

"How do you know? Were you there?" When Hannah shakes her head Tori goes on.

"You know how mad she was at Isabel for getting her in trouble with the Dean. And she always gets what she wants. Look at how she's got Clyde wrapped around her little finger, and she's got that new girl eating out of her hand. I do have an idea for cutting her down to size, though." Tori bends down toward Hannah and lowers her voice. I lean forward in my alcove to hear her above the tinkling of wind chimes and recorded water music, but I miss whatever she says.

"No way!" Hannah replies. "I'm afraid she'd put a curse on me. Let's just get this over with, okay?"

The girls approach the counter where the proprietor looks up at them placidly, seemingly oblivious to the girls' conversation and my eavesdropping. "Um, excuse me?" Tori says. "We have a list of things we need. Can you help us?"

"We don't sell curses," the saleswoman replies. Apparently she had been listening after all.

"Well, good, because we don't need any," Tori snips back. "We're supposed to get twelve candles, six brown and six white, each blessed for the . . ." She consults a folded sheet of notepaper. ". . . blessed for the ritual of the autumn equinox. Have you got any of those?"

The saleswoman turns wordlessly and disappears behind the Indian wall hanging. Something thuds, creaks, then crashes. I stay in my alcove, hoping the girls will continue their conversation. I suspect the "new girl" they mentioned is Sally and I'm also curious about Tori's plans to cut Chloe "down to size." I'm worried, too, that Chloe wants to have the equinox celebration on the ridge. It's the first I've heard of that. But the girls wait in silence until the saleswoman returns with an armful of candles and glass canisters. "You'll want these herbs to go with the candles," she says.

"We don't want any such thing," Tori announces. "Here's our list." She holds the sheet of paper an inch from the saleswoman's nose. "See, it says twelve candles. We're not here to buy anything else."

"The herbs are free," the saleswoman says. "They come with the candles."

"Oh, in that case, sure. We'll take them."

The saleswoman scoops out some dried yellow flowers into a brown paper bag. "Marigold petals," she says, "to stand for the dying sun. Ring these around your white candles." She scoops some dried seed pods into another bag. "Then strew these around the brown candles." Hannah peers into the canister the seeds came from.

"What's that?" she asks.

"Poppy husks. That's for the dark, which you're welcoming."

"Poppies? Isn't that where opium comes from?"

"Yes," the saleswoman replies, with a small smile. "Don't eat them."

"Have you got any eye of newt?" Tori asks, starting to laugh. A look from the saleswoman suddenly silences her. Hannah hands over the money for the candles and herbs, grabs Tori's arm, and pulls her out of the shop. I can hear Tori's shrill laughter exploding on the street and her clear exclamation: "Jeez, did you think she was going to turn us into toads?"

I approach the counter holding up a copy of **The Meaning of Witchcraft** by Gerald Gardner. "Would you recommend this book?" I ask the saleswoman as she closes the glass canisters and brushes some dried chaff from the countertop. An acrid smell rises to my nose and makes me sneeze.

"May the Goddess bless you," she says, handing me a Kleenex. "And yes, I can recommend that book quite highly. Gerald Gardner is the father of modern Wicca." She squints at me. "You're a teacher," she says—a statement, not a question.

I nod my head.

"So you'll want to approach the subject in a rational, scholarly way." She smiles at me as if she'd just identified an endearing but eccentric character trait in an old friend. "Come with me."

When she comes out from behind the counter I see why there'd been so much noise in the back room. Her left leg is in a metal brace and she's learning heavily on a carved wooden cane. "You'll want Margaret Murray's **The Witch-Cult in Western Europe** and Vivianne Crowley's book on Wicca. Vivianne has a doctorate in psychology from the University of London. That should be enough scholarly cred for you."

"Do you think I'm some academic snob who won't listen to anyone who doesn't possess a degree?"

The woman laughs, which makes the lines around her eyes crinkle. She's older than I thought at first. In her thirties, not her twenties. Instead of answering my question she switches her cane to her left hand. I notice that the handle is carved into the shape of a leaping deer. She holds out her hand to shake. "I'm Fawn, by the way."

"Meg Rosenthal," I say, shaking her hand. I find myself grinning as if we were sharing some private joke. "How did you know I was a teacher?"

"The way you were hiding from those girls," she says, limping back to the counter with the books she's chosen for me. "You didn't want them to see you, and I think you were interested in what they were talking about." She lifts one tawny eyebrow.

"I was," I admit. I have a feeling that lying to this woman would be pointless. "There was a death at the school last month."

"I know. That poor girl. She had come in here a few times."

"Really? I wouldn't have pegged Isabel Cheney as being interested in witchcraft."

"I doubt anyone would peg you for that, either," she says, ringing up my books and taking the bills I offer. I'm about to tell her that my interest is purely scholarly, but that would only confirm her initial impression of me as a snob.

"So what was she interested in, then?" I ask.

"She started coming in last year for charms to help her in school. She was very ambitious but sadly unsure of herself under her confident pose. When she came back to school this term, though, she had a lot of questions about local traditions. She told me it was for a paper she was writing."

"What kind of traditions was she interested in?"

"She wanted to know about the legends surrounding the clove and the woods above it, specifically about the **wittewieven**—who's supposed to haunt those woods."

Callum Reade had told me about the **wittewieven** the first night I met him. I wonder if he learned of it through Fawn . . . maybe he and Fawn . . . I silence the next thought and ask Fawn what she had told Isabel.

"It was a very old legend that went back to the days of the first Kingston settlement. A woman named Martha Drury was accused of being a witch. Rather than be hanged, she fled Kingston into the mountains. She settled in the clove, where she gained a reputation for being a healer—or, as some might say, a witch. After she died, people claimed to see a white shape hovering over the falls and said it was the ghost of Martha Drury. That's how the clove got to be called Witte Clove. **Wittewieven** means 'white woman,' but it also means 'wisewoman'—a healer, an herbalist—and as I told Isabel many people around here believe that if you enter the clove with a pure heart you will be protected and healed. I think she must have run there because I told her that."

I'm silent for a moment, then say, "It doesn't seem like the spirit of the white woman was able to protect her."

"No," Fawn says, handing me my bag. "Which makes me wonder what she was running from."

CHAPTER 17

Fawn's question haunts me all week. Who—or what—had Isabel been running from? Could she have been running from Chloe? But why? And how could a tiny girl like Chloe force a bigger girl like Isabel off a cliff? As ridiculous as it seems, I call Callum Reade to tell him what I overheard.

"You requested that I inform you of any information I might have," I say formally when I reach him at the police station. I describe the girls' conversation as best as I can recall it.

"And where were you when this conversation transpired?" he says, picking up my tone.

"Uh . . . behind a bamboo curtain in an alcove," I say, instantly realizing how silly it sounds.

He makes a noise that is something between a bark and a cough.

"If you're not going to take what I say seriously, I won't bother you again—"

"No, no, I just got something stuck in my throat. This is very useful. You were right to call. I'll question Chloe again. In the meantime, I'm concerned about this ceremony the kids are planning above the clove. Perhaps you ought to speak to your dean about it."

Dean St. Clare is the last person I want to talk to, but I realize he's right. I make an appointment to see her the next day.

"I appreciate your concern," she tells me, leaning forward with her hands clasped together on her desk. "I had my doubts as well when the students asked my permission, but then I realized that it would provide just the closure they need after such a senseless tragedy."

"But can't they reach that closure someplace **safer**?" I ask. "Someplace on flat ground instead of the edge of a precipice?"

Ivy St. Clare tilts her little birdlike head at me quizzically. "I suppose it's being a mother that makes you so . . . paranoid. Why don't I put you in charge of overseeing the event? That should channel your energies constructively. I believe the club is meeting upstairs in the Reading Room right now. Why don't you drop in on them to discuss security measures?"

Dismissed, I head upstairs to the Reading Room, wondering if the dean always responds to criticism by handing out extra work. It would be an effective deterrent.

As I approach the library, I hear a girl's voice raised in anger. "I think the whole thing is just **wrong.** I don't want anything to do with it!" As I reach the doorway, Haruko comes out in such a hurry that she collides with me. She apologizes somewhat cursorily—though she's always been cheerful and polite with me—and hurries down the stairs. I consider going after her, but then I look at the circle of guilty faces in the library and decide that these are the people I need to talk to.

"What was that all about?" I ask Sally, who's curled up in a window seat, bent over her sketchpad. She shrugs but doesn't reply. Instead Chloe answers from the depths of a velvet wingback chair in the center of the circle. "I'm afraid she's one of those girls who doesn't want to play if she can't have things her own way."

Justin Clay, who's lolling on a love seat with Tori Pratt, straightens up and untangles his legs from Tori's. "Yeah, she's kind of a drama queen."

"She **is** a bit sensitive," Hannah Weiss concedes

from her perch on the hassock next to Chloe's chair. I almost laugh at this sentiment coming from Hannah, who's about the most sensitive kid I've ever met.

I turn from student to student as each one dismisses Haruko's outburst. "That doesn't sound like Haruko at all," I say to Sally.

"How would you know?" Sally asks without lifting her head from her drawing pad. "She's not even in any of your classes."

Looking from face to face I feel as if I am watching a carefully orchestrated chamber piece: an arrangement for five voices. But the fifth member of the circle, sitting cross-legged on the floor, remains silent. I turn to him.

"Clyde? What was Haruko upset about? What did she think was '**wrong**'?"

Clyde blanches and squirms uneasily on the floor, as if he could dig himself a hole to hide in. "The rite of the autumn equinox is all about facing the dark," he says finally. "It's about accepting death as a natural part of the life cycle. . . ."

Someone in the room—I can't tell who—begins to hum the theme from **The Lion King:** "The Circle of Life." Tori and Chloe giggle. Clyde blushes. "Anyway. I guess that's what Haruko thought was wrong."

"And how exactly do you intend to 'face the dark' during this equinox ceremony?" I ask. I have a vision of the clove at sunset, the dark gash in the earth gathering the shadows into its folds. If their idea of facing the dark means going down into the clove, then I will to put an end to the ceremony right now.

"It's just a candle-lighting ceremony," Chloe says, her voice sweetly lilting. "You'll see, it will be very pretty."

"The dean has put me in charge of safety," I tell Chloe. "So pretty or not, I want your assurance that no one will go within five—make that ten—feet of the ridge."

"No problem. The main ceremony will be held in the clearing as you approach the ridge."

"You remember, Ms. Rosenthal," Hannah adds. "Right by that fallen tree where we found that piece of Isabel's dress."

"Yes, I suppose that would be far enough away from the edge," I say. "But you said the 'main cere-mony' will take place there. Is there a sideshow?"

Chloe winces at my choice of words, as if I'd just turned her sacred rite into a circus act. "The culmi-nation of the rite requires the goddess—that would be me—to approach the ridge with a candle. But I can assure you, Ms. Rosenthal, I have no intention of following Isabel into the clove."

"I'm sure you don't, but just to be safe I will go up with you."

Chloe inclines her head, for all the world like a benignant deity accepting an offering from a suppli-cant. Tori was right; I think, Chloe is beginning to think she **is** the goddess she's playing. "That will be fine," Chloe says. "As long as you are quiet and re-spectful."

"And then I want an orderly procession down the hill," I add.

"All arranged, Ms. Rosenthal. That's part of the ceremony. Then we all reconvene in the Lodge for cider and doughnuts. You can do a head count. I promise you, no one will be wandering in the woods on the eve of the autumn equinox. Not when the dark is rising."

Chloe's words follow me for the rest of the week. The coming of fall back on Long Island meant new school clothes for Sally, the migration of the elderly to Florida, and the annual PTA debate over whether to ban Halloween. Here in the mountains and farm-lands, the cast of late-September light already threat-ens cold and darkness. The sycamore leaves have turned the greenish gold of tarnished brass. The air in the morning is sharp and smells like woodsmoke. Lying in bed at night I hear geese flying overhead and the wind thrashing in the pine trees as if it wants to fly away with them. When I drive into town I see that someone has put a peaked witch's hat on the tin White Witch sign. Outside the houses I pass in town, woodpiles climb higher and higher, as if the residents are preparing for the next ice age. It's easy to see why the arts colony was originally only meant to last during the summer. According to Lily, the artists began to flee at the first sign of cold.

Mimi announced tonight at dinner that she'd been offered a job painting murals at a convent called St. Lucy's in the western Catskills. "I'm not sure exactly where it is. Some little town called Easton."

"But aren't you Jewish?" Gertrude had asked, askance.

"Yes, but don't tell the nuns. I told them that I knew the lives of the saints intimately. I'd better start boning up."

"I think St. Lucy is the one who plucked her eyes out," Vera said. "I've seen many representations of her on my travels in Italy."

"Ugh," Mimi said, making a face. "I don't want to have to paint that! But I think it might be a different St. Lucy. This one is Irish and is the patron saint of unwed mothers. St. Lucy's is an orphanage and home for unwed mothers."

Mimi's confession unleashed a torrent of winter obligations. Dora and Ada were afraid that they'd lose their lease on their apartment in Manhattan if they didn't get back soon. Mike Walsh was going out west to sketch Indians. The Zarkov brothers had been invited by a cousin to winter in Palm Beach. Virgil announced that he'd been offered a fellowship to paint at the American Academy in Rome. Last of all, Gertrude mentioned that she had agreed to go to Europe with her husband. "Of course

he's a ninny, but in exchange for my agreeing
to take some preposterous fertility cure at
Baden-Baden, he has agreed to let me start a
little art museum in the city. And I can use the
trip to collect art."

"Well, I guess Lily and I will have to keep
the hearth fires burning by ourselves," Vera
said, glancing toward me with a proprietary
smile that warmed me. Some might have re-
belled under that possessiveness, but I knew
where it came from and it made my heart swell
to see her look at me as if I were hers.

It had taken half the summer to breach
Vera's delicate sense of decorum. After May
Eve, we had continued to leave the door open
between our rooms. We called our goodnights
across the threshold but then we would speak
long into the night. I'm afraid I didn't pay attention to all she said—her talk was full of
pragmatic details of running the estate and her
plans for expanding the summer colony—but
I loved to lie in the dark, listening to the
sound of her voice. I did pay attention,
though, when she spoke of purchasing a printing press.

"I'd like to collect some local tales of the
area to print in a special edition with your
lovely woodcuts," she said.

I told her, then, about the fairy tales I'd
made up for my sisters on the farm. She

begged me to tell them to her. Then it was my
voice that filled the darkness between the two
rooms. I began with the Dutch stories I'd
heard from my mother and grandmother, and
then I told her the stories I had made up. I was
shy at first of telling her the ones about the
brave heroine I'd invented because I'd come to
think of her as Vera. It was Vera's face I saw
when I thought of those stories, even though I
had created them before I met her. Soon,
though, I gained confidence from the dark and
I began telling her my stories. I described my
heroine as part Valkyrie, part fairy queen. She
slew dragons and saved whole villages from
evil wizards. She sailed on pirate ships and discovered lost kingdoms.

When I ran out of my old stories, I started
making up new ones. One night I began one
with these words: "There once was a girl who
liked to pretend she was lost until the day she
really lost her way." As I described this girl
wandering in the woods alone, I pictured myself running through the forest on May Eve.
How had I not known it was Virgil Nash following me? Why hadn't I run from him when
I did know? How had I gotten so lost? As I described how lost and tired the girl became I
began to cry, but quietly so Vera wouldn't hear.

"At last the girl grew so weary that she
begged the spirits of the forest to turn her into

a tree. She became a slender white birch leaning against a strong beech and she never felt lost again."

When I finished Vera was silent. I was afraid I'd somehow revealed too much—that she knew all about my meetings with Nash in the barn, knew why I felt so lost—but then I heard the creak of a floorboard and turned toward the door. Standing on the threshold, in her white nightgown, she looked like the girl in my story transformed: like a slim birch swaying in the breeze as she hesitated to come farther or flee.

I stretched out my arms to her and she came forward as if pushed by an invisible wind. She was trembling when she came into my arms, quaking like an aspen in the wind. I pressed the length of my body against hers—and wrapped myself around her until I couldn't feel any space between us. Like two trees growing from the same trunk, we tossed in the same wind, shook with the same passion, were cleft by the same stroke of lightning.

"Stay with me forever," she murmured sometime toward morning.

I breathed my consent onto her skin, from the hollow beneath her collar bone to the dip above her ankle, spilling my yes into all the little pools and valleys of her body so she would be inundated by my love.

From that night on I stayed away from Nash, but on the night that Vera announced our plans to stay together for the winter I asked Nash to meet me in the barn again. I stayed with Vera into the early hours of the morning. I had learned over the summer that she reached her deepest sleep only then. Lying beside her, listening to her breathing, I studied her face. In the moonlight her noble profile reminded me of a Greek goddess carved in marble. Wise, gray-eyed Athena, perhaps, the warrior goddess. I could imagine her striding into battle, her brave heart beating steadily under her cuirassed breastplate, her eyes flashing bright as bronze. My dear brave Vera, named for truth. She would defend me to the end. And if she knew that I had betrayed her? For the hundredth time that summer I imagined telling her. The first time had been a mistake, I would tell her. I had gone to the barn looking for **her**. But then how to explain the other times? Could I tell her that I had done it for the good of the colony? After all, she was the one who had said we needed Nash and his reputation to succeed. Or should I just tell her that I was weak? He had flattered me, threatened to expose me, tricked me, taunted me, bewitched me, ensnared me. If she would only stand by me now and lend me some of her strength, I could give him up. It was her that I really wanted.

And for the hundredth time that summer I imagined her eyes clouding over as I spoke. Her clear vision of me—**her pure Lily!**—despoiled. And I imagined her turning her face from me. I knew that I couldn't bear it.

I got up. I couldn't lie beside her imagining **that.** I stole from **our room**—as she called it and I had dared to think of it—like a thief in the night. I wrapped a dark cloak over my nightgown, hiding myself from the face of the moon. Still, I felt the force of the moon's gaze upon my back as I crossed the lawn. Even when I stepped beneath the copper beech, the hot white light found me there, stippling my arms and legs with black and white leaf patterns. I let the cloak fall from me and turned around in the light, holding my arms up in it to see the leaf patterns seared onto my skin. The light fell over my rounded belly beneath my shift. I turned slowly in the moonlight, letting the leaves made from shadow and light brand me. I wanted them to leave their mark on me. Why shouldn't the darkness I felt show on my skin?

Maybe I hoped that Vera, waking and finding me gone, would come to the window and see me standing on the lawn. She would see what I had become: a tree sprung out of moonlight and shadow, carved out of light and dark. She would see what I had done, and

what I had become, but she would also see
that I loved her and not Nash. She would stop
me from going to him and telling him that I
was pregnant. Because that was what I had decided to do. I would throw myself on his
mercy and ask him to take me with him—not
because I loved him but because I no longer
deserved to be with Vera.

But then a cloud passed over the moon and
the pattern of leaves fell from my skin like
leaves falling in autumn. I put my cloak back
on and ran down the hill, through the orchard,
into the woods behind the lodge, and up the
hill through the old trees. A wind stirred the
pine needles on the forest floor into little eddies. The air smelled like rain. I went faster,
scrambling down the sharp rocks of the clove.
No moonlight lit the path that night—the
moon had hid her face from me—but I knew
the path well enough by then to feel my way
in the dark. I almost wished I would fall. I
went faster and faster, daring the now rain-
slicked rocks of the clove to dash me to the
ground, but each time my foot or hand
slipped the moss-covered rocks seemed to hold
me up, like giants passing me from hand to
hand, carrying me to him—and farther away
from Vera.

I was soaked from head to toe by the time I
reached the barn. I had lost my cloak and my

nightgown clung to my skin. He stood in the doorway smoking a cigar, his face, lit in the red glow of its burning tip, etched into a saturnine leer at the sight of me. What did he see? Did he see my swelling breasts and the curved dome of my belly? How could he not? He who always saw me so clearly.

"Finally! I knew you couldn't stay away from me forever!" He tossed the cigar away, careless of the spark that could set the barn on fire, just as he'd been careless of how he set our lives on fire for his own sport . . . but no, I told myself, I couldn't blame it all on him. I'd struck the match and held it to the tinder as well.

"There's something I have to tell you," I said, coming closer to him.

"But you're frozen!" He took off his coat and wrapped it around my shoulders. "Come inside. Let me warm you." With his hands still grasping the lapels of his coat around me, he pulled me inside into the warmth of the barn. It was full now of hay stacked to the ceiling, all the accumulated heat of a summer's worth of sun piled up against the coming winter. The coarse wool of his coat rubbed against my damp skin and I felt electricity coursing through my veins. The air was crackling between us. The hair on the back of my arms stood up and leaned toward him. I was sur-

prised to find that there was still passion between us, because I knew now that it wasn't
love that we shared. But I could still tell him I
was carrying his child and ask him to take me
with him to Rome. I wouldn't have to tell him
that I loved him; he took that much as his due.
I wouldn't have to lie—and even if I did, he
wouldn't know.

"There's something I have to tell you," I
began again.

"And I have something to tell you! I was
surprised to hear Vera say you would stay here
this winter—"

"I needn't—"

"And to tell you the truth, I was just a little
hurt that you'd made your plans without con-
sulting me."

"But you did, too!" I exclaimed. "You didn't
tell me about the fellowship at the Academy."

"My dear, I only just had the letter yesterday. You've been avoiding me half the summer.
Still, I was going to tell you tonight and ask if
you would like to come with me. I had already
begun to daydream about us drawing together
on the Palatine and riding in the Campagna."

I took a deep breath. "We could still do all
that. I could still come with you—"

I saw something change in his face. His
eyes narrowed and the muscles around his
mouth tightened. "Well, that's the problem, I

don't think it's such a good idea anymore. When I heard about your plans, I realized it was best for you to stay here. I'll have to be free to travel while I'm over there, to meet dealers and collectors. I'm not wealthy like Vera. I've got to make my reputation now when I'm young or it will be too late. Perhaps later when I'm more secure we could travel together, but for now I think it really is best if you stay here with Vera."

He stepped closer and drew his coat tighter around my shoulders. It felt like a winding sheet binding my limbs, but I didn't push him away. I shivered. He must have thought it was from the cold because he moved closer still, backing me up against the barn wall. But it was really from the coldness I sensed in him. Even as I felt the heat of his desire I knew that his heart was cold. No. I couldn't go with him, even if I told him now that I was pregnant and begged and screamed and demanded he marry me; being with him would kill me. And yet I didn't push him away. I felt a coldness in my heart answering the coldness in his. We were the same, he and I. I had deceived the person I loved and I was already planning to deceive her again.

The rough planks still held the warmth of the long day in the sun and the heat of the stacked hay. His body, pressed against mine, held that same heat. A summer's worth of passion. I let him slide his hands under my gown and lift my legs around his waist. I heard the rain gusting against the barn, like a giant trying to batter down the walls. I wrapped my legs around his back and took him into me just as the lightning flashed through the skylight, lighting us up like torches. I gasped, thinking it would strike us, almost wishing it would—I imagined the shape our bodies made emblazoned on the barn wall, our flesh dissolved to ash—but the light faded harmlessly, leaving us in the dark.

When we were done, he wanted to take me back by the road because he thought crossing the clove in the rain would be too dangerous, but I told him no.

"I'll be fine," I told him. What else could happen to me? The lightning didn't strike me while I was betraying my beloved; why would the fates dash me against the rocks of the clove now?

"I'll see you next summer," he said as I left, but I already knew he wouldn't be coming back.

I ran quickly into the rain. I didn't tell him that I wouldn't be spending the winter here either. As I climbed the slick rock path up into the clove, I made my own plans. I would get Mimi to help me. She could get me a job working on the murals at St. Lucy's. It was perfect. When the baby was born, I could give it to the nuns.

For a second I considered finding a way to bring the baby back with me. I could claim it belonged to one of my sisters. Why shouldn't Vera and I raise it as our own? Then I remembered what Vera always said: that once a woman had a baby, she lost her chance to be an artist. No, it was better this way for everyone.

As I made my way down the hill toward the Lodge I saw that one of the oldest and tallest trees in the forest had been cleaved in two by lightning. The first rays of the morning sun reached through the new break in the canopy and struck the still-smoking stump. I lay my hand on the seared wood where the lightning had carved its name into the heart of the tree—a great jagged ziggurat that looked exactly like the rend that had split my heart in two.

CHAPTER 18

On the morning of the autumn equinox Dean St. Clare announces that the last period classes will be cancelled in order to allow students to prepare for the equinox ceremony. I decide to use the time to hike up to the ridge to where the students are planning to have their ceremony. I tell myself it's because I want to have a good look at the terrain to make sure that they'll be a safe distance from the cliff, but in truth I also find myself drawn to the site after reading Lily's last journal entry. I keep reliving that night in my mind, imagining Lily entrusting herself to the slippery rocks of the clove—almost as if she'd really wanted to die rather than face the pain of Vera's disappointment in her. Certainly her desperate coupling with Nash sounded as if she was punishing herself.

It's a warm, clear day—more late summer than the first day of fall. I change out of my teaching clothes into jeans, a T-shirt, and sneakers and, at the last minute, tie a windbreaker around my waist in case it's colder on top of the ridge. I remember it as windy and cool, but maybe that was because the last time I was there I watched poor Isabel Cheney's body being carried up out of the clove—a sight that would have chilled anyone.

The hike up to the ridge takes much less time than I expect. Of course, I remind myself, the last time I was pausing every fifteen minutes to call Isabel's name. It saddens me, when I reach the fallen tree where we found the torn shred of her dress, to realize how close Isabel had been to her friends down in the apple orchard. She needn't have felt so frightened—so alone. Yet turning around in a circle I see **why** she felt that way. Deep forest rings the tiny clearing; the trees stand like sentinels blocking the way out. The only sound is the roar of the waterfall. Even if she had screamed or called for help, no one would have heard her.

I sit for a moment on the fallen tree with my eyes closed, letting myself mourn for Isabel. I've been afraid, I think, in the weeks since she died, to really allow myself to feel it. The death of a girl Sally's age is too unbearable to contemplate. But now I realize how cowardly—and selfish—my avoidance is. I let myself relive the brief glimpses I had of Isabel's blunt, friendly demeanor and her naked ambition, which I'm sure wore on people's nerves, but which I suspect would have mellowed with age and experience. Who knew how far her drive would have taken her? What a colossal waste for a girl of her talents to die so young.

When I open my eyes, a tear slides down my face. It seems like an insignificant tribute for such a tragedy. As I get up I see that someone before me has left something more tangible. A small bouquet of flowers, which I'd mistaken at first for naturally growing wildflowers, lies in the crevice of the log. It's too late in the season for lilies of the valley, though, and the bunch is tied with lavender ribbon. I pick them up and see that the crevice they were placed in is a Z-shaped gash. Was this the tree, then, that fell the night Lily said goodbye to Nash? I run my fingers along the mark, recalling that Lily had compared its jagged scar to the gash she felt in her heart. The years—and moss and rain—have softened its edges. I wonder if the years were so kind to the rend in Lily's heart.

I get up and walk to the top of the ridge. A sign

has been crudely hammered onto a tree near the head of the falls: DANGER! STEEP DROP! NO HIKING BEYOND THIS POINT.

It doesn't look like much of a deterrent. In fact, I can see a fresh path worn through the grass on the path leading down into the clove. I can only hope that it's not students who are still hiking here. I remind myself to talk to Sally about staying away from here, although a lecture on the subject might well have the opposite effect and spur her to frequent the spot to spite me.

I had thought that the clove would look less menacing in full daylight, but the black, shadowy cleft seems even darker in comparison to the blue sky above. When I look up from the clove I see the old barn in the valley below. From this angle it looks even more decrepit than from the road. The cupola leans crookedly and wide holes gape in the walls like missing teeth. Who knows how much longer it will stand? I imagine some enterprising builder—like Sheriff Reade—will eventually loot it for vintage barn wood. Then no one will watch the sunlight or moonlight paint patterns on its floors and walls ever again.

I've started down the path before even realizing I've decided to go. It's reckless, I know; I don't have the right shoes or know the trail well enough. I can hear the lecture I'd give Sally about hiking alone in unfamiliar terrain, but I can also hear—as if she'd told me her story aloud and not in writing—Lily's voice describing the moonlight spilling onto the barn floor like a pool of water.

At first the path doesn't seem so bad, but then it becomes so steep I have to grab at the tree branches along the side to keep from falling. The steep stone walls on either side of the waterfall block out all but a narrow band of sunlight that struggles to light the long descent. In the narrow chasm, the sound of falling water is deafening, like the roar of a beast crouching at the foot of the falls, hiding behind the huge boulders. It looks like a giant tossed them down the slope to make the descent impassable—or perhaps to make the **ascent** impassable. It feels like I'm climbing down into a pit. Spray from the waterfall coats the moss-covered boulders. I have to sit down on them to navigate my way. At one point, after a near miss that would have sent me hurtling down to the bottom, I look up—and immediately wish I hadn't. The steep slopes on either side seem to be closing over my head, like a giant jaw about to snap shut.

By the time I've reached the bottom, the damp from the moss and ferns has soaked through my thin canvas sneakers and into my socks, which squelch with every step. Despite my discomfort I can't help but appreciate the beauty of the place. At the bottom of the clove, the water, glowing silver and black in the alternating light and shadow that falls between the stone walls, pools into a series of stone basins ringed by ferns. A circle of weeping willows rings the lowest pool. The only sound in this perfect round grove is the splash of water on moss-covered rocks and the wind stirring the long willow branches. That recording Fawn was playing in her shop could have been made here. No wonder local legend decreed the place to be sacred; it feels like I've wandered into the apse of a cathedral.

I rest for half an hour. I only leave when I realize that if I want to make it to the barn and back before the ceremony at sunset I should get going. Before I leave the pool though, I recall what Vera told Lily at the Bethesda Fountain in Central Park—that **whoever then first after the troubling of the waters stepped in was made whole of whatsoever disease he had.** As I watch, a breeze moves through the grove, sending ripples across the still, black-green surface. Before I can question why I'm doing it, I bend down and dip my fingertips into the ice-cold water and whisper a quick prayer for Sally's safekeeping tonight at the equinox.

When I push aside the willow branches and step out of the clove I'm surprised to find a bright and sunlit day waiting for me. It's a good ten degrees warmer in the field than it was in the clove. The grass in the field is waist high and damp, the ground boggy and uneven. My legs are soon as soaked as my sneakers and flecked with seed pods. I walk quickly, trying not to think about snakes. When I reach the barn I'm surprised to find that the door is intact. I'd expected to just walk through one of the holes in the wall, but I see now that they're covered with sheets of clear plastic. Maybe the barn isn't as deserted as it looks from a distance.

The old wood shrieks against the rusted hinges and the plank walls shiver as I shove open the heavy door. As if in answer to the door's complaint something inside the barn lets out a low, eerie moan that makes me freeze in my tracks. Thoughts of angry spirits—Lily's? Nash's? The white woman's?—flit through my brain . . . and then something white takes shape out of the shadows and swoops toward me.

I shriek and duck, but the white phantom swoops back up before it reaches me. I'm poised to run— thoughts of the white woman in my head—but then I look up into the shadowy rafters where a white heart-shaped face stares out of the gloom.

A barn owl. That's all, I tell myself.

When I step into the barn, though, I'm not so sure I've escaped the white woman. In the center of the barn, in the circle of light that pours through the broken cupola, stands a figure shrouded in white. I walk toward her, mesmerized. She—I can tell from the curves beneath the cloth that it's a woman—is standing where Lily stood on May Eve. Any moment now she'll turn and shed her cloak.

"Can I help you, Ms. Rosenthal?"

I turn in the pool of sunlight to find Callum Reade, silhouetted against the doorway. "What are you doing here?" I demand.

"What am **I** doing here?" he asks, stepping out of

the bright light. I see that he's dressed in jeans and a soft blue shirt that's rolled up over his elbows. A spear of sunlight falls on his arm, lighting the red-gold hairs on fire. "I think I should be asking you that. You're in my studio."

"Studio?" I look around the barn and see, now that my eyes have adjusted to the gloom, a work-bench set against one wall. The edge of a circular saw and metal tools glint in the uneven sunlight. Slabs of wood are stacked on one side of the table; another shrouded shape crouches in the corner. "You're a carpenter?" I ask. It makes sense, I suppose, since he also restores houses.

"Nothing so useful," he says. He walks toward me, his hands on his hips, talking as he approaches as if he were trying to gentle a skittish horse. I must look as tense as I feel. It's from being startled by the owl and then Reade's unexpected appearance, I tell myself. But it's also because this scene—a woman standing in a pool of light, a man walking toward her—so vividly recalls the May Eve that Lily and Nash first met here. "My dad used to carve decoys for duck hunting. I started fooling with his tools when I was a kid. After I moved back here, I needed something to keep my hands busy." He lifts his hand and for a moment I think he's going to touch my face, but instead he tugs at the cloth draping the figure beside me. It falls to the floor like water flowing into the pool of light.

I hear the sharp intake of my own breath in the

silence of the barn. Standing in the pool is a naked woman in the moment of turning, one arm crossed over her breasts. Her face, tilted modestly downward, is unfinished. I feel Callum's eyes on my back, relentless as the barn owl's gaze. I've reached out to stroke the woman's hip before I can think of how the gesture might look, but the softly rounded curve is irresistible. The wood is warm and smooth to the touch. Running my hand along the polished slope it's hard not to think of Callum Reade's hands carving, then sanding, then oiling the wood until it ripples in the light like flesh.

I try to swallow and find my throat dry. "She's . . ." I turn and find Callum right behind me. My shoulder brushes against his arm and I feel a wave of heat coming off him along with a scent of fragrant wood. "She's beautiful," I say, trying hard to keep my voice steady. "The wood looks like skin—"

"Cherry," he says. "It's got a beautiful grain. I found a downed cherry tree in the woods a few years ago and I've been working on a few pieces from it."

I take a deep breath and catch that scent again— the same scent I've noticed coming from Callum— also on the statue. There are flecks of sawdust on the hair of his arm and clinging to a damp patch on his throat. "Um . . . it reminds me of the bronze statuette in the alcove in Beech Hall," I say.

"I was inspired by it," he says, his eyes staying on me, not the statue. When I nod he says, "But the face is unfinished on that statue and I haven't been able to finish this one's face." He squints his eyes at me and then changes his mind about whatever he was going to say. "So. I've shown you what I'm doing here. Are you going to tell me what you're doing here?"

"I wanted to see the barn. I've been reading a journal that Lily Eberhardt kept in which she writes that she met Nash here. . . ." I falter, embarrassed by the details of that first meeting, but Callum Reade rescues me.

"He painted her here," he says. "You can see in those paintings that he loved her."

"You've looked at the paintings in the Lodge?" As soon as the words are out I realize I sound as if I thought he wasn't capable of appreciating art. I'm expecting a defensive response, but instead his eyes soften as he looks toward the sculpture.

"Remember I told you how kids used to dare one another to stay all night in the woods above the clove and brave the wrath of the white woman? Well, I did it once when I was fifteen. I sat all night at the head of the falls, waiting to see her appear out of the mist. I was scared at first, but then I was disappointed when the night was almost over and I hadn't seen anything, so I hiked down to the Lodge. I think I had some minor act of vandalism in mind—something to mark the night since there'd been no supernatural visitation."

"Sheriff Reade!" I exclaim in mock surprise. "Vandalism?"

He grins. "I wasn't always so law-abiding." He rakes his hand through his hair, and I can picture him as the boy he was, those green eyes alert in the dark woods, waiting for the white woman to appear. If I were the white woman haunting those lonely woods I don't think I'd have been able to resist appearing before those eyes. "I broke a window to get into the building—it was easy, the school's never been much for security—and raided a supply closet full of paints and pencils. I was looking for something more substantial to steal in the parlor when I saw her. A life-size naked woman glaring down at me from the wall. It was how she stood there—completely unashamed, brazen as an animal—that got me. That and the way she was looking at me as if she saw right through me to my soul and knew all my secrets. I put back everything I had taken and spent the rest of the night just looking at her, wondering who she was. When I found out that she'd died in the clove I wondered if I hadn't met the white woman after all."

"Is that why you work here?" I ask.

"Partly. I first came to the barn when I found out the paintings were done here. Dymphna caught me here once—you know she and her cousin Doris own the barn and the farm stand—"

"No, I didn't know."

"Yeah." He smiles again. He seems like a different person here, more relaxed. His hand drifts to the statue and brushes a smudge of dust off the curve of her hip. A tremor moves through me, as if he'd touched me and not the statue. Do I **want** him to touch me? It has been so long since I've felt a man touch me like that—longer than the year since Jude died. We'd been having one of those **lulls**— as I'd come to think of the sexless spates in our marriage—in the weeks before he died. It might have been a whole month, but I never liked to count. Jude had been working a lot; the market had been especially volatile and he'd started trading at night. I'd started to feel a little restless and concerned, but I reassured myself that we'd always come out of these dry periods with renewed passion. That's how a marriage worked, I figured, you had to weather the ups and downs. I just hadn't figured on that particular lull stretching into eternity.

"Are you okay?" Callum Reade asks, moving closer to me.

"I just caught a chill," I say. The chill of an eternity of not being touched, I think. I look up to find Callum's pale green eyes fixed on my own, intent, as if he could read my thoughts. Again I feel heat coming off him, the heat of the sun on his skin . . . or maybe it's from the accumulated heat of Lily and Virgil's passion all those years ago. Whatever its source, I find myself leaning into it, hungry for it. I close my eyes and picture his hands carving rough wood into the shape of a woman, feel his hands cup my face as if he were measuring my contours for a mold, and then, before I can change my mind, I tilt my head up and meet his lips. They are soft but firm, as smooth as polished cherrywood. They even taste like cherries. He takes a step closer, his arms enfolding me like giant wings, which I can almost hear. . . .

And then I do hear them. And feel them. Stirring the air right above us. I open my eyes just in time to see the barn owl swooping over our heads, heading out into the fields. I step back, breaking the embrace, and glance toward the statue, away from the look of confusion and hurt in his eyes. Standing in the circle of light she looks like a woodland nymph surprised at her bath—Diana discovered in her sacred grove by Actaeon. Only instead of punishing her intruder she has been punished herself, turned into wood for all time.

I turn away from her and Callum Reade. Walking out the door I think to myself that I know exactly how she feels.

Callum follows me across the field. "Where are you going?" he calls from behind me.

"Back to the ridge," I shout without looking back. "I'm supposed to supervise the autumn equinox. I can't be late."

"That's where I'm going, too," he says.

"Fine," I say, quickening my pace. "We'd better hurry."

The climb up through the clove is longer and harder than I had anticipated. It's so steep that we have to dig our fingers into the cracks in the rock to pull ourselves up. We do it in silence, saving our breath and concentration for the climb. I'm relieved that we don't have to make small talk or acknowledge the interrupted kiss. It's not the time, I tell myself as I attack the steep rock face as if I could burn away desire like a few extra calories. Another voice reverberates in my head as we climb, though. **Will it ever be time?** Or will I always feel like this, as lifeless as a woman carved from wood?

By the time we reach the top of the clove, my fingernails are caked with mud and I suspect my face is streaked with it from wiping the sweat off my brow. My legs are trembling with effort. Callum gives me a hand up over the last boulder—and then holds on to my hand at the top of the ridge.

"Are you done running from me?" he asks. "Or are you going to find another mountain to climb to get away from me?"

"I'm sorry," I say when I see the look of hurt in his eyes. "It was a mistake—"

"Oh, I can see that!"

"I mean it was a mistake for me. I'm just not ready yet. It hasn't even been a year yet."

"Okay then, I wasn't trying to rush you. In fact, I believe it was you who kissed me."

I'm grateful my face is already red from exertion as I feel the blood course into my cheeks. "As I said, it was a mistake. I'm sorry. It won't happen again. Now if you don't mind, I have to go home and shower. . . ."

"I'm afraid there isn't time." He lifts his chin up over my shoulder. I turn and look into the darkening woods. It's like a swarm of fireflies is coming up the hill.

There must be at least forty students walking single file, each holding a lit candle. It looks like a river of light flowing uphill.

Leading the procession is Chloe, dressed in a long dark green dress that hugs her hips and breasts. A gold rope is tied over her hips, the tassel swaying back and forth as she climbs the hill. A wreath of red and gold leaves crowns her head and some kind of symbol is painted on her forehead: a circle topped with a crescent moon. When she reaches the clearing, she stops at the stump of the lightning-struck tree and sets her candle down among the twisted roots. As the other students file into the clearing, they spread out into a circle. I see Clyde Bollinger in a white dress shirt that flaps loosely around his thin hips and bony wrists, Hannah Weiss in a floaty pink dress trimmed with violet ribbons, and Justin Clay in a pink Oxford shirt and khakis, looking more like he's at a clambake on the Cape than at a pagan rite in the woods. Tori Pratt, also in a snug long dress, approaches the tree stump with a wide copper basin, which she places next to Chloe's candle.

I strain to find Sally in the crowd. I'm tempted to go closer to the clearing, but then I want to stay between the students and the ridge. Callum seems to have the same idea. With his arms folded over his chest and legs planted wide apart, he looks like he's ready to block any student's approach to the cliff edge. I finally spy Sally and Haruko among the last arrivals to the clearing. Sally's at the point of the circle farthest way from me—and the ridge—which suits me just fine. I want her as far from the edge as possible.

The last of the procession enters the clearing and I see the rear guard is made up of faculty and staff: Shelley Drake in a floaty gauze caftan, Ivy St. Clare in her usual black tunic and slim pants, Colton Briggs looking out of place in suit and tie, a woman in a Grecian style robe whom I don't recognize at first but then identify as the regal Miss Pernault with her hair down, Toby Potter looking perfectly in character in a homespun monk's robe, and motherly Dymphna Byrnes in a flowered housedress and burnt orange cardigan. The librarian, Miss Bridewell, in some kind of floral muumuu brings up the rear. Everyone is holding a candle except for Ivy St. Clare.

Behind me the sun, which has reached the line of mountains in the west, sends a gold light skidding into the clearing. As if that was the signal, Chloe picks up her candle from the stump and holds it high over her head.

"We come to say farewell to the sun," she says, her girlish voice clear and sweet in the quiet woods. "And to say a final farewell to those who have traveled into the land of shadows before us. Isabel

Cheney, we speed you on your journey and beg you to forgive any wrongdoing you suffered here. We ask all of those we have lost to watch over us in these coming days, as the nights grow longer and the shadows stretch farther and the dark rises. We promise to honor you, to look deep into the darkness in our own hearts, and pray we survive the journey into the dark until the light returns."

Chloe takes a black candle out of a pocket in her dress. She lights it from the wick of the white candle and then turns around and starts walking up toward the ridge.

"What's she doing?" Callum asks, his voice low.

"She said the ceremony required her to approach the ridge. The rest of them are supposed to stay in the clearing." As the circle of candleholders stirs, though, I have a sudden misapprehension. What if they all start walking up toward the ridge at once? I have an image of them all marching up the hill and over the edge like lemmings plunging into the sea, taking Callum Reade and me with them.

Callum must have the same thought. As Chloe approaches us holding both candles, Callum steps between her and the ridge. She stops and looks up at him, her pale face glowing in the flickering light of the candles. She creases her brow, making the painted moon ripple as though a cloud has passed over it. It reminds me of how Lily described the clouds moving over the moon on May Eve. It strikes me that just as Lily's life was irrevocably altered by an unwanted pregnancy, so the darkness of Isabel's death has fallen over Chloe's life.

"I need to go to the head of the waterfall," she says in a small but insistent voice, "to put my candles in the water."

"Why don't you give them to me?" Callum says, holding out his hand. His voice is low and gentle, too low for anyone but me or Chloe to hear. The students below us are whispering among themselves, trying to figure out what's going on.

"No!" Chloe hisses, her face distorted now by anger. "It has to be me!"

Callum tilts his head. "Why?" he asks.

The single word question seems to light a spark in Chloe. She flings herself at Callum like a small missile. Even though she's tiny and light the force of her fury knocks him a step backward toward the edge of the ridge. Before I can think, I throw myself at Chloe, grabbing a handful of her hair to pull her back—whether to save her or Callum, I have no idea. It does both, though. Chloe spins on me, the wax from her candles spraying outward in a wide arc that hits my hands and arms, and Callum regains his footing enough to step forward and restrain her. He moves her down from the ridge, commanding the rest of the students to move back. Only one manages to get past him and make it to the top of the ridge. It's Sally. I hold out my arms, which are only now beginning to register the scalding pain from the hot wax—sure that she's come to see if I'm okay. Her face is stained with tears.

"What were you thinking, Mom?" she cries, her voice breaking into a sob. "Why would you bring that man here? You ruined everything!"

She turns and hurries down the hill with the rest of the disbanded troop, leaving me to wonder which hurt worse—her angry words or the burns that I can feel already beginning to blister.

CHAPTER 19

In the weeks following the disastrous autumn equinox, the campus seems plunged into mourning for the death of summer. The gold-tinged light that slants in through my classroom window bathes my students in an amber sap as if preserving them in the moment forever. The slow drift of yellow leaves from the sycamores might be tears for the dying of the sun. Perhaps my melancholy is just the natural turning inward that marks the change of seasons. Certainly I can't complain that my students aren't . . . well, studious. Even Sally, who did so badly in school last year that I was afraid she wouldn't pass, is working hard. Whenever I see her on the lawn beneath the deep wine-colored canopy of the copper beech or in front of the fireplace in one of the lounges in Beech Hall, she bends her head down to her book or sketchpad. She still blames me for bringing Callum Reade to the autumn equinox. I can't really argue. I blame myself as well.

If I hadn't kissed him in the barn maybe he wouldn't have followed me and made that scene on the ridge. And as much as it embarrasses me to admit it, I was the one who initiated that kiss. It must be an aberration of grief that made me do it. He's not at all the kind of man I'm attracted to— gruff, bitter, clearly with a chip on his shoulder when it comes to artists, intellectuals, and New Yorkers. Certainly he's nothing like Jude. No—it's better that he hasn't sought me out since the day of the equinox.

To convince myself of that, I decide to find out just why he quit the New York police force. While my class is doing research in the library, I do an Internet search on his name and come up with the story. There's a picture of Callum Reade, looking much younger, in his uniform. OFFICER CLEARED OF WRONGDOING IN BRONX SHOOTING, the caption reads. The boy he shot had a record and a gun, which three witnesses testified they saw him pull out and aim when stopped by the police. There didn't seem much question that Callum's shooting him was justified, but then, below Callum's picture is a picture of the boy. Although he was fourteen when he died, he looks about eleven in the picture. He has a wide-open smile that reveals a gap between his two front teeth, and a mischievous look in his eyes. It's hard to imagine him wielding anything more dangerous than an MP3 player. I can't help but wonder if this is the face Callum Reade sees when he closes his eyes at night. I know I would see it. I wonder now if he was so adamant about keeping Chloe away from the ridge because he wasn't willing to risk being responsible for another young life lost.

I can't blame him. I find myself watching Chloe carefully for any more signs of erratic behavior since her outburst on the ridge. But the only thing odd about her behavior is that despite the disaster of the Autumn Equinox Festival she continues to be obsessed with pagan rites. Only a few days after the equinox, I hear she's planning a celebration for Samhain, the pagan predecessor of Halloween. I decide this time, though, that I might as well use my students' fascination with the Wiccan calendar to my advantage. I look up Samhain in the Vivianne Crowley book I bought in Seasons and read: "Samhain is the festival of the dead in Pagan custom." After an initial chill at this description, I find this cheering suggestion on the next page: "One way of celebrating Samhain is to build an altar to our ancestors and to find old photographs, mementos, medals and to put them in a place of honor for the festival."

Reading this, I'm reminded of the crafts projects I used to do with Sally when she was little and the school year was fresh: the autumn leaves we ironed between sheets of wax paper, the Thanksgiving turkeys we made out of felt and pipe cleaners. I feel my hands itching to fashion something more concrete than words on a page. And so, one day in early October, I search out Shelley in her studio and ask if she'd like to collaborate on a project.

"Since I'm researching their lives already, I could make some kind of tribute to Vera Beecher and Lily Eberhardt. Then the students could make tributes to their own ancestors. I'll have them write about the folklore of their families and the handed-down stories." I'm spinning ideas as I talk, afraid that Shelley will dismiss the project as not sophisticated enough for Arcadia's fine arts program. I realize it sounds a bit like the shoebox dioramas Sally did in the third grade. But Shelley turns away from the painting she'd been working on when I came in— another view of haunted woods—and holds the tip of her paintbrush to her lips. She looks like an allegorical figure representing the artist inspired. Just the kind of thing her grandmother might have painted.

"It's an excellent idea. They could do portraits of an ancestor or depict a scene from a childhood memory. I'll have them look at Frida Kahlo's autobiographical montages." Shelley stabs the paintbrush into her loosely knotted hair and dives down to a bookshelf from which she plucks three books in quick succession. "And we can look at some pictures of altars from the Mexican Dios de los Muertos. . . . I think I have some pictures in these old magazines."

Within minutes Shelley is surrounded by glossy **National Geographics** splayed out around her like an aureole crowning a saint's head. She's forgotten all about the painting she was working on. As I'm leaving I notice Sally's name on an index card clipped to an easel holding a covered canvas. I touch the edge of the cloth, but Shelley's voice stops me from lifting it.

"I promised Sally I wouldn't let anyone see her work—that's why she's keeping it in here. I know it must be hard that she doesn't want to share with you, but I think we should respect her wishes, don't you?"

The pity in her voice brings the blood to my face. "Of course," I say without turning around. "I didn't realize she felt so strongly about it. She's always shown me her work before. . . ." Everything I think to say just makes me sound more desperate and pathetic. When I turn around, though, I see that Shelley isn't paying the slightest attention to me. She's absorbed in an article on Roman death masks. I leave quietly, grateful that she has such a short attention span.

I'm grateful, too, for the crisp autumn air as I hurry up the hill to Beech Hall. It cools the fire in my cheeks. Why should it matter if Sally shows her paintings to Shelley Drake but not to me? The important thing is that she's found an outlet for her grief and that she's being productive. I'm glad she's found a mentor. I should also be glad, I suppose, that Shelley greeted my suggestion so eagerly, but her enthusiasm has left me feeling a bit exhausted and jittery at the same time, as if I'd drunk too much coffee or stuck my finger into an electrical socket. I think of what Shelley said about her grandmother Gertrude having a breakdown after her painting was lampooned by the Fakirs at the Art Students League, and how her mother was in and out of mental hospitals all her life. Is the history of mental instability in her family the reason Shelley is so eager not to be associated with her grandmother? Certainly, Shelley's behavior seemed a bit manic. I'll have to work hard to keep up with her.

I spend the evening alone at the kitchen table in my cottage sorting through the hatbox full of Vera Beecher's letters, looking for pictures and other artifacts that could be used in an altar. I bring down from my bedroom the May Day picture of Lily Eberhardt, Gertrude Sheldon, and Mimi Green.

Since I read about the three women—and the May Day celebration—in Lily's journal they've become more real to me. I notice now that Gertrude Sheldon has the same hectic expression in her eyes that I just saw in her granddaughter Shelley's eyes. Lily's expression, too, is not as purely happy as I first read it. The joy and excitement are there, but her eyes are shining as if she might break into tears at any moment. Only little Mimi Green—who comes across as more worldly and knowing in Lily's journal—is totally unreadable, her eyes shadowed by her long bangs and the downward tilt of her head.

I find a few other pictures of that May Day—one of Virgil Nash brandishing a cardboard sword, one of the Zarkov brothers in full Russian costume playing their balalaikas—but nothing else seems to sum up the lost days of Arcadia as well as the first picture of the three women revelers. I lean it against the hatbox with its old-fashioned spray of violets. I get up, take a step back, and see that the hatbox is the perfect backdrop. It's surrounded by a ring of old letters and notebooks that in turn are wreathed by the ivy pattern on the tabletop.

It's a nearly perfect still life . . . the composition only needs something vertical. I look around the kitchen, lighting on and then dismissing in turn the half-empty wine bottle, a cracker tin, and a ceramic vase. No, it has to continue the floral motif and connect to Lily and Vera's life. I walk into the living room and instantly spot the fleur-de-lis pattern on the fireplace tiles. Yes, that's close, but unless I want to move the whole arrangement into the living room, it's not practical. There was something else with a fleur-de-lis on it. I feel it hovering on the edge of memory, shimmering like old glass. . . .

Of course! The fleur-de-lis perfume bottle that Vera gave Lily their first winter together in New York. The image is so clear in my head that I start to look for it before I recall that I only read about the bottle in Lily's journal instead of actually seeing it.

Only I have seen one. I'd recognized the description of the bottle from ones that had belonged to my grandmother. I had played with them when I was little, filling them with colored water and lining them up on my grandmother's windowsills in her house in Brooklyn. When she died and my mother asked if I wanted anything to remember her by, I asked for one of the perfume bottles. I know I haven't thrown it out. It must be in one of the dozens of unpacked moving boxes.

I find it in the third box I try, wrapped in tissue paper among the china horses Sally collected when she went through her horsey stage. The glass is thick and mottled, tinged green, the fleur-de-lis pattern set into the neck. A tiny shred of gold and lavender paper clings to one side. Stamped on the bottom is the name of the pharmacy that made the perfume: PRIVET AND SLOE, APOTHECARIES, NY, NY. I hold the bottle up to my nose, hoping for the remembered scent of my grandmother, but it smells like old paper and dust. All that colored water I poured into it must have long ago washed away the last traces of perfume.

I grab one of Sally's sketchpads and go back to the kitchen, where I place the bottle in front of the box, overlapping the photograph a little so that Lily's outstretched arm is reflected in the mottled glass—an effect that will be hard to capture but, I immediately feel, is the heart and center of the picture. I look at the tableau for a few more minutes, then I take out my old, tattered copy of **The Changeling Girl** from my book bag. I flip through the pages, not sure what I'm looking for . . . until I see it. I lay the open book in front of the other objects. Then I sit down and do something I haven't done for many years. I draw.

When I wake up the next morning, my hands and the bed sheets are covered in pastels. It's as if a rain of spring flowers has fallen on my bed overnight. Lavender, madder red, pale green, and butter yellow are the predominant colors. I have a vague memory of dragging out Sally's old pastels late last night, but it is blurry, as if I'd been drunk. But I don't recall drinking anything and my head is clear when I get up.

The still life (it seems a strange phrase for this tribute to the dead) is lying on the kitchen table when I come downstairs. I glance at it quickly, reluctant to examine it too closely. For the first time in years I felt really transported while drawing and I'm afraid that in the cold light of day I'll be disappointed with the results. I make coffee in a travel mug that Sally and Jude gave me two years ago on Mother's Day, jam one of Dymphna's leftover scones in my pocket, and slip the picture between the pages of the sketchbook I stole from Sally's room last night. Then I head off to class before I can change my mind.

It doesn't matter if the drawing's any good, I tell myself on the path to Beech Hall. It's just a model to show the class what I have in mind for their project. If it's amateurish—as it's almost certain to be—then that will demonstrate my willingness to be open with them. We'll laugh over my efforts to draw after all these years.

But as I hug the sketchbook to my chest I know I don't want them to laugh at this first effort. I know because I'm holding it as tenderly as I would carry a child. For one creepy moment I remind myself of that picture from **The Changeling Girl** of the peasant girl cradling the beech root wrapped in cambric, her embrace already turning the inanimate thing of pulp and sap into flesh and blood.

There are a few groans when I announce an additional project, but when I explain they can get credit in two classes and that there's no writing involved they quiet down. I outline the idea and then, before

I can chicken out, tape my drawing to the black-board.

"As you can see, I haven't put pencil to paper in a while, but I wanted to give you an idea—"

"You did that?" The question comes from Chloe and at first I think she's mocking my poor effort, but then I realize she's not.

"Wow, Ms. Rosenthal," Hannah Weiss says, "we didn't know you could draw, too. It's really good . . . in a squicky sort of way."

I turn to look at my own drawing. Last night I opened **The Changeling Girl** to the picture of the peasant girl kneeling beneath the copper beech with the root cradled in her arms. Why, I wonder now, did I choose that scene? It is certainly the strangest one in the story. And I have done nothing to make the image less strange. The picture has literally bled out onto the table. Leaves from the beech tree have scattered across the surface like blood drops. The tree's bloodred roots snake off the page and creep among the scattered letters, their long tendrils eerily like fingers pawing through the pages, looking for **something.**

"I get it," Hannah Weiss calls out. "The roots show the connection between the fairy tale that Lily Eberhardt and Vera Beecher wrote and their lives to-gether as symbolized by their letters."

Tori Pratt mutters something under her breath that sounds like **show-off.** I look harder at the pic-ture. Was Hannah's elaborate analysis right?

"And the beech tree, which stands for Vera, of course, is bleeding because Lily died," Clyde Bollinger adds.

"So what does that bloody baby stand for?" Chloe asks.

I feel my own blood drain from my face at the question. Did I really draw a bloody baby? When I look at the bundle that the peasant girl cradles I see that the root is indeed red, as are all the roots of the tree. And yes, the root does have the rudimentary shape of a baby. Did I mean for it to represent the baby Lily bore and sacrificed to Vera's ideal of the artistic life? And if I did, do I really want to explain that to my students?

Luckily, Hannah Weiss comes to my rescue. "The baby stands for the school, doesn't it, Ms. Rosenthal? And it's bloody because it was born out of the grief Vera Beecher felt after Lily died."

I turn around to face the class. For once they're more interested in my answer than in checking their e-mail and instant messages on their laptops. "That's one interpretation," I say guardedly. I could point out that the school was founded before Lily's death, but Hannah's remark has made me think of something Shelley Drake said—that Ivy St. Clare has turned the school into a reliquary to pre-serve "the rotting corpse of Saint Vera." "The point is you see how much you can suggest through a drawing of inanimate objects. Do you think you can do the same with your own mementos? What objects would you pick to tell the story of your own family?"

"I have my grandfather's pocket watch." Clyde slips a heavy gold disk out of his jeans pocket. "My grandmother gave it to him when he joined the army, so he wouldn't forget her."

"That's cool," Hannah says, peering over Clyde's shoulder at the watch. "I've got my mother's Vassar ring. She's always talking about me applying there."

A few other students chime in with mementos they've inherited or borrowed from parents, grandparents, aunts, and uncles. One boy says that when his grandfather died he got all his shoes because they were both size 13. A girl says she's got the jeans her mother wore to Woodstock. I'm delighted at the class's enthusiasm. Perhaps this is just what we needed to break the somber mood that has pervaded the campus since Isabel's death—and what I needed to gain back my students' trust since I brought Sheriff Reade to the autumn equinox. I'm also touched that this group of iPod-wearing, cell-phone-obsessed teens have such a supply of sentimental objects, but then Chloe finally poses the question I've been waiting for.

"What if you don't have any family keepsakes?"

"You can use pictures or draw from memory—moments from the past you recall, that teddy bear your mother threw out, or a house you lived in when you were little and haven't seen since—" I have a sudden, jarring memory of my grandmother's kitchen in Brooklyn, the pattern on the kitchen table, the sun coming through the windows and lighting up the perfume bottles I'd filled with colored water. I turn back to my picture, curious—and a little afraid—to see what I did with the perfume bottle in the heat of my creative fugue last night.

But the bottle is untouched by the tide of red in the rest of the picture. It stands inviolate, full of clear water, bathed in light, holding a single white lily. I see now that it's the bottle and the white flower that balance the rest of the picture, but it's also the pure white of the lily that makes the red of the beech tree so startling . . . so **bloody.**

I turn away from the picture to answer more questions. Will they get credit for both classes? What percent of their grade will the project represent? Does it have to be done in pastels? Could it be executed in pen? pencil? markers? charcoal? watercolor? oils? Can they use Photoshop? By the time I finish answering all the questions we barely have time to go over last night's reading, a chapter from Marina Warner's **From the Beast to the Blonde.** The hour is up before I have a chance to remind them about tonight's reading (a chapter from Bruno Bettelheim's **The Uses of Enchantment**), and then I rush out of the room, trailed by Clyde and Hannah, who have more questions about the Dead Project, as they've started calling it.

I'm halfway to the Lodge when I realize that I left my picture taped to the blackboard. Although it will make me late to my seminar with the Merling twins, I turn back. I tell myself it's because I need to give the picture to Shelley so she can use it as an example when she introduces the project to her class, but I know it's really because I don't like the idea of it left hanging there for anyone to see.

When I get to the classroom, though, I see that the person whom I least wanted to see the picture is standing in front of it: Ivy St. Clare.

"Who did this?" she asks without turning around when I come into the room.

"I did. It's just a model for a project I'm having my students do—"

"You're not making the archival material I lent you available to them, are you?"

"No, of course not. They'll use their own family mementos." I describe the project to the dean, but she seems unable to take her eyes off my picture. When I'm done, she points to one of the objects in the drawing.

"What's this?"

I look closer and see she's pointing at the green book. I start to tell her it's Lily's journal, but then I realize I can't. How can I say I found the journal but didn't tell her about it? Luckily, the gold fleur-de-lis is half-hidden by a letter lying across its cover. "Just an old book I had lying around," I say. "I thought the color provided a nice contrast."

St. Clare turns to me, her hooded eyes peering out of her weathered face. The intensity of her look reminds me of something, but I can't think what. "Yes, it does," she says finally. "You have a good eye." Then she turns and leaves. Only then do I remember where I'd seen that look before. It was the same cold gaze with which the barn owl looked down on Callum and me.

CHAPTER 20

As soon as my last class is over, I rush back to the cottage, ignoring the tempting aroma of fresh-baked scones from Dymphna's kitchen. I really must have been in some sort of trance last night to carelessly include Lily's journal in my still life. If Beatrice Rhodes's memory is right, Ivy St. Clare has been looking for that journal since Lily died. Of course I could just tell her that I found the journal in the cottage, but I'd have to explain why I didn't mention it right away, and she might ask me to hand it over to her. I don't want to give it up until I get to the end of Lily's story. I can only hope that the dean believed me when I said that the book in the picture was mine.

I'm relieved to find the journal where I left it on the kitchen table with the hatbox and the perfume bottle, but I'm also unnerved to think how easy it would have been for Ivy St. Clare—or anyone else, for that matter—to come into the house and take it. From now on, I'll have to keep it someplace safer. I promise myself I'll only read it by myself in the cottage. I start that night, staying up into the early hours of the morning, reading Lily's account of her winter at St. Lucy's Orphanage and Home for Unwed Mothers.

When I told Vera that I had gotten a job working on the murals of St. Lucy's with Mimi Green, she was not nearly as angry as I thought she would be. She pressed her lips together and folded her hands in her lap—two gestures I'd begun to recognize as her way of reining in her temper—but when she spoke her voice was calm and cool.

"And you undertook obtaining this commission without seeking any help from me?"

I knew she was hurt, but she'd phrased her complaint in a way that offered me a way to

save face. She always did. It was one of the
things I love about her. She hated to be cornered and so she did no cornering herself.

"You've always stressed to me the virtues of
independence and self-sufficiency. I thought
you'd be proud."

"And so I am." Her lips curved into a tight
smile. "I only wonder if it's the best venue for
your talents: a religious theme and in such a
remote part of the country. I might have gotten something better for you."

"I'm sure you could have, but then I
wouldn't have gotten it myself. Mimi says she's
speaking to a friend at **Harper's Bazaar** about
photographing the murals when they're
done."

Vera sniffed. "Well, if you're really going to
do it I might as well have a word with someone at **Vanity Fair.**"

I knew then that she'd relented, but my
worries weren't over. That night she took
down her atlas of New York State and found
the little town of Easton where St. Lucy's was
located.

"Why, it's not far from here at all," she exclaimed. "An hour's drive by motor car at the
most, and you could even go by train."

With a sinking heart, I looked at the spot
her finger pointed to on the map. Mimi had
been vague about St. Lucy's location, but that

was because she was a city girl and to her upstate New York was one endless vista of dairy
farms and picturesque settings for her drawings. But I recognized where St. Lucy's was at
once, along the shore of the East Branch of the
Delaware River, not far from the farm where I
grew up.

"You could easily spend weekends here,"
Vera announced, slamming shut the heavy
atlas with a conclusive thud. "I'm sure you'll be
glad of a comfortable bed and a good meal
after bunking with the nuns all week."

What could I say? If I objected, she would
feel I was trying to escape her. I spent the next
few days debating between inventing another
commission that would take me farther away
and confessing my condition. One thing was
certain: if I waited much longer my decision
would be made for me. By mid-September
Vera was already commenting on my plumped
state. "The soft life has filled you out," she said
as we walked toward the lodge. "Perhaps living
with the nuns will be slimming."

"Ah, but I'll have Mrs. Byrnes's good cooking every weekend."

"About that," Vera began, linking her arm
in mine. We'd come to the great copper beech
tree on the lawn. The leaves had turned a
deeper purple in the last weeks but had not yet
begun to fall. The beech was one of the last

trees to lose its leaves in the autumn. By the time they began to fall, I would already be away. Suddenly I wanted nothing more than to stay right there at Arcadia and watch the leaves and then the snow fall, and to feel the baby growing inside of me, with Vera beside me. But even as I was turning toward Vera to tell her, she had gone on.

"Would you feel very hurt if I went away this winter? You could still come on the weekends, of course. Mrs. Byrnes will be watching the house—"

"Where are you going?" I asked.

"Gertrude has asked me to accompany her to Europe."

"But I thought she was going with her husband."

Vera shrugged. "Have you ever met Bennett Sheldon? He's the dullest, most tiresome man alive. I think Gertrude's afraid she'll go crazy without some other conversation for six months. And she wants my advice in collecting art for her new museum. I thought I'd begin a small collection for us here at Arcadia in order to provide models for our artists."

"I thought you couldn't stand Gertrude." My voice came out shrill. Vera turned to me with a startled look on her face.

"I can't. You know how I despise dilettantes. But she does know all the best art dealers in London and Paris. You're not jealous, are you, my dear?"

I was surprised to see her look soften toward me. I had always believed she despised jealousy, as she despised most weaknesses, but now she was smiling and drawing me closer to her. "My darling Lily, my pure Lily. You know there is no one else for me. You have nothing to fear. But if you would like to come with us, you know nothing would make me happier."

I could feel the rapid beating of her heart beneath the stiff cloth of her dress. Her arm around me tightened. I knew then that she'd planned this revelation to make me jealous and to lure me into going with her. It did not make me love her any less. If anything, it made me love her more. It was the first time I'd ever seen her do anything truly weak. And she'd done it for me. For love of me.

I returned her embrace and murmured into her neck. "How could I ever fail to trust you, Vera? Your very name is truth. Go to Europe. Bring back your treasures. I'll be here waiting for you."

Mimi wanted to go home to Brooklyn first to visit with her family, and so we arranged that we would meet at St. Lucy's in the last week of October. I decided that I would use the time to visit my family in Roxbury.

I hadn't visited since leaving for the city. I had sent letters and money all along but I'd been wary of returning to my family, afraid they'd see how far I'd grown from them. I should have been most frightened now with a secret that really could be read in my flesh, in my thickening waist and swelling breasts, but perhaps that was the reason, after all, that I went. Perhaps I had some idea that there was still a place for me and my unborn child in the home where I was born.

My parents' farm was on the outskirts of the village of Roxbury, sheltered in a hollow with rich meadows watered by the East Branch of the Delaware River. When I got off the train in Roxbury, the trim white houses seemed to reproach me with their provincial superiority. By the time I got to the white farmhouse I was almost ready to turn around and walk back to the train station. I stopped in the shade of an old weeping beech and leaned against it, suddenly light-headed at the sight of my old home. From there I watched as my sisters and mother came in and out, walking from the house to the barn, carrying pails to the barn for the milking and then the breakfast scraps and corn for the chickens. I watched my sister Rose, grown into a tall, fine woman, fetch water from the well and I watched my father, grown old since I had left, come home from the fields for his dinner. He'd gained a helper—the young man who'd proposed to me and married Marguerite—as well as a new dog who didn't catch my scent as I stood beneath the weeping beech, hidden behind a green curtain of leaves. I stood there so long that I felt I'd become a part of the tree. My limbs were as numb as if they had turned to bark, my head as heavy as if weighted down with a mane of leaves, my feet as immobile as if they had grown roots. I almost wished that I could become part of the tree, because then I could stay here always and be a part of the rhythm and flow of the farm's daily life. That was the only way, I saw now, that I'd ever again be a part of it. They didn't need me. I would only bring shame to them if I came to them now, pregnant and unmarried.

I shook off my languor by remembering Vera and the life that awaited me back at Arcadia. It seemed so far away, as if I would have to climb mountains to find it again, but I would never get there if I didn't start out. It felt like I was ripping my own flesh to move away from that tree, but when at last I pried myself away I felt I had broken the last bond I had to my old life.

I walked back to the train station and took the train on to Arkville, where I found a boardinghouse to stay in for the rest of the week. I waited there until Mimi joined me. She looked refreshed from her visit to her family, full of stories and packages of baked goods I'd never heard of before—**mandelbrot** and **rugelach**. She asked me how my visit had gone, and I shrugged and made up stories about my sisters, which I almost believed.

The next morning, we took the Delaware & Northern through a pristine country of rolling green hills populated by cows and low-lying mists that rose off the river and dewed the windows of our rail car. We were the only passengers to detrain at Easton, a pretty town with a white church and a dozen white clapboard houses on the banks of the East Branch of the Delaware. While we sat on our trunks waiting we watched a group of boys fishing in the fast-flowing river. When we inquired of one about the orphanage he responded by running away as if he were afraid we had plans to make **him** an orphan. Finally, when we were considering taking the next train back to Arkville, we heard the wheels of an approaching conveyance and out of the mists there appeared, in order: a mud-splashed pony, a hooded and hunched over driver, and a cart that might have once been painted white but was now the color of the same mud that covered the pony. The driver, a sullen young man whose face, even when he pushed back his hood, was half-hidden under a deep brimmed cap, greeted us with the words "You must be the new girls from the city." He proceeded to lift our trunks into the back of the wooden pony cart, which was redolent of hay and manure. When it became clear that we were also expected to ride in the back of the cart, Mimi balked.

"I'm not riding in that, mister."

The man tipped back his hat revealing close-set dark eyes and a beaky nose. "Oh, you're not, are you? Then you'd better start walking. St. Lu's is halfway up that mountain there." He gestured with his thumb to a hummocked slope that rose out of the pearl gray river mists only to be enveloped by a dark cloud that threatened rain. In the narrow strip of land between mist and cloud, I could make out a few white buildings clinging to the side of the mountain. As Mimi and the cart driver squared off, rain began to fall.

"I don't mind riding in the cart," I said. "I grew up on a farm so I'm used to it," I told the man, who I now saw was really only a boy of eighteen or nineteen. "There's room in the front for my friend, isn't there?"

The boy rolled his eyes, shrugged, and then performed an elaborate bow, doffing his hat and sweeping an arm to the plywood board that comprised the front seat of the cart. "After you, m'lady," he said. While Mimi struggled up onto the front seat, he helped me into the back of the cart, muttering under his breath about people who put on airs and thought themselves above their station.

The smell was really quite strong and I thought at first that along with the rocking of the cart it might make me sick, but I found that if I relaxed into the rhythm it wasn't so bad. We were climbing a steep dirt road. Facing backward, I saw the river snaking through the valley below, the green hills rolling in waves that were crested by the white foam of the ever-present mist. I felt as though I were being borne up above the sea. I thought of Vera on her ship traveling to Europe, and although I missed her I felt at peace for the first time in many months. No one would find me here. I had found a refuge. I heard Mimi laughing and I gathered that her amusement was over our driver's mistake. He'd thought we were two unwed mothers coming to St. Lucy's (St. Lu's, as he called it, as if it were a place you'd come to lose yourself) to have our babies in secret. Mimi enjoyed correcting him, telling him we were artists commissioned to paint the new murals for the chapel. The boy—Johnnie, I soon learned was his name—was profuse in his apologies, but I was glad he had made the mistake. It made me feel a little less that I had come to this place under false pretenses.

I soon discovered that the remoteness of St. Lucy's was no accident.

"Many of our girls come from the finest Catholic families," Sister Margaret, the head of the orphanage, informed us at dinner that night. We had been given seats at her table, which was on a raised dais in the cavernous dining room. "We give them privacy and a chance to return to their old lives, cleansed of their sins."

"Don't they miss their babies?" Mimi asked in between bites of roast beef. Vera needn't have worried about me losing weight here. The food was excellent.

Sister Margaret looked up from her plate. She wasn't having the roast beef. A few potatoes and beets were on her plate, but I hadn't seen her touch them. I wondered if she were an ascetic. It was hard to tell how thin she was under her black habit, but her face was long and bony, her skin as white as the wimple that framed it, and her blue eyes burned with the intensity of a fanatic. I was surprised that Mimi had dared to ask such a question of her. But she answered it calmly.

"Yes, of course they do. I imagine they think about them every remaining day of their lives.

But it is our hope that their faith in God comforts them and that, in a lesser sense, their faith in us to place the children in good homes also sustains them. We hope that in contemplating the life of St. Lucy, who was, like them, an unwed mother and who placed her child in the hands of God, they will find reassurance. That is why I've chosen to have her life depicted in the chapel, where many of the girls stop first when they come to us. I assume you've read the material I sent on St. Lucy's life."

"I have," I said, grateful to talk about something other than missing babies. I'd been so preoccupied with hiding my pregnancy and with how I could have the child in secret that I hadn't allowed myself to think about what it would feel like to hand the baby—my baby—over to a total stranger. The thought brought an unexpected pang, a sharp cramp deep down in my stomach. "I confess that I wasn't familiar with her life even though I was raised a Catholic."

"St. Lucy is not well known," Sister Margaret replied, "but our order has venerated her for more than fifteen hundred years, since her martyrdom in fifth-century Ireland when she was known by her Irish name, Luiseach. Her life is particularly inspiring for the young women who come here."

"She was raped, wasn't she?" Mimi asked.

"Raped or seduced, history doesn't distinguish, but really, don't they amount to nearly the same thing? Her seducer was a pagan chieftain. How could the poor girl defend herself against a man of such power? Many of the young women who come here are seduced by powerful men, or at least by men who enjoy exerting power over those weaker than them."

"I suppose," I said, cringing at another twinge in my belly, "that if a saint fell victim to such seduction, there is forgiveness for a mere girl who does the same."

"Exactly," Sister Margaret said, studying me closely. "That is the message I bring to my girls. The directors are not always happy with my ways. They would have me punish them for their transgressions, to make their lives here harder, but I know too well that they have enough hardness and trials to come."

"You mean childbirth?" Mimi asked. "I read in your saint's story that poor Lucy gives birth on a cliff in the middle of a thunderstorm and that she gripped a boulder so hard that she left her finger marks in it. We'll paint that if you like, but don't you think it'll scare the girls?"

It had scared me. My hand was still over my stomach where I felt now what had been causing me those twinges. The baby inside me was moving.

"That is not my intention. The important thing is to remember that Lucy survived and gave birth to a healthy baby girl. And like these girls here"—Sister Margaret waved her hand toward the roomful of young women— "she couldn't keep her child with her. When she realized that the pagan chieftain's men were upon her, she entrusted the child to the river and to God. She prayed that the river would carry her child to safety, and God answered her prayers. The child was borne downriver to a convent sacred to St. Brigit and was raised there by the nuns, where she became a great leader herself. Years later she found her way to the castle where Lucy had been taken by her seducer and heard her own mother's confession, at which point she recognized her as her mother. The two professed themselves Christians to the court and were sentenced to death by the chieftain. They were burned at the stake together, but as the smoke rose from the pyre the mother and daughter were seen borne aloft to heaven on a cloud. My hope is that the girls who come to us will take heart from St. Lucy's story."

She said those last words not to Mimi, but directly to me. Her eyes were on my belly, and suddenly I felt sure that she could see past cloth and flesh straight through to the baby inside.

After dinner, one of the younger nuns escorted us silently to our room—a plain whitewashed cell with two narrow cots. The only other furniture in the room was a pine dresser and two straight-backed chairs. The sheets on the two cots were worn thin with washing but smelt like lavender. Below a plaster of Paris roundel depicting St. Lucy and her daughter surrounded by a puffy cloud with their eyes lifted to heaven, a single window faced south, overlooking the gardens that separated the convent from the barn, the girls' dormitory, and the orphanage. Beyond the dormitory the river valley spread out below, the East Branch of the Delaware glinting in the distance. I wondered if the girls looked at it and thought of St. Lucy entrusting her baby to the River Clare. There was a creek that flowed past the convent and although I couldn't see it from our room, I could hear it—a murmuring gurgle like voices quarreling.

"A nun's cell," Mimi said when the mute nun left us.

"Would you rather stay with the unwed mothers? Or the orphans?" I asked.

Mimi snorted and lit a cigarette. "I don't suppose it matters. It's not like we're going to be entertaining any male visitors out here in the back of beyond." She waved her cigarette toward the long vista of hills and valley. The smoke wafted up to the image of St. Lucy, wreathing her like an extra layer of cloud.

"We're probably not allowed to smoke," I said. "You'd better put that out the window."

"Maybe we'll get kicked out," she said, but she opened the window an inch anyway. "I'm sorry I got you into this."

"I don't mind," I told her. "Actually, I kind of like it here."

Mimi thought I was joking, but I wasn't. I did like it at St. Lucy's—or St. Lu's, as the girls, like Johnnie, called it. I woke up early the next morning to the sound of cows lowing to be milked and thought for a moment that I was home in the childhood room I had once shared with my sisters. Only the lingering smell of Mimi's cigarettes let me know that I wasn't.

I threw on my coat over my nightgown, pulled on the fur-lined boots that Vera had given me as a going-away present, and stole outside. A low fog lay on the ground like thick cream floating on top of a milking jug. Walking through it, I felt weightless, as if borne aloft by the same cloud that rescued St. Lucy. The old gray barn leaning into the morning sun might have been built of planks from my dreams—but whether from the dairy barn of my childhood or the abandoned barn where I'd met Nash these last few months, I couldn't have said. They both seemed equally distant and unreal to me.

When I went inside, though, the sharp smell of hay, manure, and the grassy breath of cows startled me into the present. Two girls were already up, whispering and giggling over the steady hiss of squirting milk. They turned to me when I opened the door, their faces two pale half-moons against the dark flanks of the cows they milked. I saw their eyes skip right from my face to my belly. I hadn't closed my coat, and my nightgown—one of the sheer white lawn gowns Vera had made to order in England—was nearly transparent. I could have said that I was one of the artists come to paint the murals, but I didn't. I asked where the pails were kept. One of the girls—Nancy, I later learned—got up to show me. She held one hand to the small of her back when she walked. She was so small and daintily made— like a pixie in a fairy tale—that the weight of her round belly threw her off balance.

"Have you done this before?" she asked in an Irish lilt, pointing to a row of pails and stools.

I assured her that I had, setting my stool by the cow next in line to Nancy's. I rested my head against the cow's soft, warm flank and slid my hands down to her swollen udder. The barn was quiet. The girls were waiting to see if

I had told the truth. They must be used to people lying, I thought, and maybe I had been. **Did** I still know how to do this? The girl I'd been seemed like someone else entirely. Maybe I had dreamed her up the way I dreamed up my stories, the way I dreamed myself out of my childhood home and to New York City, and the way I dreamed up Vera Beecher.

I closed my eyes and listened to the cow's heart beating against my cheek. I imagined that the two girls were my sisters. They were my sisters in a way, weren't they? Right now, this was where I belonged.

The cow heaved a great grassy sigh as my fingers coaxed the milk down from her udders and I let go of my breath as well. The other girl—Jean, I soon found out—laughed and said that sound always reminded her of the sound her aunt made when she put her feet to soak after a long day's work. Nancy and I laughed, too, and we milked until our pails were full and the cows' udders were loose and empty. By the time I stood up, one hand against the small of my own back and one steadying myself against my cow, I felt as if I'd come home.

From that day on I spent my mornings sitting on a stool milking the cows and the rest of the day sitting on a stool sketching in the

background of the mural. At meals I sat with
the girls instead of at the nuns' table. Mimi
gave me a curious look when she saw where I
sat—I had been able, by always wearing a voluminous smock over my dress, to hide my
pregnancy from her—but joined me, relieved,
I think, to be free of Sister Margaret's company. She quickly warmed to the girls, who
came, almost to a one, from the city, many
from parts of Brooklyn—Bay Ridge, Sunset
Park, Coney Island, Brighton Beach—not far
from where Mimi had grown up. Mimi cheer-
fully traded street names, candy stores, parks,
and schools with the girls, although most of
them had gone to Catholic schools.

"A lot of good it did them," Mimi said to
me one day as we worked on the mural. She
had sketched in a rough cartoon of the first
four stages of St. Lucy's life we'd chosen to represent: her seduction by the pagan chieftain,
her flight from his men during which she was
hidden by a cloud, her childbirth during a
storm, and the moment when she entrusted
her newborn baby to the River Clare. The final
scene, when she is reunited with her long-lost
daughter and they are both carried to heaven
on a cloud, was to be painted on the ceiling. It
would require scaffolding, so we were leaving
that for last. I was sketching the face of
St. Lucy as she was cornered by the chieftain,

but I was having a hard time getting her expression right.

"You think their church should have
trained them better to resist advances?" I
asked. I had decided to set Lucy's seduction in
a barn—not for autobiographical reasons, but
because it was difficult to imagine what other
kind of architecture might have existed in
fifth-century Ireland. I'd have her milking a
cow when the chieftain surprised her. I'd given
her Nancy's dark little face, which looked ancient and mysterious enough to have belonged
to a pagan Celt, as I remembered it from that
first morning I came into the barn and found
her milking. The cow was looking warily at the
chieftain. I had no trouble catching the cow's
expression, but Lucy looked struck dumb in
her surprise and I didn't want her to look stu-
pider than the cow.

"Well, yes, that would be good for a start.
All this blind obedience they're taught—to take
whatever their priests tell them on faith—"

"Isn't faith what all religion is about? Aren't
you taught that in your synagogue?"

"Faith in God, yes, but not blind faith in
His representatives on earth. No, we Jews are
taught to question and argue."

"So you think a Jewish girl would argue her
way out of seduction?"

Mimi sighed. She was working on the background of the flight scene; we'd decided I was better at faces while she understood perspective better. "I know my mother taught me not to put myself in situations where a man could have the advantage over me. She taught me what men expected and how to evade their attempts to have their own way. . . ." Her voice trailed off. She was drawing the bank of the river along which Lucy ran. She'd been going out sketching the last few mornings so that she might model the River Clare on the creek that flowed past the convent. She'd managed to capture the feel of the East Branch valley even in her rough sketches.

"But?" I prompted.

"She never taught me what to do if I was the one . . . I mean if I felt . . ."

"You mean, if you wanted to be with the man?" It struck me that for all Mimi's worldliness she was still a virgin.

"Yes," she answered, blushing.

"Is it the driver?" I asked.

"John," she said, managing to inject warmth into the single syllable.

"I see."

"No, you don't." She laughed. "How can you? You're in love with Vera Beecher. At least you don't have to worry about Vera getting you with—" She turned toward me as she spoke and stopped midsentence, her eyes on my belly. I had wondered why she was the only one who didn't see it. The girls had known immediately I was one of them, and I was sure Sister Margaret also knew. But Mimi, who shared a room with me, who saw me undress every night, had remained blind to my pregnancy. Perhaps it was because we only see what we expect to see and she didn't expect to see a "lover of women" pregnant.

I dropped the hand that held my pencil to my swollen stomach and met her look.

"Oh, Lily!" She dropped down to the floor next to my feet. "How? Who?"

"Does it really matter—" I began, but I could already see the calculations being performed in her head.

"It's Virgil Nash's, isn't it? I've seen the way he looks at you, only—"

"Only you thought I'd be strong enough to resist him? Well, I wasn't. I'm no stronger than these girls here."

"But what about Vera? Does she know?"

"No, and she never can. Please, you have to promise me."

"You mean you plan to give the child away?"

I heard the disbelief in her voice—and the disapproval. To her credit, it was only then that she judged me. She was surprised—

shocked, even—that I'd been with Nash, but she hadn't judged me for that. But the idea of giving away the child was clearly repugnant to her.

"Sister Margaret says that all the babies born here are adopted into good families."

"Not all. Johnnie says some come back. Sometimes the baby doesn't 'meet with the family's expectations.' God only knows what they expect. Maybe a baby who sleeps through the night, craps flowers, and recites its ABC's at nine months."

"What happens to the children who are sent back?" I asked.

"Well, the nuns try to find other homes for them, but the older they get, the harder it is. Everyone wants a baby, not a cranky toddler or a fractious six-year-old. The ones who don't get adopted stay here until they're old enough to work, then the nuns try to place them on local farms where they're worked near to death."

"How do you know that?"

"Johnnie told me, and he should know be-cause he's one of them. He was born here. His first family sent him back because they said he didn't smile enough. They thought there was something wrong with him. The second family sent him back because he smiled too much and laughed in church. He ran off from the third when his adoptive brother tried to rape him—"

"Yes, Mimi, I understand. But most of them end up in good homes. I'll just have to have faith that mine will. I have no other choice. I can't keep it. Vera would never speak to me again if she knew I'd betrayed her, and then I'd be out on the streets. How could I support myself and a baby, too?"

Face softening, Mimi took my hand. She was still kneeling on the floor in front of me and I realized what an odd picture we'd make to anyone who came in right then. I looked toward the doors at the end of the chapel, but we were alone. Sister Margaret had promised that "the girls," as she called them, wouldn't get in our way.

"I could help you," Mimi said. "I could get you a job at the magazine and find someone to watch the baby during the day. We could share an apartment in the Village, or in Brooklyn near my family. It's cheaper out there, and the air's better for a baby. My mother would help take care of the baby—"

"And when would either of us find time to take classes or make our own art?"

She sat back on her heels and stared at me. "You really think that all this"—she waved her arms at the mural we were working on —"is more important than flesh and blood?"

I looked at the mural. The figures and the background were only outlines waiting to be filled in. They looked like ghosts flitting through an otherworldly landscape, shades wandering through Hell. Perhaps Mimi was right. But then my eye fell on the portrait of Saint Lucy I was working on. I'd been trying all morning to get her expression just right, to capture the moment she realizes she's been trapped by the chieftain, that there's no escape. I'd caught the look of surprise in her eyes, but I needed something else. Then I saw what to do. When the chieftain comes in he startles the cow and she kicks over the pail. Lucy is reaching for it as she looks up and sees the chieftain—and her fate. Her hand is arrested above the pail; the milk has already spilled.

I leaned forward and quickly sketched in the new lines over the old. This time I somehow managed to capture in her eyes fear and surprise, but also resignation. She sees her fate, the good and the bad, and she knows she's powerless to change it.

When I'd gotten it just right, I turned to answer Mimi, but she'd already gotten to her feet and gone back to filling in the landscape. I'd given her my answer.

Once Mimi knew my secret, I went to see Sister Margaret. I'd never been in her office before, and I was surprised to find it rather grand, with a big mahogany desk in front of an arched window. When I entered, she was standing in front of the window, which afforded a beautiful view of the valley. She dragged her eyes away from the view when she heard me come in and instantly her sharp blue eyes—the same color as the distant mountains—focused on my belly. She'd already guessed, of course. She held out her hands, inviting me to come closer, and when I reached her she surprised me by laying her hands over my belly.

"The baby will come by Christmas, will it not?" she asked.

"A bit later," I said, counting back. "January, I think."

Sister Margaret shook her head. "I think it will be by Christmas, dear. And are you sure you don't want to keep it?"

"I'm not married, Sister." I thought this was an easier answer than explaining about Vera and the demands of the artistic life. She didn't say anything for a minute and then she nodded and turned away from me, letting her hands fall to her side.

"As you think best. We're very careful about the families the babies go to." I thought about Johnnie's experiences but didn't say anything. "Are you able to continue working on the mural?"

"Oh yes," I assured her. "We've worked out that Mimi will do the upper parts that require standing on a ladder and I'll do the lower parts so I can sit. Then, when the scaffolding for the ceiling is built, I'll be able to work lying down. Like Michelangelo. A pregnant Michelangelo." I regretted my stupid joke the minute it was out of my mouth, but Sister Margaret didn't seem offended. She gestured toward the valley below us, to where the East Branch flowed toward the Delaware River.

"God moves in a mysterious way," she said. "Just as He sends the little streams to meet the great ones and sends them all to the ocean, I'm sure there's a reason He sent you here to paint Saint Lucy and that your kinship with her will guide you. I'm sure you will do a beautiful job."

Perhaps it was Sister Margaret's faith in me that inspired the work I did that fall. Or perhaps I really did have some special feeling of kinship with this fifth-century Irish girl. I only know that when I painted her face I felt transported. Hours would pass and I'd wake as though from a long sleep to find myself sitting in front of a completed section of the mural. Mimi said it was the best work I'd ever done. "I suppose it's because of you two sharing the same circumstances and all."

I thought Mimi would get over her anger toward me, but she remained as cold as the mountain stream that flowed past the convent. Toward the end of October, I asked Sister Margaret if I could stay in the dorm with the other girls. I didn't give a reason and she didn't ask for one. She assigned me the bed next to Nancy's. It was the last in the row and next to a window overlooking the stream that ran into the valley. I heard the sound of water when I went to sleep—a comforting sound and something to listen to when someone cried at night.

It was mostly the new girls who cried, the ones who'd just arrived. "They miss their mothers," Nancy told me.

I was shocked to see how young some of them were. One girl, Tilly (the girls weren't supposed to tell their last names), was only fourteen. She was in service in a big house on Fifth Avenue in New York City. She almost gave away the name of the family before Jean stopped her with a hiss and a slap.

"Don't go shaming your employer's household," she said, and then added in a lower whisper: "It wasn't the master of the house who got you—" She pointed toward Tilly's belly.

"Oh no," Tilly said, her eyes wide with shock at the idea. "It were the grocery delivery boy, Tom. He said I wouldn't have a baby if I said three Hail Marys while we did it."

Jean clucked her tongue. "And you believed him?"

"Aye, only I never did get to say them three Hail Marys. He was done before I'd gotten through the second."

Jean clamped a hand over her mouth and fell back on her bed laughing. Nancy tried to keep a straight face, but when she caught my eye we both started giggling. Even Tilly joined in, holding her small round belly as if to shield the baby inside from the joke that had been made at its father's expense. I felt bad about laughing at poor Tilly—I hadn't even needed a lie to convince me to give in to Virgil Nash, just a little moonlight—but I noticed that she didn't cry that night. She'd been accepted into the sisterhood of fallen women, as Jean referred to us. It happened with each new girl. Once she felt a part of the group she stopped crying. Whenever a new girl showed up, the girls stayed up later that night, gossiping and telling stories to distract the newcomer from the strangeness of the place. Soon I was the one telling the stories. I told the fairy tales I'd made up for my sisters and new stories I made up as I went along.

One night, I started a story with "There once was a girl who liked to pretend she was lost until the day she really lost her way." It was the beginning of the story I had told Vera

the first night she came to me, but the story
grew into something else this time. The girl
found a witch in the forest who showed her
how to send a likeness of herself back to her
family. The girls thought the witch sounded
like Sister Margaret and I let them think it was
her. When I told the part about the girl being
too lazy to wash the root in running water, a
few of them sighed. Who of us hadn't made
mistakes? And look where it had gotten us:
far from our homes and loved ones. I knew
then that I'd tied a knot into the story. How
would the girl in the story get home? That's
what they were waiting to hear. They sat three
to a bed, their knees drawn up to their chins
so that their white flannel nightgowns made
little tents under their crossed arms. In the
moonlight, they looked like caterpillars folded
inside their cocoons. Outside I could hear the
creek flowing past the dormitory, swollen
from a week of heavy rain. I felt bad then, but
I couldn't go back. And wasn't that what all of
us feared? That we could never go back? We
weren't the same girls who'd left our homes.
I'd seen that when I stood at the edge of my
parents' farm and knew I couldn't return.
Would I feel that when I went back to Vera
after this?

I tried to give them a different kind of ending. One that acknowledged how changed we

would be but that suggested possibilities for the future. And the child we would leave behind? She—or he—would find its own home, accepted into some facsimile of the families we had left.

When I came to the end of the story, the dormitory was silent. I couldn't see their faces because the moon no longer shone through the window. Nor could I hear the creek. Had my story put the whole world to sleep? But when I looked out the window, I understood. It was snowing. The girls unfolded their legs under their nightgowns like caterpillars breaking out of their cocoons and flitted, mothlike, to the windows where we watched the snow fill up the stream bed, muffling its voice, and then fill the whole valley, shutting us off from the world outside. We stood there until our feet grew cold and then one by one the girls went back to their beds. As each one passed I felt their fingertips lightly graze against my arms and hands. Nancy kissed my cheek and whispered, "Thank you."

I fell into a deep sleep but was woken sometime before dawn by voices. Standing by Tilly's bed were Sister Margaret and another nun holding a lantern. Someone was crying. I thought it was Tilly, but when I stood up and got close enough to see her face I saw she had gone past crying. Her face was contorted into a wrinkled ball, like an apple that's dried up in the sun. It was the young nun crying as she and Sister Margaret tried to lift Tilly out of bed. When Sister Margaret saw me there standing frozen on my feet, she clucked her tongue and pointed to a dark bloody knot in the sheets.

"As long as you're up, you can be of use and clean that up. Bring the sheets to the kitchen and tell Sister Ursula to burn them. Can you do that?"

I nodded then and quickly bundled the sheets in a ball, trying not to look at what lay inside. But I'd already seen the twisted length of red cord, like a rope dipped in carmine. Like the changeling root in my story. I carried the bundle to the kitchen and handed it over to Sister Ursula, a fat, good-natured nun from Ireland who gave the girls extra servings of pudding. When I told her what Sister Margaret had ordered, she asked me whose sheets they were.

"Tilly, the new girl," I said.

Sister Ursula clucked her tongue and laid the bundle on the fire. "Poor thing. Perhaps it will be better for her this way."

Then she seemed to recall whom she was talking to and crossed herself. She poured me a hot cup of tea from a kettle on the stove, but the smell of the tea mixed with the burning

sheets curdled my stomach. I ran outside and
vomited into the new-fallen snow. I couldn't
bear to go back into the kitchen, so I went to
the barn. It was early to milk, but the cows
didn't mind. I just wanted to lay my head
against their sides and breathe in the grass and
manure smell of them until the smell of blood
was gone. I milked all six cows. Jean and
Nancy were surprised when they found me,
but they said nothing.

I finished the face of St. Lucy giving birth
in a storm that day. The story goes that she left
her finger marks on a rock she clutched. She
still had Nancy's features, but I gave her the
expression I'd seen on Tilly's face.

"You'll scare the girls," Mimi told me when
she saw the painting.

"It's better than lying to them," I answered.

"I heard about the girl who miscarried,"
Mimi said then. I could tell she was trying to
make up for not talking to me all these weeks.
"Poor thing."

"At least she won't have to live with the
pain of not knowing what happened to her
child," I said.

Mimi put down her brush and knelt by my
side. "I'm sorry I said those things to you, Lily.
We all make mistakes. I know you're only
doing what you think is best. And after all,
some poor woman who can't have a child will

be grateful. Look at Gertrude Sheldon. She's been trying to have a baby for years."

"Oh please, don't wish that fate on my baby. Imagine what kind of mother Gertrude would make!"

"You're right," Mimi said, shaking her head, "but don't worry. I had a letter from Gertrude last week in which she hints that the waters of Baden-Baden have done the trick and she's finally pregnant."

"Well, good for her," I said. "Did she say anything about Vera?"

"Yes, she said that Vera was disgusted with Baden-Baden and all talk of babies and that she had gone to England to study pottery with Clarice Cliff. Haven't you had a letter?"

"We agreed not to write. So as to give ourselves the freedom of mind as well as geography."

"That sounds like something Vera would say." Mimi squeezed my hand and got to her feet. "From what Gertrude says, I suppose you were right. Vera wouldn't do very well with a baby. I only hope she's worth it."

I pointed to the mural. "This is worth it. This is what I'm good at, Mimi. This and telling stories. Not babies. The child deserves a mother who really wants it."

I could see tears standing in her eyes. She leaned down and gave me an awkward embrace. I hugged her to me tightly and patted her back, as if I were comforting her. I didn't tell her that when I saw that twisted red thing that came out of Tilly I'd thought: that's what's inside me. A changeling created out of dreams and pulp. A monster bred by a monstrous mother who wanted nothing more than to be rid of her own child and go back home.

When my baby was born, though, it wasn't a monster at all. She wore a splash of blood on the side of her head like a dancer would wear a rose tucked behind her ear, but otherwise she was pink and white all over. Not a gnarled root, but a plump, perfect baby. She took my breath away.

When they came to take her, I asked if I could hold her awhile. I saw the nuns exchange a look, but Sister Margaret came and said they should let me.

That night, Mimi came to the infirmary and asked if I was sure. She looked as if she was afraid I'd be angry with her for asking again, so I took her hand so she would know I wasn't. I drew her near so she could see the baby. "Look how beautiful she is," I said. "Feel how strong her grip is." I slid my hand out from under the baby's so that her fingers clasped Mimi's instead of mine. "They cling like ivy. That's what I've asked Sister Margaret to call her. Oh, I know she'll have a different name when she's adopted, but I don't want her to be without a name while she waits. And for a last name they'll name her after St. Lucy's daughter, who was carried safely away by a river. Ivy St. Clare, that's the name I'll remember her by."

CHAPTER 21

I stare for a long time at the name Lily gave her baby. When I finally look up, I see that the sky is lightening outside my window. I've stayed up all night reading and I've only gotten through half of Lily's journal. I turn to the next page and read:

When I returned to Arcadia, I found that Vera had built for us a little cottage, which she called

Fleur-de-Lis in my honor. "I name this house
for you," she said, standing on the threshold
holding a single white lily like a baton. "My
Lily of the valley, my pure Lily, my Lily among
the thorns." Then she waved me inside with
the lily and showed me the cottage, pointing
out each and every detail. She'd designed it
herself to be neat and trim as a ship's cabin and
she had it fitted out with all manner of hidden
cubbies and secret pigeonholes in which she
hid surprises for me to find.

Hidden cubbies and secret pigeonholes like the one
behind the panel on the fireplace where I'd found
the journal. If Vera had designed it, then why hadn't
she found the journal there? Or had she found it and
then put it back? But if she **had** found it, why had
Ivy thought it was lost?

All the unanswered questions make me restless. I
get up, still clutching the journal in my hands, and
pad barefoot into the hall. I come to rest in the
doorway of Sally's empty room, feeling a pang at her
absence but also a reminder of the last months of my
pregnancy. We'd moved out to the house in Great
Neck (Jude's parents, thrilled that he'd given up art
for Wall Street, had loaned us the money for a down
payment), but we hadn't had time to buy furniture
yet. I would wander through the empty rooms trying to imagine what our lives were going to be like
there. The only room we'd really furnished was the

nursery. I'd stand on the threshold, my hand resting on my swollen stomach, and try to picture the child inside growing up in this pretty pink-and-white room. There was something about the stillness of the house in the middle of the night that seemed timeless, and yet also full of **all time,** as if the empty, moonlit rooms held our future as well as our past.

How often, I wonder now, had Lily wandered through this house at night wondering what had become of the child she gave up? She'd given the baby a name so that she **could** think of her. Did she know the child still carried that name? Did she know the baby had stayed at the orphanage? For she must have, since she kept that name. Lily must have found out at some point and brought Ivy here.

I recall from my research that Ivy St. Clare came to Arcadia in 1945 when she was sixteen years old as part of a new scholarship program. I'd been sure that the program was initiated by Lily, but on my first day here Ivy had insisted that it was Vera who had chosen her, **not** Lily. Now I'm surer than ever that it **was** Lily. She must have found out that her child was still living at St. Lucy's and contrived the scholarship program as a way to get Ivy to Arcadia without arousing Vera's suspicions. But then she let Ivy believe it was Vera who had chosen her. Why? And why hadn't she ever told Ivy that she was her mother?

The answers might well be in the book I'm holding in my hand, but I can't finish reading it now. It's
already past dawn. I hear mourning doves cooing
outside Sally's open window. I turn and walk down
the stairs, cradling the book in my arms as if it is a
child I'm trying to protect. Ivy must have known that
there was something in Lily's journal of import to her.
She accused Dora and Ada of stealing the journal
after Lily's death. When she saw my still life she focused on the green book. Did she recognize it as Lily's
long-lost journal? Did she believe me when I had told
her the book in my still life was one of my own? If she
didn't, she would come looking for it—and I didn't
want her to find it until I finished reading.

I stand in front of the fireplace looking at the
central panel. Vera must have known where to look
once she got the note from Lily . . . unless Vera
never got the note. Ivy said she had given Vera the
note, but what if she hadn't? What if she'd only told
Vera that Lily had run off and kept the note with its
endearments and pledge of eternal love? If Vera
hadn't read it, then she wouldn't have known where
to look for the journal. And if Ivy had read the
note . . .

I open the book and reread the note. **You are my
heart**, I read. **I have left my story for you in the
heart and hearth of our lives together.** I had immediately assumed that she meant the hearth of the
cottage—as Vera would, I imagine, since she knew
about the secret panel—but there was someplace

else I'd read that phrase. I flip through the journal and find it in Lily's description of the early days of the colony. **Vera said she hoped the pottery kiln would become a place for the artists to gather in the evening—the heart and hearth of the community.**

If Ivy had heard the kiln referred to that way she may have thought Lily was leaving her journal with Dora and Ada. And **that** was why Ivy went to them looking for it. She didn't know about the secret panel in the hearth.

One thing's for sure. If Ivy hadn't found the journal here over sixty years ago, she wasn't going to find it here now. I open the panel and slide the journal back into its hiding place and then close the panel, brushing my fingers over the carving of the tiny baby nestled in the roots. No wonder Lily put the journal here—she'd hidden the secret of her lost child in the roots that hid the changeling baby.

I'm surprised to see how excited my students are about the Dead Project, as they're **all** calling it now. Thanks to the wonders of the Internet many have already gotten their parents to send digital copies of old photographs. They seem eager to share their pictures, so I shelve the discussion of Bettelheim for another day and ask them to hold up their photos and tell the stories behind them.

Many of the pictures are of families on vacations

or graduation shots or wedding portraits. Their stories are fairly straightforward. But some quickly become more complicated.

"This is my mother's graduation picture from
Vassar." Hannah holds up a picture of a dark-haired
girl with her own Botticelli features standing with
two other girls in dark robes on a lawn beneath a
bright red maple tree.

"Wow, she's really beautiful," Tori Pratt says.
"But you know," she adds, "that's not a graduation
picture. My mom went to Vassar and she has a picture of herself in her robe, but without that white
collar thingy they wear, and she says that's how you
can tell it's convocation, not graduation. It's something students do at the beginning of their senior
year. And look, the leaves on this tree are red. This
picture was taken in the fall, not spring when they
hold graduation."

"Huh," Hannah says looking closer at the picture
and furrowing her brows. "I'm pretty sure she said it
was her graduation picture."

"Maybe she mixed them up," I suggest.

"Maybe," Hannah echoes, her brow still fur-
rowed. "I'll have to ask."

Clyde, too, presents a story that seems to shift as
he tells it. The picture he's chosen is one of his
grandfather as a young man in an army uniform.
He's clean-shaven, his hair cropped short. He looks
so young it's hard to believe anyone would send him
off to war.

"He signed up right after Pearl Harbor," Clyde says. "My grandma says everybody did. And she always tells how she went out and got him this pocket watch so he'd take it with him and not forget her. But you know, last night I was thinking about that story and I looked at the date on my grandfather's watch. It says, 'To Harold from Sarah, June 3, 1942.' But Pearl Harbor happened on December 7, 1941. So what was he doing for those six months?"

"Can you ask them?" Hannah asks.

Clyde shakes his head. "They're both dead. I e-mailed my mother last night, but she said she had no idea. She said Poppa had always told that story about joining up right after Pearl Harbor and Grandma had always told the story about giving him the watch, but no one had ever looked at the two pieces to see that they didn't match."

"Because those stories were part of your family's folklore," I say. "You don't question the details. They take on the aura of legend. Although the story may change with each telling, certain phrases are always repeated. Like 'Back in my day, we had to walk to school—"

"Or 'When I was your age,' " Hannah interrupts, " 'we couldn't look things up on the Internet, we had to go the library.' "

"And we had to walk to it through five feet of snow," Clyde adds.

"Yeah," Tori Pratt chimes in, "my grandmother is

always going on about how little they had in the Depression compared to all the stuff we have now. And
then she always says, 'We didn't have much, but we
had each other.' " Tori's voice goes up an octave and
quavers to imitate her grandmother. She rolls her
eyes but smiles, and I find myself returning her
smile, glad to see Tori's world-weary veneer crack
a bit.

"**My** grandmother," I say, "always started her stories with 'Back in my day a woman was supposed to
choose between marriage and work.' She always said
it was good my mother had a stable job, like teaching. Grandma had worked at a magazine before
she'd met my grandfather, but she gave it up when
she got married. She'd say . . ." I close my eyes to recall the exact words. Instantly I'm seated at the
green-and-white Porceliron table in my grandmother's Brooklyn Heights kitchen. I'm drawing in
one of the blank sketchbooks my grandmother
seemed to have in endless supply. " 'When I had
your mother I gave up my job even though it was
the Depression and Jack and I had precious little to
live on.' "

I open my eyes and find that my audience has
grown. Ivy St. Clare has come into the doorway and
is listening to my story.

"But then as I got older and I was more interested in art, she'd say: 'Your grandfather kept his job
during the Depression because he was a bookkeeper.
People always need bookkeepers, but art they can do

without. The magazines laid off the illustrators and advertising staff. You can't eat art,' she'd always end by saying."

The class laughs at the last line and I realize I'd slipped into my grandmother Miriam's Brooklynese. "I grew up with both these stories, endlessly repeated, but never once did I ask my grandmother, 'Which was it? Did you give up your job in advertising to raise a family or did you lose your job in the Depression?' And I never wondered why, if she thought being an artist was such a bad career move, she gave me sketchpads and crayons on every birthday."

"Weird," Chloe says.

"Can you ask her now?" Hannah asks.

"She died when I was seventeen. And that was another strange thing. In her will she left me a small bequest to go to art school. She was specific that it be art school. My mother was ticked off. At first I thought it was because she'd left the money to me, but I overheard her telling some of her teacher friends when they paid a shivah call that what really irked her was that my grandmother and grandfather had refused to let her go to art school even when she got a scholarship."

"Damn," Clyde says, "no wonder she was pissed."

"So did you go to art school?"

"Yes," I say, "I started at Pratt. . . ." I falter, recalling only now where this story ends. "But I dropped out my junior year." I don't add that I quit because I got pregnant with Sally.

"It's like a family curse," Chloe says. "Three generations of frustrated women artists."

I try to laugh off the comment—it sounds so melodramatic!—but then I see the disapproving expression on Ivy St. Clare's face and think of what I learned about her origins last night. If she knew that her mother abandoned her in an orphanage so that she could pursue an artistic life, what might she have to say about family curses?

"Well," I say, "maybe that's why I came to Arcadia. To break the family curse."

"Do you think it's wise to use your own personal history in the classroom?" Dean St. Clare asks me when my students have left.

"I'm asking them to use their personal history. I think it's only fair that I'm willing to model the assignment by using mine."

"Did you get your ideas about teaching from your mother? I hadn't realized she was a teacher."

"She taught third grade for more than thirty-five years. She was a master of the shoebox diorama and the Palmer Method of penmanship."

"Really?" the Dean asks. "The Palmer Method? That's what the nuns taught us. I would think that it would have been out of fashion by the time your mother was around."

"She was old-fashioned," I say, not wanting to

get into the fact that my mother had me so late in life. Instead I try to turn the focus on her. "You were taught by nuns? At a Catholic school?"

"At a Catholic orphanage, to be precise. That's where I was when Vera Beecher rescued me by giving me the scholarship to come here." She touches the pin she always wears. "It's a saint's medal," she says, noticing me staring at it. "St. Lucy and her daughter, St. Clare, rising to heaven on a cloud. The nuns gave it to me when I left. Vera said it ought to reflect who I had become, not just where I came from, so she learned metalworking so she could set it in a wreath of ivy for me."

"You see, that's what I was trying to get across to the class today. We all carry myths from our family history—"

"As I just told you, I don't have a family history. I was raised in an orphanage."

"But of course you do. Vera Beecher and Lily Eberhardt were your family. You've told me twice now that Vera Beecher 'rescued' you. That's your story—"

"Are you saying I made it up?" Ivy St. Clare's small wrinkled face appears even more pinched than usual. Her hands are coiled into tight fists. Perhaps I've gone too far, but there's no way out now but to go farther.

"No, of course not. What I'm saying is that you've accepted a version of your story because it's what you've always believed to be true: that Vera

Beecher chose you for that scholarship. But mightn't it have been Lily who actually chose you?"

"Lily Eberhardt told me herself that Vera chose me," Ivy says, shaking her head.

"From what I know about Lily—from what I'm learning about her through Vera's diaries and their letters," I add quickly so she doesn't ask me again about Lily's journal, "she gave Vera credit for everything she did. She idolized Vera."

"You're wrong," Ivy says. "It was Vera who idolized Lily. So much so that it crushed her when Lily ran away. I saw Vera on the night that Lily left to meet Virgil Nash. She was mad with grief. She ran after her in a blizzard, wearing nothing but a robe and slippers—" Ivy chokes back her next words in a gargled rasp, as if her anger was strangling her.

"Vera followed Lily out into the storm?" I ask. "I thought you said that you were at the cottage all night with her and that Vera didn't realize that Lily had died in the clove until weeks later."

"I didn't say she followed her all the way to the clove. I caught up to her and made her come back to the cottage. I stayed with her for the rest of that night. We sat up by the fire. Vera couldn't sleep. She kept hoping that Lily would return. At dawn, when she realized that she wasn't coming back, she took up the fire poker and smashed the tiles above the fireplace. She was never the same after that. Lily had crushed her. So don't ask me to believe that **Lily** was the one who saved me from the orphanage. I'd rather have rotted in St. Lucy's than think I owe my salvation to that woman."

She waits a moment, as if daring me to argue, and then turns on her heel and leaves. I watch her go, speechless, wondering how much worse Ivy St. Clare would feel if she knew that the woman who destroyed her idol was her own mother.

CHAPTER 22

I have to run to make my seminar with the Merling twins. It's
all I can do to concentrate on
the day's reading—Angela Carter's
twentieth-century version of Cinderella, "Ashputtle." Carter is one
of my favorite authors, and this is
one of my favorite stories, but the
gruesome details seem especially
troubling to me today. It's a twist
on the classic absent mother story
in which the orphaned heroine re-

ceives supernatural help from her dead mother in the form of animal helpers, magic talismans, and fairy godmothers. In Carter's version, though, the mother's ghost enters the body of a bird that mutilates itself so that her daughter will have a dress to wear to the ball, and, in the final scene, the dead mother rescues her daughter from the ash-pit only to invite her to step into her coffin.

"I stepped into **my** mother's coffin when I was your age," the mother says to Ashputtle.

"I take that to mean that we're doomed to repeat our mothers' mistakes," Peter Merling says. "The mother who has died in childbirth condemns her own child to marriage and childbirth and, thus, death."

"But why doesn't the mother come back and tell the daughter to flee—live some other life that doesn't lead to entrapment and death?" Rebecca asks, her tone unusually emotional. "All this bloody sacrifice for your child—what good is it if you're condemning your child to the same cycle of sex and death?"

I think of Lily Eberhardt's decision to leave her child with nuns so that she could pursue an independent life. Then I think of my own grandmother, who gave up her ambitions to be a mother and then wouldn't let her own daughter go to art school even though she'd been offered a scholarship. And when she tried to make some sort of reparation— leaving me the money to go to art school—I ended up leaving to have a baby. **It's like a family curse,** Chloe had said. It seems to me right now that it's the curse of all mothers and daughters. We sacrifice to give them what we didn't have, but all we've done is to show them that's **all** a woman can do: sacrifice herself or sacrifice her child. It all leads to the same place.

But I can hardly say that to Rebecca and Peter Merling. Instead I let them out early and go looking for Shelley. She's in her studio arranging objects on a table.

"You've inspired me," she says. "I haven't done a still life in ages. I'm going to do my own Dead Project."

"I wish the students hadn't latched on to that name for it," I say, looking at the objects that Shelley has chosen to represent her ancestors. It's a peculiar assortment. She's chosen a copy of her grandmother's painting **Ancient Priestess Worshipping at the Feet of Artemis** and the parody of the painting that was in the Fakirs show. There are a number of references to the Art Students League and to the early days of the Arcadia Colony: a poster for the 1926 Annual League Costume Ball, a wreath of faded dried daisies that looks like the ones that Gertrude, Mimi, and Lily wore in the May Day picture I included in my own still life, a vase that has the Dorada emblem stamped on its side, and a faded scarf embroidered with gold fleur-de-lis. Shelley's tableau is clearly meant to evoke the artistic legacy of her grandmother, but I'm surprised that several of the objects she's chosen ridicule Gertrude. Then I recall how disdainful Shelley has been of her grand-mother's talent, how eager she was to distance her-self from Gertrude Sheldon's style **and** her history of mental illness. It strikes me that the Sheldon family relationship to art is even more cursed than my own.

"What's this?" I ask, picking up a small brass disk. "It looks like a saint's medal. Was your grand-mother Catholic?"

"She converted to Catholicism while traveling in Italy the year before my mother was born. It drove her parents wild! Which is why she did it, of course. She claimed that she only was able to conceive my mother after praying at a Catholic shrine in Siena."

I recall from Lily's journal that Mimi Green said Gertrude had written her from Europe saying she had gotten pregnant after taking the waters at Baden-Baden, but I don't say anything. I'm certainly not going to tell Shelley that I've got Lily's journal. But it does make me think of something. "Do you have anything your grandmother wrote about the early days of Arcadia?"

"I'll have to take a look. My grandfather Bennett burned most of her diaries and letters when she died. Her paintings and drawings, too."

"Really? That's awful." The idea of a piece of original artwork—a one-of-a-kind—destroyed has always struck me as particularly awful.

"Well, they really weren't any good. The only

things that survived were some floral still lifes and her datebooks—endless calendars full of visiting schedules, afternoon teas, charity galas, and dinner parties. I **did** find some papers once that she'd hidden in an old sewing box. I'll look through those and see if there's anything worthwhile. Is there anything particular that you're interested in?"

"I wondered if your grandmother was still in touch with Vera and Lily when Lily died in 1947, and if she wrote anything about it."

"I'll look," Shelley says again, turning back to the objects on the table which she begins to rearrange. "Through my mother's things, too."

"Your mother?"

"Fleur Sheldon. She was one of the first students here and she stayed at Arcadia over the Christmas holidays that year. So she would have been here when Lily died. I'll check my mother's diaries to see if she wrote about it. No one burned her things, no doubt because she led such a boring life no one thought there could possibly be anything scandalous in them."

On my way up to Beech Hall I spot Sally sitting with Chloe on the lawn beneath the copper beech. Although both girls have their sketchpads balanced on their knees, they aren't drawing. Their heads are bent together, Chloe's dark hair falling against Sally's deep auburn. It's a lovely scene, the deep purple of the copper beech and the chocolate and gold of the girls' hair all remind me of the palette of the Impressionist painter Édouard Vuillard. I'm tempted to stop and sketch—maybe I'll take up painting again next—when the scene is ruined completely and irrevocably. Sally looks up and I see that her face is blanched with pain. Unable to help myself, I hurry toward her.

"What's wrong?" I ask, scanning her body as if she were two and had just fallen on the playground. It's all I can do not to start patting her for broken bones.

"It's you!" Sally cries. "You told your whole class that you dropped out of art school because you got pregnant with me."

"I did not!" I sink to my knees to get closer to her and glance at Chloe. I remember how she had stared at me in class. I had been **about** to tell the class that I dropped out because I got pregnant. It is as if she had read my mind. She seems to now as well, smiling a small secret smile as the blood rushes to my face.

"Chloe's lying." I regret the words as soon as they're out of my mouth.

Chloe frowns. "I only told Sally that you dropped out of art school your junior year. We counted back and figured out it would have been about the time you got pregnant with Sally."

"**Was** that the reason?" Sally asks.

Her eyes are wide and shining, glassy with tears. "Honey," I say, reaching for her hand. "It was more complicated than that. You have to understand—"

She snatches her hand away and scrambles to her feet. "I understand perfectly. You're jealous I have the chance to do what you couldn't."

She's gone before I can say anything else, Chloe running after her, but really, what else can I say? As much as I love Sally, as much as any mother loves her daughter, isn't it the dirty truth at the bottom of every fairy tale that there's a little bit of the evil stepmother inside every mother?

I teach my next class in a fog, glad that Chloe's not in it. How could I have so baldly accused a student of lying? What if she goes to Dean St. Clare and reports the conversation? But worse than the thought of getting in trouble with the dean is the memory of the betrayal in Sally's eyes. I've always known that someday Sally would put together the dates of her conception and my leaving art school, but it couldn't have come at a worse time.

At the end of class I find I can't face the idea of going back to the cottage by myself. I'm afraid I'm turning into the evil witch who would live in such a place. So instead I climb the hill to the library, preferring to face the draconian Miss Bridewell rather than my own reflection in the mirror. When I ask her if she has all the newspaper accounts covering the death of Lily Eberhardt, she looks at me as if I've asked her to perform some impossible task like sorting out stacks of wheat and barley.

"We don't have them sorted as such," she says primly. "You'll have to do the legwork. It's all on microfilm and the microfilm is kept in the basement."

"Actually," a student aide with strawberry blond hair who's been ordering books on a cart beside Miss Bridewell's desk interrupts, "I pulled all those microfilms for a student who was doing research on Lily Eberhardt's death earlier in the year."

"But surely you reshelved those by now, Lynn." Miss Bridewell removes her glasses to glare at the poor library aide. Remarkably, the girl seems unaffected by the librarian's basilisk stare.

"Of course I did, Miss Bridewell, but it occurred to me that someone else might be interested in the same topic, so I made up a list of the pertinent references complete with the microfilm call numbers." The intrepid aide opens a file drawer and deftly pulls out a file folder. "Here it is," she says, handing me the sheet.

"That's great," I say, beaming at the girl (someone has to, I figure; Miss Bridewell is still looking at her, aghast).

"Well, then, if that's all you need, I have work to do," Miss Bridewell says.

"Um, if you could just tell me where the microfilm is kept—"

"I'll show her," the aide offers. "I'm done with this cart and I have to take it downstairs anyway."

Miss Bridewell reluctantly gives permission for the aide to accompany me and even concedes to me riding down with her in the employee elevator.

"Thank you, Lynn," I say when the elevators doors slide shut between us and Miss Bridewell's icy stare.

"Actually, it's Glynn. I've been working in the library for three years now. Miss Bridewell signs my timesheets and she's a woman who knows the Dewey Decimal System by heart, but somehow she doesn't see the G at the beginning of my name."

"People are funny that way. They don't see what they don't expect to see. Glynn's a pretty name, though."

"Thanks. My grandmother's maiden name was McGlynn. My mom just got rid of the 'Mc.' She says a girl doesn't need the '**Mc**' anyway because it means 'son of' and that it made up for me taking my father's last name."

"Your mother's quite the feminist."

"Yeah," Glynn says as the elevator door opens, "she's pretty cool. Here we are. The microfilm machine is over here. If you like, I can pull those rolls for you."

"I wouldn't want to get you in trouble with Miss Bridewell," I say, trying not to wish that Sally were more like this polite young woman who thinks her mother is cool.

"Please," she says, rolling her eyes, "she never comes down here. She says the dust aggravates her asthma. Besides, as I said, I pulled those rolls not long ago so they'll be easy for me to find."

"That would be great," I say, sitting down at the machine. While she's gone I take out a pen and

notebook. Then I play with the knobs, trying to remember how to use the archaic machine. I haven't
had to look up anything that wasn't archived on the
Internet in a long time.

Glynn returns with a stack of tiny boxes. She
takes one out and, without waiting for me to confess
my inability, shows me how to load it into the machine. Then she shows me how to make copies by
feeding coins into a slot on the side of the machine.
She waits to see if I'm able to find the first story on
her list and then tells me she'll be down here if I
need her. I listen to her retreating footsteps echoing
through the stacks of books and then focus on the
Kingston paper's account of Lily Eberhardt's death.
It's dated January 8, 1948, and the headline reads:
LOCAL ARTIST FOUND DEAD OF EXPOSURE AFTER
WORST SNOWSTORM SINCE 1888. Poor Lily. Her death
seemed little more than a side story to the weather. I
scan backward through the preceding week and see
that the storm, which began on the evening of
December 26, was indeed a dramatic event for the
village of Arcadia Falls. The area was without electricity for more than a week. The Hudson River was
jammed with ice floes from Albany to New York
City and train service was suspended.

No wonder it took them so long to find Lily's
body.

I make a copy of the January 8 article and look
for the next one on Glynn's list. This one, dated January 10, at least gives a fuller account of Lily's death

and includes her full name in the headline. LILY EBERHARDT, BELOVED CHILDREN'S BOOK AUTHOR, DIES IN BLIZZARD.

Lily Eberhardt, whose illustrated fairy tales have delighted children for many years now, was found dead last week in Witte Clove in Arcadia Falls, New York, a mile from the artists' colony where she lived and worked. Her companion and patroness, Vera Beecher, explained to the local police that Miss Eberhardt had left her residence early on the evening of December 26 just as the snow was beginning to fall.

She was meeting Mr. Virgil Nash in order to travel down to New York City by train to attend an opening for Mr. Nash's paintings at the National Arts Club in Gramercy Park. Miss Beecher didn't know that her friend had failed to meet Mr. Nash at the train station until receiving a letter from Mr. Nash on January 7 that made it clear Miss Eberhardt was not with him, at which point searchers were dispatched to look for Miss Eberhardt. Because she was known to use the path that ran through Witte Clove to travel to the village, that area was searched first.

I notice that no mention is made of Nash and Lily meeting in the barn. Nor does the reporter comment on the oddity of a woman walking on a dangerous path at night to catch a train in a village four miles from her home.

> The searchers who found her said that she was buried under two feet of snow. "She must have become disoriented in the storm and was overcome with exhaustion," Mr. Pickering of the Arcadia Falls Fire Department conjectured. "We get a few like this every big snowfall."
> Locals remember that in the blizzard of 1888

I scroll to the end of the story to see if there's anything more about Lily, but the rest is dedicated to previous deaths (a Palenville woman who died six feet from her house, a doctor from Troy who died trying to attend a childbirth) and to comparisons between this snowfall and the legendary blizzard of 1888. Only at the very end does the reporter give the date and time for a memorial service to be held for Lily at Beech Hall.

> Miss Vera Beecher requests that no flowers be sent. Donations may be made to the Lily Eberhardt Scholarship. Please address all inquiries to Miss Beecher's personal assistant, Miss Ivy St. Clare.

Interesting, I think. Ivy was only nineteen and already she was Vera Beecher's personal assistant.

After copying the article, I look down at the sheet

that Glynn gave me and see that there's one more story on this roll of microfilm. I scroll ahead and find it, dated January 15, 1948.

Ernest T. Shackleton, Medical Examiner for the Albany County Coroner's Office, announced today that Miss Lily Eberhardt did not die of hypothermia as had been conjectured, but from a contusion to her skull. Miss Eberhardt, a local artist and children's book author, was found buried beneath several feet of snow after the record-making blizzard on December 26. It was assumed that she had died of exposure to the elements, but instead she sustained severe trauma to the head and bled to death while she lay in a steep ravine only a mile from her home.

"Her death is still a result of the snowstorm," said Miss Ivy St. Clare, the assistant director of the Arcadia Colony where Miss Eberhardt lived and worked. "She fell in the snowstorm and died. It's a senseless tragedy either way."

"The world has lost a talented artist and I have lost my best friend," Miss Beecher (who declined to be interviewed for this article) said at the memorial service last week. Many notables from the New York art world were present, including Gertrude Sheldon, founder of the Sheldon Museum. A bronze statue that Virgil Nash had made depicting Miss Eberhardt, called **The Water Lily,** stood next to the casket, and a telegram from Mr. Nash was read at the service. "Lily Eberhardt was a gifted artist whose work has always been an inspiration to me. In more recent years, she has inspired me by posing for me. She has been my muse and my friend and will be sadly missed." Mr. Nash had sailed to Europe and so was not able to attend.

What a jerk, I think, yanking the microfilm out of the machine so roughly that a piece crackles and breaks near the end of the roll. I immediately look around to see if anyone has observed me destroy school property, but the library basement seems to be completely deserted. I feel ashamed at my outburst but still angry at Nash. **His muse!** If he'd gone to check on Lily when she didn't meet him at the barn he might have found her in the clove before she bled to death. What a self-centered asshole! "Most artists are," I can hear my grandmother saying. "Believe me, you're better off marrying a reliable workingman like your grandfather Jack, a man who supported his family through the Depression, rather than a flighty artist who'll spend the grocery money on paint and canvas." She wouldn't have been surprised at Virgil Nash leaving Lily to an unknown fate in the snow while he rushed to catch his train to New York so he wouldn't be late for his big show.

The idea of Lily dying as she did suddenly makes me feel cold in this damp, dreary basement. I fish a sweater out of my book bag, wrap it around my shoulders, and load the next spool of film, determined to read the rest of the articles quickly without getting lost in my thoughts. Which isn't hard. The coverage of Lily's death in the city papers focuses on her artistic accomplishments and the history of the Arcadia Colony, most of which I already know, but it's interesting to see how the contemporary press regarded the colony and Lily.

"Lily Eberhardt was one of the most renowned artists of the colony," a **New York Herald Tribune** reporter wrote. "She will be remembered for her haunting fairy tales and evocative illustrations, but also for the portraits and statues of her by Mr. Virgil Nash which were recently displayed at the National Arts Club (see review December 27, 1947)."

Ha, I think. Lily's reputation would, in fact, not fare as well as the reporter's expectations. Her fairy tales would go out of print and what credit was given them would go to Vera Beecher. As for Nash's portraits of her, they hung here at Arcadia in near obscurity. The statue he'd done of her (no doubt the same one that stood by her casket) now gathers dust in an unlit alcove. It reminds me of something else my grandmother used to say: "Artists always think they'll buy themselves immortality with their art, but there's nothing more fickle than fame. Your children are your immortality—not some scribbles on paper or canvas."

I haven't learned anything of importance and the

whole story has left me depressed. I put the last roll back in its box and take it and the others back to Glynn. I find her in a carrel in the far corner of the stacks, curled up comfortably in an old easy chair, her feet tucked beneath her, reading the fifth Harry Potter book.

"Did you find what you needed?" she asks, unfurling herself from her cozy nook.

"I think so. Thanks for your help. It was resourceful of you to think of making that list."

She smiles at the compliment, unused, I imagine, to getting any from the ill-tempered librarian. "I figured once I'd gone to the trouble of looking up the articles I might as well make a record of them. I didn't think Isabel would be the last one doing that research. Oh gosh, that sounds morbid doesn't it? Given that it was the **last** research Isabel ever did."

"Isabel? You mean Isabel Cheney was the one who last looked at these articles?"

"Uh huh. In fact, she came in here the day she died."

CHAPTER 23

The sun is already setting when I come out of the library. The clocks were set back last weekend and I'm not used yet to the earlier dusk. I hurry along the ridge trail, not wanting to be caught in the woods in the dark, especially not on the part that goes past the clove, where one misstep could send me skittering down to the rocks below. When I reach the clearing above the clove, though, the view is so spectacular that I have to stop for a moment to watch the sun sink in the west, turning the mountains into waves of blue and indigo and the clouds above them into strips of pink and lavender, like a higher range of celestial mountains. The scene is so reminiscent of the last picture in **The Changeling Girl** that when I turn back east to face the campus, I half expect to find all the landmarks of that fairy tale place: the farm the peasant girl grew up on, the orchard of gnome trees, the bloodred beech that harbors changelings in its roots, and the witch's cottage in the pine woods. And I do—it's all there. Briar Lodge is the farm; the apple trees are the gnomes; the great copper beech, ablaze in the last rays of the sunset, looks as if its roots are drinking blood; and, peeking out between the dark forest of pines, is the chimney of the cottage where I live, Fleur-de-Lis. The witch's cottage.

I looked at the picture in that book so often when I was little that it feels like home. Better than home, it's the home I always dreamed of. I suppose that's why the story exerted such a pull on my imagination. Perhaps every little girl fantasizes sometime or another that her real family is someplace else, that these strangers raising her are not her real parents and someday she will be returned to her genuine birthright—the kingdom she has lost. If I indulged in that fantasy more often than other children, perhaps it was because of the bareness of life in my grandmother's tiny Brooklyn house with its postage stamp–size yard bound by concrete sidewalks and the daily routine hemmed in by my mother's teaching hours and my grandmother's economies. It wasn't that I didn't love my grandmother and mother; it was just that I sometimes felt as though we were refugees living in exile from our true home. And while I knew that they loved me, they sometimes seemed frightened of what I might become. Like the changeling girl, I belonged elsewhere. When I learned that the place in my favorite fairy tale was real—and that my mother had almost gone to school there—I knew I'd have to go there someday. Maybe I'd hoped that here Sally and I would find a peace together that my own mother and I had never found. Instead, Arcadia has only driven us farther apart.

As the last light from the sun leaches out of the west, a full silver moon rises above the fringe of pine trees in the east and I turn toward the cottage. I can't think of it as home. It certainly doesn't look like one. It still smells musty and unlived in when I open the door tonight. Since Sally moved into the dorm, the only cooking I've done is microwaving the frozen meals I buy at the Stop & Shop on Route 30 and heating Dymphna's scones in the toaster oven.

Maybe if I made a real meal, I think, opening the refrigerator, the place would begin to feel like home. But there's nothing but a bag of apples, half a loaf of bread and a wedge of cheddar I bought last week at the farmer's market, and I'm too tired and dispirited to drive into town to do shopping. While I watch a Lean Cuisine revolve in the microwave, I promise myself that this weekend I'll go to the farmer's stand and buy fresh vegetables. I'll insist Sally have dinner here once a week. I'll lure her with her favorite foods and I'll somehow make her understand that I've never regretted for an instant having her instead of finishing art school.

I'm just taking out the tray when the phone rings. I'm so startled by the old-fashioned clang of it that I drop the tray, spilling boiling hot sauce on my hand—on the same spot, in fact, that's tender from when Chloe doused me with hot wax.

I pick up the phone and cradle it between my ear and shoulder while running cold water over my hand. I can barely hear the wispy voice on the other end over the rush of water.

"—in class. I thought you'd want to know."

"What? Who wasn't in class? Who is this?"

"Oh, sorry, it's Toby Potter. Your daughter's in my Art History class. Lovely girl. So much potential. A bit distracted, perhaps . . ."

"I'm sorry, Toby, is this a progress report?"

"A progress report? Oh no. Sorry, didn't I say? Sally wasn't in class this afternoon, and she was scheduled to do her oral report on Fragonard today. Then when I was driving into town—I live in town, you know, we must have you over someday—I saw her hitchhiking with Chloe Dawson—"

"Hitchhiking?" I ask, appalled. I instantly picture Sally climbing into a derelict van filled with homicidal maniacs.

"Yes. Luckily I picked them up before anyone

else could. I gave them a very stern lecture. After all, it's not the sixties anymore—"

"And where did you take them?" I ask, hoping against hope that he deposited them on campus.

"They asked to be let off in town—said they were going to the art supply store, but I couldn't help noticing as I turned the corner that they were heading into our town pub, the Hitchin' Post."

"Shit."

"Exactly. Anyway, I came right home to call you. I hope you don't think I'm interfering."

"Not at all. I appreciate it. I'm heading out the door to go get her right now."

I hang up and grab my purse and keys, my hand still dripping wet and stinging. It stings all the way into town, but I grip the steering wheel all the harder, preferring the physical pain to the thought of Sally sitting at a bar next to some sex offender. Already some pervert could be luring her out to the back parking lot. Although I once would have trusted her intelligence and judgment, it's clear that she's so pissed off at me these days that she might do anything to get back at me—for what, I'm not even sure anymore. It goes beyond bringing Callum Reade to the equinox or telling the class about dropping out of art school. Last year I'd begun to wonder if she somehow blamed me for her father's death, but lately it feels like she blames me for being alive when he isn't.

I pull into the parking lot of the Hitchin' Post,

spewing gravel and raking the lot with my high beams. I surprise a family of raccoons raiding the Dumpster, but no Sally. I park crookedly, next to a 4 x 4 with souped-up snow tires and a bumper sticker for the NRA. Great. Sally could have fallen in with redneck survivalists by this time. When I swing open the front door with all the force of a gunslinger entering a Western saloon, I find two old guys nursing beers at the bar and a meeting of the town's knitting circle. No sign of Sally. The bartender, a woman in her twenties with a short buzz-cut and nose ring, looks up from the glass she's polishing.

"Let me guess," she says. "You're looking for two underage girls wearing too much mascara. I never can figure out why these girls think painting their faces like raccoons will make them look older."

"Were they here? Do you know where they've gone? Did they leave with anyone? How much did they have to drink?"

"Whoa—twenty questions! Yes, yes, no, and nothing but ginger ale and grenadine. I made them for underage right away despite their rather artfully forged IDs, gave them two Shirley Temples, and called Sheriff Reade. They left before he could get here, but they were going right next door so I imagine Callum's caught up with them and brought them to the station."

"Next door? You mean to Seasons?"

"'Fraid not, honey. They were heading to Fatz

Tatz. I think they just stopped here for some liquid courage. The tall girl looked pretty nervous. The little one was telling her it didn't hurt a bit."

"The tall one's my daughter. . . . you told Callum where they went?"

The bartender narrows her eyes at my use of the sheriff's first name. "Yep. As soon as he got here. He was out on Fog Hollow Road when he got the call, though, so it took him half an hour. I don't know as he was able to get next door before Fatz did his thing."

"You know it's illegal to tattoo a minor in this state—" I start, but then seeing the bartender's eyes cool I stop. It's not her fault that my daughter is out of control. "Thank you for calling the police. And for serving them nonalcoholic drinks. Did they at least pay?"

"Yep. The tall one even remembered to give me a tip," she says, smiling. "You must've raised her right."

Great, I think, leaving the bar and heading down the street. So Sally will no doubt remember to also tip the tattooist after he gives her hepatitis B. I pass Fatz Tatz but it's closed now, so I go on to the police station. When I open the door, the scene is as solemn as I feared. Sally is huddled on a bench along the wall, her knees drawn up and tucked under an oversized sweatshirt. She looks up and I see that her face is swollen and tearstained.

"Finally!" she cries, jumping to her feet. "I

thought I was going to have to spend the night in jail. Where were you?"

"Where was **I**?" I begin, my voice climbing into the registers of disbelief and outrage as quickly as if a switch had been turned on. "I was looking for you, young lady—" I stop myself because I've just heard my mother's voice coming out of my mouth. I can feel, too, the force of someone's gaze. I turn and find Callum Reade leaning in the doorway to what I presume is his office, smiling at me. No doubt because I sound like every hysterical mother come to collect her reprobate offspring.

"I would have appreciated a call to let me know you had my daughter," I say.

The smile vanishes from his face. "I left a message and called the school. Shelley Drake just left with Chloe Dawson, but I presumed you'd want to come and take your daughter home yourself."

"Oh," I say, realizing that he's done exactly the right thing—giving me a chance to talk to Sally alone. "Are there . . . will there be . . ."

"No charges," he says, and then adds, lowering his voice an octave, "**this time**. Although, as I have explained to Sally, using a false I.D. is a class A misdemeanor. And we've had a long talk on the evils of Demon Rum and the risks of hepatitis B infection."

I look at Sally and she shudders. "He showed me pictures of drunk-driving accidents. Honest, I didn't even want a drink. I just wanted to get out of the

fracking nineteenth century and into the modern
world for five minutes."

"Next time have your mom take you to the mall
in Kingston," Callum says, and then to me, "Could
I have a word with you, Ms. Rosenthal?"

I nod and turn back to Sally. She's pulled the
hood up on her sweatshirt and sunk deeper into its
voluminous folds. I notice that it has NYPD written
in faded, peeling letters on it and realize that it must
belong to Callum. I squeeze Sally's shoulder and tell
her I'll be right back.

Callum is in his office, leaning against the front
of his desk. He motions for me to close the door
and then uses his foot to push a chair in my direction. I ignore it and remain standing. "I'm grateful
that you found Sally and that you're not pressing
charges—"

He waves my thanks away. "She's a good enough
kid," he says, "just pissed at the world for taking her
dad away. I don't blame her. The one I'm really worried about is Chloe. When I got to Fatz Tatz, she was
telling Fatz how she could make anyone do whatever she wanted with black magic. She wanted Fatz
to give her a tattoo of a figure falling off a cliff because she'd made a girl jump off a cliff just by pic-
turing it in her head."

"She thinks she made Isabel jump off the ridge?"

Callum nods and runs his hand through his hair,
now looking very tired. "I've never been one of those
locals who bad-mouth the school. Live and let live is

my motto. But something weird is going on there this year. When that girl threw herself at me on the ridge, I thought she was going to take us both over the edge. It wasn't just that she was angry, it was that she was crazy-angry. I felt like she wanted to kill us both. If I were you, I'd keep my kid away from Chloe and her little circle."

Sally sulks all the way back home. When I glance over at her, I can't even see her face because she's pulled the hood of her borrowed sweatshirt down so low it shadows her face. As we pass the rusty old sign advertising the long-gone White Witch speakeasy, I recall the first morning we drove here. I remember the fleeting enthusiasm she'd shown when she recognized her old favorite fairy tale in the landscape and the short-lived hope I had that coming here would somehow heal us. I wish now that I had a story to capture her attention. And then, as I turn up the sycamore drive, I realize I do.

"It's true that I dropped out of art school when I got pregnant with you," I say. "I thought it was what I was supposed to do. What it took to be a good parent."

She doesn't say anything, but at least she's not yelling at me, so I go on.

"I thought I'd go back when you were older—and I could have. Your dad would have been happy to pay the tuition and get me the childcare I would have needed. He used to pick up catalogs from Pratt and Parsons and the School of Visual Arts and leave them around the house."

"Why didn't you go, then?" a small voice comes from the depth of the hooded sweatshirt.

"I think I was afraid that I wouldn't be any good—that too much time had passed and I had lost my edge—"

"You mean because being a mother ruined you?"

Although I'm tempted to lie, I don't. "Yes. Being a mother does change you. Before I had you I would lose myself drawing and painting, the way you do now. Hours would fly by—"

"Like minutes," Sally finishes for me.

"Exactly," I say. "I was afraid to lose myself like that when you were little. What if I wasn't there when you needed me? Then later, I was afraid I wouldn't be able to do it anymore. Your dad still encouraged me to go back to school, so I did, when you were older, but to study literature and fairy tales. But I never regretted having you for an instant."

"And what about Dad? Did he give up his big dreams because of me?"

I sigh. I'd hoped to avoid this part. "He quit Pratt and went to work at Morgan Stanley where Grandpa Max worked. He wanted to make sure there was enough money."

"But Grandpa Max and Nana Sylvia were pretty well off. Wouldn't they have helped him?"

I shake my head. "They were of that generation who lived through the Depression—like my grandmother. Grandma Miriam saved **everything.** She even washed and reused wax paper! So even though Grandpa Max and Nana Sylvia had money, they were always afraid that they could lose it all. They wanted your father to work in business. When he went to art school instead, they cut off his allowance."

"That's awful! You wouldn't do that to me, would you?"

"I don't see why you shouldn't be able to make a living in the arts. I want you to do something you really love. But don't blame Grandpa Max and Nana Sylvia for doing what they thought was best for your father, and for you when you came along. When we knew we were having you, Grandpa Max offered to help us get the house in Great Neck if your dad would go to work with him at Morgan Stanley."

"So he gave up art school because of me, too?"

"He just wanted to be the best father he could be. And I know he never regretted it either."

I say the last part firmly, telling myself that it's not technically a lie. Jude never did regret his choice to give up art school for Sally. He thought he'd done the right thing. "And," he'd say whenever the subject came up, "there'll be plenty of time for me to take up painting again when I retire." So it's not a lie. He just didn't know that he was wrong about how much time he had.

We've arrived at the cottage. Luckily, I left the lights on, so it doesn't look too desolate. It looks almost cheerful. I'll make grilled cheese sandwiches and a pot of tea. We'll dig through the boxes of DVDs and watch an old movie. One of Sally's favorites: **Casablanca** or **Mr. Smith Goes to Washington,** which always makes her cry when Jimmy Stewart briefly gives up hope in the American Dream.

I'm about to turn to Sally to ask if she'd like to stay when I see a black silhouette appear at the lit living room window. The reason the cottage doesn't look desolate is because it's not empty. There's someone in the house.

CHAPTER 24

"You stay here," I say, trying to make my voice sound firm and confident. I squeeze Sally's hand and then reach across her to open the glove compartment before remembering that the flashlight isn't there anymore. "I'll check it out."

"But Mom, what if it's a burglar?"

"It's probably one of the housemaids that Dymphna's sent over."

I don't really think Dymphna's

sent anyone at this time of night, but I don't want Sally to be too scared—or to follow me into the house. I get out of the car, checking to make sure both doors are locked, and approach the house, wishing I at least had the flashlight to wield as a weapon. Even without a weapon though, if there's an intruder inside, I'll do whatever I have to to keep him or her from getting to Sally. I slide the key into the lock, but before I can turn it the door swings open to reveal Ivy St. Clare, wrapped dramatically in a dark shawl.

"There you are at last! We've been waiting for you to return. Is your daughter with you? Sheriff Reade said you had collected her."

I'm so taken aback by the sight of Dean St. Clare in my house that I don't answer. I peer past her into the living room and see Shelley Drake and Chloe Dawson sitting across from each other in the lettuce green chairs. Chloe looks as wilted as the leaves in the upholstery.

"How did you get into my house?" I ask the dean. "And what are you doing here?"

She adjusts the wrap over her shoulders and sniffs. "I still have my key from when I used to do little errands for Vera. As for what we're doing here—Sally and Chloe have broken school rules by going into the village at night **and** going into a drinking establishment. It's my policy to address miscreants of joint crimes together and in the same manner, but since that man wouldn't release Sally into Miss

Drake's custody we've had to wait for you to get back with her. You wouldn't want your daughter to receive special treatment, would you?" St. Clare's glance shifts from my face to something over my right shoulder. I turn and see that Sally's come to the doorway. She's not looking at me, though; she's looking at Chloe who's mouthing some silent message.

"I don't expect her to receive special treatment, but I've already talked to her and I think I can handle it from here."

"That's all very well and good, but our rules state that there are consequences for misbehavior. Vera always insisted that the students perform some work for the communal good of the school. Miss Drake and I thought that it would be appropriate for the girls to clean up from dinner tonight and for each night this week."

"Now?" I ask. "You want them to start"—I look down at my watch—"at ten o'clock at night?"

"Yes, well, if we'd been able to collect Sally earlier they would have already been done. Still, there's plenty of time for them to finish and I did expressly tell Dymphna to leave the cleaning."

"But I wanted to talk some more to Sally—" I begin, turning to her. If I expect her to look grateful for my intervention I'd be disappointed. She's staring at a spot on the ceiling, ignoring me. Any connection we began to make on the drive back from town has vanished.

"Do you want Miss Dawson to do all the work herself, then?" the dean asks.

"Mom, that wouldn't be fair. Let me go with Chloe. I'm perfectly ready to scrub some dishes."

"I'll make sure they get back to the dorm all right," Shelley says, speaking for the first time. She gives me a small smile, glancing nervously at the dean to see if she's looking, but Ivy's attention is fixed on the mantel above the fireplace. I feel a guilty flush steal over me as I recall what's hidden there, and I have to forcibly remind myself that Ivy St. Clare doesn't know about the hiding place behind the carved panel. I turn back to Sally, catching Shelley's eye as I do.

"Is that what you want, Sally?" I ask.

She shrugs. "I guess it's what I have to do. Can I change, though? Someone spilled beer on my jeans in that skanky bar."

Dean St. Clare nods and then, when Sally's gone upstairs, turns to me. "I hope you understand why this is necessary. If Sally learns that she can hide behind you she'll have a very hard time here. And, if you don't mind me saying, Sally is a very troubled young girl."

"She lost her father a year ago," I respond, the blood rushing to my face.

St. Clare gives me a pitying look. "I grew up an orphan. My mother abandoned me at birth and God knows if my father even knew I existed. The first family who adopted me **returned** me. I could have spent my life making excuses for bad behavior, but instead I determined to make something of myself. You've got to let Sally realize that for herself."

"Of course I understand that, and I admire what you've been able to accomplish. But you did have help. Lily Eberhardt and Vera Beecher gave you a second chance when they gave you the scholarship to study here."

"That's true, but it was never a free ride. I knew from the minute I stepped foot on the grounds that I'd have to work to earn a place here. And I have worked every day of my life to maintain that place. You have no idea what I've had to do." She's holding herself so rigid the skin seems stretched taut over the bones of her face. Her hands are coiled into fists and her collarbones stand out as sharp as stone ledges. It's as if something inside her were struggling to be free of the thin layer of flesh and blood. Something sharp cracks and for a second I think it's Ivy herself, held so taut that she's snapped like a branch in the wind, but it's only Shelley fiddling with one of the pokers by the fireplace.

"Sorry," she says. "It looked like it was about to fall."

I glance nervously at the mantel, afraid that the secret compartment has sprung open and disgorged Lily's journal and all its secrets of Ivy's orphaned past, but it's securely closed. I turn to find Sally coming down the stairs in sweatpants and Jude's Pratt sweatshirt (she must have been dying to get out of Callum Reade's), tying her hair back in a workmanlike ponytail. As she lowers her arm I catch a glimpse of red and green on her right wrist. I assumed that Callum had gotten to Fatz Katz before Sally could get a tattoo, but stepping forward and grabbing her wrist I see I assumed wrong.

"It's no big deal, Mom. And don't start in about hepatitis. Fatz uses sterile needles."

It's a tiny rosebud—about the most innocent image she could have chosen—but still I feel just as I did when I saw the scars left over from the chicken pox she had when she was three, like life was leaving its mark on her all too soon.

After they leave I prowl around the cottage like a mother cat who's had her kittens taken from her. I walk from room to room, unable to rid myself of the idea that Sally's in danger. I try to reassure myself that Shelley Drake will keep an eye on the girls, but Shelley, although well-intentioned, is a bit of a flake. In Sally's room, I pick up Callum Reade's discarded sweatshirt and clutch it to my chest as if I could fill it with Sally again. Instead I inhale the scent of wood shavings and lemon oil, the same scent I'd caught on him the day at the barn. Shivering, I pull the sweatshirt on and go back downstairs.

I head straight to the fireplace and open the secret compartment. Lily's journal is right where I left it. It was ridiculous to think that after going undetected for forty years Ivy would stumble upon it now. Still, I didn't like having her so close to the hiding place. It makes me realize how disappointed I'd be if the journal was taken from me before I got a chance to finish it. I take the journal out, curl up on the living room couch, bundled in Callum's sweatshirt and one of my grandmother's old afghans, and settle in to read, determined to get to the end of Lily's story at last.

Our lives in Fleur-de-Lis were full of little surprises. Vera delighted in giving me small presents and in finding ways to make me happy. She had made good on her promise to buy a printing press and that fall she invited a printer from the city, Bill Adams, to teach us how to print our own books. Anita Day from the Guild of Book Workers came for the next three summers to teach us bookbinding. In the fall of 1930 we published our first book, **The Changeling Girl,** in an edition of one hundred copies. We were still new to the process and made so many mistakes that only seventy were worth keeping. We sent them out that year to friends for Christmas presents. Vera thought the story was appropriate to the times and to the economic hardships that so many were experiencing. In our Christmas card (also printed on our new press) Vera wrote, "I hope you will enjoy this little story about a poor girl who helps her family through hard times and finds happiness in good, honest work." I was glad that was all Vera saw in the story.

In the card we sent to Mimi Green, who had married Johnnie and moved back to Brooklyn, I wrote an extra note. "You'll perhaps see something else in this story."

We didn't hear back from Mimi—not even a thank-you note—which annoyed Vera, who, for all her championing of the unconventional artistic life, was a stickler for the conventions of good manners. "You see what happens when women marry and have children," Vera said, striking Mimi off our Christmas list. "They abandon all their old friends."

"Gertrude hasn't abandoned us," I pointed out mischievously.

"If only she would," Vera groaned. Having a healthy baby girl in the spring of 1929 had done nothing to make Gertrude Sheldon more maternal or stable. When she came back from Europe, she'd retreated with the child to the Sheldon's country estate on an island in Maine, telling everyone that her daughter's constitution was delicate and couldn't risk the contagion and heat of New York City. Later there were rumors that Gertrude had actually spent the summer in a sanatorium and that she was suffering from nervous exhaustion following her confinement. She was still in seclusion the following summer, which also annoyed

Vera—not because she missed Gertrude's presence, but because Gertrude had lured Virgil Nash to her home in Maine. We heard she had promised him her patronage, and Nash did indeed become wealthy from painting portraits of the Sheldon family and their circle.

I was relieved that I wouldn't have to face Nash. Even when Gertrude returned to Arcadia a few years later, Nash stayed away. Perhaps he was avoiding me, or perhaps he was embarrassed by the paintings he was doing. His society portraits had made him rich, but they were facile and flattering. He must have felt the gap between him and his fellow artists widen as many of our friends' fortunes declined in the coming years.

Vera told me in the beginning of 1930 that she'd lost a great many of her holdings in the stock market and that she would have to give up the New York town house, but that if I was willing to practice some basic economies, we could still afford to live simply at Arcadia all the year round. I told her that nothing would make me happier than to spend the whole year at Arcadia. In truth, I enjoyed the economies forced upon us. At last I could be useful to her! I knew how to cook and clean and grow vegetables. I even convinced her to get a cow and some hens so that we could produce our own milk and eggs.

Many of our artist friends were not as fortunate as we were, and so we gave them a home in the summer, a place that would relieve them of the day-to-day struggle to survive, where they could still draw and paint and make pottery and books and furniture. There were many who survived off the goods they produced at Arcadia during those summers.

And so, although I was not ignorant of the need around us, I have to admit that the decade of the thirties was the happiest time of my life. We had enough while many did not, we had the means to help our friends a little, we had our work, and, most of all, Vera and I had each other. It was Vera now who received commissions for important murals—for post offices and banks, colleges, and even one state capitol. I was her assistant and her model, but after the chapel of St. Lucy's I never again wanted to work on such a large scale.

"I am content with my fairy tales," I told her, "and my drawings of my make-believe places." It was true: I was happy.

Until the day I learned about Ivy.

Of course I had thought about her. Sister Margaret had been right about that. There wasn't a day that went by that I didn't wonder where she was, what sort of family had taken her, what she looked like. But I knew that the rules of St. Lucy's strictly forbade any of the mothers to make inquiries concerning the babies they gave up. I knew, too, that it was a foolish wish. What if she wasn't happy? Or worse, what if she had gotten sick and died? So many children did in those years. Gertrude was always talking about the dangers of polio, meningitis, measles, and a host of other illnesses that could carry off a child if a mother didn't enforce the most stringent sanitary practices in her household. I wasn't sure if I wished my child a mother like Gertrude, who kept her daughter physically safe but turned her into a fretful neurotic, or a more loving, but relaxed mother who might not anticipate every ailment. However, once I had the thought in my head that Ivy could have died, I had to know.

In the summer of 1944 Vera received a commission to paint a mural for a women's college in northeastern Pennsylvania. When we arrived there I saw that the college was not far from St. Lucy's. I told her one day that I wanted to visit the convent to see the mural that Mimi and I had done to see how it was holding up. "I'd like to get some good photographs," I told her. I was afraid she'd offer to go with me, but I made sure that I picked a day when the models for the frieze she was working on were there so she couldn't leave. Vera was clearly annoyed that I wouldn't be there to mix her paints, but I'd found a re-placement.

"But no one knows how to get the colors right but you," she complained.

I assured her that I'd left the precise formu-las with my replacement (an art student at the college who seemed levelheaded) and left be-fore Vera could think of any other objections. As I traveled east on the same train line I had taken in the other direction sixteen years be-fore, I thought about how dependent on me Vera had grown over the years. It was not that I minded doing things for her—I would have gladly laid down my life for her—but it sad-dened me to see a woman of her strengths grown petulant and demanding. She ought to have some other outlet for her domineering spirit.

It was then that I began to conceive in my mind the idea of a prepatory school for the arts. We had long attracted young artists who came for the summer to study with our more experienced artists, but it was a haphazard arrangement that occupied only a few months of the year. There was no consistency of in-struction, no organized course of study, no philosophy. After a summer or two, many of the most talented young women drifted away, married, had children, and gave up their art, or treated it as a hobby to fill an idle hour instead of their vocation. I felt that we—Vera and I and Arcadia—could do better. If we formed ourselves into a school we could really prepare young artists—especially young women, I couldn't help but think—to support themselves. We would teach the fine arts, of course, but also illustration, graphic design, textiles, printing, bookbinding . . . the decorative arts that could provide a practical income while also making the world a more beautiful place. By the time I arrived at Easton, I had mapped out a plan for the Arcadia School of the Arts. I had already decided that there would be a scholarship program for poor girls who exhibited remarkable talents in the arts.

The town of Easton felt oddly deserted when I alighted at the train station. A driver met me at the station and drove me up to St. Lucy's in a rattling and rusted old Buick instead of Johnnie's pony cart. He told me the town had been given its death sentence.

"The buildings are all to be razed and burned down to make way for the new reservoir," he said. "They'd have started on it already if not for the war, but it's only a matter of time now. This whole valley will be underwater in another ten years."

"What about St. Lucy's?" I asked, thinking of the girls who found their way here from the

city. Where would they go if St. Lucy's was
gone? What would happen to the orphans?

"St. Lu's is right on top of the taking line,
but it's not likely the city will want a bunch of
nuns perched over their water supply. There's
talk of moving it to the other side of the
mountain, but Sister Margaret, the old nun
who runs the place, don't like the idea. She
says the place was chosen because it was like
the spot in Ireland where the original St. Lucy
put her baby in the river. She says that if
St. Lucy could entrust her only child to the
waters, she can entrust the convent to these
waters. She refuses to make plans to move.
Frankly, I think the old bird—no disrespect
meant," he said, crossing himself, "has gone a
bit touched in the head."

I was alarmed at the driver's description of
Sister Margaret. I had hoped that she would be
able to tell me what had become of my baby.
But then, maybe it was better if she didn't remember me too well, since it was not permit-
ted for the unwed mothers of St. Lucy's to ask
after their lost babies.

By the time I arrived at St. Lucy's I had devised a plan. I would tell Sister Margaret that
my benefactor, Vera Beecher, had decided that
her new school would save a spot for any child
born at St. Lucy's. I would need a list of children born there from, say, 1927 to 1930, with

their birthdates and present addresses. I should be able to figure out from her birthdate the present location of my daughter.

When I came to stand on the threshold of the convent door, though, I found that I was frightened. I was afraid of what I might learn about my child's fate. As the driver carried my suitcase inside, I went instead into the little chapel of St. Lucy's, the one that Mimi and I had painted. I remembered that Sister Margaret had said that many of the girls went into the chapel first to collect themselves before entering the convent. That was why she'd thought it was so important that the paintings there should be inspirational and comforting.

There was one person in the chapel when I entered it. I thought at first that she must be one of the pregnant girls, praying to the saint for guidance, but then I saw that she was only a child and that she wasn't praying. She was drawing.

She was an ugly little thing in a threadbare flannel jumper that hung loosely to her bare and scabby knees, worn over a starched white shirt buttoned high around her thin neck. Her short black hair looked like it had been hacked into the shape of a bowl. She was hunched over her sketchpad and I thought at first that she might be deformed—a hunchback, per-

haps, or a polio survivor. I walked up behind
her quietly so as not to startle her. When I
looked over her shoulder at her drawing,
though, all of her imperfections faded into
nothingness. The scene she had chosen to
sketch was of St. Lucy giving her child to the
River Clare. Not only had she captured the
likeness of what I had painted years ago,
but she had made it into something new—
something better. She'd managed, as I had not,
to imbue the face of the saint with a combination of love, despair, and hope. The mother's
and baby's eyes were locked on each other with
a force that seemed unbreakable.

"You've done that beautifully," I said. "You
have a wonderful way of capturing gesture and
expression."

The girl did not seem to register that I'd
spoken. She went on drawing, meticulously
cross-hatching the shadow of St. Lucy as she
knelt by the river. Perhaps she was deaf, I
thought, or simpleminded. But when she finished shading in St. Lucy's shadow, she looked
up at me with dark eyes as black and sharp as
the point of her pencil.

"I've had my whole life to get this bit
right," she said in a high-pitched, slightly
nasal, voice. "I should hope I'd gotten it down
by now."

"You need other models," I said, smiling.

"And better paper and pencils." I noted that the paper she drew on was coarse and her pencils sharpened down to tiny nubs. "I think I can help."

I held out my hand to her. "I'm Lily Eberhardt, and my friend Vera Beecher and I are starting a school for girls like you."

The girl tucked her pencil behind her ear and put her cold and grimy hand in mine without smiling. "I'm pleased to meet you, Miss Eberhardt. My name's Ivy St. Clare, and I think you'll find that there aren't too many girls like me."

CHAPTER 25

I left Ivy in the chapel sketching another scene—she informed me she sketched three a day and spent the afternoons teaching drawing to the younger children. I went to find Sister Margaret, trying to calm myself as I walked through the long stone hall to her office. "She spends her mornings in there 'working,' but really I think she just stares out her window," Ivy had said. "She hasn't been right in the head since they told her the convent has to be moved. Good luck getting anything out of her."

I tried to persuade myself that if Sister Margaret really had gone senile I couldn't blame her for not telling me about Ivy. At any rate, there was little to gain in chastising an old woman. After all, I had left my child in her care and clearly she had been cared for. In the short conversation I had with Ivy, I sensed that she was the pet of the nunnery. She had her own room, she told me, disdainfully dismissing the notion that she would share quarters with the babies; she ate with the nuns, and she had her mornings free to draw. When I asked if she wouldn't prefer to live with a family, she sniffed and said she wasn't the family kind. "I prefer to be on my own."

Perhaps I should have been glad for her self-sufficiency, but I felt chilled by it.

I knocked on Sister Margaret's door, but when there was no answer I opened it myself. Ivy had been right. The old nun was turned away from her desk so that she could look out her window. It was a lovely view, just as I remembered it from the day I had told Sister Margaret that I was pregnant. You could see the East Branch rolling through green hills, past the white steeple of Easton's church, and toward the blue mountains beyond. Was she

imagining, I wondered, the valley flooded
and turned into a lake? When she turned to
me at the sound of my footstep I was startled
to see that her once-sharp blue eyes were covered with a milky film, as though her eyes had
been flooded as her beloved valley soon would
be. She couldn't see the view at all.

"Sister Margaret," I said gently, all my
anger dissolving, "you probably don't remember me. I'm Lily Eberhardt. I came here sixteen
years ago—"

"Lily Eberhardt," she said, her face creasing
into a web of lines as she smiled. "Of course, I
remember you." She reached out her hands
and I realized she meant me to put my hands
in hers. That must be her way of "seeing" people, I thought, stepping closer. As I laid my
hands in hers, though, I had a strange and
sudden fear that she would place her hands on
my belly as she had the time I told her I was
pregnant. But of course she didn't. She gripped
my hands in hers and crooned, "Such talented
hands! They gave us St. Lucy. I told the man
from the water company that they couldn't
possibly think of putting such beautiful paintings under the water. He had no answer for
me." She smiled slyly. "So you see, your pictures have saved us. I knew it was a good day
that you came here. You brought us such
beauty!"

I sank down to my knees in front of Sister Margaret, still clasping her hands. "I brought something else here," I said. "Do you remember? I had a child here—a baby girl."

The old woman raised her hand, index finger pointing to the sky. I thought for a moment she was pointing to heaven, admonishing me to God for my sins, but then she touched her finger to her pursed lips and said, "Shhh. It's a secret. The baby girl that the painter took. She's a secret."

"You mean the baby girl that the painter had," I said, but Sister Margaret waved my correction away, her crabbed arthritic fingers trembling in the air. "Yes, I did tell you to keep her a secret. But when no one came to take her—"

"Such a beautiful baby, of course someone wanted her."

"But she came back, didn't she?"

Sister Margaret tilted her head to one side and then placed her trembling hands on either side of my face. "You came back. I thought you would."

I sighed with exasperation. What difference did it make? "Yes, I came back. I'd like to take Ivy back with me now."

"Ivy?"

"Yes, Ivy, my . . ." I couldn't say it. I couldn't own my own child to one of the only

two people alive who knew she was mine. I
knew then the terrible truth: I'd felt no bond
of love or affection toward that strange,
homely girl I found in the chapel. Except for
one thing. **I'm not the family kind,** she had
said. Well, we had that in common. I was no
better at being a mother than she had been at
playing someone's daughter. "Ivy St. Clare," I
said, beginning again. "My new protégée. I'd
like to offer her a scholarship at our new arts
school."

And so I brought Ivy to Arcadia . . . oh, not
right away, of course. First I had to convince
Vera that we could single- (or double-) hand-
edly start our own school. She was skeptical at
first, but when she saw how determined I was,
she gave way.

   "I suppose this is your way of making up
for not having children," she said one evening
as we sat before the fire in Fleur-de-Lis. "I'm
afraid we women can't avoid the mothering in-
stinct in the end." When she said that, it occurred to me for the first time that Vera might
regret not having children. Had I been wrong
all those years ago not to trust her with my secret? Might she have accepted my child? It was
an awful thought given how things had turned
out, but I banished it from my head as I went
forward, putting my plan into effect. I had

plenty to keep my mind occupied in the coming year if I wanted our new school to open by
the next fall. I needed teachers, classrooms, art
supplies and, of course, students—some of
whom, it became immediately clear to me,
would have to be paying students.

"I hate to say it," Vera said when she looked
over the figures with me, "but if you ask Fleur
Sheldon to come, a dozen of the Sheldons'
friends will send their daughters as well. With
their tuition, we'll be able to support a dozen
scholarship girls."

I had to agree, even though I hated to
admit Fleur Sheldon. It wasn't that I had anything against the girl. In fact, I felt sorry for
her. She was so clearly talentless, but Gertrude
would not see that and forced Fleur to apply
herself to her artistic studies day and night. No
expense was spared. The most exclusive in-
structors were hired and the poor girl was
dragged around the great museums of Europe
and forced to copy the masters. What a waste!
If only poor little Ivy had been given Fleur's
education and opportunities! But I would rec-
tify that imbalance now—and if it meant
fleecing the Sheldons' pocketbook, so be it.

It happened just as Vera predicted. Vera
wrote a letter that Christmas to Gertrude Sheldon inviting Fleur to join the Arcadia School
of the Arts. By March, we'd gotten applica-

tions from fourteen full-paying students.
I posted notices at the Art Students League
inviting applicants, and Dora and Ada re-
cruited from the city schools and settlement
houses where they taught pottery. Then I
wrote to Sister Margaret inviting Ivy—and
whatever other deserving girls she might recommend.

"I'm afraid no one's more deserving than
Ivy St. Clare," she wrote back. "She will be
missed here, but I'm confident that she is
going where she belongs."

Was that, I wondered, a veiled reference to
our relationship?

It hardly mattered. By late spring we had
chosen eleven scholarship students including
Ivy and enrolled fourteen paying students.
When I sent out the final notices to our accepted applicants, I sent one more to a girl
who hadn't applied at all—Mimi Green's
daughter, who I figured must be close to sixteen by then and who, if she had any of her
mother's talent, would be just right for the
school. I suppose I wanted Mimi to know that
I appreciated how she'd kept my secret all these
years. Mimi's response was a terse "No thank
you." I never again tried to contact her.

The girls arrived in the last week of July.
We had no dorms yet, so they stayed in the
main house, sharing two or three to a room.
All except Ivy.

"I had my own room at the orphanage," she told me on the first day. "I can't sleep with the sound of other people **breathing.**" If it had been anyone else I would have told her to make do, but how could I deny her anything when her whole life had been one of want because of me? I gave her the room I had before Vera and I moved to Fleur-de-Lis.

Mrs. Byrnes sniffed with disapproval when I asked her to get bedding for Ivy's room. "Will the lady be having her breakfast in bed as well?" she asked. "Shouldn't the girls here on scholarship have to work to help earn their keep?"

"I want no distinction made between them," I told Mrs. Byrnes. She raised her eyebrows but didn't say a word. I knew what she was thinking. I had already made a distinction. I realized then that I would never be able to treat Ivy dispassionately. I would always be trying to make up for what I hadn't given her. And yet I could tell that being indulged was **not** what she needed. She'd already been the pet at the convent. Here she needed to be challenged—but someone else would have to do the challenging.

After dinner that night, while Vera and I were sitting by the fire going over the accounts, I casually mentioned my idea for Ivy. "I've been thinking you should have one of the students as your personal assistant. Someone

who can take care of the little details that distract you from your work—appointments and
correspondence and such."

"You always take care of those things," Vera
said, looking up from the account book.

"Yes, but I'll be too busy now with the
school and I think it would be good if someone else knew how to attend to such things—"

"You sound as if you're thinking of
leaving."

I looked up and saw she'd gone pale and
her jaw was clenched. The hand that held the
pencil above the account book was trembling.
I was startled by how frightened she looked.
Was she that afraid of losing me? It should, I
suppose, have flattered me, but instead it made
me feel a little frightened myself. Not that I had
any thought of ever leaving, but what if I did?
What would Vera do? Would she let me go?

I shook the thought off. After all, I had no
intention of going anywhere. Where, at any
rate, would I go?

"Of course not, darling," I said, trying to
sound casual. "You can't get rid of me, Vera.
I'm yours for life. I only thought . . .
well, that poor orphan girl, Ivy St. Clare, she's
used to doing odd jobs for the nuns. She's like
you. If she doesn't have enough to engage her
energies, I'm afraid she'll become broody. I
think she'd make a good assistant for you."

"Yes, she does seem quite bright. Tell her to come to my office tomorrow after class. She can help sort through next year's applications."

The next day I found Ivy at breakfast and told her that Miss Beecher had asked specifically that she be her assistant.

"Me?" she asked, looking none too pleased. "Why would she want me? She doesn't even know me."

"Ah, but she does know you through your drawings and paintings. She looked at all the submissions of the scholarship applicants and she was most impressed by your work. She chose you especially for the scholarship and she'd like to get to know you better. And she really does need help sorting through all the paperwork. I'm afraid I'm hopeless with such things."

I saw the girl thaw a bit under the warming influence of praise. "Well, I am good at organizing things," she said a trifle condescendingly. "Of course, I'd be happy to be Miss Beecher's assistant."

And so, with only a few lies and a little flattery, I fitted Ivy and Vera together as neatly as I might fit together the pieces of a puzzle. And fit together they did. It was almost as if she were Vera's child and not Nash's, they suited each other so well. Vera was demanding, but Ivy thrived under her orders. She worked day and night to make things just right. Vera had only to voice an idea and Ivy would make it happen. At the end of the fall semester, for instance, Vera mentioned that it was a shame there was no sculpture class. By January Ivy had found a teacher and ordered marble and clay. Her only fault was that at times she was so single-minded in carrying through Vera's wishes that she didn't care whom she stepped over to get her job done. When the marble arrived for the new sculpture class over the Christmas break, she had it delivered to the pottery shed without a thought to how it would inconvenience Dora and Ada. When I mentioned it to her she stared at me as though I were speaking a different language, as if the feelings of two people meant nothing. I often think she has something missing. Like the girl in the fairy tale who's been raised by wolves, she seems to lack an essential part of being human.

I do regret that I was never able to form a close bond with Ivy myself. I blame my own self-consciousness around her and my fear of overfavoring her. At the end of that first year, I admitted to myself that I had lost the opportunity of telling her that I was her mother. She wouldn't thank me for the knowledge and she wouldn't forgive me for deceiving Vera. Nor could I ask her to keep such a secret from Vera, whom she clearly idolized. I settled for knowing that I had given Ivy a good home. A year-round home. As the other girls made their plans for the summer vacation, Vera asked Ivy to stay on. "She has no place to go," she said to me when she explained that Ivy would be given her old suite of rooms in Beech Hall.

I would have been content, I think, if Virgil Nash had not reappeared on the scene.

His name had come up in our initial lists of teaching candidates. "I'm sure he's grown too rich and famous to stoop to teaching at a girls' school," I had said, hoping to discourage Vera. The truth was I didn't want Virgil coming into contact with Ivy. Although I could not detect any resemblance to him in her odd pixieish features, I had a superstitious dread that he would sense a kinship to her. Vera, however, had insisted on writing to invite him. I promptly deposited the letter in the kitchen stove. When he didn't respond to Vera's invitation she concluded that I was right; he had grown too important for the likes of us. All would have been well if Gertrude Sheldon hadn't conceived a desire for her child to be taught by the great Mr. Nash. Over the summer break she approached him herself about teaching at Arcadia. I'm not sure what she said to persuade him (whether she offered him money or threatened to withdraw her patronage from him), but whatever she did, it worked. When the school reconvened in August he showed up unannounced, driving a Cadillac convertible and smelling strongly of gin. He was still a handsome man, but his face had a sort of cast over it, like the wax mask we used to make bronze models, and his eyes had lost their keenness. When he reached into his car for his valise and paint box, his hands trembled. I almost pitied him. But then when Vera turned to tell Mrs. Byrnes to get a room ready for him, he looked me up and down as if measuring me for a suit of clothes and I stopped feeling sorry for him.

"We can't have Mr. Nash stay in the Hall," I said. "Not with all these young girls."

"Afraid I'll prefer the young ones to you, eh, Lily?" he asked. "You needn't be, y'know. You're still looking fit."

I felt the blood rush to my face and I turned away to hide my reaction, coming face to face with Ivy, who had stolen up behind me. She stared from me to Nash and back again. For the first time I saw that they **did** resemble each other in one feature. They had the same cold eyes.

"Ah, Ivy, just in time," Vera said. "You can take Mr. Nash down to Briar Lodge. He can share accommodations with Monsieur Paloque. I'm sure you won't want the noise of

a houseful of silly girls distracting you from
your work."

Nash smiled at Vera and then he turned to
Ivy. "You are completely right. How could I
work surrounded by such loveliness?" he asked
Ivy with a rakish tilt of the head.

I saw Ivy take in Nash with her cool assessing gaze and then I watched in horror as that
cold shell broke. She blushed and returned his
smile. Poor Ivy! She had encountered only a
handful of men in her cloistered life and never
one remotely like Virgil Nash. She instantly
fell under the spell of his careless flirting. I was
so horrified that I blurted out, "I'll show Virgil
to the Lodge."

Vera looked surprised, and I knew that later
I'd have to come up with some reason for my
seeming eagerness to spend time alone with
Virgil Nash. For now I just wanted to get him
away from Ivy. "Ivy's much too busy greeting
the new girls." I caught Ivy glaring at me, but I
slipped into the Cadillac obliviously and
drummed my fingers on the armrest while he
took his leave of Vera and Ivy. When he
backed the car up, he rested his arm on the
back of my seat and I felt his fingers graze my
neck. I only hoped Vera hadn't seen. He left
his right arm draped indolently over the back
of my seat as he piloted the car down the drive
toward the Lodge. I swatted his arm away

from me as soon as we were out of sight of the Hall.

"Stop that! Pay attention to the road. You'll get us both killed!"

"Your solicitude for my welfare is touching," he said. "And all these years I thought you'd completely forgotten about me."

"I have."

"So why so quick to be my escort, Lily? What was all that about? You couldn't possibly think I was seriously interested in that little monkey."

"That little monkey—" It was on my lips to tell him she was his daughter, but I stopped. Nash would never be able to keep such a secret to himself, certainly not when he was drinking. "She's special to me . . . to me and Vera. I don't like to see you playing with her feelings. She won't understand. She grew up in an orphanage, taught by nuns. She has no experience with men like you."

"So it's not because you're jealous?" he asked, stopping the car in front of the Lodge. I was relieved to see that it was quiet. Monsieur Paloque, the drawing master, had not arrived yet from his summer on the French Riviera.

"No. You know I don't feel that way about you. All that happened between us is in the past. If you have any idea of taunting me with it, then I'll go to Vera and tell her everything and ask her to make you leave. I don't know what you think by coming here anyway."

"I had hoped," he said, his voice suddenly somber, "to recover my muse. I haven't painted anything worth a damn since the summer I was here eighteen years ago."

"But you've made plenty of money," I told him. "That was your choice."

"Yes, it was my choice." He sighed. "Maybe it is too late. I thought if I came back here I might capture a little of that old magic."

I glanced at him and saw that he was staring at me, but it wasn't with lust. There was longing there, but not a longing for things of the flesh. "If you're really here to paint, and not to run after the girls . . ."

"I've had my fill of girls. I'd give 'em all up for one painting I wasn't ashamed of. I'll tell you what: I promise to stay away from the girls—and especially your little monkey—if you do one thing for me."

"I won't betray Vera," I told him. "I've been faithful to her since that summer with you—"

"I don't mean that. Believe it or not, Lily, that's not how I want you. I confess, I do think of those nights we spent in the barn. But what I want is to paint you—there in the barn—with the light coming through the cracks in the walls, making patterns on your skin. . . . I've been doing some sketches. . . ."

He reached into the backseat of the car and took out a worn leather portfolio. He untied it and shook out loose sheets of drawing paper. They fluttered into my lap like autumn leaves. I picked up one and saw a figure of a naked woman standing in a doorway, her back to the viewer, her body striated with bars of shadow and light. I knew at once that the figure was me.

"You promise to leave Ivy alone?" I asked.

"Ivy who?" he asked in return.

I like to think that I said yes to Virgil to keep him from Ivy, but I have to confess that when I saw that drawing I knew what I had been missing since the summer I'd spent with him. I didn't miss the physical intimacy we'd shared. I was much happier with Vera on that account. I missed what he saw in me: I missed that part of me only he seemed to see—a part that was more animal than woman. I felt that way again when I began posing for him and I felt it when I saw the paintings. Nash was right. His muse had been waiting for him here at Arcadia. The paintings he did of me that year were the best he had done since that first summer. Even Vera, when she saw them, had to admit that they were the real thing.

My darling Vera. I knew it made her jealous that I was posing for Nash, but she withstood the pangs of her jealousy for the sake of the art that came out of those sessions. I believe she was able to because she trusted me so well. She would never suspect that I was capable of betraying her. Her trust so humbled me that I was more than ever determined she never know what happened between Nash and me so long ago.

It was Ivy whom I had the most trouble with. True to his word, Nash never flirted with her again, but the damage had already been done. She was clearly smitten with him. She took all his classes and sought him out in his studio at the Lodge whenever she could. She would even sneak down to the barn to watch him painting me. When I scolded her for spying she accused me of being afraid of what she might see—and what she might tell Vera. By spring I was grateful when school ended and Vera suggested that she and I go away for a few months before the next school term.

"We can't be slaves to the school," she told me. "And besides, Ivy will be here to watch over things. We can afford to go away for a while."

I was relieved to get away from Ivy's prying eyes, but even that made me feel guilty. How could I resent my own child when she was what I had made her? I resolved during our travels that I would concentrate on getting

closer to Ivy when we returned. I would find a
way to befriend her.

When we returned to Arcadia just a few
days before the start of fall term, though, I
found that Ivy had become more than ever set
in her dislike of me. She had used the time we
were gone to establish herself as the mistress of
Beech Hall and the ruling force of Arcadia.
She'd pried out of Mrs. Byrnes all her stories of
arcane festivals and rites and declared that the
school year would begin with a pagan bonfire
at which she, Ivy, would play the winter goddess. I laughed when I first heard her plans,
but then she reminded me of the May Day festival of our first summer here and asked why it
was any different. Was it that I wanted to play
a role? If so, I could play the summer goddess
who cedes her power to the winter goddess. I
assured her that I wanted nothing to do with
such a charade, but when Vera heard of the
idea she insisted I go along with it. "You'll look
lovely as the summer goddess, and it will set a
good example to the girls. Unless . . ." She fal-
tered, looking uncharacteristically unsure.

"Unless what?" I demanded.

She sighed. "Unless you're really afraid that
Ivy is taking your place. You know it's not like
that. No one could ever take your place
with me."

I blushed to think she would suspect me of

such petty jealousy. Especially when it was my own child I'd be jealous of—although of course she couldn't know that. I'd have to go along with Ivy's little play now, or else I'd look spiteful and insecure.

I wore the same white dress that I'd worn for May Eve so many years ago, with a wreath of daisies in my hair. When I appeared at the bonfire I was startled to see that Ivy was wearing an almost identical dress. She'd found an old photograph and copied the dress. On her the simple shift hung straight and severe. Instead of flowers in her hair she wore a wreath made up of twisted holly and ivy. Standing before the bonfire, she was a forbidding figure— a wrathful pagan deity. I gave a little speech about passing the mantel of inspiration to the next generation and ended it by handing her my wreath of flowers. She tossed the flowers into the fire and then called on the other girls to chase me from the campus.

I knew that this would be part of the "rite" so I wasn't surprised, but I was taken aback by the energy of the girls who chased me. I tried to make light of it, but I wasn't as young as I was on May Eve. I ran through the orchard and then ducked behind the Lodge, hoping that I wouldn't have to run uphill, but Fleur Sheldon spotted me and alerted the other girls. I could have just turned myself over to the girls and then been escorted up the ridge, but I hated to show my age—plus I had gotten my second wind. In fact, I ran so fast that soon the shrieks and laughter of the girls faded behind me. Caught up in the spirit of the game, I decided to play a little trick on them. At the top of the ridge I tore a strip of lace from my dress and draped it over a bush right by the edge of the clove. I was planning to hide behind the bushes and let them all think for a minute that they'd chased me over the ridge. Then I'd show myself before anyone became too worried.

As I turned around, though, I found Ivy standing at the edge of the clearing watching me. She'd outrun the other girls, but because she was so quiet I hadn't known she was so close.

"You've spotted my little trick," I said. "Unless you'd like to be a part of it." I smiled, hoping to establish a bond by sharing a secret together. She approached slowly, her eyes on the piece of cloth fluttering on the branch at the edge of the cliff.

"Miss Beecher would be upset . . ." she began.

"Oh, Ivy! I wouldn't play a trick like that on Vera. We'll tell the girls I'm all right before the news gets back to Vera."

". . . but she'd get over it in time," she finished. She looked up, her eyes meeting mine.

The look I saw there was as cold and empty as the night sky. I became immediately aware of how close we stood to the edge, how easy it would be for her to push me over . . . and then the clearing was full of the loud jubilant cries of young girls.

"Be off, Summer!" they cried. "It's Autumn's time now!"

"That's right," Ivy said, too low for anyone to hear but me. "It's my time now."

After the First Night bonfire I knew I'd have to do something to change the relations between Ivy and me. I would never gain her friendship as long as she saw me as her rival in Virgil's affections. I continued to pose for him—he was working now on a series of three bronze statues for a show at the National Arts Club to be held just after Christmas—afraid that if I stopped, Ivy might push herself forward into his attention. And although I'd come to trust Virgil not to take advantage of her, I couldn't bear to think of her making advances to the man who was in reality her father.

This, then, was the burden I endured these last few months. How could I turn Ivy away from Nash without telling her the truth? Throughout this fall I fretted over this conundrum until I made myself quite sick with worrying. Vera could not help but notice how preoccupied I was and it raised in her once more the old demon of jealousy. She began to resent the time I spent posing for Nash and would even remark upon it over dinner, asking Nash quite pointedly if he wasn't done yet, and hadn't he committed his subject to memory enough to be able to continue without a model.

"Every time I look at Lily, I see something I hadn't seen before," he answered.

Vera's face turned an angry red. Nothing infuriated her more than the idea that Nash knew me better than she did. The truth is that Nash **did** see me more clearly than Vera did. I'm afraid it was obvious to everyone that she was jealous of him, although I think that the girls mostly thought that she was jealous of his talent and success, not of **me.** Ivy wasn't so blind, though. She watched me carefully whenever Vera and Nash and I were in the same room, and she noted the growing hostility between Vera and Nash. I could see how uncomfortable it made her. She might be infatuated with Virgil Nash, but she still idolized Vera. She couldn't bear to see the two of them at odds. Finally last week I went to Nash and begged him to leave Arcadia. I said nothing about Ivy but spoke only of Vera's jealousy.

"As long as you are here, there will be no peace between us," I told him.

He looked up from the clay model he had

sculpted of me—the last of the three and the smallest. In this one I stood in a pool of water, looking over my shoulder, as if I were Diana surprised at my bath. The pool at my feet was full of water lilies, a reference to my name. It was my favorite of the three statues and it was hard to be angry with Nash while looking at it. "You're throwing me out of paradise?" he asked.

"It won't be a paradise if you stay," I replied.

Nash sighed. He turned the statue around on its revolving plinth. Then he looked up and grinned at me. "To tell you the truth, I was getting a bit restless. Teaching Fleur Sheldon is enough to drive a man mad. It's like trying to teach a monkey to paint. If I make my escape, do you promise not to give the Sheldons my forwarding address?"

"I'll tell them you disappeared without a trace!" I promised, "On one condition." I touched the head of the little statue. "Would you make another copy of this for me to keep?"

He put his hand to his chest. "I'm touched you want a reminder of me. Of course! I'll have it ready for you at the barn the day I leave." I didn't tell him that it wasn't of him I wanted a reminder; it was of myself as I once had been.

We agreed that his imminent departure

would remain our secret until after the Christmas Day dinner that marked the end of term.

That was yesterday. After dinner, Nash followed me into Vera's office where I'd gone to retrieve a book she wanted me to bring back to the cottage. She had gone on ahead of me, so I wasn't afraid of her seeing us together, but I asked him to close the door anyway.

"Your statue will be ready by four tomorrow," he said. "Will you come to the barn to take it as my farewell present to you? My train leaves at five."

"Yes," I told him. "I'll be there by four."

"And have you kept your promise to me and kept my new address a secret from that little monkey?"

"You shouldn't be so cruel to her," I said. "She can't help how she is. It's how she was raised—"

"Or not raised," he said.

I had to agree. For all her hovering over Fleur, Gertrude Sheldon was a curiously neglectful mother. She left the girl alone here over the break while she went to Europe on a skiing holiday, for instance.

"It's just that I feel sorry for the poor girl," I said. "If only she had a little talent—"

"Dear Lily." He put his hand to my face and for a moment I was afraid that he would embrace me, but he let his hand drop. "Always looking after everyone but yourself. I hope that will change now. I'll see you tomorrow then, at four in the barn."

I spent last night and this morning writing in this journal. Vera has gone to the Hall to finish replying to the Christmas cards we received. I chided her for working on the holiday, but in truth I was glad that she gave me the time and privacy to complete this. Or almost privacy—Fleur Sheldon was here earlier, wanting to show me some of her drawings. I felt bad for the girl, abandoned by her mother for the holidays, and spent a half hour with her. I had to tell her I had an urgent appointment in town with Dora and Ada in order to get her to leave.

I will put this journal behind the beech panel in the mantel, above the hearth that has been the center of our lives together. Ivy is coming soon to pick up some papers and I will send a note to Vera telling her—in language only she will understand so it will be safe from prying eyes—where to find it. Then it will be up to Vera to decide whether she will still have me or not. I can't continue to play a role. When I look at the paintings Virgil Nash has done of me this last year and a half, I see a woman who stands naked in the sunlight as if she has nothing to hide. That is the woman Nash sees when he looks at me and that is the woman I want to be again and I can't be that woman if I continue to keep the truth—about Nash, about Ivy—from her. Even if Vera can't forgive me—and yet I can't believe she won't have the heart to—it is better to live honestly than continue to live a lie.

And so, my darling Vera, this part of my story ends here. It's up to you what the next part of my story will be. I put myself entirely into your hands.

CHAPTER 26

When I finish the journal my face is wet with tears. Is it because Lily hadn't betrayed Vera after all? Or because somehow her plans all went awry? Did Vera read the journal and reject her pleas for forgiveness? Did she force Lily out into the storm? Or did Lily flee and throw herself from the ridge into the clove after Vera rejected her?

I get up off the couch and cross

to the fireplace. I run my fingers along the broken tiles as if they were a braille message that could tell me what happened in this room sixty years ago. But the only answer I get is a knock at the front door which makes me nearly jump out of my skin.

In the seconds it takes me to answer, I've posited half a dozen disasters that could have befallen Sally. Finding Callum Reade on the other side of the door doesn't dispel any of them. He must read the look of panic on my face.

"It's nothing to do with Sally," he says. "I got a call from the dean saying she was handling the girls' punishment and thanking me for not summonsing them. I just wanted to make sure everything was okay. She sounded pretty severe. . . ." His voice trails off and I realize he's staring at me—at my chest, to be precise. I look down, afraid I've answered the door in my nightgown, but it's worse than that. I'm wearing his sweatshirt—and nothing else under it.

When I look back up, his eyes lock on mine and I feel something click inside of me, like a bolt sliding home. As if he'd heard it, he steps toward me and stops when he's an inch away. I don't move back. He moves his hand to my face, his fingers stroking my cheekbone, his palm cupping my jaw. I feel as if I am one of his wood carvings, taking shape under his hands. Then he tilts my face up and leans down to kiss me.

For a moment, as his lips first brush mine, I feel

as if we are suspended in time. We've both become statues frozen in the moment of the kiss. I almost want to stay like this forever. Almost.

I'm not sure who moves first, but suddenly we're both moving. His arms wrap around my back, pulling me tight against him; his hands slip beneath the heavy sweatshirt. When he finds bare skin beneath, he moans. Or maybe I'm the one who moans. He takes a step back—somehow we're at the foot of the stairs—and places his palm flat against my sternum.

"I don't want to rush you," he begins. "I don't know if you're ready."

Instead of speaking—I'm not sure I can—I press my hand over his and move it over my heart so he can feel how fast it's beating. Then I interlace my fingers in his, turn, and lead him upstairs to my room.

Sometime in the early hours of the morning, he asks, "When you answered the door you looked like you'd been crying. Was it Sally you were upset about?"

"Partly," I answer. "But also about something I'd been reading . . ." I stop, unsure if I should go on. For a few hours I've forgotten that a world exists beyond this bed. Now I'm reluctant to let it in. But then I glance toward the window and see that the sky is lightening above the tips of the pine trees. The world will be with us soon enough anyway.

I tell him about finding Lily's journal and all that

I've read in it, along with what I learned from Beatrice Rhodes. By the end I'm sitting cross-legged on the bed—in his sweatshirt again—reading the last bit of the journal to him. When I'm done, Callum doesn't say anything right away. He lies with one arm bent beneath his head, looking up at the ceiling. I resist the urge to trace the lines of his face with my hand or push my fingers through his short hair that seems to bristle with electricity when I touch it.

"So Lily didn't mean to leave Vera after all," he says about three seconds before I would have completely changed the subject. "I'm glad. I always thought less of Lily for it."

"So now we have to think less of Vera. She must have read the journal and been unable to forgive her."

"Maybe," he says, frowning. "But if she'd read the journal then why has it been lost all these years?"

"Do you think Ivy kept the note from Vera?"

"I think Lily was foolish to trust her. Make me a promise: if you ever have something important to tell me make sure you do it face-to-face, okay?"

I smile at the implication that we will have important things to tell each other in the future. He grins back at me. "You mean," I say, leaning down so that my lips are inches from his ear, "if I have to tell you **this**, for instance?" I whisper the rest in his ear. I'm not sure who blushes the most.

"**That**," he says, pulling me down beside him, "should definitely **never** appear in writing!"

———

When we finally get out of bed, I find I've barely got enough time to shower if I want to have time to run by the dorm and check on Sally as I was planning to do before class.

"I'm coming back here to keep an eye on the Halloween bonfire," Callum says at the door, "Or Samhain bonfire, as these crazy pagans are calling it."

"Oh, I guess if you **have** to come back here—"

He grabs me and burrows his head in my neck. "I'll be back here for you if you want me," he murmurs, brushing his lips against my clavicle.

I shiver and press my lips against his earlobe. "Yes, I want you to come back," I say. "After the bonfire?"

"After the bonfire." He lifts his head and grins at me. "As long as roast sheriff isn't on the witches' menu tonight." Then he turns and leaves before I can tell him it isn't a very funny joke.

I stop at Sally's room, but Haruko tells me that Sally went out early. "She was meeting Chloe to talk about tonight's **thing**." She rolls her eyes on the word **thing.**

"You're not too into these rites, are you?" I ask.

"Not really," she says. "I thought they were kind of fun at first, but now I think some people take them too seriously."

"By 'some people,' do you mean Chloe?" Haruko

looks visibly uncomfortable. If Sally finds out I've been grilling her roommate, she'll never forgive me. "Forget I asked you that," I say. "It's none of my business."

"No," Haruko says, "actually it is your business. I think there's something really bothering Chloe. Someone ought to talk to her and you're probably the best one to do it."

"Why me?"

"Because Sally says you know how to listen without judging people. I think Chloe's afraid to tell anyone about what happened the night Isabel died because people will judge her, but she might talk to you if you tried."

"Okay." I want to ask Haruko if Sally really said that about me, but don't. "I'll try to talk to Chloe."

I leave Haruko, determined to repay the girl's trust by talking to Chloe. First, though, I have to get through Folklore. Fortunately, there's only one report left and the students are all anxious to get out early so they can get ready for tonight's festivities. I'm hopeful that I'll be able to end the class early and have enough time to talk to Chloe before my seminar. Since she's the one giving her report today, it will seem natural to ask her to stay after.

She comes to the front of the room carrying a large artist's portfolio. "I don't really have all that many mementos and photographs that I felt like sharing," she begins. "My parents travel a lot—my father works for the State Department—and so I've been in boarding schools since I was, like, ten."

A few students make sounds of agreement and I realize that many of these students must have been sent here by parents too busy to deal with them at home.

"So I decided I wanted to do something a little different for my project. I hope that's okay with you, Ms. Rosenthal?"

Chloe should have cleared a change of topic with me first, but I can tell her that when I talk to her after class. "I'm curious to see what you've done," I say.

"I started thinking that the Arcadia School was more like my family than my own family and so I did the project on the school's history. Isabel and I were working on a paper together about the history of Arcadia before First Night, but then . . . well, after Isabel died the dean said she didn't need to see the paper and that I should just forget about it . . . but I haven't been able to. I mean, Isabel did a lot of work on the project—more than I did, honestly, and I thought it would be a sort of tribute to her to finish it."

Someone in the classroom snorts. I turn to glare at Tori Pratt. "Do you have something you want to share, Victoria?"

"Isn't what Chloe's done, like, plagiarism? She's just taking Isabel's work and trying to pass it off as her own."

"Isabel wrote the paper, but I've illustrated it." Chloe opens the portfolio and takes out several pieces of stiff bristol board. She places them on the easel. The first picture facing out is a watercolor of a woman holding a baby beneath the copper beech tree.

"Is this supposed to be from **The Changeling Girl**?" I ask.

Chloe shakes her head. "Not exactly. You see, Isabel had this theory that **The Changeling Girl** was autobiographical and that it was really a story about what women had to give up to become artists. She thought Lily Eberhardt had given up her own child in order to stay at Arcadia with Vera Beecher."

I'm so stunned to hear the same version of events that I've just read in Lily's journal that I don't say anything. Chloe removes the first picture and slides it behind the others. The new watercolor shows Lily standing on the edge of the ridge, still holding the baby. With her is another figure, which I guess is supposed to represent Vera Beecher. The tame, bucolic landscape of the campus lies below them on one side, the wild rocky cleft of the clove on the other. Vera is gesturing toward the clove as if demonstrating the view, but I already have a queasy feeling that something else is going on in these pictures.

"Vera Beecher believed a woman couldn't be an artist and a mother, too," Chloe says, "so she asked Lily to give up her baby. But Lily wouldn't. . . ."

Chloe slides the last picture in front. As I feared, it shows Lily Eberhardt leaping into the clove, her white dress billowing about her like a cloud, her baby floating beside her like an angel in a baroque altarpiece. It's strangely beautiful but also very disturbing. The class seems stunned by it as well. Any minute now they'll recover and start asking questions about how Isabel could have come up with this bizarre story—and I don't want that. I want to find out first.

"Okay," I say, "that's a really original way to approach the topic and I'm sure you all have a lot of questions for Chloe, but I wanted to give you extra time today to get ready for the Halloween celebration, so why don't you save your questions for tomorrow? Class dismissed."

The class is quick enough to shake themselves out of their stupor and leave. Chloe starts to slide her pictures in the portfolio, but I tell her to wait. "I want to talk to you about your project," I say.

As they pass on their way out, Tori Pratt says something to Justin Clay and then laughs. Chloe glares at them as they leave, but as soon as they're out the door, Chloe's lower lip begins to quiver.

"I know I should have okayed the project with you before I did it, but I thought you'd like it!" she wails. "You're so into that changeling story and Isabel's paper was all about that."

"It's okay, Chloe, I'm not angry, I'm just curious. Where did you get Isabel's paper? I thought she was

delivering it to the dean the afternoon of the bonfire."

"She was . . . I mean she did. But when I checked
my e-mail the next day I saw she'd also sent it
to me."

"Huh. I'm surprised. When I saw the two of you
I thought you were mad at her because she hadn't
given you the paper."

"I was, but I guess she figured that if she sent it to
me before she went to the dean's office it would look
like she'd done what she was supposed to do. She
knew I wouldn't get it until after she turned the
paper in to the dean. The whole thing backfired, because when Dean St. Clare found out we hadn't
worked on it together she gave us both Fs anyway."

"And the dean kept the paper?"

"Yeah . . . I guess so." Chloe furrows her brow,
confused at the direction I've taken.

"And do you know where Isabel got the idea that
Lily Eberhardt had a baby that she gave up?"

"No. Isabel was really secretive about her sources.
She kept bragging that she was doing **original** research, but she wouldn't say what she meant. And
then she didn't even send the bibliography with the
paper when she e-mailed it to me."

"I see. Do you have the paper?"

Chloe nods and takes out a folder from her portfolio. "I'm really sorry I didn't talk to you about it
first. I thought it would be a way of making it up to
Isabel. . . ."

An anguished look crosses her face. I put my hand on her arm and lean toward her. "Is there something you're not telling about what happened that night?" I ask. "I remember that you were mad at Isabel."

Chloe looks up at me, her eyes wide, frightened at what she's let slip. I'm frightened, too. If Chloe admits to hurting Isabel, what will I do? "She was always so sure of herself," she says, looking miserable. "I just wanted to give her a little scare."

"What kind of a scare, Chloe?"

"You know those white dresses that Ms. Drake made for us? Well, there was an extra one for a girl who had to go home. I took it and hung it from a tree near the edge of the woods. Then I made sure Isabel ran in that direction—"

"So she'd think it was a person hanging in the tree and be frightened by it?"

"Yeah. She was a wuss about that kind of thing."

"So did it work?"

Chloe bites her lip and nods. "She went into the woods right where I'd rigged up the dress, and a minute later I heard her shriek. I thought she'd run straight out again, but instead she must have run deeper into the woods."

"And you didn't follow her?"

Chloe shakes her head, her eyes filling with tears. "We're not **allowed** in the woods and I'd already gotten in enough trouble."

I sigh, exasperated at the fractured logic of

teenagers. They often choose the most inconvenient times to follow the rules. Then I notice that Chloe still looks fidgety. It's a look I know well from Sally.

"Is there something else you're not telling me, Chloe?"

"It's nothing really. It's just . . . I thought I saw someone—another one of the girls—farther up the hill, but then she vanished and I thought I must have imagined it. . . ." She looks embarrassed.

"What is it Chloe? What did you see?"

"It's stupid. . . . It was just one of the girls in a white dress. But when she vanished I thought of the story about the white woman who haunts the woods and it kind of freaked me out. **That's** why I didn't try to follow Isabel. Pretty stupid, huh? I was trying to scare Isabel, but I ended up scaring myself."

After I send Chloe on her way, I start walking toward the Lodge, but halfway across the lawn I stop at the bench beneath the beech tree and sit down to think. Although Chloe's pictures depicted a garbled version of Lily's story, it bore enough resemblance to the real thing to make me wonder if Isabel had had access to Lily's journal. I take out the paper now and read the first paragraph.

Lily Eberhardt wrote in her private journal, "We carried the seeds of destruction into paradise." She was referring to the romantic triangle between herself, Vera Beecher, and the painter Virgil Nash. In fact the seed of destruction that she and Vera Beecher brought to Arcadia was their assumption that motherhood and artistic creation were mutually exclusive—an assumption that was tested the first year of the colony when Lily Eberhardt became pregnant. Lily's attempt to hide her pregnancy is what brought about her death.

I put down the paper and exhale. How else could Isabel have learned about Lily's pregnancy unless she read Lily's journal. But how could she have gotten it? Then I remember: the week before I arrived Isabel and Chloe were cleaning Fleur-de-Lis . . . or at least they were **supposed** to be cleaning. Hadn't Chloe said that she found Isabel with her nose in a book when she was supposed to be cleaning? Isabel must have found the journal behind the panel in the fireplace. She must have thought she'd struck gold and that the dean would be impressed when she saw the paper—but she hadn't been. I imagine Ivy's reaction to this first paragraph. Her first question must have been where had Isabel found the journal. Had Isabel realized then that she would be blamed for stealing the journal from Fleur-de-Lis?

Chloe wasn't the only one who caught a glimpse of a figure dressed in white on the night of the bonfire. On my way back to the cottage I saw someone in white flitting through the woods. I thought it was my imagination—as Chloe did—and then, later, when Callum told me about the **wittewieven** I thought I'd spied the white woman who haunted the clove. Now I wonder if it was Isabel Cheney coming back from Fleur-de-Lis after putting Lily's journal back where she found it. It's the kind of thing a teenager would do—repairing a wrong by hiding the evidence. Did she think the dean wouldn't keep after her to find out where the journal was?

I look up toward the dean's office. In full sunlight the glass is an opaque surface reflecting trees and sky; it's impossible to tell if anyone is looking out. On First Night, though, I saw the dean silhouetted against the dark windowpane. **She's always watching,** Callum had said. Had she watched from her window on First Night, waiting for a chance to confront Isabel and take the journal? Was she the white woman Chloe had seen in the woods behind the Lodge? Had she followed Isabel into the woods and confronted her at the top of the ridge?

I get to my feet, agitated by the picture in my head of Ivy St. Clare cornering a frightened girl on the edge of the cliff . . . but my mind balks. Ivy couldn't want the journal enough to kill for it, could she? I wonder what Callum would think. If my cell phone worked I could call to tell him what Chloe's told me, but as it is I can't think of anyplace private enough to make that call. I'll call after my last class, I promise myself as I cross under the copper beech. The thought of talking to Callum later—of seeing him again—sends a pulse of desire through my core so strong I have to stop and put my hand on the beech's trunk to steady myself for a moment. Images from last night flood through my mind as steady as the fall of wine red leaves from the tree. Have I gone too fast? What do I really know about this man? The force of my desire scares me. I take deep breaths to calm myself, and then, recovered, I give the tree a farewell pat. Its bark is smooth and curiously warm. Then I walk briskly to the Lodge.

I reach the Lodge, still deep in thought. Peter and Rebecca are in the lounge, dark heads bent together, whispering. They look up when I enter, four identical brown eyes staring at me like the eyes of deer caught grazing. I look from them to the paintings above their heads: Nash's last three portraits of Lily.

As I look at the paintings I think of a young Callum Reade, held spellbound by the force of Lily's gaze. **She was looking at me as if she saw right through me to my soul and knew all my secrets,** he had said. Could the man who painted her like this have abandoned her in the snowstorm to die?

I look back down at Rebecca and Peter, who are now exchanging quizzical looks at my behavior. "The first day we met you said it was fascinating that the man who did these paintings of Lily **killed** her. Tell me again why you said that," I ask.

"Everyone knows that she died on her way to meet him—" Rebecca begins.

"—and that he left for the city without telling anyone she didn't show up," Peter finishes for her.

"It was in the middle of a blizzard and he must

have known that she was coming through the clove," Rebecca adds.

"But he didn't even go back to check if she was okay."

"He must have felt guilty because he killed himself later."

I shake my head. "You're right. It would have been as good as killing her not to look for her. But what if she came and then went back because she never intended to leave with him in the first place?"

"Then it wouldn't have been Nash's fault at all," another voice says.

I turn and find Shelley standing in the doorway. She's wearing her smock, which is spattered with white paint. As she comes into the lounge I see that her face and hair are also paint-splattered and her pupils are unnaturally dilated. She looks like she's waking from a trance.

"The tragedy is that everyone blamed him," Shelley continues. "No one would have anything to do with him after Lily's death. My mother, who had taken classes with him here at Arcadia and very much admired him, said she saw him in Europe the next summer. He was a drunken wreck, she said. He killed himself on the one-year anniversary of Lily's death."

"That **is** tragic," I say, thinking of Lily's description of how full of hope Nash had been while making these last paintings.

"Yes," Shelley agrees. "Even more so if Lily didn't

die going to see him. Do you have some reason to think that she was on her way back from Nash when she died?"

I start to answer but then remember the twins. "Peter, Rebecca," I say, "would you mind if we canceled class today? I need to talk to Professor Drake."

Two identical heads shake in perfect unison. "No problem. We still have to work on our costumes. We're going as the Scarlet Witch and Quicksilver."

"Wait, I know this," I say, proud to possess this bit of esoteric knowledge. "They're the twin children of Magneto."

Peter and Rebecca exchange one of their unreadable looks, and then reward me with identical smiles. "Pretty slick, Ms. Rosenthal."

Shelley, though, is staring at me. "I've never heard of them. What body of mythology are they from?"

"Marvel Comics," I answer. "One of the advantages of having a teenager."

On the way to Shelley's studio I tell her about Isabel's paper and my fear that the dean might have confronted Isabel to get Lily's journal back. "What I don't understand is why Ivy would want the journal so desperately," I conclude.

"I think I have an idea why. There's something my mother says in her letter. . . ." When she opens the door, I'm so dazzled by a burst of white light that I don't quite follow what she's saying. At first I think the light must be coming from the windows, but the light at this time of day is still subdued. The glare is coming from the dozen or so high-powered spot-lights arranged around the room. Shelley sees me squinting and apologizes.

"Oh, my, let me turn these off," she says, scurry-ing from lamp to lamp. "I borrowed them from the film department so I could paint last night. You know how it is when the muse hits you; nothing else matters, not even sleep."

I nod, but really, what do I know of that kind of single-minded devotion to one's art? I've barely fin-ished a thought—let alone a drawing—in the past sixteen years without being interrupted by some-thing I had to do for Jude or Sally. I feel a bit envi-ous looking at what she's done. Clearly the source of her inspiration was the May Day photograph of Gertrude, Mimi, and Lily. She's reproduced the fig-ures of the three women on an enormous canvas. On such a large scale they look like goddesses—the Three Graces, perhaps. But she didn't stop there. The white-clad women have wandered into her paintings of the woods where they slip in and out of the shadows like shrouded ghosts.

"Wow, all this from one photograph?" I ask.

"The photograph gave me the idea for the first painting, but it was my mother's letter that made me decide to let the women wander through the woods."

"Her letter?"

"I was just telling you!" She sounds annoyed and I realize that lack of sleep has made her irritable. "Here," she takes a cream-colored envelope out of her smock pocket and shoves it into my hands. "You'll see."

I slip the heavy pages out of the envelope and read.

January 15, 1948

Dear Mother,

I apologize for not writing sooner, but the last few weeks have been very upsetting. You'll have heard by now about poor Lily Eberhardt. A few days after Christmas, I found Ivy in the Hall foyer placing a statue Mr. Nash had done of Lily in a dark alcove. It was so beautiful—it depicts Lily as a water nymph standing in a pool of water lilies. I asked where it came from. Ivy said that Lily had left it behind when she ran away with Mr. Nash, but I didn't believe a word of it. I thought Ivy was just jealous—why else would she hide the beautiful statue in a dark alcove as if it were some ordinary piece of bric-a-brac?

A week later, a package arrived with three paintings of Lily that Nash had sent to Miss Beecher. It was clear from the letter Mr. Nash enclosed that Lily wasn't with him. That's when they began to look for her. It took three more days before they found her body frozen in the clove. I was in the Rose Parlor working on my portrait (you were right about staying here over the vacation—I've learned so much that I wouldn't have if I'd gone with you and Father to Chamonix) when her body was brought into the main hall. I thought that a wild dog had gotten loose in the house, there was such an inhuman howling echoing through the halls, but when I went to find the source of the noise I came upon this most extraordinary tableau. The body was laid out on the big oak refectory table upon a red and gold tapestry runner. From her long blond hair that was spread out all about her, I knew at once that it was Lily. Her face was white as snow. Vera was knelt before her, and Ivy stood behind Vera with one hand on her shoulder. I came from behind so neither of them saw me.

"She looks like she froze to death," Vera said. "Are you sure the fall is what killed her?"

"Of course I'm sure," Ivy answered. "Remember? I checked to make sure."

Today the medical examiner confirmed what Ivy said. He's decreed that Lily died of a blow to the head, caused most likely when she slipped and fell in the clove and struck her head on a rock.

I thought perhaps that the term might be postponed (and waited to write you until I knew), but when I went to Miss Beecher's office to ask I found Ivy there—sitting behind Miss

Beecher's desk!—and she told me no, it was Miss Beecher's wish that the school continue as usual.

I wondered, though, if you would wish me to continue here as it was primarily for the sake of studying with Miss Eberhardt and Mr. Nash that you sent me, and now both of them are gone. I feel the loss of Miss Eberhardt, most especially as she behaved like a mother to me. Nor do I like the way Ivy is taking over. I'm sure you'll agree that it's better for me to leave here. I think I've learned all that I can from this place.

Yours truly,
Fleur Sheldon

I look up from the letter and meet Shelley's intense blue stare. "Do you see what's wrong?" she asks.

I'm tempted to say that what's wrong is that her grandmother had clearly abandoned her daughter in this school and had such a stilted relationship with her that Fleur felt it necessary to sign her full name on a letter to her mother. But I know that's not what she means.

"Ivy says that she checked to make sure that the fall killed her. So she and Vera must have been in the clove when Lily fell."

CHAPTER 27

"Maybe Vera went looking for Lily, saw her coming back through the clove, and then saw her fall."

"Then why wouldn't she have gone for help?" Shelley asks. "Why would she have left her beloved Lily lying in the clove and pretend that Lily had run off with Nash? Why did she wait for the searchers to find her body?" With each question, Shelley stabs her finger at her mother's letter.

"If it wasn't an accident," I say. "If Vera struck her . . ."

"Or if Ivy did," Shelley adds.

"That would be awful."

"Why would it be worse than if Vera struck her?" she asks. "Vera was her lover."

"But Ivy was Lily's daughter."

Shelley's eyes widen. "She was? But they look nothing alike!" She points to the May Day painting. Shelley has perhaps idealized Lily's beauty, but the lithe, blond woman in the painting is not far from the photographs I've seen of Lily—and she's the polar opposite of tiny, dark-complected Ivy St. Clare.

I shrug. "Not all kids look like their parents," I say. "Ivy didn't know she was Lily's daughter. If she did have something to do with Lily's death, and she found out that Lily was her mother—"

"It would destroy her!" Shelley's tone is horrified, but there's a gleam in her eyes that seems almost gleeful. I remind myself that she's overworked and overtired.

"There's no telling how she might react. She might have already killed Isabel trying to get the journal back. We have to tell Cal—Sheriff Reade. Can I borrow your mother's letter to show him?"

I hold out my hand for the letter, but she holds it closer to her body. "Perhaps I should talk to the sheriff as well to back up your story."

"That's generous of you," I say, looking at her

paint-splattered clothes, her tangled hair and wild, shadow-ringed eyes. She hardly looks like the most reliable person to have as an advocate. "But I think I can handle it." She hands over the letter reluctantly. "I'll be careful with it," I say. "I'll show it to Sheriff Reade when he comes here tonight to supervise the bonfire." I look down at my watch, more to hide the blush that I can feel creeping into my face at the mention of Callum's name, but then I'm genuinely startled by the time. "Damn! I'm going to be late for my class. Please don't tell anyone what we've talked about. If Dean St. Clare thinks we're on to her, she might completely flip and hurt someone else. . . ." I falter, wondering if I should tell Shelley that Chloe saw someone in the woods that night, but Shelley's already grasped the importance of protecting Chloe.

"You mean if Ivy knew that Chloe read Isabel's paper she might hurt her. Chloe's in my drawing class next period. While you're teaching your class and meeting with Sheriff Reade I'll keep an eye on Chloe and make sure she's okay. I'll help her with her costume and stay close to her at the bonfire."

I hesitate for a moment, wondering if Shelley in her overexcited state is the best one for this job, but then realize I've no other choice. I can't be everywhere at once. "Okay, thanks. Just make sure Chloe doesn't go anywhere near the dean's office. Once I've talked to Sheriff Reade and he goes to see the dean, I'll come find you."

"Tell Sheriff Reade that Dean St. Clare always has tea in her office at four-thirty. That's the best place to find her alone."

"I'll tell him. Just make sure you keep an eye on Chloe . . . and if you can, Sally, too. She's in your drawing class, too."

Shelley gives me a reassuring smile. "Of course it's natural for you to worry about your own daughter, but what possible reason could Dean St. Clare have to hurt her?"

Throughout my last class of the day Shelley's words echo in my head, but they fail to reassure me. If Ivy suspects that I've had Lily's journal all along (and she **did** ask about the green book in my still life), she might be crazy enough to threaten Sally to keep me quiet. I only manage to keep myself from running to the Lodge by reminding myself that Sally is in class with Shelley. There's no reason to think she's anywhere near the dean. So I finish class as best as I can, then cross the sunlit lawn in front of Beech Hall and approach the site of the bonfire, where I see Callum standing with Shelley Drake.

From his posture—head tilted to one side, one hand resting on his hip a few inches from his holster—I can tell he's biding his time while Shelley, silver hair flying in the breeze, flails her arms and points at the wood piled high inside the stone circle. How strange, I think, that I've known this man only a few months and I can already read his body language. How strange that after only one night with him I feel an electric thread stretching from me to him as vibrant as the gold bars of late-afternoon sunlight sweeping the lawn. Before I reach him, he lifts his head and looks right at me as if he feels it, too. He smiles and I feel that thread pull tight inside me. Then he slants his eyes back at Shelley, who's paused to see who Callum's looking at, and turns his attention back to her, his face assuming the appropriate gravitas of a law enforcer.

I dodge around them when I see Sally. She's standing in a circle of students—some in Halloween costumes, others in jeans and T-shirts, all underdressed for the brisk air—huddled around an urn of hot apple cider. She looks like she's freezing. I take off my sweater and offer it to her, but she shakes her head. "I'll be fine when they stop artfully arranging the logs and light the bonfire."

"Artfully arranging?"

She nods. "Ms. Drake has been overseeing the construction since we got here. At least it got her unstuck from Chloe's and my side. She attached herself to us like Velcro after class until we promised we would stay right here."

"I'm afraid that's my fault," I admit. "I asked her to keep an eye on you."

"Really, Mom? What did you think was going to happen to me here? Did you think I'd fall into the bonfire?"

The irritation in her voice immediately triggers a

corresponding emotion and before I can stop myself I snap back. "Do I have to remind you that a student died the last time the school had a bonfire?"

She rolls her eyes at me. "I promise not to jump off a cliff. Okay?" She turns and heads back to the group of students who are now removing the top layer of wood from the bonfire. I consider following her but realize that in my present state of anxiety more talk will just escalate into an argument. I join Callum, who's lecturing Shelley on fire safety and bonfire construction.

"It looks so much more picturesque the way we had it, Sheriff Reade. But if you insist . . ."

"I do," he says. "That is, if you don't want to burn down the campus. And make sure the students maintain their distance so they don't light themselves on fire. Especially these kids in their long robes and capes." He points to a girl wearing a flowing red cape whom I recognize as Rebecca Merling dressed as the Marvel superhero Scarlet Witch. Her brother Peter is in a blue bodysuit emblazoned with a silver lightning bolt and wearing a silver wig that makes him look more like Andy Warhol than a superhero. They're standing behind a girl in a long white robe that's been painted with grayish veins to look like marble. When she turns, I'm startled to see that her hair is dusted with white powder, her arms are painted gray, and her face is a deathlike blue.

"Christ, what's Chloe Dawson got up as?" Callum asks.

"I'm surprised you don't know, Sheriff Reade, what with your Celtic ancestry," Shelley answers. I get the feeling she's glad to have something to lecture him on after his intrusion into her bonfire construction. "That's the Cailleach Bheur, the blue-faced hag, also known as the Queen of Winter. I was a little surprised when she came to me today and told me that she intended to dress up as this particular version of the Goddess. She asked me to help her draw marble veins on her robes and then she wanted to borrow marble dust from the sculpture room to rub on her arms and dust her hair so that she looked like a statue."

"Why a statue?" I asked.

"The Cailleach Bheur rules the land through the winter, but at Beltane—or May Day, as you may know it—she turns to stone. Tonight, on Samhain, she's reborn. Chloe plans to throw her marble robes in the bonfire to symbolize the transformation of the goddess from stone to flesh."

"It sounds a bit morbid, if you ask me," Callum says. "But I guess no one's asking. Did you want to talk?" he asks, catching my eye.

I nod and start to follow him, but Shelley grabs my arm and holds me back.

"Sheriff Reade is right. This idea of Chloe's to play the blue-faced hag **is** morbid," she hisses in my ear. "She clearly blames herself for Isabel's death. Perhaps if she knew that it was really Dean St. Clare who was responsible she would stop torturing herself."

"I think we'd better leave that to Sheriff Reade."
I glance over at Chloe, standing motionless and
apart from the group, her face an expressionless
mask under the blue paint. Maybe I **should** have a
word with her, I think, but when I glance in the direction of Beech Hall I see Callum, who has stopped
on the lawn and is waving impatiently for me to
join him.

"I'd better go," I tell Shelley. "When I'm done
with Sheriff Reade, I'll come back and talk to Chloe.
Just keep an eye on her, okay?"

"I won't let her out of my sight," Shelley assures
me, squeezing my arm with a surprisingly firm grip.
She turns and strides away, toward Chloe. When
I look down at my arm, I see white fingerprints
where she's touched me. It must be the marble dust
she used for Chloe's costume.

I start walking toward Callum, but stop one
more time to look back at Chloe. She's standing on
the crest of the hill overlooking the apple orchard.
Motionless in the last rays of sunlight she looks
eerily like a stone statue, an ancient one at that. I
understand why she's chosen this role. After Jude
died, I felt for the longest time as though I had been
turned to stone. I imagine Chloe feels much the
same. Maybe she thinks that by burning her marble
robes in the bonfire, she too will be reborn.

I turn away, brushing marble dust from my arm.
I wish Chloe luck, but I could tell her that recovering from her grief and guilt won't be that simple.

CHAPTER 28

I meet Callum under the beech tree and as we cross the lawn stoward the hall, I tell him what I've learned from Chloe and from Shelley about Fleur's letter. He listens attentively, nodding as he holds the door of Beech Hall open for me. As soon as the door closes behind us, he pulls me into the alcove in the foyer and kisses me. He pushes me against the wall and I push back—not to resist him but to press myself harder into his mouth, his skin, his scent. That pine and lemon and musk scent that I seem to have developed an addiction to. For a moment our desire is so perfectly matched that we hover in place like dragonflies with linked wings, and then he pushes a little harder and something hard jams into the small of my back.

"Ouch," I say, swiveling to remove the obstacle. It's the bronze statue of Lily standing naked in a pool of water, her long hair crowned by a wreath of flowers and streaming down her back. It's the water lily statue that Nash promised her on his last day at Arcadia.

"Lily seems to be coming between us," he says, placing the statue back in its dark niche.

"Maybe she's brought us together. If I hadn't gone to the barn that day . . ."

He strokes my face. I close my eyes, wanting to melt into his arms again, but mentioning the barn reminds me of what I've learned. I push him a few inches away and tell him what Chloe told me about the trick she played on Isabel and seeing someone else in the woods. Then I take out Fleur Sheldon's letter. "See?" I say, pointing at Fleur's account of the conversation between Vera and Ivy above Lily's body. "Ivy says she checked to see if Lily was dead, so she and Vera were there when Lily fell in the clove. And yet they left her body there. They must have had something to do with Lily's death."

"It's not much in the way of evidence," he says,

shaking his head. "And Chloe only saw a glimpse of a woman in white. Everyone was dressed in white that night. We have no way of telling if it was Ivy or not. Even if it was her, it doesn't mean that she pushed Isabel from the ridge."

"So you're not going to do anything?" I ask. "That woman might be guilty of murdering a **child**. How can we let her stay here in charge of all these young girls if that's possibly true?"

He strokes my arm, trying to calm me down. "I'll question her about that night again. You should go back to the bonfire. That's the best thing you can do to keep Sally and the other girls safe."

As frustrated as I am not to go with him, I have to admit he's right. "Okay," I say, "but will you come find me at the bonfire when you're done?"

He grins and pulls me tight against him. "I'll find you wherever you are." He kisses me again—hard and quick—and then leaves before I can think of an excuse to go with him. I watch him disappear down the long shadowy hallway and then turn to go out the front doorway.

As I do, the statue of Lily catches my eye. The bronze gleams where Callum's hand has rubbed away the dust. I pull a tissue out of my pocket and rub the statue until it glows. It should be someplace where the light catches it, I think as I return it to the niche. Fleur had said in her letter that Ivy hid the statue in a dark alcove because she was jealous of Lily.

I pick the statue up again.

Fleur had seen Ivy placing the statue in the alcove **before** Lily's body was found. But that had to be wrong. Nash had promised the statue to Lily on the last day before he left for his show in the city. She'd been going to the barn so he could give it to her, but she never made it back. The only way Ivy could have been in possession of the statue before Lily's body was found was if she had taken it from Lily in the clove. Together with the letter, the statue proves that Ivy and Vera met Lily in the clove. If Callum confronts Ivy with the statue, he'll have a much better case.

I start off down the hall, clutching the statue in my hand. The figure's hip fits smoothly in my palm, its weight a reassuring heft. . . .

I stop dead in the hall, a picture forming in my head of Lily climbing up through the snow, seeing Vera at the top. . . . Lily's holding the statue in her hand. What would Vera think when she saw her holding Nash's gift? Did they fight over it? Did Vera take it from her? Did she strike her in anger?

I hurry on, hoping I'll reach Callum before he goes into the dean's office. I find him standing in front of her door, paused there to collect his thoughts. I'm afraid he'll be angry when he sees me, but his first response is a smile, which he quickly schools into a frown.

"I told you to wait—"

"I know, but I realized something." I explain how

the statue couldn't have been in the alcove before Lily's body was found unless Ivy and Vera were in the clove that day. He takes the statue from me and turns it over, studying the ornately carved wreath on the figure's head.

"Can DNA survive from blood over sixty years old?" I ask.

Callum smiles and slips the statue into the deep pocket of his coat. "I'm not sure," he says. "But I'll tell you one thing: Ivy St. Clare won't know for sure either. Thank you. This might be just the thing to get her to confess. Now you should get out of here—"

Before he can finish, the door swings open and Ivy St. Clare appears in the entrance.

"Are you two going to stand there gossiping outside my door all night or come in?" she asks.

"I was just going," I say, but Ivy shakes her head.

"I think you'd better come in, Ms. Rosenthal," she snaps. "After all, you're the one who's been reading Lily's journal, haven't you?"

"How did you know I had it?" I ask, following Ivy into the office.

"From the still life you did," she says, walking to the window seat where her sketchpad lies open. She sits down and looks up at me. "Vera and I looked all over for it after Lily died, but we finally decided that she must have given it to someone for safekeeping. I always suspected it would turn up someday."

"Do you know what's in it?" I ask.

Ivy shrugs. The motion makes the hollows above

her clavicle bones deepen. She looks, I think, almost skeletal. "I imagine she unburdened herself about her affair with Virgil Nash. She seemed to think that Vera would forgive her if she confessed all, but she was wrong."

"How do you know that?" Callum asks.

Ivy looks up, pursing her lips. "I'll tell you if you tell me what else you've found. There is something else, isn't there?"

Callum takes out Fleur Sheldon's letter and hands it to her. She squints at it and then fumbles for the reading glasses hanging around her neck.

"Ah, Fleur Sheldon. I'd recognize her precious schoolgirl handwriting anywhere. Let's see what she wrote home to **Mummy.**" We wait while she reads. Callum looks poised to spring on her if she so much as smudges the letter, but she merely hands it back to him and takes her reading glasses off. "She always was a little snoop," she says. "And remarkably talentless. I hired her daughter out of pity—"

"It's clear from this that you and Vera Beecher knew of Lily's death before her body was found," Callum says, cutting short what's bound to be a long list of Shelley Drake's failings.

Ivy sighs. "I suppose one could deduce that from Fleur's ramblings, but what of it?" She shrugs and smiles. "Surely even an officer in a backwater like Arcadia Falls knows that doesn't constitute evidence of a crime."

Callum smiles and removes the statue from his

pocket. "No, but a murder weapon with the victim's blood on it does." He brandishes the statue so close to Ivy's face that she blinks and presses herself back against the window. For the first time since I've known her, I see a flicker of uncertainty in her eyes. But she quickly recovers.

"That's Nash's statue of Lily. An idealization, if you ask me, and rather amateurish. He sent it back to Vera with his paintings of Lily."

"No, he didn't," I say, pointing at the letter that she's let fall in her lap. "Fleur says that she saw you putting the statue in the alcove **before** the package with the paintings arrived. Nash gave it to Lily the night he left Arcadia. That was why Lily went to the barn. She was carrying it when you and Vera found her on the ridge."

"Was Vera angry when she saw her carrying Nash's statue?" Callum asks. "Did she grab it from Lily? Is that when Vera struck her?" I'm startled that Callum has imagined the scenario as I have, but when Ivy pales I realize why he's accused Vera and not Ivy.

"Vera would never have hurt Lily! She worshipped her. Look at her!" Ivy tilts her chin toward the painting behind her desk where Lily, as the Muse of Drawing, stands in her Grecian robes holding a pencil to her lips, her long golden hair flowing around her like a halo. "Lily wasn't human to Vera. She was an ideal. Vera would never have hurt her."

"Then we won't find Lily's blood on this statue

when I send it to the lab in Albany?" Ivy's eyes flick from the head of the statue back to Callum's pale eyes. It's a tiny motion, but Callum sees it and pursues his course. "You realize that you'll be charged as an accessory. If you tell us what happened now, though, the judge would take your assistance into consideration. After all, Vera's dead. What difference does it make if the world finds out that she killed her lover sixty years ago?"

"What difference?" Ivy leans forward, the tension in her small, wizened body evident in her clenched fists and the cords standing out on her neck. "Vera's memory is what holds this place together. It's what I've worked my whole life to preserve. I will not allow you to soil it with some sordid story the two of you have cooked up."

"Well, this is the story we'll tell," Callum says, slipping the statue back in his pocket and plucking Fleur's letter out of Ivy's lap. "Let's go, Ms. Rosenthal. I'll take you to the station and you can make your statement." He lays his hand on my arm and steers me toward the door, but before we've taken two steps Ivy springs to her feet. "It was me," she cries. "I killed her. Vera did nothing."

We turn. I'm grateful for Callum's hand on my arm because Ivy is terrible to look at. Her lips are stretched tight in a grimace that could be a scream, but I realize with horror is actually a smile. Every tendon in her neck and arms stands out like a road map of the secrets she's kept hidden all these years.

She's triumphant, I realize, to have this one service left to do for her idol. This must be what Callum counted on. "Tell us," he says softly.

Ivy sinks back down onto the window seat. She looks out the window toward the lawn where the students stand around the newly lit bonfire. "I heard Nash and Lily agree to meet at the barn in this very room," she says. "I was here, in the window seat, with the drapes closed. They never knew I was here."

I think back to what Lily had written in her journal about that last conversation with Nash. "Then you knew that Lily wasn't planning to go with Nash?"

"Yes, I knew. I was disappointed. I had hoped that she would leave with him. I knew that eventually she would turn Vera against me. I'd never be safe here—and where else could I go? She even had the nerve to make me her go-between. She gave me a note to carry to Vera—"

"But you never gave it to her, did you?"

Ivy smiles. "No, I didn't. Why should I? I told Vera that I overheard Lily planning her **elopement** with Nash and that I'd seen her heading toward the barn to meet him. She was standing right where you are now, Ms. Rosenthal. When I told her that, Vera swayed like a tree in the wind and collapsed to the floor. I sat by her and took her hand. I asked if she wanted me to go to the barn to see if I could bring Lily back. I meant to go and tell Lily that Vera didn't want her, but when Vera realized that she might still be able to catch up to Lily, she rushed from the Hall. She didn't even stop to take a coat, but ran out into the snow. It was coming down hard by then. I had to run to keep up with her. I was afraid I'd lose her . . . afraid, too, that if she saw Lily coming back from the barn she'd think she had decided not to run away with Nash. That Vera would forgive her. It was snowing so hard I could barely see the ridgeline above us. I held Vera back, afraid she'd fall over the edge if she went farther. Afraid she might throw herself over. 'She's gone,' she cried. 'Gone, gone, gone.' But then Vera gasped and looking up, I saw a shape appear out of the swirling snow, like a ghost appearing out of the fog, like those stories the villagers tell of a white woman rising out of the mist in the clove—" Her voice trembles at the memory, the image still horrible to her after all these years. "It was Lily standing on the edge of the ridge. I was so shocked I forgot to hold on to Vera and she ran toward Lily—only to welcome her back, I think—but Lily must have been startled to see her. She stepped back and fell."

"Are you sure she fell?" Callum asks.

"Yes. I'm positive. Vera would have thrown herself over into the clove with her if I hadn't stopped her. We could see her below us. I was sure she was dead, but Vera wanted to go down and check. I told her she was too upset to make the climb. I even told her she was too old! I told her I would go down. I made her sit on a fallen log below the crest of the hill. 'If I know you're watching me,' I told her, 'you'll make me nervous.' I promised that I'd call for her if Lily was still alive."

"And was she?" Callum asks.

Ivy doesn't answer right away. She looks out at the lawn toward the bonfire that is now burning in full force. She cranks open the narrow casement on the left side and the room is suddenly full of the sound of young voices raised in song. The sound seems to help her come to a decision. "Yes," she says, her back to us. "She was alive. She opened her eyes when I knelt down beside her and she said my name. I saw the statue where it had fallen beside her."

I cover my mouth to keep from crying out. I can picture the moment all too well. Lily, lying hurt in the snow, looking up to see her own daughter, thinking she had come to help her.

"I raised it and struck her." She turns away from the window. Her right fist is clenched as if she is holding the statue she had used to kill Lily.

"But why?" I ask, unable to stay quiet anymore.

"I did it for Vera. So she would be free of her at last."

"But you didn't tell Vera that," Callum says, his voice cold. "You let her think that Lily had died from the fall. You let her think that her lover had died running away from her."

"I didn't think that through at the time," Ivy

says. For the first time since she began her story, she looks ashamed.

But Callum doesn't let the point go. "You soon found a use for Vera's guilt, didn't you? You were the only one who knew her secret. She thought you were protecting her, but you were controlling her."

"It wasn't like that." Ivy turns away again and startles at something she sees through the window. Silhouetted against the orange glow of the bonfire are two figures walking briskly across the lawn toward Beech Hall. I recognize Chloe from her flowing robes and Shelley Drake from her mane of kinky hair lit red by the firelight. She's trying to catch up to Chloe.

"Whatever can be wrong with that girl?" Ivy says. "She's been a wreck since Isabel Cheney's death."

"You mean since her murder," Callum says, getting to his feet. He moves between the Dean and the door, blocking her exit.

Ivy frowns, creasing her face into a cluster of wrinkles. "Murder? But Isabel fell from the ridge."

"Isabel had Lily's journal," I say. "You knew that as soon as you read her paper."

"Her paper? Once I knew that Chloe and Isabel hadn't collaborated as they were supposed to, I didn't bother reading it. What was the point?"

Callum glances at me and I shrug. I can't tell if Ivy's telling the truth or not.

"So you weren't in the woods that night?" he asks.

She looks like she's about to deny it, but then she sighs. "Yes, I went to the ridge for a little while. I often go there."

"The scene of the crime," Callum says.

Ivy smiles. "No, young man, that's not it at all." She turns to me. "Do you remember what I told you the night they brought Isabel's body up from the ravine? That Vera believed Lily's spirit haunted the ridge?"

"Yes, I remember," I answer. "But then why would you go there when it was you who killed her? I would think it would be the last place you'd want to be."

"I go there because I think that if there is such a thing as spirits and if Lily's spirit is in those woods, then that's where Vera's spirit is, too. That's why I was in those woods on the night of the bonfire, to be close to Vera, not to hurt that silly girl. Really, what kind of monster do you think I am?"

"The kind that would kill her own mother!" The words come from the doorway where Chloe Dawson stands robed in sepulchral gray, one arm held straight out, only the tip of her pointed finger showing under the belled sleeve of her robe. In her blue face paint, she looks like an avenging fury. Ivy utters a strangled cry and takes a step back, but then she recovers herself.

"What nonsense! I didn't have a mother. I'm an orphan," Ivy cries. I look angrily at Shelley, who's come in behind Chloe.

"I didn't mean to tell Chloe," Shelley says, "but she was asking so many questions that it just came out."

"That's why you killed Isabel," Chloe says, taking another step toward the dean. Callum grabs her arm to keep her from getting any closer. "She read in Lily's journal that Lily was your mother, and you couldn't bear for anyone to know that you had killed your own mother."

Ivy drags her eyes away from Chloe and toward me. Her face, framed against the black window, is white with shock, her black eyes bottomless pits of dark. "Is that what Lily wrote in her journal?" she asks.

I look to Callum for help, but he's busy with Shelley, who's tugging at his sleeve. I look back at Ivy. What can I do? It's all bound to come out now. "Yes," I say. "Lily had a baby with Nash. She gave birth at St. Lucy's while she was working on the murals there. She named you Ivy because of the way your fingers clung to her." I've included this detail as a proof of Lily's love, but Ivy's look of horror deepens. "She thought you'd been adopted, but when she found out you hadn't, she brought you here—"

"Vera brought me here!" Ivy cries. She holds up her hands, clenched as if she were trying to hold on to the story as she knows it, but the sight of her own hands, curled in like tendrils of ivy clinging to a wall, makes her cry out again.

"Lily wanted you to think that," I say softly. I

step toward her, but she backs away. Her legs hit the window seat and she falls backward, her shoulder hitting the frame of the open casement window. She grasps the frame to keep from falling out. She looks around the room, at the ring of faces, and then her eyes move from the live faces in the room to the painted one behind the desk. The monumental figure of the Muse of Drawing looks back at her with Lily's eyes. Ivy gasps and then she swings her legs around and deftly slips out of the window and onto the lawn.

Callum is immediately at the window, but he's much too big to get through the narrow opening. Through the glass of the middle section I can see Ivy running toward the bonfire. We're all too busy watching her to notice that Chloe has opened the casement window on the other side. I grab for her as she slips through, but get only a handful of mottled gray sheet for my trouble. I quickly measure the narrow window with my eyes and decide I'll just fit.

"I'll go after them," I say.

I jump to the ground before anyone can object. I look back and see Callum framed in the bay window, scowling at me and yelling something, but I don't wait to hear what he's got to say. I turn just in time to see Chloe's pale robes, aglow in the light of the bonfire, disappearing over the rim of the hill. I run after her, skirting the edges of the bonfire, threading through the groups of students sitting on the lawn. When I reach the crest of the hill, I see

Chloe running between the skeletal shapes of leafless apple trees. She's heading toward the edge of the woods near the Lodge, presumably because she's seen Ivy St. Clare run in that direction.

I turn back toward the Lodge and see Callum and Shelley coming out of the Hall. If I wait, I'll lose Chloe. And if she catches up to St. Clare at the ridge, one or both of them might end up dead in the ravine. Just then, I glimpse Sally sitting with Clyde and Hannah. Sally looks up at me, her mouth a round O of surprise. I shout at her to tell Sheriff Reade where I've gone, and I run down the hill, keeping my eyes fixed on Chloe. I've underestimated the slope of the hill, though. About halfway down, I lose my footing, fall, and roll to the bottom.

Luckily I don't seem to have injured anything. I get to my feet, dizzy but with both feet firmly planted on the ground, facing the rows of apple trees. Their bare branches gleam silver in the light of the newly risen moon, their shadows all pointing west as if directing me toward the woods. When I look that way, I catch a glimpse of Chloe's pale robes slipping between the deeper shadows of the pine trees.

I try to run straight in that direction, but the apple trees block my way. In the moonlight their gnarled trunks assume contorted faces, much like Ivy St. Clare's wrinkled pixie face, scowling and grimacing at me. The dark pine woods are a relief in comparison. The moonlight that filters through the treetops onto the forest floor casts only the straight shadows of the tall pine trees. The ground is covered by soft pine needles that glisten under my feet. I see Chloe ahead of me, her white robe silver now in the moonlight. I follow her, climbing steadily uphill. She slips in and out of view between the broad-trunked pines, but it's clear now where we're headed.

It must seem natural to Ivy to head for the top of the clove, the place where she goes to commune with Vera's spirit. How must she feel tonight, though, going to the place where she killed Lily, knowing now that Lily was her mother? What state will Ivy be in when she gets to the top of the ridge? And how will she react to Chloe if Chloe gets there before me?

Which she will at this rate. As hard as I push, I can only run so fast uphill. Chloe has the advantage of a head start and youth.

Her one disadvantage turns out to be those flowing robes. I catch up to her at the fallen tree because the roots have snagged the hem of her robes. She's cursing and yanking on them when I reach her.

"Chloe, wait!" I call, my voice coming out in hoarse, breathless gasps.

She turns her head in my direction and I stop, frozen to the spot. I've forgotten about the blue face paint. In the moonlit clearing her hair, robe, and marble-painted arms gleam, but her face is invisible. There's only a black hole where it should be.

My call has also caught Ivy's attention. She's

standing on the top of the ridge, just above Chloe. "Both of you leave me alone," she calls. "This is none of your business. It's between Vera and me."

Chloe turns away from me, toward Ivy, and I see Ivy scream, her hands rising to cover her mouth. I can guess what she sees—an empty, faceless shroud. From the look of horror on her face I imagine that it's Lily's face she sees in the darkness. I reach for Chloe to keep her from going any farther. I manage to grasp her arm, but just then I hear a voice behind me.

"Mom?"

In the moment I take to turn toward Sally, Chloe escapes my grasp. Shielding Sally with my arm I watch as Chloe takes a step up the hill and Ivy takes a step backward, placing her on the edge of the cliff. She totters, looking backward over her shoulder into the deep drop. She seems to gain her balance for a moment, but then she looks again at Chloe. She sets her mouth in a firm line and takes one more step backward into thin air, choosing the sharp drop into the abyss over the abyss that's staring her in the face.

CHAPTER 29

Callum finds us on the edge of the cliff, my arms clamped so tightly around Chloe and Sally that my biceps will ache for a week. He shines his flashlight over the edge of the cliff, illuminating Ivy's broken body a hundred feet below us. Then he shines the flashlight on each of us in turn— Sally, Chloe, and then me. He holds it on me.

"Are you okay?" He practically

barks the question. Chloe shields her eyes from the light and whimpers at the harshness of his voice, but I understand the fear underlying it.

"We're okay," I say. "Ivy jumped. She killed herself."

Callum nods—one curt bob of his head—and then stands up. Waving the flashlight over his head he calls into the night, "We're over here!"

Here echoes in the chasm below us. Chloe begins to shake and I relax my grip enough to pat her back. Callum kneels down next to us and I whisper in his ear, "Can you get Chloe away from the edge?"

As soon as he puts his arm around Chloe, I put both of mine around Sally. Callum turns Chloe firmly away from the clove and guides her downhill. The second her gaze is torn away from the drop, she begins crying, as if she'd been held transfixed by the dizzying abyss and only now realizes how close she came to going over. I hear voices coming up the hill—Shelley Drake, Toby Potter, Dymphna Byrnes—all of them ready to take care of her. And us, I suppose, but I don't turn to them just yet.

"Honey," I say to Sally, "it's okay. We can go now."

"I was afraid that something was going to happen to you." She speaks so low I have to lean my head toward her mouth. "That's why I followed you. But if I hadn't . . . you could have stopped her. . . ." She begins to shake and I pull her tight against me.

"I don't think anyone could have stopped her."

I'm not sure if it's true, but Sally doesn't argue. I hold her to me as the moon rises high enough in the sky to reach down into the chasm. I can feel it, an icy wave, moving through me the way a current of cold water sometimes comes over you in the ocean, only this wave is made of light, flowing into the clove, sweeping over the waterfall, the tumbled rocks and, finally, the broken body of Ivy St. Clare. Just as the snow covered Lily's body sixty years ago, so the moonlight blankets Ivy now. They're down there together, I think. As if Lily had been lying there all these years waiting to pull her daughter— her murderer—down into the clove with her.

I, too, start to shake. Then I feel myself covered with warmth. Callum's behind us, wrapping a blanket around both our shoulders, coaxing us away from the edge. I have to close my eyes before I can break the pull of the clove and go with him. But even as I walk down the hill I carry its chill with me, like a lump of ice lodged in my gut.

For the next few weeks every time I close my eyes I see the clove covered in moonlit snow. At night I dream of it. Each night it's the same: I'm standing on the edge of the cliff, looking down into the clove. Lily in her white May Day dress stands at the bottom. Instead of a wreath of flowers around her head, her blond hair is rimed with frost. She holds out her arms and another white-clad figure joins her. It's Ivy St. Clare. She has a wreath of ivy in her hair.

The two women link arms and then they both hold out their arms. They're waiting for the third member of their party—the third Grace—and I suddenly know it's me they're waiting for. I feel the pull of their wills dragging me down into the clove, my feet move closer to the edge, my weight leans over . . . and then I see, to my relief, another figure is joining them.

Thank God, I think, it doesn't have to be me. But when the third robed figure lifts its head, I see that beneath her cowled hood there's nothing. The third figure has no face.

Then I fall.

I wake up flinching against the sensation of plummeting downward. Unable to go back to sleep, I go downstairs, creeping softly so as not to wake Sally. Since Ivy St. Clare's death, Sally has stayed in the cottage with me. At first I was glad to keep her close, but as the days have passed and she's shown no sign of wanting to go back to the dorm, I've begun to worry. Is she staying with me because she thinks I need her? Or because she's frightened of something? Should we just leave the school altogether? Or would running away only make it worse? I feel as if we're still on the ridge, clutching each other to keep from falling over the edge. I'm afraid that if I let go we'll both fall; but if I don't we'll never find our way to safety.

I almost hoped in the first few days that the school would close and take the decision out of my hands. After all, it wouldn't be surprising if parents withdrew their children after two deaths. Then we could all disband, leaving Arcadia to its ghosts and its stories. But that's not what happened.

I was surprised by how many people came to Ivy's funeral. I recognized some from the village—Doris from the Rip van Winkle Diner, Beatrice Rhodes, Fawn from Seasons—but there were many more who looked far too stylish to be locals.

"Alums," Dymphna informed me in a hushed whisper as we stood in line to file past Ivy's casket. "And the trustees. There's a meeting afterward. If you ask me, which no one did, they could've waited a day."

Looking around, I recognized some of the faces of wealthy and influential arts patrons I'd seen in the society columns of the **Times**. Toby Potter, in a Victorian morning coat, told me the names of those I didn't know. Apparently, many alumni of Arcadia had gone on to become curators, collectors, dealers, and critics. A good many of them had come from wealthy families or had married into wealth and wielded power and influence in the New York art world. A few were artists themselves.

"They must be very dedicated to the school," I whispered to Toby.

"They probably want to make sure she's really gone." Toby whispered back while keeping his eyes on the procession heading toward the open casket. "I think some of them are afraid she'll pop out of the casket and demand more money for the endowment."

I shuddered at the image. I found this viewing of the corpse macabre. The few funerals I'd been to over the years had been Jewish ones, all closed-casket. I was dismayed to find myself steered by Toby into the line for the viewing. The last thing I wanted to do was look into her face. I was wondering if I could somehow file past **without** looking, but when I reached the casket, I found it impossible not to. I was shocked then at how peaceful Ivy seemed. Her face, which had been so wizened and lined in life, had relaxed, whether from some trick of the mortician's craft or because death had released some tension in her features. Still, I couldn't look at her for long without recalling that look of horror I'd seen on her face as she stood on the edge of the clove. I let my eyes drift down to the collar of her suit, on which I saw the pin she'd always worn in life: the wreath of ivy surrounding the two saints borne aloft on a cloud. I said a little prayer that she had at last found some peace.

At the end of the service the minister asked if anyone would like to say a few words about the deceased. There was an awful silence and I thought that no one would come forward. But Shelley Drake cleared her throat and rose to her feet. She was oddly dressed for a funeral, in a lavender floral print and matching lavender shoes. The chapel felt horribly still and I wondered if I was the only one afraid of what Shelley might say.

"We've come here today as a community broken by grief and tragedy," she began, her voice thin and wavery as the light filtered through the old stained-glass windows. "Many are perhaps wondering if there is a future for Arcadia after the terrible events of these last few months. But I know what Ivy St. Clare would say if she were alive." Shelley looked toward the open casket. "She would ask, What is the purpose of art if not to offer a refuge in times of loss and disillusionment? These recent deaths, of one who was at the beginning of her artistic career, and one who was reaching the end of hers, are all the more tragic because they are linked to each other. We may never know what really happened, if Ivy St. Clare was guilty of Isabel Cheney's death, but it's clear from her suicide that she felt responsible for it and for the death of Lily Eberhardt. She believed her actions would preserve the institution of the Arcadia School. We know that she was tragically misguided, but should we then throw away this refuge for the artistic spirit? We may never understand why Dean St. Clare did what she did, but we can hope that in the years to come the artists who come here, and who are nurtured here, will redeem her sins. After all, what is art but a way to shape and corral the chaos and senselessness of tragedy and disappointment?"

It was a strange speech for a funeral, but I realized it was perhaps meant more for the board meeting that occurred later that day. It must have seemed appropriate to the board, because they unanimously appointed Shelley Drake interim dean.

At the tea and reception that followed the board meeting, I expressed my surprise to Toby Potter. "I wouldn't have thought Shelley had the organizational skills to run a school," I said. And then, because I was afraid I sounded too critical, I added, "I mean, her skills seem more artistic than bureaucratic."

"In other words, you think she seems too flaky to run anything more complicated than a bake sale," Toby deftly rephrased my reservations about Shelley with a malicious grin. "Don't worry. I believe the whole 'distracted artist' air she cultivates may be a pose. I imagine she's found it convenient in getting out of unpleasant responsibilities. I wouldn't be surprised if she turns out to be an able and even draconian administrator."

I was surprised at Toby's assessment given what he'd told me the first time we met about Shelley's history of mental instability, but then I remembered how well organized she'd been when she led the search for Isabel. She'd even managed to produce pink bandanas and whistles. "Do you think the board elected her as interim dean because of her organizational skills?"

"No." Toby rocked back and forth on his heels like a wind-up toy, grinning gleefully. "They elected her interim dean because the Sheldons are the largest endowers of the school."

"Really?" I looked over Toby's head to where Shelley stood between a middle-aged woman in pearls and cashmere and a man in a navy blazer, pink pressed shirt, and khaki slacks—a couple who looked like they could have wandered in here from the Greenwich Country Club. Shelley was wearing the same loose flannel dress she wore to the funeral, and I noticed that its floral print was splattered with paint. She had tamed her kinky gray hair into a bun, but stray pieces stuck out like an ill-trimmed hedge. "I remember her telling me that part of the reason she taught at Arcadia was because it infuriated her upper-crust family. But if her family supports the school financially—"

"Then why would her teaching here make them angry?" Toby finished my question, then lifted his eyebrows, pursed his lips, and held up both hands. "No reason at all, I'd say. It's hard to imagine what family she was speaking about. Her mother, Fleur Sheldon, died in a mental institution years ago. Our Shelley was appointed a guardian by the family law firm and brought up by nannies and boarding schools. No, Shelley might affect the role of rebellious artist when it suits her, but she's done exactly what her grandmother Gertrude Sheldon would have wanted to do herself: take over Vera Beecher's role as mistress of Arcadia."

I looked over at Shelley to see her ducking her head, smiling shyly, and patting down her straying bits of hair. She seemed entirely in her element. Recalling Gertrude Sheldon's jealousy of Vera Beecher, I had to conclude that Toby was right: she would have been delighted to see her granddaughter take over Arcadia.

In the days and weeks that follow I find that Toby is also right about Shelley's hidden knack for organization. Or rather, reorganization. She seems to be everywhere, popping unannounced into classes, holding informal sessions in the dorms to see what direction the students want for Arcadia, even invading Dymphna's kitchen to suggest vegetarian meal choices and lower-calorie desserts.

She even asks Callum Reade to come in to give a talk on campus safety. I attend because it's mandatory, but I feel awkward and spend the session pretending to take notes so that I don't have to meet his gaze, which seems focused in my direction whenever I look up.

I didn't mean to leave things so awkward between us. At first I was so focused on Sally that I couldn't spare the attention for him. When he came by the cottage, I kept him at the door and explained that Sally was there and that I had to concentrate on her. "She's afraid that she could have lost me," I explained, hating the hurt look in his face. "Now's not the time to introduce anyone new into her life."

He respected my wishes and stayed away. After a few weeks I began to wonder if they weren't his wishes, too.

On those sleepless nights that I spent by the fire in my cottage, I told myself I couldn't blame Callum for staying away. It was probably for the best. Sally doesn't need to see me with another man yet, and, really, how much do I have in common with Callum Reade?

I've nearly convinced myself that I am over him when I run into him on the path to the cottage in the last week of the term. The leap my heart makes comes from being startled.

"What are you doing here?" I ask. It comes out more rudely than I meant it to. He tilts his head and stares for a moment before answering. There are deep shadows under his eyes, but otherwise it's hard to read his expression. It's dark here under the pines in the early dusk of approaching winter.

"Dean Drake asked me to have a look at this path to suggest where she should have security lights installed," he answers after a moment.

"Oh," I say, feeling stupid, as if I'd accused him of stalking me. "Isn't that a little . . . I don't know . . . presumptuous?"

He laughs. "You mean, don't I have anything better to do? Yeah, well I thought so, too, but for years I told Dean St. Clare that there should be lights on this path so I figured there was no sense acting proud. Besides, I had another reason for wanting to come out here. I wanted to talk to you."

"I see," I say, forcing myself to look him in the eyes. "About that . . . I should have told you. I'm thinking of leaving after the winter break. Sally seems unable to get over seeing Ivy fall to her death.

She'll hardly leave my side. I think that maybe it would be better if I got her away from a place with such bad memories. So you see, there's really no point . . . I mean . . . for you and me . . ."

Throughout this increasingly fragmented speech Callum has stood with his arms crossed over his chest, seemingly content to watch me blather on, making a fool of myself. When I splutter to a halt, he gives me a sad, condescending smile, as if I'm the village idiot.

"I figured you might not come back after the break. That's why I wanted to talk to you before you go. I need to ask you something about the night Isabel Cheney died."

"Oh," I say, hoping the light's not good enough for him to see me blush. "Of course. What can I help you with, sheriff?"

He seems to wince at my use of his title, but it might just be from the glare of the setting sun, which is slanting low through the pine trees. He shields his eyes and looks away. "You saw Dean St. Clare before the bonfire, right?"

"Yes, in her office."

"And do you remember what she was wearing?"

"Um, a tunic and slacks."

"What color?"

"Dark green, I think. Why—"

"And later when we saw her standing in the window, was she wearing the same thing?" Callum's looking straight at me. The sun that had been in his eyes has lowered, but the amber light reflected off the lower half of his face has turned his eyes a piercing green-gold, their fix on me so unnerving that I have to close my own eyes. When I do, I picture Ivy St. Clare standing in her darkened window.

"I couldn't tell. The lights were out in her office."

He sighs. "Neither could I. Chloe said she saw a woman in white in the woods. But why would Ivy have changed into a white dress? She didn't take part in the bonfire ceremony."

"What does it matter?" I ask. "Ivy admitted that she was in the woods that night."

"She admitted she was on top of the ridge, but she didn't say anything about running into Chloe down by the apple orchard."

"Maybe Chloe imagined the woman in white because she'd worked herself up into believing the legend."

"Or maybe there was someone else in the woods that night, someone who pushed Isabel off the ridge."

I realize now where the dark shadows under his eyes come from. Callum Reade was responsible for a young man's death in New York City and he can't bear the thought of leaving another young person's death unsolved, even if it means chasing after a legend.

"Is that why you're being so obliging to Dean Drake—so you can look for more evidence on the campus?"

He smiles. Unlike the smile of a minute ago, this one is sad and rueful. "You've found me out, Ms. Rosenthal. I'm searching the woods for signs and portents." He holds his arms out, palms extended to the sky, and then looks up as if the signs and portents he spoke of might be hiding in the tops of the pine trees. Then he sniffs at the air and dismisses me. "Best get home," he tells me. "It smells like it's going to snow."

I wake up that night because it's too quiet. I've become accustomed to the sigh and creak of pine trees in the wind and the murmur of the Wittekill as it flows past my cottage, but when I wake up in the middle of the night there's no sound at all. The cottage is wrapped in thick silence. I get up to look out the window, half expecting the whole forest to be gone, the trees come to life and walked off as in Lily's fairy tale. Instead I find the trees shrouded in heavy white robes, their limbs muffled by the steadily falling snow. It reminds me of the night Lily first told the girls at St. Lucy's the story of the changeling girl and Lily thought she had put the whole world to sleep with her story, only to find it was the snow that had muffled the creek. She'd described the girls as caterpillars breaking out of their cocoons and flitting mothlike to the window. For a moment, standing in my own darkened bedroom looking out at the white-robed trees, I feel them around me: those girls who had come far from their homes to leave their babies with strangers, listening to a story about a girl who lost her way in the woods. I feel them waiting for me to finish the story.

But I think they wouldn't like the ending I would have to tell them.

Climbing back into bed, I burrow under the blankets, muffling the silence of the waiting girls, but I feel it all around me: a sense that time has been suspended and that I'll be here forever, alone and insulated in the quiet of the snowstorm. It takes a long time for me to fall back asleep.

In the morning it's still snowing. When I wake Sally up, I tell her to look out her window, remembering how her face would light up at the first snow each year. But when she looks out at the beautifully transformed world, she only sighs. "I guess they don't have snow days here," she says and hides back under the covers.

Sally turns out to be wrong. At breakfast, in the Dining Hall, Shelley—or Dean Drake, as she likes to be called now—announces that since it is the last day of the term, classes are canceled. "I don't want anyone falling into the clove," she says. She doesn't have to add **like Dean St. Clare, like Isabel** for those names to reverberate in the silence that follows her announcement. The only one who does speak is Dymphna, but it's a muttered whisper that only I hear because I'm standing next to her by the tea urn.

"Dean St. Clare would never cancel classes for a smidgen of snow like this."

Surprised by the edge in her voice, I glance at her. Her round dimpled face is pink with suppressed anger. She may be the only one at Arcadia who really misses Ivy St. Clare.

"It's probably Dean Drake's inexperience that makes her a bit overcautious. I'm sure she's just doing what she thinks is best to keep the students safe."

"Are you saying that Miss St. Clare didn't have the children's safety in mind, then?" she asks, turning an even brighter shade of pink. "Don't tell me you believe that nonsense about her hurting Isabel Cheney? She'd never do something like that."

"But she confessed to killing Lily Eberhardt," I say as gently and softly as I can. I notice that Shelley, while outlining the guidelines for how the dorm rooms should be left, is glaring in our direction.

"Well, yes, I wasn't entirely surprised to hear that. My mother always said that Miss St. Clare couldn't abide Lily—that she was horrible jealous of her from the day she set foot here. But that was something altogether different. Arcadia was everything to the dean. She wouldn't do anything to harm it—or one of the students."

I could point out that she might have thought killing Isabel was her way of protecting the school or that it was an accident, but Clyde Bollinger has come up to the urn, holding his mug out for a cup of tea.

"Arcadia blend?" he asks.

"Sorry, love, it's all gone and the new dean says

we've got to serve decaffeinated beverages from now on," Dymphna informs him. "So it's chamomile or raspberry leaf, the latter being most beneficial in the toning of the uterus."

Poor Clyde blanches. "Uh . . . no thanks. Could I have a word with you, Ms. Rosenthal?"

"Sure," I say. "Why don't we go up to the Reading Room? It should be empty while everyone's here."

Clyde nods gratefully and precedes me, giving a wary backward glance at Dymphna in case she might be planning to "tone" any other of his organs. I have to hurry to keep up with his long-legged lope out of the Dining Hall and up the stairs to the Reading Room. "If you're after me to fix the tea and coffee situation, I'm afraid I can't help," I tell him when we get to the lounge, "but if you come by my cottage I will brew you a strong cup of Earl Grey." It occurs to me that it might be a nice gesture to invite some of my students to the cottage since Shelley's decision to cancel classes on the last day has robbed me of a chance to say goodbye to them.

"It's not about the tea, Ms. Rosenthal. It's about Chloe."

"What is it?" I ask, motioning for him to sit down on the couch and pulling a chair in front of him.

He folds his long lanky body awkwardly down onto the low couch and crouches forward, elbows on knees. I can't help but feel a pang of guilt. I was worried about Chloe when I learned that she was not going home after the dean's death, but I've been too busy tending to Sally to keep more than a cursory eye on Chloe over the last few weeks. She's seemed subdued, but not overly upset. She handed in her assignments on time, answered questions in class, and even looked like she'd put on a few pounds, although that might have been a trick of the heavy sweaters and baggy corduroys she started wearing when the weather grew cold.

"She doesn't still blame herself for Isabel's death, does she? I tried to tell her that it's likely the dean pushed her and that she couldn't have done anything to stop her."

"I don't think she buys that," Clyde says. "She says that if she hadn't played that trick on Isabel she wouldn't have run up to the ridge. And now she says it's her fault, too, that the dean died. She wants to perform some kind of purification ceremony on the winter solstice to stop the cycle of guilt and retribution."

"I think we've had enough ceremonies," I tell Clyde. "And besides, the solstice is tomorrow. Everyone will be leaving for winter break."

"But she's staying here for the break. She's asked Ms. Drake—I mean Dean Drake—if she can stay on in the dorms and Dean Drake's said yes."

Getting up to my feet, I tell Clyde not to worry. "I'll talk to Chloe. If I can't convince her to go home, I'll have her stay with me and Sally. We can observe the winter solstice together."

It's not hard to find Chloe. As soon as breakfast is over, the students abscond with the dining hall trays and run to the hill above the apple orchard for sledding. I pass Sally and Haruko heading back to our cottage.

"We still have Dad's old sled, don't we?" Sally asks. "You didn't give it away, did you?"

Did I? I wonder with a stab of guilt. I'd gotten pretty ruthless by the end of packing in Great Neck, and I dimly recall placing a price tag on Jude's old Flexible Flyer in the garage. But then I also remember going out in the middle of the night and taking the price tag off. He'd had it from the time he was eight and he'd pulled ten-month-old Sally on it around the backyard the first year we lived in Great Neck. "I'll take her sledding when she's older," he'd said. Long Island winters being mild and most of our vacations being spent in Florida, the sled didn't get much use over the last sixteen years, but at the last minute I couldn't bear to let it go. It felt freighted with all the things we hadn't gotten to do with Jude.

"I think it's in the garage," I tell Sally.

"I told you," she says to Haruko. "My mom saved all the important things." Then she turns and gives me a small smile that nearly breaks my heart. I'm afraid to speak lest I say something to ruin the moment, but then I see her shiver in her thin jacket and, unbidden, the words "You'd better get your down parka while you're at it" pop out of my mouth. Sally rolls her eyes at Haruko, but her smile widens and the two girls turn to go. I watch them for a minute, saying a small prayer of thanks for the resiliency of youth. When I turn and see Chloe standing at the top of the sledding hill, though, my faith in that resiliency is shaken. She's standing just where she stood on Halloween night, only in a powder-blue North Face parka instead of a white robe. Her face looks as haunted as it did that night. How could I not have noticed the deep blue bruises under her eyes and her swollen pink eyelids?

"Aren't you going sledding?" I ask when I reach her. "It looks like fun."

She shakes her head. "I don't like the feeling of falling. It reminds me . . ." She doesn't have to finish. I wonder if she has the same falling dreams that I do. We stand for a minute watching her classmates speed down the hill on their makeshift sleds, whooping with a mixture of fear and delight, laughing when they wipe out at the bottom. I can't imagine being young enough to enjoy the sense of weightlessness, the rush of gravity, but it makes me sad that Chloe has lost that ability at such a young age.

"Look," I say, "I hear you're planning to stay here over break. Why don't you stay at the cottage with Sally and me? It'll be more comfortable than the dorm and I'm sure Sally will be glad of the company."

"Really? You wouldn't mind?"

"Of course not," I say, wondering if it will really be the best thing for Sally to share the house with such a morose roommate. "Bring your stuff over tomorrow."

As I'm walking away from Chloe I run into Shelley. "I saw you talking to Chloe," she says. "Is she all right?"

"I'm not sure," I admit. "She still holds herself responsible for Isabel's death."

"For Isabel's death? But she knows it was Ivy's fault."

"Yes, but if she hadn't played that trick on Isabel—" The blank look on Shelley's face reminds me that I never told Shelley about the dress trick. I tell her briefly, ending with the apparition of the white woman. "Of course she might have imagined that part."

"No doubt. These girls can be quite hysterical."

"Yes, they can," I say, stifling the urge to laugh at Shelley Drake calling anyone else **hysterical.**

CHAPTER 30

Sally decides to stay in the dorm that night because the students are having an end-of-term party. I'm grateful she feels ready to leave the safety of our cottage, even if the cottage feels lonelier without her. I will not be one of those mothers who cling to their children, I repeat to myself a dozen times as I make my solitary dinner, grade my students' final essays, and watch the snow fall outside.

I'd asked them to write their own changeling stories and then examine what the changeling myth meant to them. I'm impressed with the variety of responses—there's a a sci-fi story from Clyde Bollinger and a heart-wrenching story from a girl who's barely spoken all term about her brother in drug rehab. (**Sometimes I think he's not the same brother who used to play Candyland with me . . . that he was snatched in the night and replaced by an alien.**) The one I like the best, though, is Hannah Weiss's.

She'd told me that when she asked her mother about the picture, her mother admitted that she hadn't graduated from Vassar at all. She'd dropped out when she married Hannah's father. She told Hannah that she had never told her because she didn't want to be a bad example. And she'd hoped that Hannah going to private school in the East would give her a chance to do what her mother hadn't. In her paper, Hannah writes:

What I like about the changeling stories we've read this semester is that the real child always comes back in the end. Your mother isn't fooled. She knows who you really are. Sometimes you wish she didn't. Sometimes you'd rather belong to another family—a family of fairies who live under a tree in the woods—but in the end your real family are the people who recognize who you really are.

I'd never thought of the changeling story as a story of belonging. It makes me wonder if that's why my grandmother kept the book around. It always seemed like a weird choice of children's story. When I take out the old dog-eared copy and run my hands over its worn pages I'm reminded of my grandmother's soft, worn hands touching my forehead when I had a fever or brushing away my tears when I was hurt.

In the morning the snow has stopped, but the thruway is closed and the radio forecasts another big storm on the way. Sally arrives back at the cottage with Haruko around noon.

"Haruko's parents can't make it up here because of the snow. Can she stay here tonight?"

An hour or so later Chloe shows up with Clyde and Hannah Weiss in tow carrying her many suitcases. Clyde's parents have been delayed by the snow and Hannah's flight to Seattle has been cancelled.

"Hey," Sally announces, "we have enough people to play Risk. My dad and I used to have marathon sessions. Mom, do we still have—"

I've got the game out before Sally can finish her sentence, grateful that the tattered board game (missing some infantry and half of Kamchatka) was spared in the tag sale purge. I saved the **important things,** she'd said yesterday. A sled, a game, some pots and pans—a few magic talismans as protection against the dark. How could you ever know what the **important things** would turn out to be? I leave the five of them sprawled out on the living room floor with enough cocoa, popcorn, and imperial ambitions to last the afternoon while I go into town to stock up on provisions before the next storm.

The thruway might be shut down, but the road into town is well plowed and the town itself is bustling. Trimmed in white, the faded Victorians and Greek Revivals look like they've acquired a new coat of paint. The shoveled sidewalks are full of pedestrians walking briskly between the grocery and hardware, stocking up on supplies for the coming storm. The windows of the Rip van Winkle Diner are steamy with the exhalations of locals filling up on Dymphna's pies and hot coffee.

In the grocery store I buy the ingredients for lasagna and salad and garlic bread, figuring I might have all those kids staying for dinner. It'll be nice, I think, to have a full house. I add an extra carton of milk and two pints of Ben & Jerry's ice cream— Chunky Monkey for Sally, Karamel Sutra for me— and then pause, wondering if any of the kids have any food allergies I should know about.

I use the pay phone in the pharmacy to call home. When Sally picks up I hear laughter in the background and Haruko shouting, "I eat your country for breakfast!"

"Everything okay there?" I ask.

"Yeah," Sally says, breathless, as though she'd been laughing, too. "I had no idea Haruko was so bent on world domination."

I laugh. "It's always the quiet ones. Hey, I thought I'd get dinner for everyone—are they all still there?"

"Just Chloe and Haruko. Clyde's parents came and took Hannah, too. She's going to stay with the Bollingers until she can get a flight to Seattle. Dean Drake was with them. I told her you were in town—" I miss whatever Sally says next because the operator comes on telling me I have to deposit another quarter for five more minutes. I feed in the change and hear Sally saying, "—so I got out our **Yahrzeit** candles, but I wanted to ask if it's okay to use them?"

Dean Drake must have been checking that we had supplies in case of a blackout. I'd bought the **Yahrzeit** candles to light on the anniversary of Jude's death and realize now with a guilty qualm that I'd forgotten. "Sure," I say. "As your great-grandmother Miriam used to say, 'It's gotta be the anniversary of someone's death.'" I make sure that neither Haruko nor Chloe are lactose intolerant (they're not), find out their favorite ice cream flavors (Cherry Garcia for Chloe, Phish Food for Haruko), and tell Sally that I'll be home soon.

Walking toward my car on Maple Street, I notice that there's smoke coming from the chimney of the blue Queen Anne that Callum Reade was renovating. There are curtains in the window and an evergreen wreath on the door. Some couple from the city must have bought it. I'm happy that Callum's turned a profit on it, but I feel a little pang that someone else is living the cozy familial dream I'd briefly entertained when I passed the house last summer.

Great, now I'm sentimental not only over my past with Jude but over an imagined future. The sight of Beatrice Rhodes's little bungalow lifts my spirits, though. Here is a woman who's made a happy life for herself on her own. She also has a wreath on her door—holly, not pine—but the smoke is coming not from the cottage chimney, but from the studio chimney out back. She must have gotten to work early this morning. The scene is so inviting that I decide to drop my groceries in the car and then pay Beatrice Rhodes a visit—maybe do a little Christmas shopping while I'm at it.

I follow a narrow track—one shovel's width—around to the studio. Thick white smoke is pouring out of the studio's chimney. Despite the cold, the door is propped open by a ceramic urn.

"Miss Rhodes?" I call as I step through the doorway. I don't want to startle the woman. "Beatrice?"

"In back," a reedy but strong voice calls from the back room.

I go around the counter and enter the workroom. Beatrice Rhodes is bent over the door of the kiln, silhouetted against the orange glow. She's removing a tray of blue glazed bowls, each one glowing like a Chinese lantern. When she sets down the tray on a wire shelf, she straightens up, sees me, and gives me a wide smile that creases cheeks pink with the heat of the kiln.

"Miss Rosenthal, I was just thinking about you."

"You were?"

"Yes, I thought of something you might find interesting." She peels off her heavy leather gloves and takes my hand in hers. I'm struck once again by how soft her hand is, like an old flannel nightgown. She makes me sit down on one of the two Morris chairs in front of the kiln and then rummages through the pigeonholes of an old secretary desk. "It's here somewhere," she says. "This business about Ivy's death brought it back to me, but then all the Christmas orders came in and I haven't had a moment to breathe. Help yourself to a cup of tea while I look."

There's an earthenware teapot glazed in celadon green and two matching cups on the little table between the two chairs, as if she'd been expecting me. There's also today's **New York Times** folded to the crossword puzzle, which has been completed in ink. Not bad for Saturday's puzzle, I think. Beatrice Rhodes must be pretty sharp even if she's not making much sense right now.

"It started at Ivy's funeral. That pin she was wearing reminded me of something, but I wasn't sure what, but I know it's here somewhere in this desk because that's where I hid it."

"What's in the desk?" I ask, unable to hold my tongue any longer. "What are you looking for?"

Beatrice turns and straightens to look at me. "The pin, of course. Didn't I say? Ivy's pin." She turns back to the desk as if she'd explained everything, but I'm more confused than ever. I think I know what pin she's talking about—the silver brooch surrounded by ivy leaves that Ivy always wore—but I clearly remember seeing it pinned to Ivy's collar in her casket.

"Ivy's pin? But she was buried with it, Miss Rhodes. It can't be in your desk, too."

"Well, of course I know that. . . . Aha! Here it is!"

Beatrice turns to me, unwrapping something from old, yellowed paper, and then holds out her hand. She's holding a silver pin that's identical to the one Ivy St. Clare wore—the same two saints, mother and daughter, borne aloft on a cloud—only without the wreath of ivy leaves around it.

"Where did you get this?"

"From Fleur Sheldon," she tells me, sitting down in the other chair. "I'd forgotten all about it until I saw the one Ivy had on at the funeral. Fleur left it here the day Lily died."

"She came here? But why?"

"I'm not sure she knew! She seemed very confused. I was sitting right there"— Beatrice points to a window with a deep ledge hidden behind heavy drapes, a place where a child would hide—"watching the snow fall, and I saw her coming down the path. She looked . . . I don't know . . . **wild** somehow. Her hair had come down and was covered in snow and she was weaving back and forth on the path as though she were drunk, just as I'd seen my father walk when he came home from the bars. It scared me. I'd seen people do awful things when they were drunk."

Her voice flutters and her hand, still cradling the pin, is trembling. I pour out a cup of tea for her and insist that she drink some before going on. As eager as I am to hear her story, I see that its recollection has affected her deeply. After she's taken a sip, though, she goes on. Throughout, she holds the pin cradled in her hand, close to her chest.

"I'd only been here a few days, you see. My mother had died in October and my father wasn't coping very well. When Aunt Ada sent for me to come for Christmas, I knew there was talk of me staying on, but I had the idea it was only if Ada's friend Dora liked me well enough. To tell the truth, I didn't know whether I wanted her to like me or not. I loved my father, but he scared me when he drank . . . but I was also afraid of what might happen to him if I wasn't there to look after him. So I didn't know whether I wanted Aunt Ada and Dora to take me. One minute I acted like an angel, the next I was the devil himself. That morning, the day after Christmas, I'd broken all the ornaments on the tree and was in disgrace. So I was hiding in the window seat behind the drapes when Fleur came. She was soaking wet from the snow so the aunts sat her in front of the kiln—right where you're sitting." Beatrice points at my chair. "They made tea for her. When her teeth stopped chattering enough for her to speak, Fleur took this pin, wrapped in this paper, out of her pocket." Beatrice holds her hand open to show me the pin again. " 'Do you know what this is?' Fleur asked in a queer voice. Dora took the pin from her and examined it and then passed it to Ada. They looked at each other in that way they had of communicating without words, and then Ada said, 'It's a St. Lucy's medal. The Catholics think she protects orphaned babies so they pin this to the swaddling of a baby when it's sent out to be adopted. Where did you get it, Fleur?' But Fleur only began to cry."

Beatrice looks up from the pin in her hand and I see that she, too, has begun to cry. "It scared me— her crying and the aunts talking about an orphanage. For the first time it occurred to me that if my father couldn't keep me and my aunt didn't want me I would end up in an orphanage. I was sorry then that I'd been so bad."

Beatrice stops and takes another sip of tea. Her hand is shaking as she lifts the cup. No wonder she'd blocked out the painful memory of this scene. I lean forward and put my hand over hers, the velvety, clay-worn softness of it speaking of all the years that have passed, but her eyes are the eyes of a child afraid to be left in the world alone. "Some people came into the shop then and Ada went to wait on them while Dora minded the kiln. I stayed behind the drapes and prayed that I wouldn't be sent to an orphanage. I promised God I would be good." She laughs and wipes her eyes. "Oh my, I believe I promised all manner of improbable things. And the whole time I was afraid that if the aunts found me hiding in the window seat they'd be angry. They thought I was up in my bedroom. So when Ada called Dora to come up front into the shop I decided to make my escape. I didn't think that girl would even notice me she was so distraught. But when I slid down from behind the curtain, the girl looked up like I'd caught her doing something bad. She was holding something in her lap—a green book."

"A green book? Did it have a design on the cover?"

She nods. "I was too young to know what the design was, but now I know it was a fleur-de-lis. That was Lily's sign."

"You think the book Fleur had with her was Lily's journal?"

"Yes! That must have been why Ivy St. Clare thought the aunts had it. She must have known that Fleur took it and came here." She shakes her head sadly. "And to think all that time Ivy was accusing the aunts of taking Lily's journal, I could have told them Fleur had it. But honestly I didn't know it was the same book!"

"Fleur took it with her when she left?"

"Yes. When she saw me she shoved it back in her pocket and ran out, but she didn't take the pin back, or the paper it had been wrapped in. She left those here on the table. I heard the aunts running after Fleur, and I went to the table and picked up the pin." Beatrice opens her hand and looks down at the pin. She's been holding it so tight that there's an imprint in the soft flesh of her palm. "I thought the mother on it looked kind. I'd heard Ada say that she protected orphans. So I prayed to her. I prayed first for her to take care of my father, but then I asked to please let me stay here with Dora and Ada. That was when I knew that I wanted to stay with them."

Beatrice looks up from the medal to me. Her face is wet with tears but she's smiling now. "And then I wrapped the pin back in this piece of paper and hid it in the desk. I had some idea that in order for my prayer to be answered I had to hide the medal. No one else could touch it. And there it's been all these years. I'd clean forgotten all about it until I saw it on Ivy. Why do you suppose Ivy had one?"

"Because Ivy grew up at St. Lucy's," I tell her. "But I can't imagine why Fleur Sheldon would have one."

"I think," Beatrice says, handing me the crumpled piece of paper, "that the answer is here."

I look down at the yellowed paper. It's an adoption certificate for a baby dated January 15, 1929. My heart flutters at the date—it's only a few weeks after Ivy's birth. And when I look down I see that, yes, the birth mother is listed as Lily Eberhardt. I read further and see that the names of the adopting parents are Gertrude and Bennett Sheldon.

"But if this is right Fleur Sheldon was Lily's child, not Ivy. And if Fleur was Lily's child, then Shelley Drake is Lily's granddaughter—"

I stand up, knocking against the table in my haste. The teacups chime like bells tolling the hour. "I have to go, Miss Rhodes. I want to thank you for telling me all this. I know it wasn't easy to dredge up those old memories."

Beatrice waves her hand in front of her face. "It's done me good to remember how scared I was when I first came here. It's reminded me to be grateful for what I was given. My poor father drank himself to death. I could have wound up lost and abandoned; instead I had two loving mothers to make up for the one I lost. Here." She takes my hand in hers. I feel something hard press from her soft palm to mine. When I open my hand I'm holding the St. Lucy's medal.

"But don't you want to keep it?" I ask.

"What for?" she asks. "It's answered my prayers already. Maybe now it will answer yours."

CHAPTER 31

I run back to my car, heedless of the slippery inch of new fallen snow, the pieces of the story coming together in my head as fast and urgent as the steadily falling flakes. Lily wrote in her journal that Fleur had come by the cottage on the day after Christmas. Fleur, who was always **nosing around,** according to Ivy. Clearly Fleur idealized Lily—not just because of Lily's beauty and talent, but because she'd found a birth certificate (Careless Gertrude Sheldon—she must have left it somewhere that Fleur could find it!) that identified her as Lily's child. When she came by the cottage she must have seen where Lily hid her journal. Who could blame the girl for wanting to know more about her real mother? She must have gone into the cottage after Lily left, taken out the journal, and read it. What a disappointment it must have been to find that Lily thought that Ivy was her daughter. She must have wanted to find Lily right away to tell her she was wrong. She'd run to where Lily had said she was going—to Dora and Ada's house—through the snow.

I can well imagine Fleur's frantic flight through the snow because it's snowing hard now as I pull out onto the highway. Heavy white flakes, each the size of a baby's fist, spin toward my windshield out of the gathering gloom. I turn my wipers on high and put the high beams on, surprised at how dark it is. I went into town around 1:30. Surely it can't be later than 3:00. . . . I look at the clock on the dashboard before remembering that it hasn't worked in years. I twist Jude's watch around to see its face—and nearly run into an approaching snowplow. I pull over to the side of the road to wait for my heart to stop hammering in my chest . . . and to check the time. It's 3:30. No wonder it's getting dark. There's only another hour or so of daylight left.

I pull back onto the road, desperate now to get

back to the cottage before dark, as if I could outrace the trajectory of my thoughts.

Fleur must have been heartbroken when Lily disappeared, even more so when Lily's body was found. I replay the letter Shelley showed me again: Fleur watching Ivy and Vera standing over the dead body of the woman she believed was her mother. I imagine her looking for answers to her identity and being told by Gertrude that she was crazy to imagine herself Lily's daughter—and crazy to think that Lily had been killed by Vera and Ivy. What a horrible life she must have led after that, and what a horrible life for her daughter.

As I think of Fleur's daughter the Jag swerves on the road, the tires fishtailing in the slick snow, on the bald tires I should have replaced at the beginning of the winter. I grip the steering wheel and lean forward, willing the car to straighten out. I try to make myself go slower, but I can't. Not while Shelley Drake is on the same campus as Sally and Chloe.

I try to calm down by telling myself that I have no proof that Shelley was behind Isabel's death, but the pieces keep falling into place with a relentless logic. Fleur Sheldon was the last one to have Lily's journal. Shelley must have found it with her mother's things, along with the letter that described the discovery of Lily's body. Shelley realized that Ivy St. Clare was responsible for Lily's death—for her **grandmother's** death. She would have blamed Ivy for her mother's crumbling mental health. Why, though, didn't she accuse Ivy herself? Maybe she was afraid that it would look like she had been trying to get Ivy fired from Arcadia so that she could take over her position, which is what she ended up doing. So she'd found someone else to make the connections and accuse Ivy: Isabel Cheney, a bright, ambitious history student who'd be sure to learn from the journal and letter that Ivy St. Clare was Lily's daughter and figure out that Ivy had killed Lily. But Isabel had also been smart enough to figure out what Shelley was trying to do and to confront her. Only someone truly unhinged would respond by following Isabel into the woods and pushing her from the ridge, but I am beginning to suspect that Shelley is just that. Shelley must have been the woman in white I glimpsed near the cottage and whom Chloe had seen in the woods.

As I told Shelley yesterday.

Shelley now knew that Chloe had seen her. Would she wait for Chloe to figure out that it had been Shelley or would she arrange another accident on the ridge?

I've just passed the old barn and am climbing the hill to the school when I remember two things simultaneously: Chloe wants to perform a rite honoring the solstice, which is today, and Sally said that Shelley had come by and asked a question about candles. Not, as I had assumed, to use in case of a blackout, but candles to use for a solstice rite.

At the thought of Shelley taking Sally and Chloe

into the woods I press my foot down on the
gas . . . and the car veers sharply left. I wrench the
wheel to the right, but that only makes the spin
worse. As if in slow motion, the Jag drifts onto the
other side of the road and then begins to spin. I feel
like I'm inside a snow globe only the snow is on the
outside of the glass. I have time to curse Jude—
**Could you have at least left me with a car with
decent tires?**—and to wonder if that will be my last
thought.

When the car comes to a stop I'm looking at the
snow-covered cornfield and the old barn. I'm miraculously unharmed, but when I try to back up, the
tires spin in the deep snow without traction. I get
out of the car, sinking into a foot of snow, and look
up and down the road for a passing car, but the
storm has cleared the traffic. I'm grabbing for the
cell phone in my bag before I remember there's no
signal here.

The sensible thing to do is walk up the road to
the school's entrance and then walk up the Sycamore
Drive to the cottage. If I'm lucky, someone will drive
by and give me a lift, but if I'm not, it could take me
an hour to get back home.

I look down at my watch. It's ten minutes to four.
What time does the sun set on the shortest day of
the year? 4:20? 4:30? I turn west and squint into the
blowing snow, but the storm has turned the horizon
into a gray blur. Would Chloe be foolish enough to
go out to the ridge when you can't even see the sun-

set? But then I remember the haunted look on Chloe's face and know that all she would need is a little prompting to get her out to the ridge—and only a little push to get her over it. It would be easy afterward for Shelley to say that Chloe slipped in the snow, along with any witnesses who had come along. Like Sally.

I look toward the clove. At first I can barely make out anything in the snow, and then, miraculously, the wind stops and the snow lightens. I can make out the waterfall, encrusted with ice but still flowing, and the snow-covered path next to it. It would be crazy to try climbing up in these conditions—as crazy as Lily going back that way after she had said goodbye to Nash in the barn, but she had. And she'd made it. If she hadn't fought with Vera—if Ivy hadn't kept the note from her and Fleur hadn't stolen the journal—she would have been fine. She risked the climb to be with her beloved; I can risk it to make sure Sally and Chloe are safe.

Where the wind has blown the snow thin, I start walking across the field. The stubble of dried grass crunches beneath my feet. It feels like years, not weeks, since I last walked through the waist-high grass. The terrain is utterly changed. The willow trees surrounding the first pool at the foot of the falls are bare, their long, ice-covered branches clicking in the breeze like the bamboo curtains in the Seasons shop in town. I recall what Fawn said about the legend of the clove—about the **wittewieven** who haunted it. She told Isabel that anyone with a pure heart would be safe.

As I climb the steep path beside the frozen water-fall I wonder for the first time what that really means. How could you tell if your heart was **pure**? Did Lily wonder as she made this climb if her heart was pure? She'd said her last goodbye to Virgil Nash. She'd left a confession of her transgressions for Vera to read—or at least she thought she had. I imagine her scaling this icy slope, feeling cleansed of her sins, unafraid of any specter of retribution. When she reached the top and saw Vera, Lily must have thought that her beloved was coming to welcome her. What a cruel shock it must have been to find her angry and betrayed. And then, after Lily had fallen, to look up into the eyes of the woman she thought was her daughter and see her raise her arm to strike her! She must have thought in those last seconds of life that the avenging white woman of the clove had come to destroy her for the sin of abandoning her child.

I'm so caught up in imagining the last moments of Lily's life that I'm not watching my footing care-fully enough. I step on a snow-slick rock that tilts under my foot and lose my balance. My arms flail as I fall, reaching for something to keep me from slid-ing down the steep slope, but all I find is air. My knees hit jagged rock and then my stomach slaps hard against the snow-packed trail. A plume of snow surrounds me as I slide. As long as I stay on my stomach I'll be all right, I think, but then I hear the rush of water close by my ear and realize I'm sliding into the water. If I go over the edge of the falls I won't have a chance of surviving. I try to dig my nails into the ground, but the snow's too deep. The roar of the fall comes closer, filling me with a blind panic.

I throw out my arms . . . and hit something hard, a branch or tree trunk. The pain reverberates all the way up into my shoulder, but I ignore it and grab for the limb. Rough bark scrapes my hands and the limb bends with my weight, but I stop sliding down. It takes a moment for the swirl of snow I've stirred up to settle enough for me to see. When it does, I'm sorry that I can. The sapling I've gotten hold of is growing out of a ledge above the second cascade, just where Isabel's body was found—and Lily's. Below me is a sheer drop to the bottom.

I try to pull myself up, but I slip another few inches. I feel the roots of the tree I'm holding on to give way. A few pebbles, dislodged by my movement, drop over the edge of the falls and plummet dizzyingly down into the mist. I close my eyes, willing my body to be still and weightless. Behind my eyelids I see Sally's face wearing that look of betrayal it's had so often since Jude died. If I die here, will she blame me? I know she blames Jude for dying because I feel the same way. I blame him for dying and leaving me to raise Sally on my own and—I hate to admit it to myself even now—I blame him for leaving us in debt and need. It seems so petty right now, but I know it's true. Just half an hour ago when I'd skidded on the road, I'd cursed him for leaving me with bald tires.

I wonder if Jude, in the moments before he died, was afraid of how he was leaving us. The thought floods me with sorrow for him. How horrible if his last thoughts on earth were fear for Sally and me over something as petty as money. If I could, I'd tell him now that I don't care. I'd tell him that I understand he'd been trying his best to provide for us and that we've done just fine without the big house in Great Neck and all the trappings of wealth.

Something loosens inside of me—a clenched muscle that I've been holding tight since Jude's death. It feels so good that I almost laugh out loud. And then, opening my eyes, I do laugh. I'm hanging on for dear life to a two-inch thick sapling above a raging waterfall having a moment of closure. The sound echoes against the rock walls of the clove, loud in the snow-shrouded silence. I stare up into the swirling snow that spins down to mix with the mist rising off the falls. Where they meet the air thickens and sways, a column of undulating vapor. Perhaps this is what makes people say they've seen the white woman of Witte Clove. I can almost make out the shape: a tall, slim woman in a white dress, her back to me, in the moment of turning and looking over her shoulder. . . .

Snow and mist and shadow shift in the half-light, forming the shape of a face. Eyes made up of emptiness look straight into mine. I feel as if she sees all the emptiness and fear inside of me—sees but doesn't judge. Sees and forgives.

Tears stream down my face. When I blink them away the face has vanished, but another shape has taken its place. I think it's another illusion—she was an illusion, wasn't she?—but then strong hands grip my shoulders and pull me onto solid ground.

"I've got you," Callum Reade says. "Now why don't you tell me what in the hell you're doing here in the middle of a blizzard."

CHAPTER 32

"I'm trying to get back home," I say, rubbing my hands up and down my arms to get some feeling back into them. "What are **you** doing here?"

He takes his coat off and drapes it over my shoulders. I can feel the warmth from his body still clinging to it. "I saw your car crashed in the field—I nearly had a heart attack!—and then I followed your footsteps. I could hardly believe you'd headed into the clove. Why didn't you go around by the road?"

"I was afraid it would take too long. I have to get to the ridge. I'm afraid that Shelley Drake is going to bring them to the ridge at sunset to celebrate the solstice."

"I can't believe that even Shelley Drake would be crazy enough to drag those kids out in this storm."

"That's just it—she **is** crazy." I explain as quickly as I can what I learned from Beatrice Rhodes, showing him the St. Lucy's medal and the birth certificate, and recount the story I've constructed on the drive back. I have to admit it all sounds a little farfetched. I almost hope he'll dismiss it, but he doesn't. He nods once, gravely.

"I've always thought that Shelley Drake was a bit **unhinged,**" he says. "We've got to get up there. You go first. That way if you slip, I'll be able to catch you."

The look in his eyes spurs me on. I start up the trail, going as fast as I can over the slippery rocks. I hear Callum's footsteps and breathing close behind me. Knowing he's there to catch me gives me the confidence to go faster. A few yards from the top of the ridge, where the trail splits in two, he grabs my arm and holds me back.

"Wait. If they're on top of the ridge we don't want to startle them." He points to the path that veers off to the left. "This path goes around to a stand of trees a little below the head of the falls. We can get a better look at what's going on and size up the situation." The idea of taking a detour—of taking any longer to get to the top—makes my skin itch. What if Shelley's already there with Sally right now? I try to listen for their voices, but I hear nothing but the rush of water.

"Okay," I say, "but let's hurry."

He goes first now to show me the way, which is a good thing because the woods are utterly transformed. The pines, muffled in snow, stand like white-mantled sentinels guarding the secrets of the forest, the only sounds they make the occasional **shoosh** of snow sliding off their boughs.

Be quiet, don't tell, they seem to be saying. I think of Fleur Sheldon wandering through the snow after reading Lily's journal, realizing that Lily had no idea she was her real mother. I think of Lily finding Vera waiting for her at the top of the clove, believing Vera had read her journal and learned her secrets, then seeing the look of betrayal on her face that sent her over the edge into the clove. I think of her looking up to see the girl she thought was her daughter raising her arm to strike her dead. I think of Ivy's face when Chloe told her that the woman she killed was her own mother. All these women undone by their own love.

I wonder when Shelley Drake first heard she was Lily's granddaughter. Was it from her mother? Did she think it was the claim of a crazy woman who hated the mother who had raised her? Or did she, too, prefer to identify herself with Lily Eberhardt, the beautiful artist, rather than the rich and talentless Gertrude Sheldon?

If I confront her now, will it make Shelley even crazier?

Shoosh, the trees say as we make our way through the dark woods. **Be quiet, don't tell.**

As we approach the head of the clove Callum stops and puts his hand out to keep me back. Then he holds up one finger. He's listening to something, but I hear nothing except the snow sliding off the boughs. Then, faintly, I hear what Callum does. It's a girl's voice, thin as the icicles hanging from the pine branches, singing. A wisp of a line floats through the still air: **Let it out and let it in . . .** It sounds like the pines breathing.

"That's a Beatles song," Callum says. " 'Hey Jude.' "

"It's Jude's favorite song. He used to sing it to Sally every night at bedtime—" I pause, listening to the quavery voice. "—and that's Sally singing it."

I rush forward. Callum tries to hold me back but I dodge under his arm and he slips on the snow trying to grab me. I don't care about "sizing up the situation," I just want Sally.

I head straight for the sound of her voice, off the path, crashing through thick underbrush that turns out to be thorny holly, and come flailing out into the clearing about five feet from the edge of the ridge. Chloe and Haruko are standing below the ridge, each holding a lit **Yahrzeit** candle. Sally stands farther up, near the edge of the cliff, holding a candle in a mittened hand, singing the last refrain of "Hey Jude." Shelley stands beside her.

I call Sally's name and she turns.

"Mom, you're back! I was singing Daddy's song. Dean Drake said it was a good way to say goodbye to him."

"Yes," Shelley says, stepping closer to Sally and putting her arm around her shoulder. "This is a good place to say goodbye to all the things we've lost."

I open my mouth to ask her if that's what she was doing when she met Isabel here, but I stop myself. I don't want to make Shelley mad or defensive while she's standing on the edge of a precipice with my daughter. "Yes, it is," I say instead. "I think I understand how you feel."

"Do you?" She tilts her head and looks at me quizzically. Then something flares in her eyes. "You've figured it out, haven't you? I wondered how long it would take you."

I could pretend not to know what she's talking about, but I have a feeling that wouldn't work. There's a hungry look in Shelley's eyes that I guess—hope—is the desire to talk to someone who knows her secret. If I can show her I understand, perhaps she'll let Sally go.

"I know what it's like to lose someone you love," I say, taking a tentative step forward.

"You mean your **husband**?" Shelley laughs. "That's not the same thing at all. You didn't grow up with your mother in an insane asylum. You can't tell me you know how **that** feels." Shelley tightens her grip on Sally's shoulder and I see Sally wince.

"No," I say holding up my hands, palms out. Out of the corner of my eye I spy Callum at the edge of the woods, hidden in the shadows. He makes a circular motion with his hand: Keep her talking. "I don't. Tell me about it."

Shelley smiles. In the glow of the candle Sally holds it's a ghastly grimace, like that of a crazed jack-o'-lantern. "My mother grew up feeling like a stranger in her own home. She always suspected that she was adopted, and then she read Lily's journal and she knew that she'd finally found her real mother, only to lose her again. And then after Lily's death no one would believe my mother because she had no proof."

"But you told me Lily was **Ivy's** mother!" Chloe's voice comes from behind me. I'd almost forgotten that she and Haruko are there. Without looking around—I couldn't take my eyes off Sally if I tried—I put my arm out to stop her from coming any closer. My hand brushes the silky nylon of her down parka.

"Yes, so you would tell our revered dean," Shelley says. "I knew that if Ivy thought she had killed her own mother it would drive her over the edge." Shelley laughs. "And it did—literally!"

Damn. Although I wanted Shelley to talk, I don't want her to say so much she's got nothing to lose.

"That was **her** decision," I say, "not yours. Ivy must have been haunted by Lily's murder all her life. Anyone would have been. But you don't have to be. Come away from the edge." I hold out my hand, palm up, as I would offer it to a strange dog. "Both of you."

Fear springs up in Sally's eyes. Although I've chosen my words carefully so as not to sound like my only concern is her safety, she's realized for the first time why Shelley is holding her there at the edge of the cliff. The candle in her hands shakes, the melted wax sloshing against the sides of the glass.

"So you and your police officer friend can accuse me of killing Isabel?"

I shrug, desperately trying to make the gesture look casual even though I can feel the muscles in my neck and back spasm with bottled-up tension. "Why would we do that when Chloe and I saw Ivy take her own life?"

"That's right," Shelley replies, grinning smugly. "And after all, it was Chloe here who goaded our poor dean into doing it." Shelley turns her jack-o'-lantern grin on Chloe and I feel her stiffen under her parka.

"But you were the one who told me Lily was Ivy's mother," she cries. "You made me accuse her!"

"Oh, Chloe," Shelley says, clucking her tongue. "Can anyone really make a person do something they don't want to? Are you going to blame me for the trick you played on Isabel, too? You should have seen her face when that dress came hurtling out of the tree at her! And then when I told her that you were the one who played the trick on her she was furious at you. She was most eager when I offered her a chance to get back at you."

Shelley switches her gaze from Chloe to me. "I got the idea from Lily's journal, from the trick she planned to play on the girls. I helped her rip a piece of her dress and leave it on the roots of the fallen tree, then we went up to the head of the falls to see the view—"

"You killed Isabel!" Chloe surges forward. I grab a handful of her parka to keep her back. Shelley takes a step backward toward the edge, pulling Sally with her. **Why is she doing this?** The question screams inside my head. I've tried to give her a way out, but she's deliberately teasing Chloe into accusing her of Isabel's murder. Then I understand. On some level, Shelley wants to die—dying as Lily died after avenging her murder.

I risk a glance in Callum's direction. He's managed to inch within a few feet of Sally. He's crouched, poised to spring, but will he be able to save Sally if Shelley tries to drag her over the cliff with her?

I can pray that he will, but I can't count on it. I have to offer something else to Shelley to give her a reason to live.

"You said no one believed Fleur when she said Lily was her mother because she didn't have proof. I have that proof."

The cold gleam in Shelley's eyes turns warm. She takes a step forward, jostling Sally with her. I take an answering step forward—I can't help it!—and Shelley stops.

"How do I know you're not lying?"

I take out the birth certificate that Beatrice gave me. "I could show it to you or—" I turn to Chloe, the strain of letting my eyes off Sally physically painful, and hold the page above her candle. "Or I could burn it. What do you think, Chloe? Shall we burn it? The only record of who was really Lily Eberhardt's daughter?"

I hold the old document close enough to the candle so that the edges begin to crisp. The pine glade immediately fills with the scent of charred paper. Later, I'll think it was the scent that galvanized Shelley. She moves forward so quickly that Sally is knocked over. Callum springs toward Sally. Dodging Shelley's attack, I follow him, letting the paper fall from my hand. It's only chance that at that moment a wind blows through the glade. It seems to come from the trees, a breath of snow crystals and pine-scented air that snatches the paper and tosses it high in the air. **Shoosh,** the trees whisper. **Be quiet, don't tell.**

Shelley reaches for the paper but it slips from her grasp, climbs higher, and gusts toward the edge of the cliff. She follows it, like a child trying to catch a balloon, her eyes on it, not the edge of the cliff she's approaching.

I try to stop her but a hand pulls me back. Shelley goes right past me—arms out, face aglow, as if heading into a mother's embrace—and over the edge of the cliff.

There's no scream, no cry of terror, only a sickening thud as her body hits the bottom of the icy ravine and then a final movement of snow sliding off the trees to cover up the sound. **Shoosh,** the trees say. **Be quiet. It's done.**

CHAPTER 33

Sally and I spend Christmas
morning on a Jet Blue flight to
Fort Lauderdale, eating blue corn
chips and watching a Will Ferrell
movie called **Stranger Than Fiction** that turns out to be ten times
better than I'd expected. Sally and
I both cry buckets at the end, upsetting the stewardess and the elderly woman sitting next to us. I
could tell them we're crying for
much more than Will Ferrell's fate,

but I realize that if I tried to account for all we've been through it would be less believable than the fanciful events of the movie.

Even getting these last-minute tickets seems highly improbable, but when I called Max and Sylvia Rosenthal and asked if we could spend the holidays with them, the e-mail confirmation for the tickets arrived in my inbox twenty minutes later. I hated to think what they cost, so I didn't think about it.

The atmosphere at Boca West proves conducive to not thinking. The neon-colored impatiens that grow waist high and hibiscus blooms the size of dinner plates make the whole place look like a Disney cartoon. Sally and I spend our days at the pool with Max or shopping in the air-conditioned malls with Sylvia. We eat out every night at a cheerful array of chain restaurants. It's hard to believe, in this mild climate, that places like Arcadia Falls even exist.

But I know that this particular paradise comes with a price. On our last day, Sylvia suggests she take Sally school shopping alone while I have a chat with Max. I grimly sit down at the poolside table usually reserved for Max's cronies from his days working on Wall Street. The guys are absent today, no doubt alerted to the conference Max and I are to have.

I've always admired Max. He put himself through college on the GI Bill and rose through the ranks of Morgan Stanley on the strength of his uncanny math abilities and chutzpah. He's as slim as he was the day he got out of the army and has a full head of white hair. He still plays a round of golf every day to keep fit and a game of bridge to keep his mind sharp. When I look at him, I see how Jude might have aged.

"You should have told us that Jude left you with so little. We had no idea. Sylvia thought you sold up in Great Neck because you never liked it there."

"I didn't want you to think badly of Jude," I tell him. "He would have hated for you to know that he mismanaged the money."

Max nods, his shrewd brown eyes acknowledging the truth of what I've said, but then he raises one finger and shakes it at me. "Still, he would have hated more to see you and Sally going without."

"We haven't been starving," I say. Feeling the first prickles of anger needling my skin, I take a deep breath. "We had enough after I sold the house to move upstate, and I want to teach—"

"Sure, teaching's fine, but let's face it, you coulda picked a better place to do it. Three deaths in the first semester. I went to some rough schools growing up in the Bronx, but that's meshuga. Anyways—" He waves a bronzed hand, his Columbia University ring glinting in the bright sunlight. "That's all over now, thank God. Sylvia and I would like to give you the money to move back to Great Neck. Let Sally finish out high school there. I'm sure you can find someplace to teach on Long Island, if that's what you want."

"That's very generous of you, Max, but I have to finish out the year," I surprise myself by saying. I hadn't realized until this moment that I need to go back—at least for the next semester. "I have a contract," I add.

"Of course, that's the honorable thing to do. But after that. And, of course, we've got a college fund for Sally. She's a bright kid. With her art skills, she could work in advertising."

I bite back the urge to say, Or she could be an artist. Conceding that advertising is a worthwhile career is a big step for Max Rosenthal.

"Is it all right if I take the semester to think about it?" I ask, smiling with as much charm as I can muster. "I have to talk to Sally."

"Of course, sweetheart." He leans forward and pats my knee. "But if I know my granddaughter, she'll be happy to be back in the vicinity of a good mall."

Sally does seem to enjoy being cosseted and fawned over by her grandparents. We arrive back in upstate New York with two more suitcases than we took with us. I don't mention right away the offer of moving back to Great Neck. I'd like her to finish off the year at Arcadia with as much commitment as possible. If she knows she's leaving I'm afraid she won't take her classes seriously enough.

She does, though. The new drawing teacher, Emanuel Ruiz, a young graduate of The School of

Visual Arts, is rigorous, talented, **and** incredibly good looking. At first I think Sally's devotion to the class is due to his looks, but soon I realize that he challenges her in ways she's never been before. Her figure drawings transform from cartoons to lifelike portraits and she branches out into landscape, an area she's always avoided.

"That was a brilliant hire," I tell Toby Potter, our new interim dean, over tea one day in March.

"I saw his work at the SVA Student Art Show last year. We were lucky to get him. I had to tell the board they could use my salary to pay him to be able to offer enough to get him here."

"That was gallant of you," I say.

"Not really. I knew they'd be too embarrassed to cut my salary, so I demanded raises for everyone else while I was at it."

"Thanks for that," I say, sipping my cup of Arcadia blend tea. "It's come in handy."

I've used the money to enroll Sally in a summer arts program at Parsons in Manhattan, my way of making up to her the months of rural shopping deprivation. I didn't tell her—and I don't tell Toby Potter—that I've got applications in at a dozen high schools on Long Island and in New York City. I feel disloyal thinking about leaving after all he's done to rescue the Arcadia School, but I have to do what's best for Sally.

Because even though Sally's thriving in Emanuel Ruiz's drawing class and doing well in most of her other classes, I'm afraid that the atmosphere at Arcadia is unhealthy. I feel it most at night alone in the cottage, reading through the notebooks Vera Beecher kept in her final years. Her dry accounts of students and teachers, supplies and projects, give me plenty of facts to supplement my thesis, but they're not exactly inspiring. Although she strove to keep the school alive, her heart went out of it once Lily was gone. Late at night I sometimes go downstairs and sit in front of the fireplace, looking up at the shattered lilies on the tiled hearth. I think of how it hurts to find that the person you loved wasn't who you thought they were and how that grief—the loss of the person you thought you loved—can be worse than death. I realize now that if Jude had lived I probably would have been furious at him for gambling all we had to start the hedge fund. We would have fought, but I like to think our marriage would have survived. But we never had a chance to find out. If Lily had lived, would Vera have forgiven her for her infidelity and for the child she had in secret? I would like to think that forgiveness would have allowed Vera to become a greater artist. Instead, she spent her life fossilized in that last moment of betrayal and anger.

It's a fate I want to avoid for myself.

I try to hold on to the forgiveness I felt for Jude in the clove, but it comes and goes, mingled with regret and pain, as transient as the first signs of spring in this cold climate. I can see that Sally is struggling with the same feelings and that a great deal of her anger toward me is displaced anger toward Jude. Instead of making me feel better, though, it makes me sad that she doesn't have a purer memory of her father.

At least that's how I feel until the spring art show. It's on a day in late April full of cold sunshine that coaxes the first green buds from the sycamores and snowdrops from the forest floor. The show is held in the parlor of Briar Lodge. The student work hangs on foam board partitions, Lily Eberhardt's painted images looking out over the watercolors and pastels. I imagine she would be proud of the school she and Vera founded. She might smile at some of the more pretentious efforts, like Tori Pratt's portrait of a headless mannequin standing in front of a rain-slicked window entitled **Soliloquy in Blue,** but I think she'd laugh at Hannah Weiss's portrait of herself as the evil stepmother from Disney's **Snow White and the Seven Dwarfs.**

"Last semester, Ms. Drake assigned us two self-portraits," Hannah explains to me when I compliment her on the painting. "One showing how others see us, and one of how we see ourselves."

"And this one is how other people see you?" I asked.

"That's what I thought at first, because I thought my mother and stepfather saw me as selfish and ugly because I'm not patient enough with my little brothers. But then I realized it was really how I saw myself. This one is how I think they see me." She points to the next painting on the wall. It's a brightly colored cartoon of herself as Snow White surrounded by birds and forest creatures. After a minute I realize that all the characters in the picture—the deer, the rabbits, the robins and bluebirds—all have Hannah's features.

"I like that," I tell Hannah, laughing, "but I'd rather you saw yourself as Snow White than as a witch."

"Oh no," Hannah cries. "The witch is much, much cooler. Besides, Ms. Drake said not to be surprised if you kept changing your mind about which portrait is which. It's not always easy to tell the difference between how you see yourself and how you think other people see you."

Maybe that was Shelley's problem, I think, leaving Hannah to look at the rest of the show. She worried so much that people would see her as the child of a crazy woman that she became crazy. I have to admit, though, that her assignment produced some interesting results. Clyde's two portraits show him as a pasty computer geek eating Twinkies in the glow of a video game and then as Mr. Spock from the **Star Trek** series. The headless mannequin of Tori Pratt's painting is her "how other people see me." Her "how I see myself" is the same setting without the mannequin, just a pile of discarded clothes lying on the floor. Chloe has done a single painting of herself looking into a mirror. The twin images are identical except that the one in the mirror has aged about fifty years. I can't blame Chloe for feeling older than she looks after the year she's been through.

I'm almost afraid to look at Sally's painting. This is the project, I surmise, that she's been hiding from me all year long. Is there something about how she sees herself that she thinks will upset me?

I see her standing in front of her paintings laughing at something with Haruko. Their heads block Sally's portraits as I approach, but then Sally moves and I see one of them. It's Sally standing alone in a desolate landscape underneath a lowering sky. She looks sad and pathetic and lonely. My heart contracts at the thought that **this** is how she sees herself. But then, when I get closer to the painting, I see that the label beneath it reads: HOW OTHER PEOPLE SEE ME—ALONE. I look to the right at its companion piece. It's a group picture of Sally flanked by Jude and me. We both have our arms around Sally, but my face is level with hers, while Jude's floats a little above and behind us. It's from a photograph that Jude took of us on a trip to Florida a few years ago. He'd set up his camera with a timer and rushed to get into the shot. As a result, he had come out blurry in the photograph—and spectral in this painted version, as if his ghost were watching over Sally and me. Eyes blurring, I look down at the title of the painting: HOW I SEE MYSELF—LOVED.

"Do you like it?" Sally asks. "I wanted it to be a surprise."

"I love it," I tell her, slipping my arm around her waist. For once she doesn't pull away at a public display of affection. She leans in and rests her head lightly on my shoulder for just a moment but long enough to make me feel as loved as the woman in that painting—secure in the embrace of her family.

That feeling of being loved makes me feel strong enough to do something I've been putting off. A few days after the art show I go into town to see Callum Reade. I go to the station because I'm afraid that if I meet him anywhere else I'll fall straight into his arms—and I can't do that. I think he must recognize my reasoning when he looks up from his desk and sees me standing in his doorway. The gladness in his eyes barely reaches his mouth before he reins it in.

"I was hoping you'd come before the end of the term," he says. He waves to the chair in front of his desk, but I shake my head and stay in the doorway.

"I got a job offer at a school in Queens," I blurt out. "And my in-laws have offered to help us get an apartment in Great Neck."

"I see," he says, bowing his head to retrieve something from his desk drawer. "Is that what you're going to do?"

"I'm not sure," I say, trying hard to resist the urge to run my hands through his hair. "I haven't told Sally yet. I wanted her to finish out the term first, and then I'll ask her what she wants. I want her to have a choice."

He looks up, his green eyes flashing. "Don't you get a choice?"

"This **is** my choice," I answer.

The light goes out in his eyes. He bows his head again and looks at the piece of paper he's holding. "Then I'd better give you this now." He holds out a crumpled sheet of paper. I have to cross the room to take it from him. When I look down I see that it's the adoption certificate that Beatrice Rhodes gave me.

"Where—?"

"We found it clutched in Shelley Drake's hand," he says. "That's how badly she wanted it."

I nod. "Being Lily's granddaughter must have made her feel like she belonged here. Like she had a home."

"I guess so. I got to wondering, though, why there were two Ivy St. Clares. So I did a little research at the Andes Historical Society—that's where all the archives from St. Lucy's went after the valley was inundated—and at the County Records Office. I found these." He holds out two sheets of paper. "I think you'll find them interesting."

"What—?" I begin as I reach out to take the papers from him, but when he takes my hand in his I find I can't say anything else.

"I'll stay away until you tell me otherwise," he says. "But I wonder if Sally would want you to make this sacrifice any more than you'd want her to sacrifice her happiness for you." Then he lets go of my hand. With the two sheets of paper in hand, I leave before he can see the tears in my eyes.

Callum's question haunts me on the drive back to school. I think of my grandmother sacrificing her career to raise my mother and then of my mother sacrificing her chance to go to art school so she could be secure. Would they have been happier if they had done what Lily did—sacrificing her own child to live the life of an artist with Vera? Could you lop off one half of yourself and expect the other half to thrive?

When I get home I read the two documents he's given me and everything I thought I knew turns upside down. I spend the rest of the afternoon making phone calls and doing research online. I reread Lily's journal far into the night. When I finish reading I look up from Lily's journal and see the sky turning pink outside. It's May 1—May Day. And even though I could have sworn that I've had enough of pagan celebrations, I decide there's something I have to do.

I go to the dorm to wake up Sally. She's bleary-eyed, but I hand her a travel mug full of hot cocoa and promise her doughnuts when we get where we're going.

"And where's that?" she mutters, stepping into the jeans I've picked up off the floor. Haruko snores gently in the other bed, oblivious to our talking.

"You'll see," I tell her. "A surprise."

She falls back to sleep as soon as we're in the car.

I put a blanket over her and drive down to Route 28 and turn west. In Pine Hill, I stop at a bakery and buy bear claws, jelly doughnuts, French crullers, and two more cups of hot cocoa. The car fills with the aroma of chocolate and yeast and sugar—better than incense any day. The road spools out beneath us, like a ribbon extending into our futures. I feel like we could just keep going. What's to stop us?

The dawn drive reminds me of when we left Great Neck last August, but I felt then as if we were fleeing the wreckage of our old lives and going to the one place that would have us. Now I feel the world is open to us. All we have to do is choose.

But I want Sally to be part of making the choice this time, and in order for her to do that she has to know everything. I feel in my sweatshirt pocket for the folded pieces of paper. They crinkle at my touch, brittle as fall leaves and as crackling with energy, as if they might spontaneously combust in my pocket.

When I pull off Route 28 Sally stirs and stretches. "What smells so good?"

"I told you there would be doughnuts," I say, wafting the wax-paper bakery bag under her nose and then snatching it away. "But first there's a hike."

She groans, but gets out of the car good-naturedly enough. Even when she sees how steep the path is, she doesn't complain.

What a good kid she's turning out to be, Jude, I find myself whispering under my breath as I pant behind her on the steep trail. **You'd be proud of her.**

She gets to the top before me and I can hear her little cry of delight and surprise. At the top of the hill is a small stone chapel standing all by itself.

"It's like something from a story. How did it get here?"

"It's the chapel from the convent of St. Lucy's. It was moved here when the valley was flooded," I say, waving toward the view, which is just emerging out of the darkness. The sun has crested the ridge to the east, lighting up the high outcropping we stand on, but not the valley below yet. "A group of artists got together and saved it because of the paintings inside."

Sally swings open the door, ignoring the view of the valley, and begins opening the shutters. I haven't seen her this excited since Jude bought her a plastic playhouse on her fifth birthday. The pictures silence her though. She walks from frame to frame, following the story of the fifth-century Irish girl who probably wasn't any older when she ran away from home than Sally is now. I fill in narrative details when needed, but mostly Lily and Mimi's paintings tell the story with remarkable clarity.

"So she had to give up her baby and her daughter grew up without her! That's awful!" Sally cries with the outrage of the young at unfairness and injustice.

"But look, they're reunited later." I gloss over the part about mother and daughter getting burned at the stake for preaching Christianity. "Here they are on a cloud ascending to heaven."

Sally shakes her head, displeased. "You mean they find each other only to die? Ugh, what an awful story! Imagine if I'd grown up with strangers instead of you, Mom." She leans against me for a moment and I squeeze her shoulder. Then she's gone, kneeling in the corner, looking at the artist's signatures. "Lily Eberhardt and Mimi Green," she reads. "The same Lily who was one of the founders of Arcadia?"

"The same," I say.

"Who's Mimi Green?"

"She was one of the first artists who worked at Arcadia. She did the landscapes. They're pretty, aren't they?"

Sally takes a step back and stands in the middle of the room to get the full effect of the landscapes. The gently rolling green hills, the verdant valleys, the flashing river, and the thick forests that serve as backdrop harmonize so well with the figures in the foreground that they seem to fall away, like half-forgotten places slipping behind mist and cloud. But looked at closely, little details emerge: yellow jewelweed and blue cornflower growing in the meadows, foxes and rabbits hiding in the woods, red-winged blackbirds and yellow finches in the branches of the trees. It's a paradise—but it's also real: the East Branch valley before it was inundated, a little paradise on earth captured on the stone walls rescued from the flood.

"Wow, she was really good," Sally says. "I've never heard of her. Did she go on to paint anything else?"

"She gave up painting," I say, steering Sally out of the chapel and to the bench. I take out the luke-warm hot cocoas from the bag and hand Sally a cruller. "And she went back to using her real name. Mimi Green was a name she used for working at magazines because her real name was too . . . well, too ethnic." I take out the adoption certificate that Callum found in the County Records Office and smooth it out on my lap. I point to the name on the line for adopting mother.

"Miriam Zielinski," Sally reads. "That sounds familiar—"

"Zielinski means 'green' in Polish," I tell her. "And Mimi's a nickname for Miriam—"

"Wasn't Grandma's mother named Miriam? And wasn't Zielinski her maiden name?"

"Yes. Her married name was Kay. I always thought that was a funny name for a Polish Jew, but I figured that my grandpa Jack's father's name had gotten changed from something long and unpro-nounceable when he landed at Ellis Island. I asked once, but Grandma Miriam pretended she hadn't heard me and my mother said she never knew. But now I do." I point to the name of the adopting father: John McKay. "He was Irish—or at least they gave him an Irish name at the convent when he was left there. He died when I was only five, so I don't re-member him much, but everyone said he adored Miriam, so I figure he didn't mind blending in with her family in Brooklyn—"

Sally shakes the paper in front of my face, cutting me off. "But this says they adopted a baby girl whose birth mother was Lily Eberhardt!"

"Yes. You see, Miriam—your great-grandmother Miriam—was a friend of Lily's. She was at St. Lucy's when Lily had her baby—a baby she couldn't tell anyone about. Lily left before her baby was adopted, but Mimi—Miriam—stayed. She had let on to Gertrude Sheldon, who was a patron of the convent—that Lily had had a baby and then Gertrude, who I think must have gotten pregnant in Europe only to lose that baby, wanted to adopt the baby." I take out of my pocket the adoption form that poor Fleur Sheldon had found and then left at Dora and Ada's house, the one that listed Gertrude Sheldon as the adopting mother of Lily's baby. "What I think must have happened is that Mimi decided at the last minute that she couldn't bear to see Lily's baby go to Gertrude, who was, by all accounts a pretty awful woman." I shudder, thinking of poor Fleur spending her holidays alone at Arcadia while her parents skied at Chamonix. Inside my pocket is the letter Callum had found in the St. Lucy's archives.

Dear Sister Margaret, I am sending the infant we obtained from you back, as I have had the good fortune to conceive my own child. A sure sign of God's grace, you will agree! You will understand, I am sure, that I can't possibly attend to two children. At any rate, the infant's personality is not suited to mine—it seems unusually leaden. I regret any inconvenience this has caused and enclose a check to be applied toward the needs of your orphans. Yours truly, Gertrude Elizabeth Sheldon

I imagine that Gertrude Sheldon wrote the same sort of note when she was forced to return a hat that didn't "suit." But I don't show Sally this egregious example of inhumanity. I continue with Mimi and Jack's story instead.

"So she convinced the nun to switch the babies and give another girl the name Ivy St. Clare. And she and Jack, who she met and fell in love with while she was working on that mural, took Lily's child. They named her Margaret, in honor of the nun who ran the convent and helped them take the baby in secret, and that's how your grandma Margie got her name. And how I got mine, for that matter. I always thought it was an odd name for a Jewish family. They moved back to Brooklyn and Mimi—or Miriam, as she called herself— gave up painting. I guess she thought that's what she had to do because that's what women did back then."

I consider adding something like: Thank goodness women don't have to make those choices now! But I don't. Who knows what choices Sally will be faced with in the years to come? I hope she'll draw and paint and work and fall in love and have children, but whether she'll do those things all at once, or in some completely new and different order and combination that I can't begin to imagine, only she will be able to decide. Right now, I only have one choice I need her to make.

"So Lily Eberhardt is—"

"My grandmother and your great-grandmother. Yes. But that's not the only reason I brought you here. We've got a decision to make."

I tell her our options. The job in Queens. Max's offer of an apartment in Great Neck. Our options here. We hash it all out. When we're done we're covered in powdered sugar and the mist has cleared from the valley.

"So you're sure?" I ask, brushing the sugar off my hands.

"Yeah," she says. "Come on. Let's go home."

I feel a little light-headed on the drive back, but that's probably all the sugar I've consumed. Or the brightness of the morning sun we're driving straight into. When we arrive in Arcadia Falls, the town looks fresh-washed, not like the decaying Catskills town I saw it as months ago at all.

"Hey, there's Haruko and Hannah—they must be going to the used-record store that just opened in town. I told 'em we have a real turntable. . . . we still have it, don't we?"

"Yes," I say without hesitation. It's another relic of Jude's I hadn't been able to give away. "Do you want to get out and catch up with them?"

"Yeah . . . if you don't mind?"

"Not at all," I say. "I have some errands to run in town. I'll see you back on campus."

I park and walk toward the Rip van Winkle Diner, my heart thudding in my chest. I try to put that down to the sugar, too, but I know it's because I'm hoping to find Callum there so that I can tell him we've decided to stay. When I open the door to the diner, though, my heart suddenly feels as heavy as the lumps of dough in my stomach. He's not there. It's ridiculous, I know, to think he'd be sitting here waiting for me—as ridiculous as it is to think he's been waiting for me all these months, but still I feel unaccountably let down by his absence. Too discouraged to stay and eat, I start to leave, but Doris Byrnes sees me and waves me in.

"Are you looking for Sheriff Reade?" she asks.

I consider trying to deny it, but she's looking at me as if she can see right through me. I remember Callum telling me that Dymphna Byrnes was a bit of a witch and I have the feeling that her cousin has just as much uncanny power.

"Yes," I say. "Do you know where he is?"

"He'll be working on that house," she says.

"The blue Queen Anne on Maple Street?" I ask, as if there's any doubt which house she's talking about.

She nods, but is distracted by someone calling for a coffee refill. I leave before anyone can notice how flushed I am. The people Callum fixed the house up for must have hired him to do more work on it, I tell myself as I turn onto Maple Street and spot the blue house. Daffodils line the front path and the lilac bush in the front yard is leafing out—there will be lilacs in a few weeks. I walk up onto the porch under the watchful enigmatic gaze of the Greek goddess who has been returned to her carved acanthus bower in the gable. Her face has been completely restored now, but she still looks like she's keeping a secret. The front door is open. Music comes from a radio playing inside, something mournful and Irish that suddenly erupts into a hard rock beat.

It's no use knocking with that music blaring— and the owners are probably not here if Callum's playing the radio so loud—so I go in. The house smells like fresh-sawn wood and lemon furniture oil. The hardwood floors in the foyer and living room gleam in the sunlight pouring through the freshly washed windows. The house looks newly scrubbed, as if waiting for something, but there's no furniture in the living room and my steps echo in the foyer as if the whole place is empty. Only the statue of the wood nymph stands in the living room. Her face, which has been finished now, looks oddly familiar. I stare at it for a few minutes, trying to decide who she looks like until I realize that she has the same face as the painting over Ivy St. Clare's desk. It's Lily's face, but it's also mine. Callum had seen the resemblance before I had.

I follow the radio music, recognizing beneath the hard rock beat the familiar strains of "Amazing

Grace," into the kitchen. Callum is standing on a stepladder wiping clean an empty cabinet. He turns when he hears me come in, but he doesn't step down. He gazes at me as if there's a story written on my skin he's trying to read.

"I thought you were getting this place ready for some couple from the city?" I ask, surprised myself that this is what I choose to ask him first.

He drops the cleaning cloth on the counter and steps down from the ladder. I take a step forward and catch the scent of lemon from the oil on the cloth that's now on his hands. Cherrywood. Lemon. And something else I can't name. Him.

"You and your Sally, you're the couple from the city. I thought this place would be perfect for you. I can give you a pretty good price on it . . . that is, if you're staying."

For answer, I step closer and rest my hand on his chest. I feel his heart beating beneath the thin fabric of his T-shirt and smell the warm musk of his skin beneath the cherry and lemon scents on his clothes. The roughness of his cheek brushes against the top of my head as I lay it on his chest. His arms come up around me. I feel as if I'm fitting myself into a mold I've been shaped from. I feel as if I've come home.

ABOUT THE AUTHOR

Carol Goodman is the author of **The Lake of Dead Languages, The Seduction of Water, The Drowning Tree, The Ghost Orchid, The Sonnet Lover,** and **The Night Villa. The Seduction of Water** won the Hammett Prize, and others of her novels have been nominated for the Dublin/IMPAC Award and the Mary Higgins Clark Award. Her fiction has been translated into eight languages. She lives in New York State with her family.